Girls From Da Hood 13

Girls From Da Hood 13

Ms. Michel Moore,
Treasure Hernandez, and Katt

URBAN
BOOKS

www.urbanbooks.net

Urban Books, LLC
300 Farmingdale Road, NY-Route 109
Farmingdale, NY 11735

ISBN 13: 978-1-60162-095-8
ISBN 10: 1-60162-095-0

First Mass Market Printing March 2019
First Trade Paperback Printing July 2018
Printed in the United States of America

10 9 8 7 6 5 4 3 2 1

Distributed by Kensington Publishing Corp.
Submit Orders to:
Customer Service
400 Hahn Road
Westminster, MD 21157-4627
Phone: 1-800-733-3000
Fax: 1-800-659-2436

Girls From Da Hood 13

by

Ms. Michel Moore,
Treasure Hernandez, and Katt

Get It, Get It!

by

Ms. Michel Moore

Chapter One

Once a dopefiend, always a dopefiend! Recovery my ass! I'm so tired of this bullshit!

"Mama, please! Mama, please wake up! Why you keep doing this stupid stuff all the time?" Monica was distraught. Confused by reality, her mind raced. Screaming at the top of her young lungs, the young teen violently grabbed her mother's frail, sunken face. She slapped it repeatedly in an attempt to get her bloodshot eyes to reopen and once again take in life. Monica exhaled. She worked steadily as would a seasoned, trained surgeon.

Like clockwork, she then jumped to her feet. Running to get a cold washcloth, the teen knew time was essential. With water dripping from the drenched dirty rag she grabbed off the bathroom floor, she pushed through the growing crowd of nosy neighbors. She placed the cloth on her mother's sweating forehead. Immediately it caused her small frame to slightly jerk from the shock of the sudden temperature change.

"You won't be happy until your ass fucking die and leave us all alone," Monica angrily shouted, while pounding down on Jenette Howard's chest.

Everyone packed inside the tiny apartment, which was done in ghetto decor. Each stood motionless, waiting for this week's near-tragic outcome. Even though Jenette was no more than a bona fide run-of-the-mill drug addict, normally Monica never would've cursed at her mom, let alone raised her voice. However, this was a special occasion. Today was one of those all-too-famous "first of the month" kinda special occasions. It was one that everyone in the hood waited and prayed for. Jenette had gotten her food stamps at nine o'clock that morning. And instead of stocking the cabinets with even a few cans of soup, let alone a tiny loaf of bread, she copped her usual choice of nourishment: dope.

Never once thinking about anything else but self, less than two hours later it was what it was. She was surrounded by all three of her innocent, hungry children. Jenette was laid the fuck out on the living room floor, damn near overdosing. She was seconds away from meeting her Maker. Tragically, if given the chance to cop another pack of the same shit that had her knocking at death's door, she'd ask for double her money's worth.

Same shit, different day, Monica thought, frustrated, as she went through the regular routine of bringing her mother out of her drug-induced trance. *I swear to God she's really testing me! How long she gonna do this dumb shit?*

With each passing episode of her mother's over-the-top antics, the scary temptation was growing greater daily for Monica not to come to her mother's constant aid. Monica was fighting with her conscience about calling protective services her damn self. The only thing stopping her was the risk of being separated from her little brother and sister in the system. The teen knew the callous system cared even less about keeping family together than Jenette did.

It would be different if this weren't the norm, but unfortunately, it was. Jenette was famous for overdoing it like it was in her DNA. Whether it was a fifth of five o'clock gin and she was drunk, passed out cold, or her showcase specialty: the needle left dangling half in her arm after a good, strong hit. The single mother of three was good for bugging out, spazzing into full-blown convulsions. Poor Monica didn't know which she hated to witness more: her mother with too many drugs in her system, or the days when Jenette was bold, craving a blast, throwing up, scratching her skin 'til it bled, sick, with the eerie, dead glare of a zombie in her eyes.

Under both circumstances, Monica was left to play nursemaid to her mother, who was once halfway decent. Jenette's hopeless search for love and acceptance led her to depend on anything she could get her hands on to try to escape the grim certainty of her life. Her indulging in every drug, drink, random sex partner, and reckless behavior known to man had torn her family apart. And the saddest part of the god-awful, gut-wrenching story was that Jenette was lost in her own world and couldn't care less.

Monica was the oldest of the three of Jenette's children. She was extremely small for her age, standing barely four feet seven inches tall. Her skin was dark brown and her hair, which matched her eyes, was light brown. Monica was a few months short of turning fifteen but had the knowledge of someone twice her age. She had no choice but to grow up quickly, especially being cursed with a mother like Jenette.

Like most of the other illegitimate children in the economically stressed Detroit neighborhood, Monica's mother was a 100-percent alcoholic crossed with an addicted junkie and proud of it. She had no shame whatsoever. Day or night, Jenette could be found jumping in and out of cars, trying to get money by hook or by crook. If it was a blowjob, no matter if the trick was five or fifty-five, Jenette was on call, no questions asked. That creepy, foul bullshit sadly left Monica to be both mother and father to her little sister and brother.

Of course, all three children had different sperm donors. They never came around or really gave a shit about their kid's well-being. Considering Jenette's known slutty ways, each questioned if they were even really the father. Jenette, always depressed, seemed to take their absence out on her children. Getting cursed at, spit at, and all-out ignored was the norm in their household.

Life in Monica's small corner of the world was based on a lot of chaos. With all the different tricks Jenette would have parading in and out of their small one-bedroom apartment to support her habit, Monica was fed up. The teen didn't know how much more she could take. She was at her wits' end. Instead of going to the movies, hanging out at the mall with friends, or even trying to do her homework assignments, only one thing would fill Monica's long days: scheming to put food on the table and clothes on Dennis's and Kayla's backs.

Monica couldn't help but think back to the first time her mother taught her to "borrow stuff" from the store. Always on the come up, Jenette had her daughter stuffing packs of expensive steaks and family-sized pork chops down the back of her pants at an early age. When Jenette would be too sick to get out of bed or off the floor, curled up in a ball throwing up in her mouth, she'd have Monica going to the dope house to cop for her. In the worst-case scenario, sometimes Monica would reluctantly have to cook the drugs up. And more traumatically than that, she'd sometimes shoot it into her mother's thirsty veins. That was if she could find one that wasn't tapped out.

Monica was only eight years old at the time Jenette's addiction began, but her youth and innocence never once mattered to her mother. That was life in the hood and Monica had to get used to it if she wanted to survive. After all, she and her siblings weren't the only kids who lived like that in their part of the city. It was a "get in where you fit in" situation. Nothing more than Jenette's live-in babysitter and from time to time her hustle partner, Monica was often hungry. She was left in the house to watch her premature baby brother for days, sometimes weeks at a time. When her unfit, drunken mother, unfortunately, got pregnant again, Monica got on her knees nightly. With eyes closed tightly, she hoped and prayed to God that all of that running the streets and getting high her mom was doing would cease.

Jenette, on the other hand, had a much different game plan and agenda. True to the game of chasing that ultimate high, pregnant or not, she wouldn't hear of missing a day of clowning in the streets. Monica's heartfelt wishes meant nothing to her mother. No sooner than Jenette gave birth, she was out the door back on the hunt.

Now she was leaving Monica with two kids instead of one. It was nothing short of a small miracle the hospital even released the baby into Jenette's care. Unfortunately for Monica, they did. The teen was still just a child herself, a baby raising babies as the saying goes.

Chapter Two

"All right, Dennis, I'm not playing. Y'all need to get up before you're late." Monica roughly shook his arm to show him she meant business.

It was six forty-five in the morning, and Monica was busy trying to get Dennis and Kayla out of bed. This was their everyday early morning routine. The school they attended served free, piping hot breakfast at 7:30 a.m. sharp. Monica wanted her brother and sister to make sure to eat a balanced meal before they started class. Even though most days she missed eating a healthy breakfast herself, her siblings were her top priority in life, no ifs, ands, or buts about it.

After the kids were up, Monica lifted the thin, filth-stained mattress from the full-sized bed all three of them shared, and she removed Dennis's and Kayla's blue jeans. She always remembered to place them there the night before so they could have somewhat of a crease in them. Unfortunately, since Jenette would sell every iron that Monica would bring in the house, or anything else for that matter that had a plug on it, keeping their clothes neat was a constant struggle.

Monica, a survivor, had been forced to adapt to a few more "broke as shit" conditions, and she hated every minute of doing so. It consisted of a vast range of everything, from putting milk on the window-sills in the winter months to begging the old fart who owned the corner store for credit until the first of the month came around. It was that type of daily demeaning action that caused Monica to ultimately make the decision to step up her game.

Going in the stores month after month beg-ging was trifling and beneath her. The teen was getting older, and her developing body was start-ing to attract the Arab store owners' attention in more ways than one. Her new outward appear-ance caused them to expect and demand way more in exchange for small favors than a virgin Monica was willing to give up. Dennis and Kayla were also growing each day and needed a lot more things than ever before. They each wanted to wear clothes that were just as nice as what the other kids at school wore. Monica hated to let them down. The youthful surrogate mother had to make some shit happen fast for her family before things started to spiral out of control even more. And, as luck would have it, it didn't take long.

***

Monica was sitting on the front steps when Dennis and Kayla got home from school that day. They had barely rounded the corner when Monica saw something was wrong.

"What happened to you, Dennis? Who put their fucking hands on you?" Monica was heated as she practically leaped off the stairs running toward her little brother. She was overly protective of her siblings. Instantly pissed seeing that Dennis's shirt was torn and his lip was bleeding, Monica demanded answers.

"Jeff and 'em was talking 'bout me and Kayla. They said we be wearing the same stuff to school all the time." Dennis had tears forming in his eyes as he told the story, but he was much too proud to let them drop. "I told them so what and we all started arguing. Then they jumped on me." Dennis bravely stood tall. "I wasn't scared of none of them."

"Where the fuck they asses at? Let them jump on me and shit." Monica started dusting the dirt out of her brother's hair. "I'm tired of them little motherfuckers. They clothes ain't all of that. Y'all shit be clean, with a crease."

Kayla was standing on the sidewalk, crying and wiping her nose with her sleeve. Her face was beet red, and her eyes were full of pain. Wanting her older sister to know it all, Kayla marched over and yanked down on her brother's arm. You could tell she was aggravated with every tug.

"Dennis, tell Monica what else they said. Tell her what they said about Mama," she whined, looking at him and shaking her head.

Dennis stared at the ground, not wanting to look up at his older sister and make direct eye contact. He started slowly wasting time by kicking at the broken concrete curb, hoping and praying that Monica would stop the miniature interrogation she insisted on going through. However, it didn't work. Monica was growing angrier as the seconds passed and she waited to hear the entire story.

"Dennis, you better stop playing with me and tell me what all the fuck happened before I jump on your ass. Now, what was it that they said?" Monica folded her arms across her chest as she shifted all her weight to one hip. "I'm waiting!"

Dennis took a deep breath, hesitated a few seconds more, then let it out. "They said that mama was nothing but a ho. And then they said she was in the alley by the park, sucking an old man's dick. Now you happy?" The brave boy unfortunately lost his battle with his pride as tears started to pour from his eyes. "Fuck Mama's dopefiend ass. I hate her. I wish she was dead," he yelled while running up the stairs. He disappeared into the slimy-ass apartment building they were forced to call home.

Hearing those cruel words come out of Dennis's mouth caused both of his sisters to also cry.

Fuck living like this! Monica thought. *Shit gotta get better!*

Reaching out, she took Kayla's tiny hand as both girls slowly walked up the stairs. Monica looked down at her little sister and felt an almost unbearable sharp pain in the pit of her stomach. She was the oldest, and their survival was on her. Jenette and her despicable behavior was completely inexcusable, and Monica had to take charge.

"Don't worry, Kayla. Dennis will be all right." They entered the building. "We all will, I promise. I'm gonna fix it."

Chapter Three

Two years had passed since the day Dennis had wished their mother would drop dead. Sadly, as life would go, nothing much had changed. Jenette was still a poor excuse for a mother, or even a human being for that matter. Confusion still daily filled Monica's world. Thankfully Kayla was doing well in school. Monica, still the sole provider of their dysfunctional family, rewarded her younger sibling every chance she got with brand new dresses and lots of books Kayla yearned for.

But Dennis was a horse of a different color and flat-out on the nut. He was straight-up out of order. A certified little thug in training, he was hanging out until all times of the night, skipping school, and constantly fighting. Dennis stayed in some shit. Even though Monica would go out and steal him the hottest gear that was popping, it didn't seem to matter at all to Dennis. He was determined to go against the grain of any rules that his big sister tried to set for him.

"Damn, boy. What's your problem? I try to keep your bad ass fresh as can be. You got brand new Tims in every color. You own every throwback I can get my hands on, and I give you something to keep in your pockets on the regular." Monica was pacing the room as she preached to her hard-headed younger brother. "What else do you want? Do you want the social worker coming back around here again? Would that make you happy?"

Dennis couldn't deny that his big sis kept him tight. That wasn't really his problem. Truth be told, he was still pissed about having been cursed with a junkie for a mother. Rubbing his hands together, he nodded. "Naw, Monica, I don't want that bitch to be bringing her nosy ass over here, but dang."

"Dang what? And stop cussing, li'l boy."

"You know what I'm talking 'bout, Monica."

"Listen, boy. I done told you a thousand times before that's Mama with her bullshit. That ain't got jack shit to do with you, me, or Kayla." Monica went across the living room and sat on the couch next to her brother. "Pay attention, Dennis. This is my last year in high school. I'll be eighteen in a few months, and then I can try to get custody of both you and Kayla. I know it's hard, but just chill. It's our only hope, so don't fuck it up."

Dennis truly loved his sister, without question, more than he loved his own mother. Monica was the one who put fly gear on his back, food in his stomach, and always kept his pockets off craps. Leaning back on the worn, tattered couch, he stared up at the paint that was peeling off the ceiling of the run-down apartment. "All right, Monica, I'll chill," he said, smiling, "if you braid my hair again tonight."

"I'm not fucking clowning around with your li'l ass. Don't make me bust you dead in your mouth." She pushed his head over to the side playfully.

"Stop touching a grown-ass man," Dennis laughed as they started to play wrestle. The two were not only brother and sister. They were best friends.

As they continued laughing and joking, they barely noticed Jenette stumble in through the front door. Monica and Dennis could both smell the gin from across the room. Jenette, obviously out of her mind, fell against the kitchen counter and slid down onto the floor. Bumping the side of her face on the refrigerator on the way, the drunken mother never cried out as a small gash instantly started to bleed.

But so what? That was her problem and hers alone. Neither Monica nor Dennis moved to come to her rescue. They were used to their mother being passed out on the floor. It was her second home. Jenette seemed to sleep better there anyhow. After a second of them staring at her with utter disgust, they tightly held their noses and stepped over her body as if she were no more than a puddle of piss in the street. Jenette, knocked out cold, didn't even move one inch. She would be left all night to keep the mice and cockroaches company.

It was 8:10 a.m. and Monica had just made it inside the classroom before the bell rang. She had been in the hallway taking orders from some of her friends for new outfits. Over the past few months, Monica had been knocking them stores in the head something hard. She was getting anything her heart desired. Monica Howard had gone from being the girl the ignorant guys in her classroom nicknamed Dusty Drawers to being one of the best-dressed chicks in her school. Monica was known on a daily basis to floss top-notch designer jeans and other expensive outfits while carrying every new high-profile bag that came out on the market. Most of the clothes she stole were from neighborhood department stores or local malls. Whenever she could find time, Monica hustled. She would even take the Greyhound bus to New York every other week for all the high-priced items people ordered.

Monica was a little wild when it came to stealing. Having no true method to her madness, she was often careless and disorganized. Monica was cocky and took way too many unnecessary risks in the pursuit of getting what she or others on her list wanted. Most of the security guards were more than familiar with her face, and many knew her by name. The seasoned thief was used to the method of "borrowing things" that Jenette had taught her. However, balling up clothes and sticking them in her loose-fitting overalls was starting to play out. Stuffing belts and baby tees in her oversized purse would often result in the store confiscating their own merchandise and her expensive designer bags as evidence of her crime.

Monica would often breeze into a shop and try on a coat. She would walk around the store for a few moments or so and then make her escape by bolting out the door. With God on her side, Monica would make it to the parking lot sometimes, but other times she didn't. Often, the only thing that saved her from jail was that she was under eighteen and all the youth homes were always filled to capacity.

With trying to take care of Kayla and Dennis as well as herself, Monica was truly catching it. With only a few months left before she graduated, Monica was planning on going to City College, getting her own little apartment, and having her brother and sister move in. Their "Jenette nightmare" would soon be over if all went as planned. In the meantime, Monica made her money the best way she knew how: by "borrowing."

**

That night, lying across her bed, Monica was on the phone. "Okay, girl, tell me one more time." Monica grabbed a pencil out of her designer book bag and began to scribble on a small piece of paper.

"First, see if you can get me those new jeans they got out. You know, the ones with the different-color design on the pocket," her best friend expressively explained.

Kanina was Monica's number-one customer. She always was first in line to get Monica's hottest pieces. Monica knew all of Kanina's sizes by heart. She knew her measurements better than any man Kanina had ever fucked around with. Over the months that passed, the two girls had become close friends. Even when Monica had no clothes to sling to earn dough, Kanina would loan her money.

Jenette was still getting high on the regular, and if Monica didn't have the money to give her mother for drugs, she would and often did take Monica's or Dennis's gear out of the house. Whenever Dennis's belongings went missing, he damn near would try to kill Jenette, mother or not. One day, he hit Jenette so hard upside her head she was unconscious for what seemed like an eternity. For one reason or another, she never fucked with Kayla's stuff. Monica always tried to keep the peace. But Kanina was a true friend and looked out when need be.

"All right, I got that. What about the top?" Monica questioned. "Do you want long or short sleeves? They come in both and in every color."

Monica was past careful in taking exact orders so she could make sure to have a definite sale for the stuff right away. Having the money in her hand was a lot easier than clothes to hide from Jenette, especially when the clothes still had price tags on them. Jenette could and often would trade them at the dope house for some product. The dudes who worked inside of the spots loved to see Jenette's good dopefiend ass coming. They would always end up paying way less than what Monica would have sold the garments for, but that was that old dopefiend mentality Jenette swore by: get high by any means necessary.

Kanina took her time in answering, because she was lying back, picturing the hookup in her mind. "Girl, if you can get both of them, go right ahead. Matter of fact, try to see if you can get the jacket, too." Even though she only wanted one blouse, she knew it was near the end of the month and that Monica needed the extra loot. Kanina was an only child. Both of her parents worked at a factory and gave her just about everything she asked for. She lived the life that Monica often would daydream about.

"Okay, Kanina, I'm gonna finish this list then go to sleep. I'm tired as hell. I was trying to wait up for Dennis, but you know how that shit goes. Ain't no telling when he gonna show his li'l punk ass up." Monica started yawning in the middle of her sentence. "I'm 'bout to fall asleep on you."

"Monica, girl, I ain't even gonna front with you. I don't see how you do all that bullshit. Balls to the wall, flat-out, you better than me. I would go fucking crazy." Kanina couldn't help but feel sorry for her friend. Everybody has got a lot of shit to swallow at one time or another, but Monica seemed to stay in line to have a double-hard lump shoved down her throat.

"I know, but don't worry. I got a game plan. See you after school, and don't forget to take notes for me." Monica flipped her cell phone closed and fell back across the bed. The next morning she was going to skip class so she could go "borrowing" and get her pockets back right. There was no food in the house, and of course, she had to fix that.

As she lay in bed, Monica started thinking of graduation, prom, and all the changes that would soon happily come with turning eighteen. She was content in knowing that the clock was ticking and a new life was waiting for her and her siblings. It was only a matter of time before they would be all good.

Her little brother wasn't quite as patient as Monica. Dennis was in the streets every night getting into some bullshit that would end up costing him and his family dearly. Having Jenette for a mom meant a constant fight around every corner in the hood. She ran scams and fucked over everyone she could, so Jenette kept enemies. Taking up for her time and again was getting on Dennis's last nerve.

Chapter Four

"Oh my God," Monica screamed while look-ing at the calendar she kept hanging on the wall in the bedroom. "It's less than two weeks away from the prom, and I still haven't found the per-fect dress yet. I'm seriously slippin'."

"So what, crazy? Stop all that noise. I can't con-centrate." Kayla was trying her best to study.

"Don't hate. One day your little butt will be out searching for a prom dress too."

"Maybe, but if I do, I'm gonna make sure that I won't go with no dumb boy. I am gonna go by myself," Kayla huffed as she buried her face in the book she was reading.

Monica laughed at her sister. "You say that now. I'll wait and see what you say in about another two or three years."

"You better not hold your breath waiting. I hate boys." Kayla twisted her lips up, folding her arms in protest of Monica's words.

Monica had Kayla sit down on the floor so she could start to braid her hair. She made sure to keep up her little sister's appearance. Jenette didn't have time to care about anything but a good hit. By looking at Kayla, you could never tell that her mother was a junkie.

After about an hour or so, she finally finished. Kayla got up to stretch her legs. "Monica, don't forget about the awards ceremony tomorrow evening." She walked over to the mirror to admire her hair. Kayla was swinging her braids from side to side as she twirled around and around until she got dizzy and fell down. "I really want you to come, okay?"

"I won't forget, I promise. I'm going to the big mall later to get us both something to wear. What color dress do you want?"

"Can you see if you can find a yellow dress?" Kayla leaped to her feet. "I want to wear the sandals you got for me last week, and a yellow dress would match. Please, Monica?"

Monica kissed Kayla on her cheek. "Not a problem, baby girl. You know I got you." She walked over to the dresser and got out her book. *Damn, these orders are piling up! Everybody and they mama wants a prom dress.*

She double-checked the list and made calls to the people she knew had cash on hand. Monica wanted to make sure that she would have no problem at all going straight from the mall to their houses, dropping off the items, and getting her loot. If the price tag said $150, then they would pay half. That was the way shit worked.

The senior prom would be the last time to show off in front of all the people in her and Kanina's class. Even the bitches who didn't like Monica were putting their orders in. If she would be able to get everything on her list, her pockets would be on bump by nightfall. Monica picked her phone up off the charger and started dialing.

"Hey now, this is Monica. Will you be ready to see me about six o'clock this evening or what?"

"I'll be here waiting. Try to get red or sky blue. It really doesn't matter as long as it's a size eight," replied the first person on her list.

Monica went on to have similar conversations several times before changing her clothes to head out to the mall. She threw on a pair of Seven jeans, which hung loosely on her body. After pulling a light jacket out of the closet and getting Kayla together, she was out the door.

Monica often paid Miss Lila, the nice old lady who lived across the hall, to babysit her little sister. Sometimes the good neighbor would even fix them plates of food on Sundays when Monica was broke and couldn't provide. Miss Lila was a true godsend.

After making sure that Kayla was tight, Monica made her way down the piss-infected stairwell. Jenette, drunk as hell, was on her way inside of the building. Monica walked right past her, not speaking or even acknowledging her presence. The young girl was on a mission and didn't have time or patience for any of her mother's crackhead, dopefiend games.

When Monica emerged from the "Apartment Building from Hell," as she and Dennis had renamed it, she found Kanina parked in front of the building, waiting for her. Usually, Monica would roll by herself on the bus to do dirt. She hated to involve anyone else in her bullshit, but she had too many things on the list to haul back on the iron pimp.

"Hey, chick, what's good?" Monica showed all her teeth, smiling when she hopped into the car.

Kanina shook her head and busted out laughing. "Why your little ass always in such a good mood when you about to steal?"

"Fuck, I don't know. I guess 'cause I know I'm about to make some loot afterward." Monica shrugged her shoulders as she reached over and put her seat belt on. "Buckle up for safety, bitch. I don't wanna break the law."

"Shut up, trick. You the last female who gives a fuck about the law." They both had to laugh as Kanina pulled off.

Kanina and Monica gossiped and speculated about the prom all the way to the mall. When they pulled into the lot, Kanina found a parking space near one of the entranceways. Before going inside, Monica pulled the list from her purse and carefully went over it. Monica was almost out of breath as she went over the list repeatedly so she wouldn't have to look at it inside. "Okay, Kanina, you know the drill. After I get the five dresses out of the boutique on this side, I'll meet you around at the other entrance. Make sure to have the door unlocked just in case they be on my ass."

"Girl, you know I got you." Kanina winked at Monica, who was getting out of the car.

"Hey, I almost forgot. Keep your cell phone on loud, not vibrate. You never know when there might be a change of plans." Monica winked back at her best friend as she shut the car door.

Monica made her way toward the boutique door as Kanina slowly pulled the car around to the other side of the mall entrance to wait. She turned the radio all the way down and watched every single person like a hawk. Kanina was scared shitless and worried about her friend. She loved all the fresh clothes her homegirl would steal for her, but she didn't want her to get knocked doing it. She knew Monica was good at stealing, but everyone was subject to bad days, and her girl was no exception to the rule.

Monica put her small hands around the door handle of the boutique and entered with pride. She acted as if she had a million dollars in her pocket and not a care in the world. As soon as she stepped in the store, she headed straight to the formal dress section. She had been in the store three days prior to see if they had exactly what she needed and fortunately they did. Just as she remembered, the gowns were hanging toward the back near the fitting rooms. This was perfect for Monica. She went right to work.

Okay, I've got both the red ones, she thought as she swiftly searched the garment for any hidden sensors. Most stores didn't put bulky security tags on dresses and gowns because the weight of it could alter the material. She learned that from watching a fashion special on cable at Kanina's house.

Monica scanned the store to see if anyone was paying attention. When the coast seemed clear, she rapidly balled up both dresses and stuffed them in her Coach duffle bag. Quickly looking through rack after rack, she finally found the black dress in the right size. It was a little more out in the open than the others, but Monica was determined not to let that stop her. She pretended to browse some more until a few older white women came into the somewhat upscale boutique. This was the break she was hoping for. Any time older people came in, especially white folks, the saleswoman's attention would immediately turn toward helping them. Salespeople were just like Monica in many ways. They hustled, trying to sell all the overpriced items they could ring up, and Monica hustled, "borrowing" all the shit she could stuff in her purse and down her pants.

Oh, this shit is gonna be easy now. She waited until the perfect time, when everyone's back was turned, and she made her move. Monica had the black dress off the hanger and into her purse in no time flat. She threw the hanger under the display and kept it moving. Getting the two yellow sundresses would be a piece of cake after that. Monica glanced over and slightly smirked at the saleslady, who was busy catering to everyone else in the store except for her black ass. Ol' girl was occupied trying to get a commission from a big sale.

After scanning the store one more time for any signs of security, with all five dresses in her possession, Monica nonchalantly walked out the door. There were no alarms, no buzzers, and most importantly, no security guards chasing behind. Ecstatic, she pulled out her cell phone and dialed her friend's number.

Kanina saw the number flash across the screen, and she felt an instant sense of relief. "Hey, are you straight?" she nervously questioned her friend as soon as she answered. She stared at the mall doors to see if there was any sign of Monica.

"Not a problem, girl. I was in and out just like that." Monica snapped her fingers as she pushed open the door with her back. No sooner than she stepped in the parking lot, she felt the warm sun touch her body.

Kanina smiled and nodded. *Hell, yeah!*

Monica hastily made her way to the car to drop off the dresses and get ready to go back into a different store to fill the rest of her orders. She pulled the dresses out on the back seat and smoothed them all out. Monica didn't want them to wrinkle any more than needed. People always tried to pay less for a wrinkled garment.

"Damn, these motherfuckers are off the chain, Monica. We'd look hot." Kanina smiled.

"I know. When I saw them the other day, I was bugging out. I started to get them for you and me. You know how ya ass love this color."

"I wish you would have. I'm tripping on this one, for sure. I should just buy this myself." Kanina had the money in her purse and was serious as hell, but Monica had an order to fill.

"Don't worry. Let them hoes have this cheap-ass bullshit. I'm gonna hook us up on some hellava dresses I saw at Saks Fifth Avenue last week."

"That's what I'm talking about. I wanna floss on them hating-ass bitches."

"Dig dis here: when I get finished and we both walk into that prom, every last female in the place is gonna have her face cracked." Monica raised her hand and waved it all around her face, imitating the thought.

"Your ass is truly crazy." Kanina almost choked from laughter as the gum she was chewing went down her throat.

"I'm serious. Wait 'til you see them. I'm telling you, we gonna rock that bitch." Monica grabbed her purse and jumped back out of the car into the sweltering heat. "All right then, let me run into this other store and get the rest of the stuff on the list, and we can be out. I want to get back and get rid of this gear before them busters spend my money. And God knows I need every single penny."

"I'll be right here." Kanina held up her cell phone and reassured her girl. "Don't worry, it's on." She knew the routine and sat back and waited for Monica to return.

It was hot as hell outside, but Kanina didn't want to turn the air conditioner on. She wanted to hear any and all noises around her. She was completely paranoid. Everyone who walked past looked like the police to her. Monica always told her that she wasn't built for this type of shit, and Kanina knew that her friend was right.

The clock in the car said 3:45, and by the time it read 4:15, Monica was on her way out the door with a big Kool-Aid smile plastered across her face. She opened the car door and slid inside.

"Here, girl, this is for your scary ass." Monica was still cheesing as she threw a huge bottle of Burberry perfume onto Kanina's lap. "All right,

chick. Now let's roll. And damn, turn on the air."
Monica pulled item after item out of her purse and
pants as the two girls hit the highway. Not only did
she get everything on her list, she managed to get a
few extras as well.

Monica pulled out her calculator and started
punching in numbers and smiling. She and her little brother and sister would be able to eat good for
the entire week. She neatly folded the items on the
back seat and placed them in their own separate
bags. That way, any person spending money with
her would have to take exactly what they ordered
and not have a chance to grab someone else's shit.

Chapter Five

It was two days before prom, and Monica still hadn't gotten her and Kanina's dresses. After she stole the first three gowns and word got around, every girl in school started pressuring her to get theirs. Monica barely had time to braid Kayla's hair or get Dennis the new Jordans that came out. Nothing else seemed to matter but the grind of getting paid. Kanina, on the other hand, was starting to panic about not having a dress to wear.

"Dang, Monica, I know you said that you was gonna get us the hookup, but when?" She had a puzzled look on her face. "I don't know what color shoes to buy or what color to get my nails done. Can you clue a bitch in or what?"

"Yeah, you right. I'll tell you what, as soon as the bell rings, we can be out. We can swing by the mall out off the interstate, and I can grab both dresses and purses to match. How about that?"

"Thanks, Monica. You know I like to be prepared, but if you want, I've got enough money saved from my allowance to just buy both our prom stuff."

"Girl, bye." Monica frowned. "Fuck spending money you don't have to."

The last bell rang, and Kanina beat Monica to the car and waited patiently for her to arrive.

"Your ass is on it, ain't you?" Monica joked as she slowly approached her friend.

"Girl, you ain't never lied. I can't wait."

Monica grabbed the keys out of Kanina's hand. "Let me drive. Your behind goes too slow."

"Shut up, girl," Kanina yelled out while she jumped in the passenger seat.

When they got in the car and drove off, Monica turned the radio to a jazz station so that she could concentrate. Normally she listened to rap at home when she was chilling, but she was about to go to work and wanted to keep her mind free and clear of any distractions. Jazz, with all its power, soothed her thoughts.

After about twenty-five minutes on the interstate, dodging in and out of traffic, they pulled off at the mall exit. Monica found a space near the front and turned the music all the way off. She unfastened her pants and took her shirt all the way out. She then proceeded to pull the sun visor down, fix her hair, and put on a little bit of bubblegum-flavored lip gloss. Monica had stolen every flavor that the corner store carried. Even when she had money, she would pocket it. Stealing was fast becoming a force of habit with her. Monica was almost addicted to it.

"All right, I'm ready. I didn't want to go all up in Saks looking a hot freakin' mess." Monica dumped the contents of her expensive purse in the back seat of Kanina's car. "I need all the free space I can get."

"Monica, please be careful. We never came out here before. I thought that you was gonna get them at the other mall. It's only down the road. We should go there. This is where all the rich white folks hang out. You know they don't play." Kanina was pleading with Monica to change her mind.

"I got this. I told you that your ass wasn't built for this type of shit, but for a bitch like me," Monica said, "it's in my blood. I'm gonna get it how I live, that's a given." She was tilting her head from side to side as she geeked herself up. "Now stop fucking with my karma and sending me bad vibes."

Kanina knew there was no talking Monica out of going in, so she didn't have any choice but to go along with the game plan. She was starting to sweat and feel nervous. "Monica, I'm sorry. I didn't mean to throw you off. It's just that I have a bad feeling about this mall."

"Listen, the prom is in less than two days. Now do your ass wanna turn around and I go into JCPenney, or worse than that Sears, to cop our outfits? Or do you want me to march my little cute ass in Saks and get us some shit that will make them bitches howl?" Monica was in rare form. She was hyped and confident in her stealing abilities.

For all of ten seconds, Kanina sat back in the seat, thinking about wearing a dress from the window at Sears, before she immediately straightened her ass up. "Girl, you know I ain't even with that. I wouldn't even go to that motherfucker if I was sporting that kinda gear. I put that on everything."

"Now, that's more like it, bitch. Now you know the routine. Keep your phone on and the door unlocked. I'll be back as soon as possible."

"Okay, I'll be parked right here waiting."

Kanina climbed over to the driver's seat as Monica exited the car and made her way to the store entrance. Once inside, Monica quickly glanced around to see where and if she spotted any guards. She was not familiar with the layout of this particular Saks, and she had to look at the store directory. Unfortunately, the formal attire was located on the second floor. *Damn!*

Monica headed toward the escalator. On the way up, she made sure to take Kanina's advice, and she started paying careful attention to all of the other customers. She knew any one of them could be an undercover security guard. Just because they weren't all out in the open sporting a fake badge and a uniform, they still could hold a bitch damn near hostage until the police showed they punk asses up. Most of the time, the wannabe police store-bought rent-a-cops were worse than the real ones. They always had something to prove just because they couldn't make the real police force or their ass got their teeth stumped out of their mouth by the school bully. Stealing off the second floor of the store was definitely a risk, but Monica was determined. *A bitch gotta do what a bitch gotta do!* she reasoned with herself as she got off on her floor.

Monica took small steps as she casually strolled around all the high-priced clothes that were carefully arranged on the tables and racks. Monica, hood raised, knew she was out of her league as she took notice of the outrageous price tags. She didn't want to overplay her hand and rush over to the gowns like she would have done in the ghetto. Taking her time and giving the illusion that she was a regular shopper and not a brazen, overzealous teenage shoplifter was always in her best interest. Monica had to play it cool.

After ten or fifteen minutes of pretending to look at silk blouses and lace handkerchiefs, Monica nonchalantly strolled to her ultimate destination: formal wear. It was filled with other teenagers her age accompanied by their well-to-do parents. Monica both resented them and felt envious of them at the same time. You could tell that they had

money and were rich by her standards. Because
it was prom season, that section of the store was
crowded, and the sales staff was busy, trying to
help as many people as possible. Monica instantly
took notice of two gowns that were on a rack near
the counter. She moved like a cat in and out of the
displays. When she finally got close, Monica saw
that both the dresses had big hold tags on them.
That didn't stop her from feeling the material and
imagining her and Kanina rocking them at the
prom.

"Damn, this is the shit," she mumbled under
her breath. "I can see us in these bitches already."
She was in deep thought when she was calmly
interrupted.

"Hello, dear, can I help you with something?"
The aging saleswoman was very polite and cordial
as she addressed Monica. "Do you see one that
catches your eye, sweetheart?"

Monica was immediately thrown off by the lady's
demeanor. She seemed like someone's grandmother.
Monica gave her a weak smile. "Um yes, ma'am,
I do. I think I like one of those two, right there."
Monica stumbled over her words while pointing to
the dresses with the brown tags on them.

"I'm very sorry, sweetheart. Those are on hold
for our special VIP customers. We have a few more
that you might like and would be better suited for
you. Please follow me."

The lady guided Monica over to the side of the formal department that was obviously less expensive. The clothes and displays lacked the amount of care put into those sprawled out on the "in" side of the store. When Monica saw the way the garments on that side were hung, she rolled her eyes and immediately caught feelings.

Who do this old bitch think I am? Doesn't she know that this is a fucking $500 purse on my arm? I ain't wearing this cheap shit to my prom!

Monica started going through the countless tacky, discontinued gowns, and she gave the old hag the phoniest smile that she could half-ass muster up. Monica's mind had kicked totally into "I don't give a fuck" mode, and the game was on.

"You take your time looking at these on this rack, and I'm sure you can find something a little bit more suitable for a girl like you. They're on clearance. Maybe the markdown can help you."

The saleslady's nice, grandmotherly manner soared from kind to low-key insulting in a matter of seconds. No sooner than the saleswoman was out of Monica's sight did she laugh at the thought of the young girl being able to afford the lavish gowns she originally pointed out. *Imagine that. Why would she even waste her time dreaming about that gown? She could never save up enough at that McDonald's job she probably works at to buy a $3,500 Christian Dior gown.*

Back on the other side of the store, where Monica had been systematically ushered to, she had to think quickly. She had to have those dresses now, point blank. It was the principle of the situation. Monica rubbed her sweaty palms on her blue Eddie Bauer slacks and proudly marched back to the side that she had just been banished from. The two expensive gowns were hanging there and seemed to be calling out her name. Monica was pissed off and determined to reply. Recklessly and most certainly with no signs of remorse, Monica boldly snatched the two gowns off their hangers and stuffed them into her purse.

Fuck that old bitch. They on hold all right! On hold for my black ass! Monica stormed off and headed arrogantly to the escalator and stepped on. She was on a mission and couldn't care less about who or what was around her. It was as if she had a receipt in her hand and couldn't be questioned.

When Monica got off the escalator, the doors to freedom were just a few short steps away. *I don't know why that old bitch acted like I couldn't have afforded some dresses like this.* Monica patted her purse and held it snugly against her body as the automatic doors swung wide open. She got out to the parking lot and saw Kanina flash her lights twice. Monica was almost home free. She felt a sense of relief, imagining all her classmates sucking her socks when they saw her and Kanina in their prom dresses. It was on. *Damn, I made it. Don't they realize I can't be fucking faded?* She had a devilish smirk on her face. *Them motherfuckers can't stop me!*

Monica started taking big strides as she took notice of Kanina's face dropping. All of a sudden, out of nowhere, all hell broke loose.

"There she is. That's her right there." The old saleslady who'd pretended to be kind was now screaming at the top of her decrepit lungs. "She had to have taken them. Get her." Within a matter of seconds, the group converged on the brash, unpolished thief, Monica.

"Miss! Excuse me, miss! We need to talk to you for a minute," one of the men explained in a loud, boisterous tone. Three huge security guards were starting to surround Monica. There was nowhere to run. She was trapped, and she unsuccessfully tried to flip the script.

"I don't know what the fuck you want," she yelled. "Now leave me the hell alone." Monica was infuriated and continued to act as if they were truly unjustly bothering her.

One man grabbed her arm, while the other one snatched her purse out of her hands. "What is this, young lady?" He pulled the two dresses out of her purse and shook his head. "Did you pay for this? Where is your receipt?"

She was busted. After a few moments of struggling to get free from the guard's strong grip, Monica finally gave in and stopped resisting the inevitable. The real police were pulling into the parking lot, but Monica still wasn't fazed.

"Do whatever you gonna do. I ain't scared." Monica spat directly in the saleswoman's face as she was being handcuffed. "That's for being so rude."

Kanina was frozen in shock as she watched her best friend being practically thrown in the back of the police squad car and driven away. She sat in the parking lot, in total silence, for close to an hour, in denial over what had just taken place.

Damn, she thought as she finally pulled off. How was she gonna tell Dennis and Kayla? She had no earthly idea what to do next. Kanina knew off the jump that informing Jenette would be like talking to the wind. She couldn't care less what happened to Monica or anyone else who wasn't the dope man. Kanina drove home in silence and prepared herself to confess to both of her law-abiding, hardworking parents what exactly she and her best friend Monica had been doing and, regretfully, the outcome of their actions. Hopefully, they could help Monica. One thing was for certain: both girls would miss going to their senior prom. Kanina would more than likely be put on some form of punishment, but it would not be as harsh a penalty as what Monica was facing. "This is so fucked up." Kanina bit her lower lip nervously as she pulled in the driveway of her suburban home.

Chapter Six

"All rise. The Honorable Judge James P. Thorton presiding." The bailiff waited respectfully until the judge took his seat on the bench. "Please all be seated."

Case after case was called in the crowded courtroom before she heard her name called.

"Monica Howard, case number 781921H, will you please approach the microphone?"

"Yes, Your Honor." Monica made her way front and center and found her way next to the inexperienced public defender who was assigned her case. Monica had already made a deal and was ready to face the music and accept the consequences of her actions.

"You are being charged with grand larceny in the amount of seven thousand dollars, which is a felony. Do you understand the charges against you?"

"Yes, I do." Monica frowned.

"How do you plead, Miss Howard?" The judge had a grim and stern look on his aging face.

Monica hung her head as she mumbled her response. "No contest, Your Honor."

"Can you please speak up in a tone that can be heard by this courtroom, Miss Howard?"

"I said no contest, Judge Thorton, sir."

"Are you clearly aware of what you are saying to this court today, young lady?"

"Yes, sir, I am."

"All right then, let's proceed, shall we?" The judge glanced over every document that was placed in front of him, and he nodded in agreement. "Can each lawyer please approach the bench?"

After a few formalities and a pile of papers being signed, Monica's fate was decided. The young girl would spend the next fourteen months at a prison for women offenders, which was located far north of the city limits. That was that, point blank, done deal.

When Monica was led out of the courtroom, she saw Kanina's parents holding Kayla's hand and Kanina wiping her eyes. Monica had one phone call when she got arrested, and she placed that call to Kanina's mom, Mrs. Cooper, begging her to take care of her sister and brother until she was set free.

Jenette was not a factor. Living her life as she did, Jenette could barely take care of herself. No one had seen or heard from her in three or four days. Dennis opted not to leave home and Jenette. The wayward teen promised Monica that he would go to school and do the right thing. Dennis reassured everyone that he could hold himself down and take care of things on his own. Considering her present situation, Monica really didn't have any true say-so. She had to go with the flow and hope for the best.

On the bus ride to prison, Monica thought about the prom that she missed as well as the graduation ceremony she couldn't attend. Tightly closing her eyes, Monica imagined each and every person in the auditorium cheering and applauding for her. She'd worked four hard, long years and wanted badly to walk across that stage with her peers. Monica felt as if she had earned that privilege. Now she had been robbed of it.

Although not taking part in those events caused tears to well in her eyes, Monica was saddened the most by being taken away from her siblings. The only thing that gave her comfort was she knew they would be in good hands. Well, at least Kayla would. Monica prayed that Dennis would change his mind after a few days of Jenette and all her mess. Mr.

and Mrs. Cooper could provide all the things that Kayla and he both deserved to have.

The road the criminal-minded group of women were traveling on was filled with potholes, and the small bus seemed to purposely hit each one. Every bump caused the handcuffs on Monica's tiny wrists to tighten, cutting off her circulation. They were both starting to feel numb and turn purple. She wasn't in any real rush to get caged up behind bars like an animal, but she wanted to arrive at the prison soon so that her hands could freely move around.

As the bus finally crossed into the confinement of the walls of the prison, Monica braced herself for the unknown. When all the female inmates entered the facility, they were asked to strip down naked, and they were hosed off like cattle at a market. They were then searched and assigned a number. Each woman was given two dingy washcloths, a towel, a blanket, and two sets of mismatched sheets. All the items were old and worn, and they had a stale smell. Monica slightly rubbed the washcloth and quickly frowned at the abrasive texture as she was led down the long, twisted concrete corridor.

Monica reflected on the days when she was younger and Jenette had them sleeping on the floor with one blanket to share. Those times were in the past for her or so she thought. After all the "borrowing" Monica had done, she had become accustomed to a fluffy mattress, a thick triple-layer goose comforter, and silk linens, but she was a trooper. It was time for her to man up, so to speak. Monica was determined not to let a place like jail fuck with her mind or her spirit. This wasn't somewhere she wanted to get used to. It was just a bump in the road.

The female officer opened the cell and proceeded to slam it shut loudly as soon as Monica crossed inside its closed-in, damp walls. Reality was quickly starting to set in. She was really locked the fuck up. Not on a punishment for the weekend, like no watching television or not being able to go out to play, but in prison for fourteen months.

"I can do this time standing on my head, with my eyes closed. The man can't hold my black ass down," Monica said out loud as she finally reached her bunk and plopped down, trying to convince herself of her own words.

"Oh, is that right, Miss Lady?" The woman on the upper bunk startled Monica when she spoke. "You think it's just that easy, do you? You think you've got all the answers and this joint figured out? Well, I'll be damned." The voice grew stronger with each word.

Monica jumped up and swiftly went on the other side of the small cell to get a better look at the person talking. "Dang, G, I ain't see your ass." Monica paused when the woman on the bunk sat all the way up, and she noticed that she was an older woman. "Oh, I'm sorry. I didn't mean to cuss. I just didn't know anyone else was in here."

"I understand, dear, but take it from me, while you're locked up in this cage, try to pay attention and always beware of these other females. I don't care how tough you think you are. These bitches in here can be just as treacherous as any man, if not more. But then again, I don't have to tell you that, do I?"

The older woman was being sarcastic as she slowly got off her bunk and was now standing face-to-face with Monica. They were just about the same height and weight. Most of their features were similar, having the same eye color and complexion. The only major difference was the forty or so years of age separating the two.

"How old are you? You look like a baby." The woman tilted her head sideways as she awaited the answer to her question.

"I'm eighteen, ma'am."

"Eighteen, are you sure? You don't look old enough to spit at a barn fire."

Monica started smiling at the lady's comparison and her Down South, country accent. "Yes, I'm sure I'm eighteen, unfortunately for me! The judge reminded me right before he sentenced me to come here."

Both women started to laugh because they knew that Monica, being of legal age, guaranteed her a spot in the penitentiary instead of juvenile hall lockup.

"Well, all I can tell you is now ya rolling with the big dogs. A pretty young girl like you is gonna get tested, believe me." The old woman grinned as if she knew some sort of ancient Chinese secret.

"I ain't the one." Monica sucked her teeth and twisted her lips to the side. "Nan bitch in dis motherfucker betta not try me. That's my word." Monica started pacing back and forth around the tiny cell that she would now call home. Angry as hell, Monica threw respecting her elders out the window as she cursed.

"Okat, Miss Betta Not Try Me. Calm your little ass down. I don't even know ya name."

"It's Monica. Monica Howard."

"All right then, Monica. My name is Sandra."

The older of the two sat down on the lower bunk and schooled Monica on everything from the guards and the inmates to the food and the phone.

After close to three hours of Sandra holding court, putting Monica up on game, the cell gates were cracked for lunch and yard time.

"Remember what I told you, Monica. Don't ask for or look for any kinda trouble, but don't back down and show any signs of weakness. This ain't the playground at school. This is ya life."

"I got this, Sandra. I ain't gonna hesitate not once on none of these bitches! I'm gonna go hard."

Even though Monica was completely overwhelmed by her present circumstances, she held herself down. The inmates poured into the hallway. Mothers, sisters, daughters, cousins, nieces, and even great-grandmas, all fell in line. Both Monica and Sandra did the same, making their way into the chow hall, where they got in line without incident. But like they always say, "I knew it was too good to be true," well, it was. Another inmate brushed past Monica extremely close and made sure that her breast touched Monica's shoulder. Sandra was right. It didn't take long for someone to test Monica. Now she had to react and set the tone.

"Damn, what's your fuckin' problem? Are you crazy or something?" Monica was pissed off as she yelled at the girl.

"Oh, sorry, my bad." The girl tried to play it off and act as if she had made a mistake.

"Listen, you big bitch. I ain't gonna tell you but once that I ain't the one to be fucked with. If you even daydreaming about some dumb shit with me, you better check ya'self." Monica was hyped as hell. She was holding her tray sideways and made sure that the girl fully understood that she wasn't in the mood for no foolishness or games. She would split her shit to the white meat.

"Look, I said that it was my fault. Why you tripping?" The girl was towering over Monica and pointing in her face.

The two were about to come to blows. Sandra jumped in between them in hopes of defusing tension and stopping any more physical contact. She wanted to make her presence felt.

"Come on, you two. There's no need for all this arguing and carrying on." Sandra had a huge smile on her face. "Monica, calm down. This chick already said that she was sorry, and I think she knows that she will be even sorrier if she ever, ever makes that same fucked-up mistake again. Am I right?" Sandra gave the girl a treacherous look, and the girl turned around quickly, deciding to be on her way before Sandra really got pissed. "Well, I guess we told her, didn't we?" Sandra smiled.

After giving a slight nod in agreement, Monica got her food, and they found a seat. Monica and Sandra ate their lunch and walked around the yard talking the entire time. It was if they had known one another their entire lives. Sandra had a daughter who was Monica's age, but she was taken by the state over five years ago. Sandra was constantly in and out of jail, and she was deemed unfit, losing her parental rights. This time, she was doing a four-year bid for shoplifting. It was one more thing that she and Monica had in common.

By the time the bell started ringing, Sandra had found out Monica's entire horrible life history. She was determined to put her new cellmate up on game. As soon as they got back inside their tiny concrete home away from home, the lessons began.

Chapter Seven

Week after week passed, and Monica and Sandra grew closer by the minute. Sandra was like the mother Monica never had. Everything a person needed to know to walk inside a store buck-ass naked and come out suited and booted without even being noticed was instilled into Monica's brain. Sandra was giving her some true knowledge that the average petty shoplifter dreamed of acquiring.

"Listen, Monica, I know all that snatch-and-run, smash-and-grab bullshit makes you think that you did something big, but it ain't shit. Fuck all that drawing attention to yourself. It only makes them stores be on the lookout for you." Sandra was in the middle of one of her famous speeches of the day. "That type of wild bullshit don't do nothing but make ya li'l ass hot."

Monica was trying her best to pay attention. She was tired and was being tormented by a headache that had been pounding all day long. "I know, Sandra. When I go home, I'm gonna run my shit a lot differently. I got a plan for they ass." She tilted her head back and rubbed both sides gently, trying to change the subject. "Something ain't right. My head won't stop hurting."

"Girl, it's probably from all that worrying. You have to learn to pace yourself on calling home."

"Yeah, I guess you right. It's just that I have been trying to call my friend Kanina and the answering machine keeps picking up. She always accepts my calls." Monica sighed as she sat up on her bunk.

"Stop jumping to conclusions. People on the outside have a life to live. You might have stolen for them, given to them, and looked out for them and they mama, but all bullshit aside, your ass is in jail, not theirs. Your young behind has gots to walk this time down on your own. They can't do your time for you, so stop pressing your bid and mine!" Sandra was finally succeeding in calming Monica down when Miss Sims, the night guard on duty, slowly approached the cell gates.

"Howard, come with me."

"What's wrong, Miss Sims? Did she do something?" Sandra questioned.

"Stay out of this. It doesn't concern you." Miss Sims rolled her eyes. "Now come on, Howard, you have a visit."

"A visit?" Monica was confused. It was four hours past visiting time. "Who is it? It's not even my day for a visit."

"Just hurry up." Miss Sims opened up the cell gate and let Monica slip out into the corridor.

"Sandra, I'm scared. I don't know what this is about." Monica was hesitant to move her feet any farther. She looked at Sandra for help.

"Whatever it is, don't worry. I'll be here waiting for you." Sandra was determined to help Monica feel as safe as possible. She had seen this type of circumstance occur repeatedly over the years she was locked up. When an inmate was called out this late on a visit, it could only mean one thing.

Sandra held her head down in her hands as she waited for her cellmate to return. *Damn, it's gonna be one long-ass night!* She felt chills rush throughout her entire body. Sandra leaned back on the bunk and listened to the sounds of the prison. She imagined who had died in Monica's family. After all the horror stories Monica had told Sandra, Jenette was the first and only one to come to mind.

Miss Sims put her key into the huge steel door and turned the handle down toward the floor. "Howard, visiting room one," Miss Sims bellowed. During all the months that Monica had spent locked up, Miss Sims never really seemed to make eye contact with her, let alone show any sort of kindness, but today was different.

"All right, Howard, remember that God never gives you more than you can stand."

Monica looked into Miss Sims's eyes as she pushed the heavy door open and revealed Kanina's mother and the prison chaplain on the other side. They were seated at a table in the far corner of the room near the window. Monica's face started to stiffen up, and her already-pounding headache intensified. She turned around and glanced back at Miss Sims one last time before she made her way across to her visitors. She was glad that at least she'd had her hair braided earlier that morning. She made sure to get it tightened up every few days. Monica didn't want Kanina's mother to see her looking like a wild child.

"Hello, Monica." The chaplain was the first to speak as he stood up and patted her on the shoulder.

"Hello, Chaplain Davis," she replied, looking over at her best friend's mother.

Before Monica could get a chance to sit down, she saw Mrs. Cooper lower her head and start to cry. Monica immediately started sobbing and pleading with them to tell her what was wrong.

"Oh my God, what's wrong? Is it my mother?" she cried out. "I knew if I wasn't there, something bad was gonna happen to her. I knew it, I knew it." Monica's screaming was uncontrollable.

"Calm down, Monica. Jenette is fine, I guess. No one has seen her in days." Mrs. Cooper wiped her eyes while handing Monica a tissue to do the same. The tension in the room was still intense as Monica's total, undivided attention was focused on the two people across from her at the table.

"Can one of you please tell me?" Her heart was racing.

"Listen, dear, the doctors did everything they could, but it was too late. The injuries were far too severe and so much blood was lost. Kanina wanted to answer the phone and tell you everything, but I wouldn't let her. I thought it would be better to break the news to you in person," Mrs. Cooper sobbed.

"What news? What the hell are you talking about? What do you mean so much blood? What doctors?" Monica leaped out of her seat and practically knocked the table over.

Miss Sims watched from the security booth as the loud, somber exchange of words took place.

"It was Dennis. He was shot and injured badly in some sort of street altercation yesterday evening. He died on the operating table. I'm so sorry."

"Dennis? Oh my God." Monica's eyes grew wide, and her heart slowly broke as she took in all the details of her younger brother's death. After hearing that he was shot in the head as well as his back, Monica let the tears flow. She hated that Dennis was dead and she couldn't be there to protect him. That had always been her job. Guilt took control of her body as she wept.

Kanina's mother assured her that Kayla was doing as fine as could be expected considering all the horrible events that had taken place over the past months of the year. She then hugged Monica for close to ten minutes. Monica asked Chaplain Davis if she would be allowed to attend her brother's funeral service.

"Yes, it should not be any problem at all. I have to check your file, but if my memory serves me correct, you aren't a high-risk prisoner. I will inform your family of the cost of you attending."

Monica put a frown on her face. "How much do you think it will be?" Her eyes were swollen and puffy from all the tears. "I don't have but twenty dollars in my account."

"Don't worry about the money, Monica. My husband and I will cover it."

Monica managed a slight, half-hearted smile. "Thank you. I don't know what I would ever do without you. Kanina is so lucky to have a mother like you."

Before the tear-filled visit came to a close, Monica learned that Kanina's mom would try to find Jenette to finalize the services. She was, after all, dopefiend or not, Dennis's next of kin and had to sign off on the body and give the mortician some vital information. Monica knew that the state of Michigan would step in and pay a portion of the cost to bury her little brother, but Jenette would have to fill out the proper documents.

Miss Sims marched Monica down the long, twisted hallway back toward the row of cells that housed the women. Suddenly all the awful, foul odors that engulfed the air no longer mattered. All the late-night noises that ruled the environment were silent to Monica's ears. She was in somewhat of a trance as she reentered her cell and fell on her bunk. Sandra cringed with pity as she witnessed her young friend ball up into an instant state of depression.

"Monica, you have to listen to me. I know it appears as if your entire world is being ripped apart at the seams, but it's gonna pass. You just need time. We both know that I don't read the Bible on a daily basis or go to the services they hold here, but I do know one thing. God will never give you more than you can stand."

It was the same thing that Miss Sims had just told her. Sandra, true enough, wasn't an overly religious woman, but she cared about Monica's well-being and fully understood that at a time like this there was only one place or person one could turn to: the Lord.

After waiting three days for an update, Monica put in a request to see the chaplain. She still hadn't received any word about the day or time when her little brother's funeral would be held. She wanted at least to have her hair braided and be prepared. While she awaited his response, she called Kanina.

"You have a collect call from an inmate at a state prison. To accept the charges, press one. To decline, just hang up to disconnect." The automated operator clicked on no sooner than Kanina had gotten the phone up to her ear. She immediately, without hesitation, pressed the number one button on the keypad. After a few brief clicks, she heard Monica's voice.

"Hello. Hello."

"Hey, girl, I'm here," Kanina belted out.

Monica heard her best friend's soft-spoken voice, and she started to cry. "Kanina, damn I miss ya ass so much. I am so fucking lonely in this place."

"Don't worry, girl. It'll be over soon. You almost at the end of your bid. Remember you got an out date. I mean it ain't like you killed somebody."

"I know, but being away from home is so messed up, especially now." Monica sighed.

"I feel you. You know, Kayla really misses the shit out ya ass too." Kanina was trying her best to keep her girl's spirits up. "She'll be back shortly. My mother took her shopping to get a dress to wear to the service."

"That's why I'm calling. I haven't heard anything yet. I don't know what day or time it is. They don't tell us shit until the very last minute."

"Dang, Monica. I thought they said they would let you know that no one can find Jenette, not the state, me, or Mom. It's as if she dropped off the face of the earth. Ain't nobody around the way seen her since the night Dennis got killed, and you know they needed her to sign all those papers. A lot of people are looking for her for some reason."

"So what does that mean? I'm confused. What, he can't be buried?" Monica started to feel a chill go throughout her entire body. The cold concrete walls that surrounded her small body started to spin.

"The state stepped in and took control. They paid the funeral home that's up on Dexter Avenue to hold the service. It's tomorrow morning, at ten o'clock sharp. I thought you knew. My mother called the prison two days ago, and the chaplain explained the process."

"What?" Monica screamed out. "At ten tomorrow? They ain't told me shit. See what I'm talking about? If I hadn't called you, they would have shown up early as hell, no warning, and my hair would have looked like hell on a stick."

"Listen, Monica, I don't know if—" Before Kanina could get her words out, the phone went dead. "Hello, Monica? Hey, girl, can you hear me?" Kanina tightly closed her eyes and lay back in the chair she was sitting in. *I swear to God I hope she can call back.*

Monica was left on the other end of the line, still holding the phone in her hands. "What the fuck? What happened?" She was frantic as she looked up at the guard who was standing in the doorway mean mugging her. "Why you do that? I wasn't done yet!"

"Shift change, Howard. You know the rules. Hurry up and get back to your cell for count."

"I didn't realize it was so late. I'm trying to get some information about my brother's funeral service. I need about five more minutes of phone time and I'll be done," Monica pleaded.

"Listen, Miss Thang. I know all about your circumstances, but rules are rules, and I'm not about to risk losing my job for you or your dead brother. Now move your ass!" The guard placed her hand on her stick as she seemingly dared Monica to challenge or oppose her orders.

The outrageous and insensitive comments struck an already-tender nerve and Monica couldn't resist. It was on! "Who in the fuck are you talking to? What's your problem?" Monica lunged toward the burly guard and tried to damn near smack the taste out of her mouth. "That's my fucking little brother your ho ass is talking about. I should kill you." Monica was out of control.

She and the guard began a short-lived battle. Monica was, without a doubt, outsized and completely overpowered. Even with the rage that filled her spirit, she had no win. The guard threw Monica around the narrow room without even breaking a sweat.

"I think that I had about enough of your little ass." She laughed while pulling out her baton and putting her tactical training to use.

Without any remorse or sensitivity to the situation at hand, the guard struck Monica across her forehead, causing her to fall against the wall and become unconscious. The callous guard reached down on her waistband and grabbed her radio to send for assistance, as she kicked her young, immature attacker once in the stomach. When help finally arrived, they found Monica, delirious, bleeding from an open cut and spitting up blood. She was taken to the prison clinic in handcuffs, open wounds and all. Monica was roughly handled by all the guards on her way.

Almost three entire days passed since the time the battle had taken place. Monica regained consciousness and was back in her right mind. She had been transferred to the state hospital for observation. Not only did she suffer a busted lip and a severe concussion, but Monica had missed her brother's funeral. When that reality set in, that's when her real pain began. She felt an overwhelming sense of guilt. The girl, once strong and confident, was now reduced to constant tears and thoughts of suicide. Monica felt that if she could have just controlled her temper, she would have been able to at least say good-bye to her only brother.

Kanina and her mother were allowed twenty minutes to visit Monica before she was shipped back to prison. Upon entering the hospital room, Mrs. Cooper was astounded to see Monica handcuffed to the tiny bed's steel railing.

"I can't understand why you need to go to these extremes. This doesn't make sense. You act as if she's an animal."

The day nurse shrugged her shoulders as she went on performing her daily duties. "Listen, lady. I don't make the rules for the way they choose to treat unruly and hostile prisoners. I have a job to do. Now if you will excuse me, I have to continue with my rounds."

Kanina and her mother were left standing dumbfounded and confused. What did the nurse mean by unruly, let alone hostile? That wasn't the Monica they both knew.

Monica turned her head toward her two visitors and let out a sigh of relief as they cautiously approached her. They had no idea what to expect. Kanina was shaking. She didn't want to see her girl with any bumps or bruises, looking wrecked. Monica had been waiting to apologize to her extended family for letting them down and not being able to stand by Kayla's side at the funeral. She tried her best to look her visitors in the eyes, but she couldn't bring herself to do it. The shame took over, and the tears started to pour.

"Listen, sweetheart. Please don't cry. I'm so sorry about what happened. We tried everything in our power to find your mother. Kanina and I searched and searched until the very last minute. These heartless prison officials wouldn't budge one inch on their so-called rules." Mrs. Cooper was overly apologetic as she rubbed Monica's forehead.

Monica sat up in the bed. Squinting her eyes, she dried tears that had soaked the thin hospital gown that draped over her body. "I don't understand, Mrs. Cooper. I'm the one who couldn't keep my temper under control. I know I messed things up. It's my entire fault. I don't know what happened. Things just went haywire. I'm sorry."

Kanina came in between her best friend in the world and her mother. "Monica, I was trying to tell you, but the phone went dead, and you never called back. The next call we got was from the ho-ass warden."

"Kanina, watch your mouth," Mrs. Cooper was also definitely pissed off, but she didn't condone using profanity under any circumstances.

"Sorry, Mom, but I'm mad," Kanina continued as Monica remained in the dark. "I was trying to tell you, girl. Without your mother's signature on Dennis's burial paperwork, the stupid warden refused to grant you a temporary release."

"He refused? What do you mean he refused?" Monica was livid. "I can't believe that bullshit." As soon as the words came out of her mouth, she quickly turned toward Mrs. Cooper. "I'm sorry, but I've been lying in this bed night after night, chained up, depressed, ashamed, and blaming myself, and all along the warden was the one who stopped me from going to the funeral? I can't freaking believe it."

"I tried to tell you, Monica. I promise. I swear to God, I looked all over town for Jenette." Kanina held her head down. "She finally showed up at our door a few days after the service, drunk as hell and high as a kite, asking for the obituary and a couple of dollars. Kayla went to the door and gave her one before slamming it right in your mother's face."

Monica hated to hear her mother still hadn't changed one little bit since she had been away. Jenette was destined to be nothing more than a piece of shit, and Monica was now ready to completely shut the door on her just like her little sister had done.

"Kanina and Mrs. Cooper, I wanna thank both of you. Thanks for always being in my corner and especially for taking Kayla into your home."

"It's our pleasure, Monica. Kayla is so smart and sweet. We love her. She's just like part of our family." Mrs. Cooper was beaming with pride as she spoke about Kayla. "I always wanted another daughter. Now I have three: Kanina, Kayla, and you."

All three of them talked and made plans for the future until the nurse came back in the room. "I'm sorry, ladies, but you have to bring this visit to a close."

"Okay. Can we maybe have one more minute to say good-bye?" Mrs. Cooper was now being polite to the nurse.

"Sure. Let me give this other inmate her medication, and that will give you a few more minutes."

The three of them decided that from that point on they wouldn't shed any more tears. After a couple of minutes, the nurse returned and escorted Kanina and Mrs. Cooper from the room. The remaining days Monica spent in the hospital sped by, and she was soon returned to the prison.

Chapter Eight

"I missed you, Monica." Sandra wrapped her arms around her small friend, welcoming her back. "I know this is no place a person wants to get used to, but I'm still glad to see ya ass."

"I'm glad to see you too. The hospital was quiet, and a chick definitely got a lot of rest, considering the circumstances, but I was lonely." Monica broke loose from the brief embrace and stared Sandra directly in her eyes. "Listen. You know all that stuff that you were trying to teach me? Well, I'm more than ready to learn. I want to get back out there and really do my thing. I want to dominate all they asses."

Sandra was a little taken aback, to say the least, by the sudden change in Monica's normally meek personality. "Damn, baby girl! That bump on the head must have really knocked some sense into you. If you gonna be out there, you might as well hit 'em hard."

"I'm gonna pay attention and study your every move." Monica kicked off her state-issued shoes and got relaxed.

Sandra smiled as her young protégé reached for a pencil and got ready to take notes.

After what seemed like an eternity, Monica was less than thirty days away from freedom. She had managed to keep her temper in check and not to get any more bad behavior tickets. Sandra had schooled her on everything she needed to know. Monica and she practiced eye contact with the salespeople and security guards. They practiced how to give off the appearance of belonging in your surroundings. Sandra wanted her student in crime to completely grasp the importance of fitting into any crowd. She explained the art of shoplifting as if it were a science, and to Sandra it was. Every ingredient that Monica learned was combined in one master plan after another.

"All right, Monica. I'm gonna demonstrate once more. Now pay careful attention to my eyes and my hands." Sandra briskly moved past the magazine table in the day room and smiled at Monica. "Did you notice?"

"Notice what? What did you want me to notice?" Monica sat up in her chair with a puzzled expression on her face.

Sandra started to laugh out loud at her confused young friend as she raised her sweater. "Did you notice this?" She slid one of the magazines that

was just on the table out from her side and threw it
on the empty chair next to Monica.

"Damn, your ass is quick. I didn't see that shit.
How did you do that?" The questions kept coming.

All of Monica's praise and compliments added
fuel to the seasoned criminal's ego. "Listen up,
youngster. Remember what I told you when you
first came in this rat hole. All that smash-and-grab,
'shoot 'em up, bang bang' shit don't do nothing
but increase your chances of getting knocked and
catching another case. Real bad boys always move
in silence. Be confident, not cocky."

Sandra hated that her cellmate would soon be
getting paroled, but she was dying to see if all her
late-night lessons in thievery would pay off. If they
did, great! Monica would be off and running and
would soon be able to make a new home for her
little sister Kayla. If they didn't, she'd see her little
friend back behind the walls. Only time would tell.

One day and a wake up, Monica thought as she
brushed her teeth and looked into the foggy mirror
in the huge community bathroom that she and
the entire cellblock H used. She finished her daily
routine and made her way in line with the other
inmates. The first thing on Monica's agenda once
she was free would be to lock herself in a bathroom
and take a nice, hot bubble bath for at least an

hour. Taking a semi-warm shower in a huge, open stall that fit ten prisoners at a time was starting to get on her last nerve. Monica failed to understand how some women seemed to love being incarcerated. *Forget this mess! No privacy and no peace of mind? They can have this bullshit!*

When Monica and Sandra got back to their cell, they decided to skip breakfast and go over the various skills that Monica had acquired. Besides, Monica was much too anxious to eat.

"Well, little one, I ain't gonna lie. An old lady like me didn't think that you could go the distance, but you ended up doing it like a champ. I'm proud of you." Sandra was tearing up as she spoke.

"Don't cry, Sandra. You gonna mess around and make me cry too." Monica tried not to look her bunkie in the face. "You've been just like a mother to me. You accepted me for who I am and not once did you try to change me. I appreciate all the knowledge that you have given me, and I swear to God that I'm gonna make you proud."

Sandra refused to hold back her tears any longer. "Monica, let me try to explain something to you. I am a bona fide thief. That's all I know, and nine out of ten times, that's all I'll ever know. I don't want this life for you. I love you like my own daughter, and I pray to God that you don't come back here."

Sandra took a small balled-up tissue out of her worn sweater pocket and blew her nose. "If I thought for one half of a second that I could point you in a direction other than stealing, I wouldn't hesitate in doing it. You are smart. Your mind is sharp, and you could do so much more in your life than taking a chance with catching another felony charge."

Monica never had any one person care about her so much or even put the notion in her head that she could do better. From the beginning of life, she always held herself down. "Sandra, I know what—"

Sandra cut her off in the middle of her sentence. "I know that at this point there's no reasoning with you. That's why I gave you the only gifts I could: technique and a method to all this madness. I only want the best for you." After Sandra finished her heartfelt speech, both of them were crying.

"I just want you to know that I will never forget you. As soon as I get something going on, I'm gonna look out for you, Sandra."

Monica meant every word that was coming out of her mouth, but Sandra was a jailhouse veteran. She knew that out of sight always meant out of mind, but it didn't matter. She still loved Monica unconditionally. They had formed an unbreakable bond.

The two women decided that there would be no more long goodbyes and that when the morning came, it would be a happy occasion and not sad. They spent the day packing up some of the few things that Monica wanted to take home, including her letters from Kanina and handmade cards that Kayla had sent. The rest of her belongings she gave to Sandra.

Daybreak came, and both Sandra and Monica slowly got out of their bunks. They quietly gathered Monica's duffle bag and bedding, which had to be rolled up and turned back in at the front intake office. She'd received it from there more than a year ago.

Sandra was only allowed to the inmate contact door and had to say her good-byes at that point. "Don't forget everything that you've learned." She placed her hand on Monica's shoulder.

Monica dropped her bag on the ground and hugged her cellmate, her teacher, her friend, and her substitute mother all rolled tightly into one. "I love you, Sandra. I promise that I'll write. I'll never forget about you. I'll be waiting for you on the other side when you get released."

With all that being said, the guard opened the heavy black door and ushered Monica through. She glanced back one last time and waved at Sandra as the door slammed shut. After a few more doors being opened and closed and a couple of long hallways, freedom was close. When they got to the office, Monica had one last taste of prison life. While a part of her was more than ready to leave, part of her was scared to death of her new life on the other side of the wall.

The guard at the front desk was the same one Monica had fought with and lost to. Of course, it goes without saying there was no love lost between the two.

"Well, I guess we won't have the pleasure of your company anymore, huh?" She was being a real, true smart-ass, sloppy bitch.

"Naw, sorry about that, Guard Shit Bag! You won't be able to watch my pretty, young ass take a shower no more." Monica smirked. "It must be extra hard being old, fat, and out of shape. Your man must really love you." The once-cocky guard's jaw dropped to the ground. Monica had obviously struck a nerve. "I guess it's true what they say. Words do hurt, don't they?"

Monica made sure to give the guard the finger as soon as she got on the other side of the gates and felt freedom kiss her face. She took a deep breath and looked across the street. There sat her girl Kanina flashing her lights. Monica dashed over to the car with her bags and jumped inside, smiling from ear to ear. It was like Christmastime.

"Okay, let's hit the mall," she teased.

"Dang, girl, I missed your crazy, silly ass being free."

"I missed being free. I ain't never going back to that motherfucker. I put that on everything I love. Now, chick, put me up on all the four-one-one that I done missed."

The entire ride back to the city limits was consumed with gossip and conversation about everyone and anyone Kanina could think of. Monica lay back and enjoyed the scenery and the contentment of just being free. She had the window down, and she tightly closed her eyes as the warm wind blew on her face. After months of sleeping with one eye open, Monica could finally relax.

Soon all of Kanina's words were lost as Monica dozed off to sleep. She and Sandra had been up for two days straight, and it had taken a toll on her. Monica dreamed that Dennis was still alive and she was braiding his hair in a new style that he had seen in a rap magazine. They were laughing and joking just like old times. She was so happy. It all seemed so real, so true, until Kanina pulled into a gas station and woke her up.

"Dang, Monica. Your behind was snoring up a storm and smiling at the same time. Who was you dreaming about, Drake's cute ass?"

"Girl, you's a fool." Monica started cheesing. "Naw, I swear to God, I was dreaming about Dennis.

He was still alive. We were chillin', watching television, and I was braiding his hair some kind of way."

Kanina didn't know exactly what to say at that point. She had been trying to avoid any conversation involving Dennis or Jenette. Soon enough Monica would find out that her mother had literally sold Kayla to her parents. She would also find out that not one time since Monica had been locked up had Jenette thought to inquire about her daughter's location or the date that she would be released from prison.

Night after night of showing up at the house, threatening to take Kayla if they didn't give her money that she needed to buy dope, Jenette finally played herself. They knew she was bluffing, but they wanted to be protected with a little insurance just in case. Mr. Cooper had a lawyer friend of his draw up a legal document giving him and his wife temporary custody and guardianship of Kayla. It would be important to have if Jenette ever pushed their hand.

One of their neighbors was a notary public, and the next time that Jenette showed up having one of her crack attacks, the Coopers had him come over to bear witness to and notarize Jenette's signing of the paperwork. She was so happy and elated to get $500 in her weather-beaten hands, Jenette never once glanced up the staircase to notice her youngest child shaking her head in disgust at yet another despicable act. Kayla was ashamed to been conceived and birthed from such a rotten monster's infested womb.

Kanina was sympathetic to her friend. She knew the next few days would be kinda hard and full of plenty of major and minor adjustments. After twenty more minutes of driving, they got into the city.

"I know that you're probably tired from driving, but can you do me a favor?" Monica had a serious look on her face.

"Yeah, girl. What is it?"

"Can you take me to the cemetery where Dennis is buried? I want to say good-bye."

"You don't even have to ask that, Monica. I understand."

When they reached the gravesite, Kanina left her best friend to mourn as she walked quietly back to the car. Monica sat on the ground and made her peace with her little brother. She needed to get a lot of things off her mind, and she promised him that she was gonna make him proud of her one day.

"Dennis, I'm sorry that I left you alone with Mama," she whispered. "I was only trying to make sure that we ate and I could keep clothes on y'all's back. You know that I loved you more than life itself. I won't let Kayla down like I did you, I swear to God!"

Monica had to try to rid herself of all the remorseful feelings she was carrying around. She needed closure to get on with the task of living. Going back to school and getting a degree was on top of her list. Dennis was gone, but she still had Kayla to consider. Now it would be just them. Monica knew Jenette was a lost cause, and she had no desire to share her life with her mom. As soon as she could get on her feet, she would be out of Jenette's sight for good.

Chapter Nine

Kanina and Monica soon continued their journey home. The mood inside the car was upbeat considering the fact that they'd just left Dennis's gravesite. Monica had found the closure she'd been seeking for months. Kanina turned onto Malcolm X Boulevard and was passing Monica's block.

"Hey, you're missing the turnoff."

"No, I'm not. My parents want you to come and stay with us, Monica."

"What are you talking about? Your mom and pops done already did enough. I can't put them out anymore. I already owe them so much." Monica was sincerely in their debt and humbled.

"Girl, stop bugging. We family. I know you didn't think that we were gonna let you go back to Jenette's crib, did you? Be for real!"

"I really hadn't thought about it. I'm just happy to be free, even if I have to sleep on the floor. It's better than being locked up." Monica had a chill run through her body as she spoke.

"I know Jenette is your mother and all, and I don't mean to talk shit about her, but come on now, Monica. Living back with her is like being in hell." Kanina was giving it to Monica straight no chaser, regardless of hurting her friend's feelings. "Your mother ain't changed. She still ain't shit. Now stop tripping and let's go home. Besides, Kayla is out of school now, and I know she's waiting for us."

Monica agreed with one condition attached. "Okay, Kanina. I feel you, but can you at least swing me past Jenette's to grab some of my stuff if it's still there?"

Kanina busted a U-turn, drove down the drug-infested street, proceeded to pull up in front of the old, half-occupied apartment building that Monica used to call home. Litter filled the walkway, and a drunk was passed out on the curb as usual.

"Do you want me to go upstairs with you?" Kanina was leery about staying outside by herself, even in broad daylight. She hoped that Monica would say yes.

"I could use your help carrying my things."

They both jumped out of the car after Kanina made sure to put her Club on the steering wheel and the alarm on alert. "Better safe than fucking sorry." Kanina smirked. "These folks are off the chain on this block. Do ya ass still wanna lay ya head down in this hood now or what?"

"Girl, you ain't never lied. These motherfuckers look even rougher than I remembered." Monica giggled.

They jumped over the drunken derelict on the curb and ran up the stairs. As soon as they stepped foot in the door and took a whiff, they stumbled. The smell was almost unbearable, and both girls felt nauseated. Kanina placed her hand over her mouth and nose to try to block the odor. Monica's eyes started burning from the stench, which was worse than prison. Being back in the place she once called home was starting to take her back down memory lane. Unfortunately, all her memories were not so great. She got a strange chill but shook it off. The pair went up flight after flight until reaching the fifth floor. Monica led the way as they got to Jenette's door. She starting knocking repeatedly and got no response.

"Maybe I should leave a note." Monica tried to sound optimistic as she looked over at Kanina.

"Knock harder. Maybe she's asleep." Kanina removed her hand from her face all of three seconds to talk before she felt dizzy.

Monica started pounding again and soon heard a door open across the hall. It was Miss Lila.

"Monica, is that you?" She was cautiously peeking out in the hall.

"Yes, Miss Lila, it's me."

Miss Lila opened her door all the way and stepped out in the hall to hug her former little neighbor. "Baby, how are you? I'm so glad to see that you made it home." She pinched Monica's cheeks and kissed her forehead. "Come on in and have a seat, you and your friend. I can fix y'all some cookies and milk or maybe a sandwich."

They sat down on the couch that was covered with plastic, and they revealed their visit would be short.

Miss Lila, regardless of company, went through the routine of turning every single lock that was on her front door. She then went and sat down in her favorite chair. "It's so good to see you, child. How is my little Kayla doing?"

"She's fine, Miss Lila. She's doing just fine."

"That's so good." Miss Lila shook her head. "I always think about her and you. Y'all was always such good girls. I even say a prayer for Dennis every now and then. God rest his tormented soul."

Monica was growing restless with all the formalities of going back down memory lane, and she cut straight to the chase. "Excuse me, Miss Lila. I don't mean to interrupt you, but have you seen my mother today? I knocked on the door, and she didn't answer." Monica sighed. "Did she come in late? Do you think she's asleep or something?"

"What are you talking about, child? What door?" Miss Lila seemed confused. "I haven't seen Jenette in over four or five months now," she huffed.

Monica and Kanina were sitting all the way up on the edge of the couch, bewildered by her statement. Monica was close to being frantic. "Four or five months? What are you taking about, Miss Lila?"

Miss Lila hated to be the bearer of bad news, yet she had no choice. "I'm sorry, child. I thought you knew. That's when the court bailiff came and enforced the eviction notice. They threw all of the contents of the apartment on the curb." Miss Lila was getting disgusted as she spoke. "Your mama was somewhere getting high or drunk, and by the time she showed up, the neighborhood had taken what they wanted, which wasn't much." Miss Lila got up from her chair and got a box out of the closet. "Jenette had sold just about everything that wasn't nailed down no sooner than they put your little brother into the ground."

Kanina sat motionless as she watched Monica go into temporary shock. After a moment or two, Monica shook it off and thought about what Sandra and Miss Sims had said to her: "God never gives you more than you can stand." Keeping that in mind, Monica gathered her thoughts and finally spoke.

"Well, Miss Lila, I really didn't expect anything more than that from my mother. It should be against the law for some women to give birth, and Jenette is a perfect example. I don't feel any animosity or resentment toward her, just pity." Kanina and Miss Lila both nodded in total agreement with Monica. The bottom line was that Jenette was a lost cause. Monica tried her best to conceal the heartache that she was truly feeling. Jenette was still her mother, crack or no crack. "Well, Miss Lila, we have to be going now. I'll make sure to bring Kayla by next time for a longer visit."

"Okay, sweetheart." Miss Lila reached down and picked up the box that she had gotten out of the closet. "Here, Monica. This is yours."

"Mine? What is it?" Monica opened it up and instantly started crying like a baby.

"I went and got it off the curb. Nobody should be throwing away pictures." Miss Lila smiled.

Monica was elated that her pictures were safe and sound. She opened up a manila envelope that was on the bottom, and a huge grin replaced the tears. "Thank you!"

"I figured that you would need that one day, so I took that, too." Miss Lila chuckled.

Monica couldn't believe it. The high school had mailed her diploma. With her box of snapshots and her high school diploma in hand, Monica and Kanina waited patiently as Miss Lila let them out of her fortress. They practically ran down all five flights and out the door to fresh air. They got in the car, and Kanina sped off as the two headed home.

Monica and Kanina finally arrived to a house filled with love. Mr. and Mrs. Cooper were standing on the front porch, waiting to greet their new houseguest. Kayla was doing cartwheels on the grass and didn't see the girls turn into the driveway. Monica peered out the window and thanked God for keeping her little sister safe. When Kayla stopped doing flips and twists, she was dizzy. No sooner did her eyes focus on Kanina's car than she darted over and almost pulled Monica out of the car.

"I missed you, Monica. Promise me you won't go back to jail anymore. I was so lonely and sad. First you left, then Dennis got killed, and then Mama gave me away."

It was obvious that Kayla had been through a lot of hurt and pain in a short matter of time, but she had still managed somehow to maintain an upbeat attitude.

"I like it here. I've got my own room, lots of books, and even my very own computer."

"That's great, Kayla. I'm glad that you're happy." Monica was trying her best to be brave, just like Kayla. "You know that I won't ever leave you again. I swear."

The two sisters hugged for what seemed like hours before the Coopers interrupted. "Come on now, you two. We have an entire lifetime to hug. I fixed a nice, big welcome-home dinner for Monica." Mrs. Cooper was smiling while wiping her hands on her apron. "Everybody go and wash up, and I'll put the food on the table."

Kanina and her father grabbed Monica's two small bags out of the car. Kayla snatched her big sister's arm while practically dragging her in the house. Mrs. Cooper had prepared a feast fit for a king. Monica was in heaven and ate second helpings of everything.

After dinner was over, Kayla showed Monica every single book that she owned and also every A paper that she had received from school over the past year. By the time that was over, Monica was exhausted. Kanina already had taken Monica's things to her room. It was the first time that she could have privacy.

Monica went into the bathroom and ran the hottest water in the tub that her body could stand, and she filled it with bubbles just like she daydreamed about night after night in prison. Kanina and her mom had purchased Monica pajamas and a room full of personal items that she needed. Monica undressed and eased her way down in the bath. She soon fell fast asleep, while soaking the entire jail ordeal off of her body.

Chapter Ten

A few months had passed since the day of Monica's release, and a lot of changes had taken place. After some rest and getting situated, she'd enrolled at the community college just as she had planned before her arrest. Although Dennis was gone and Kayla was happy living with the Coopers in a stable household, Monica still wanted to pursue her dream of obtaining a degree in business management. One day she hoped to own her very own dress shop and make something more of herself than being a common shoplifter.

In between classes, she would write letters to Sandra, keeping her informed of what she was up to. Monica knew how vital mail was to a person who was locked down. If it weren't for the letters she received from Kayla and Kanina, Monica knew that she'd have been lost in the system. Monica had yet to find a job, so sending any money to her former cellmate was temporarily put on hold. She intended to, but shit was tight. Being young and black was hard enough, but when you mixed in a felony record, finding a job was damn near an impossible feat. Mr. and Mrs. Cooper weren't putting any pressure on Monica, but she still felt under foot and wanted to be on her own. She was used to being independent and taking care of herself.

Every night, Monica and Kanina talked about moving out and one day getting their own apartment. They calculated that they needed a little over $1,400 to get them started. Kanina didn't have a criminal record, so getting a job was slightly easier for her, plus she had savings bonds that her parents had been purchasing for her since she was born. Monica just had to come up with her half.

Time and again, the expressions on employers' faces when reviewing applications ranged from sympathetic to downright rude. Monica was now no more than an awful statistic. She was one of many released from prison who were shunned and looked upon as a throwaway citizen. Aggravated by being unemployed, and having no apparent job prospects in sight, Monica decided to return to the only thing she knew would earn her a constant flow of money: "borrowing." It was in her blood, and Monica was ready to put everything she'd learned from Sandra to work and go hard!

Monica sat in the parking lot alone inside of the used car that she'd managed to get on the humble from a crackhead for a hundred bucks. If they were trying to get on, they'd sell their own mama for a hit. The filthy car had rust spots on the doors and a huge dent across the hood. Three of the tires were bald, and the interior was fucked, but the only thing that mattered to her at the time was that she had sounds. The radio was at least able to pump out Monica's favorite jazz station.

She sat back meditating and getting herself in the zone so that she could accomplish the task at hand. It had been almost eighteen months now since the young girl had been caught, arrested, convicted, and thrown into prison. It was no way in hell that she was ready for a repeat performance of that ordeal. Monica reached down in her slightly oversized purse and pulled out a tube of cherry-flavored lip gloss. After checking her face in the mirror, she was set to put Sandra's plan into effect.

Monica confidently strolled to the front of Macy's and took a deep breath. She swung open the doors and did her thing. First stop was the men's department. Doing exactly as Sandra had instructed, Monica made sure to ask the security guard at the entrance directions to where she was going. She asked him if he could show her the way because she was running late for her father's birthday lunch and had to get him a present. Just as Sandra had predicted, the guard was disarmed by Monica's act of being helpless, and he quickly jumped in to be her knight in shining armor. Sandra was correct. All men, black or white, old or young, short or tall, loved to feel important or needed. They loved a woman in distress or in search of their help, especially the ones who were young and pretty like Monica.

The saleslady saw Monica walking with the guard, and she went on pricing merchandise on the other side of the aisle.

"Thank you for being so nice to me." Monica gave the middle-aged man a sexy grin as she touched his arm. "I truly appreciate it."

"Anytime, young lady." His eyes were glued to Monica's tight-fitting sweater. "Anytime at all." He watched her round ass sway from side to side as she walked away in her snug-fitting jeans.

"Okay, that part was easy. Now for part two," she mumbled to herself.

Upon entering menswear, she marched directly to the leathers that were displayed near the back corner. She slipped out the miniature wire and bolt cutters that were tucked and concealed in her sleeve, and she went to work. Monica made her first target a cream quilted three-quarter-length coat, priced at $980. That was followed by a black butter-soft jacket with a silk lining, priced at $875. She pulled a Macy's garment bag discreetly out of her purse and smoothly slipped it over the two leather coats. Just like that, it was done with, no noise and no fuss.

With both in tow, along with a couple of eighty-five-dollar belts that matched the coats, Monica smiled at the guard. She thanked him once again as she pranced out the door all in less than fifteen minutes.

"Damn, that shit really worked," Monica laughed as she climbed into her car. "I can't believe it. Sandra was right."

Monica turned the radio on in the struggle buggy. She bounced her head as she drove to the one place that she knew, without a doubt, she could get both coats off at. She turned into her old neighborhood and pulled up, parking three doors down from her destination: the dope house. The windows were boarded up in the front, and the grass was never cut. To an unsuspecting person driving by, the home looked abandoned, but to those who knew differently, they went around the back and entered through the rear door. There were a few people ahead of Monica waiting to get served. Although the coats in her arms were heavy, she waited with patience for her turn to talk to the guy who was working the door.

"Well, I'll be damned. Is that you, Monica?" Black Billy was licking his lips as he looked her up and down. "Your ass done grew the fuck up." He smiled while holding the gate open in hopes that she would rub her body across his. "Shitttt, in all the right places, too." Locking the gate again and grabbing the bag out of Monica's hands, his dick got hard at the thought of hittin' that.

"How you doing, Black Billy? I ain't seen you in a couple of years now. What's been up?" Monica felt slightly uncomfortable with the way he was looking at her, but since she had known him from way back in the day, she brushed the feeling off.

"It ain't nothing, Monica. Just chillin', trying to make a little loot. You know how it is."

"Yeah, me too." Monica took the bag from his hand and pulled the coats out. "What you know about this here?"

"Awww shit! This motherfucker right here is hot." Black Billy snatched the black jacket out of Monica's grip. "I got to have this bitch. Black is my fucking color." He put it on and zipped it up. "What you think? Is it me or what?"

From his reaction, Monica knew that coming to the dope house would pay off. The dudes here always had cash on hand. "Stop playing with me. You know your ass is killing that shit." Monica grinned. "Get you some of them new black Mauri Alligator hiking boots and you good to go." She was straight in hustle mode.

Black Billy couldn't resist copping the jacket. He went in his pocket and pulled out a huge stack of cash. "What's the ticket?" he asked, trying to act like he was Big Willie as if Monica couldn't see that they were all singles.

"The tag says $875, so give me $435."

"Damn, girl, I thought we was fam." Black Billy threw his hands up and twisted his lips. "Look out for ya mans. What's up, Monica?"

Monica stepped back and laughed at him. "Look, guy. You know I just really got back home. I'm trying to be on the come up and shit, so just drop down. You got it like that. You can have these two belts on me." She threw them across the room on the table. "Now run my cash, playa!"

Black Billy started counting out the singles while Monica tried to convince him to buy the other coat, but unfortunately, he wasn't going for it. He told her that cream wasn't a good color for him. "My little workers are in the back taking care of a li'l somethin'-somethin'. Maybe one of them wants to get on. They both pretty boys. They'll rock that cream. I'm too hard for sissy colors like that." In the excitement of getting a new jacket for half off, it slipped Black Billy's mind just who was in that back room and what exactly was going on.

"Good looking. Call they ass out here. I gotta get home and study for a test."

"Monica, when you gonna let me take your fine ass out to dinner or the movies? I need a smart, hustlin' girl like you on my team. You be 'bout ya shit. I always liked that about you."

Monica blushed. "Maybe one day, Black Billy. Now can you call your boys out here?"

Black Billy shouted into the next room as Monica plopped down and leaned back on the couch. "Hey, y'all! Bring ya asses. My new woman got some gear for sale." He winked at Monica, who had no choice but to smile.

After a minute or two, the door cracked open, and one of the young boys emerged from the room, pulling up his pants and drinking a forty ounce. "Damn, dude! Can a nigga get his dick sucked in peace or what? I was first in line with that old freak ho."

Monica looked into the boy's face, and she busted out laughing. He couldn't have been any older than fourteen. Black Billy tossed him the coat, informing him that the ticket was half off the price tag. While he was busy trying it on, Monica glanced into the other room and got sick to her stomach. At first sight, she thought she was seeing things. She knew that it couldn't be, but it most certainly was. It was Jenette, her mother, down on her knees giving the other young boy some head. Her own mother was the "old freak ho" the boy was just talking about. Monica was speechless, and her heart dropped to the ground. She was frozen and couldn't move.

The boy in the room felt Monica's eyes on him and blew her a kiss as his body started shaking. "What's up, baby? You want some of this dick? You looking mighty hard." He smirked as he pulled his hook up out of Jenette's now cum-filled mouth.

Jenette turned to see exactly who the young boy was talking to, and she made eye contact with Monica, her firstborn. Slowly getting off the floor and walking toward the door, Jenette remained emotionless as she wiped her face. She was almost twenty pounds lighter, and her skin was a shade darker, but one thing ceased to change: Jenette's eyes. They looked the same as they always did, dark, cold, and harsh. Monica watched the awful nightmare get closer to the door, and her entire body felt numb. After turning her back on Kayla, not showing up at Dennis's funeral, and of course, robbing Monica of her childhood to raise her kids, Jenette should have been running to her daughter to apologize. Monica was ashamed, but the skinny, dirty, and repulsive creature was still her mother, and deep down inside she still loved her. Jenette put her hand on the door and showed no signs of remorse as she looked Monica dead in her face, slamming the door shut without saying a single word.

Ain't this about a bitch, ran though Monica's mind repeatedly. She was crushed. Monica jumped to her feet and moved to the other side of the living room. As soon as the boy paid her for the second coat, she got out of there as fast as she could and rushed back to her car. "That bitch is foul," Monica screamed out loud as she drove away, never shedding a tear. "Fuck that bitch. Her ass really don't exist anymore, flat the fuck out. She's dead to me!"

Monica had no intention of mentioning to Kayla or Kanina what she had just witnessed. Some shit was better off being left in the dark and never spoken of, and flat the fuck out, this was one of them.

Black Billy saw what had just taken place. He felt sorry for Monica, but not so sorry that he didn't take his turn getting some of Jenette's toothless head.

Monica got back to Kanina's house in record time. She took a quick bath and got her books out to study for her exam. Rightly so, she couldn't stay focused and kept reliving the sight of seeing her mother degrade herself with boys young enough to be her own kids. Jenette was a disgrace to herself and everyone she knew. Monica had no appetite and chose not to go down for dinner or even help Kayla with her homework. Flashbacks of that foul bullshit were consuming her every thought. She kept picturing Jenette slamming the door.

After swallowing three extra-strength aspirin, Monica tried her best to fall asleep. The only things that gave her some peace of mind were that $925 tucked in her purse and the thought of her and Kanina getting that apartment.

Chapter Eleven

The weeks that followed were filled with two things in Monica's life: school and getting paid. She studied at night, attended class in the day, and stole all evening. Never once letting a week go by without writing a letter to her friend and mentor, Sandra, all was well. Every letter had at least a twenty-five-dollar money order enclosed. Monica made sure that Sandra wanted for nothing. After all, it was her schemes that kept her on top of her game and paid.

It was finally moving day for Monica and Kanina. They leased a three-bedroom apartment on the lower east side of the city. It was right off the river, and the view was spectacular, to say the least. Each girl had her own private bathroom, and Monica would use the third bedroom to house the surplus of items that she was stealing daily. She was bringing way too many bags into the Coopers' house, and they were both starting to suspect that Monica was up to her old tricks.

Kayla was sad to see her big sister and Kanina move out, but she felt more than enough love where she was living. Mrs. Cooper had filed papers trying to legally adopt Kayla. Jenette was still MIA and had not been seen or heard from in several months, which was good, considering the hatred Monica and Kayla both felt toward her. No court in the land would give Kayla back to Jenette, who nine out of ten times wouldn't be sober enough to show up to fight anyhow.

The last box was stacked in the living room. Both of the girls' brand-new bedroom sets had arrived and were set up. They each picked one that showed their individual taste and flair. They felt like they were on top of the world.

"We should go out and celebrate." Kanina was excited, and it showed.

"Yeah, you right. We are almost grown as a motherfucker," Monica clowned. "Let's go down to Tina's Tavern and see if we can get in. I heard they don't be carding."

"Yeah, I heard that shit too. Let's get dressed."

"All right, but damn wearing jeans! Let's get real on them old hoes and show 'em what's really good!"

The girls disappeared into their bathrooms to transform themselves into queens.

Monica and Kanina got up to the front door of the club and put their game faces on. They were on a mission to get in without any embarrassing stuff happening. Stepping inside, Monica pulled out a knot, handing the guy at the door a crisp hundred-dollar bill. She made sure he got a good look so he knew that her and her girl came to spend money and not sit at the bar, hoping some nigga would buy them a drink. They came prepared to get their party on. Just as she figured, they were let in. No ID and no checking their purses. It was true what they say: "Money talks and bullshit walks."

As they walked through the sea of people who were partying, all eyes were suddenly on them. Every woman wished they were able to afford clothes like Monica and Kanina were wearing, and the men all lusted for them. They were like ghetto superstars. Both of the young women found an empty booth near the dance floor. Sliding around the table and crossing their legs, both Monica and Kanina tried to give the impression that they belonged. They couldn't have been sitting alone and enjoying the music playing for more than five minutes when the waitress came prancing over to the table. She had a tray with two drinks on them.

"Excuse me, ladies." She smiled as she chewed her gum. "The two young men at the bar sent these over to you." The waitress put napkins in front of them and set the tall red drinks down.

"What exactly is this?" Kanina inquired before taking a sip. "We were planning on ordering a bottle of champagne."

Monica chuckled at her friend acting all uppity, and she decided to join in on the fun. "Yeah, we were, but I guess we don't want to hurt anyone's feelings, so let's drink them."

Monica then asked the waitress to bring them two bottles of Moët anyway and a bowl of strawberries. They were gonna get fucked up and party 'til the club closed down. As the waitress left the table, the girls raised their glasses at the guys to acknowledge their slight but thoughtful contribution to their celebration.

"Dang, Monica, both of those dudes are fine as hell. I wouldn't mind getting with that."

"Yeah, they are some cute brothers, especially the one with the big emerald cuff links on that sweet button-up." Monica was undressing him with her eyes. "He is hot."

The guys, with drinks in hand, made their way over to the table before any of the other men gathered the courage. Most of the guys there would most likely have to work an entire two months to be able to afford dressing just one of the girls. Yet these guys were the exception to the rule. Their gear was also top-notch. It was easy to see they weren't the average nine-to-five brothers. The clothes, the jewelry, and the way they carried themselves were dead giveaways that they were straight-up ballers.

After the introductions were made, the guys took a seat. Quinton sat next to Monica, and Latrell made himself at home just about on Kanina's lap, which was fine with her. Conversation about each other's gear was getting under way when the waitress returned.

Now we gonna see if these dudes really got some cash or if they are frontin', Monica thought as she reached for her purse. Thankfully she was abruptly stopped by Quinton's strong, muscular arms.

"Come on now, sweetheart. Do you think you ladies are paying for anything tonight?"

"You don't have to do that. I got it," Monica played it off. She loved that he was picking up the tab.

Quinton gave the waitress the bill, plus he threw in a big, fat tip. He had her bring two more glasses so that they could toast their new friendship. Kanina and Latrell were totally engulfed by one another and paid no attention to anything else going on in the club. That left plenty of time for Monica and Quinton to get better acquainted. They discussed everything that came to mind.

Two hours, three bottles of Moët, and two rounds of shots of Hennessy later, all four of them were faded and made the decision to call it a night.

Besides, the fellas claimed they had some business to take care of and were running a little late.

Quinton and Monica were hand in hand as they exited through the doors and stood at the valet, while Kanina and Latrell were exchanging numbers as well as good night kisses.

"I guess they really like each other, huh?" Monica nudged Quinton.

"Damn, you ain't ever lied. They might as well get a room," he joked, tapping his boy on the shoulder when the valet drove up in their car first. It was a brand-new triple-gold Corvette with spinning chrome rims, the kind of car that got girls' panties instantly wet just by looking at it, let alone touching that motherfucker.

The valet handed Quinton the keys, to Monica's relief. She was glad that he was the driver and not Latrell. Monica imagined herself cruising around town making all the females jealous of the whip she could be bouncing and Quinton's fine ass.

The guys waited for them to bring Kanina's car up front before they pulled off. The two friends were tipsy and fell into the car laughing. They had managed to go out, get fucked up, and meet some real money handlers. The night was a total success.

The weeks that followed involved Kanina and Latrell spending every free minute they had together.

The two were practically inseparable, which like it or not, caused Monica and Quinton to be thrown together. Monica did like spending time with him. She even missed him when he wasn't around, but she had to stay on top of her game. Making money wasn't a choice for Monica. She'd been poor her whole life, and she refused to slip down to that level of living ever again. Kanina had her parents to fall back on, but Monica depended on herself and only herself. She had to go out and hustle, point blank.

Neither guy knew what Monica was doing for a living. They just knew the women in their life had their situation tight, just as both girls had no idea where Quinton and Latrell would go at times. They guys often received calls on their cell phones and disappeared. All parties involved were living secret lives, which over time would have to be revealed.

Night after night Kanina and Latrell slept together, sharing a bed, while Quinton and Monica camped out in the living room. He was aware that Monica, although street smart and book smart, was still a virgin. She explained that growing up in her mother's household made her want to be extra careful about whom she chose to give her body to. Monica wanting to wait, true enough, was driving him crazy, but he respected her wishes.

Quinton was proud that he had a "good girl," and he knew that when he finally would get his chance to hit them guts, he was gonna damn near rip the frame out of Monica's little ass. Quinton realized she was special and well worth the wait, so he made up his mind to let his good girl come to him. He just hoped that she would hurry the hell up!

Chapter Twelve

It was nearing Christmas. The snow was falling lightly, and Kanina and Monica were enjoying the vacation break from school. Monica took the free time to catch up on her letters to Sandra. For a Christmas present, she sent her a money order for one hundred dollars. She'd promised that she would look out for Sandra, and she was doing just that. Kanina made sure to spend a little time with her aging grandparents and show them some love.

The fellas had become a permanent fixture in their lives, and for once, Monica was completely happy and satisfied. Quinton and she had yet to have sex, but he was still hanging in there. He worshipped her like a queen. In his eyes, the fact that she was a virgin only made her stock shoot up. She was nothing like the hood rats who usually chased him. She was loyal and dedicated. He helped Monica with her bills and spent mad loot, showering her with jewelry and fresh flowers every week. Quinton knew she was the one. It was true love. Quinton was her everyday Santa, fuck waiting for Christmas!

They were all going to pick out a huge tree that would sit directly in the picture window of the girls' apartment. Latrell had a candy apple red custom Navigator, and they planned on the tree being secured down on his roof. Although he wasn't in favor of the method of transporting the tree, he went along with anything Kanina wanted. She was his lady, and whatever it took to make her content, he was with it. They say pussy is a bad motherfucker, well, Kanina must have had a beast, because Latrell never ever let a speck of dust get on his whip, and now he was hauling trees.

Monica and Kanina picked out the biggest, fullest tree they could find. Quinton and Latrell came up with just about every reason they could to persuade the girls to purchase a small tree. After all, they were the ones who had to lug it inside the crib. The game plan was for the women to decorate the tree and the men to cook. Unfortunately, seeing the two guys fumble around the kitchen, the decision was made, and they were quickly removed from their assignment. The night was perfect. After eating the meal the girls ended up preparing, the two couples sat hugged up for hours, watching the lights twinkle on the tree.

Monica was scanning over Kayla's Christmas list. She was in high school now and no longer wanted toys. Everything on the list consisted of clothes or electronics. Between Mr. and Mrs. Cooper and big sisters Monica and Kanina, Miss Kayla was a hot mess. You couldn't tell her shit. Thanks to them she rocked every designer who crossed the runways. Her days as a high school student were nothing like Monica's. Kayla was the best dressed the first day she entered the building. There was no Jenette around to fuck things up for them any longer. She deserved the very best that Monica could steal. Kayla had always knuckled down, hitting the books, staying on the honor roll, and now was her payoff.

Christmas Day was filled with lots of presents and promises. Monica and Kanina spent the night in their old rooms so they could be with Kayla early in the morning and see her face as she opened her gifts. Mrs. Cooper baked chocolate chip cookies and made hot chocolate. Monica chopped the celery and onions, while Kanina peeled potatoes. Of course, Miss Kayla watched. It was the perfect day. To top it off, Mr. Cooper had everyone around the dinner table take turns saying what was the best gift they had received. When it got to his turn, he held up an envelope.

"What is that, honey?" Mrs. Cooper blushed.

"Yeah, Dad, is it for me?" Kanina was getting excited.

"I bet it's for me." Kayla smiled, rocking back and forth in her seat.

Monica remained calm because she really didn't care what the contents of the envelope were. She had everything she needed: a caring family and a good and patient man who adored her.

"All right, ladies, settle down," Mr. Cooper commanded. "This is a present for the whole family." He opened it up and snatched the documents out. "This paper in my hands says that as of December 23, 2017, Kayla Marie Howard shall now legally be known as Kayla Marie Cooper. The adoption is final."

Everyone jumped from their chairs and embraced each other. Kayla was shedding tears of joy. In spite of all the high-priced gear Monica put on her back, she still hadn't seen her little sister so happy in her whole life. Being loved, feeling safe, and having a true sense of belonging was what Kayla always wanted. Now her dreams had come to pass.

Quinton and Latrell were on their way over. Monica and Kanina had just made it home. It was ten-thirty Christmas night, but there was still enough time to exchange presents. Kanina made two healthy-sized platters of food for the guys. Her mom always prepared more food than could feed an army, so bringing a couple of meals to their men was easy to do. Monica wanted the fellas to have a full stomach and feel happy. That way they might be a little more generous with the cash flow. With all the presents she had stolen the past month, her money reserves were close to depletion.

"Merry Christmas, Kanina baby," Latrell yelled as he burst through the doorway with his arms full of gifts. There were boxes of all sizes wrapped in different paper with bows of different colors on each. "Look what daddy has for that ass!"

"Oh my God, Latrell! All of this is mine? Did you carjack Santa's fat behind?"

"Naw, boo boo, but come sit on my lap and tell me if you been naughty or nice."

Kanina helped him set the boxes down, and he hardly had time to take his coat off before she pounced in the pile. "I love you, Latrell." She beamed as she started her assault on the presents.

Monica heard noises in the hallway outside the door and went to investigate. There she found Quinton. In his arms was a small puppy with a huge bow around his tiny neck. "Hi, sweetie. This is for you."

"Quinton, who told you I wanted a dog?" She took him from Quinton and held him tightly. "He's so soft and fluffy. Is it a he or she?" Monica asked while rubbing noses with her new little brown funny-face, fluffy friend.

"First of all, no one told me. It's my job to know what you need or want and then provide it. Secondly, he is a he. I thought you needed a man around here twenty-four-seven to guard your fine self." Quinton smiled as he swooped several bags stuffed with presents off the floor and went inside the apartment, with Monica and the puppy on his heels. They found a still-childlike Kanina on attack, and without asking twice, the boxes were losing. Neither she nor Latrell even glanced upward to acknowledge their friends' presence.

"I guess you like your shit, huh, Kanina?" Quinton yelled out to her as he leaned back in his favorite chair.

Monica came out the kitchen with a bowl of water for the puppy. "I love him, Quinton. What should we name him?"

"You'll think of something, princess, by the time we get back. You can have your little sister keep an eye on him for us."

"Back?" she questioned. "Back from where?"

Quinton reached into one of the bags, handing Monica a flat, long box with a tiny ribbon attached. "This is for you. I hope you'll want it."

Monica was nothing like Kanina and slowly opened the package. She was slightly puzzled as she stared at the small folders inside.

"What's wrong? Don't you like your gift?" Quinton reached for her hand and rubbed it gently.

"What is it for? I don't understand." Monica shyly stated and lowered her head from embarrassment.

"Baby, they're plane tickets for us to Miami. Me and Latrell have to take care of some business next month, and I thought you could use a break from all this bone- chilling cold."

Monica was overjoyed as she ran around the room. Kanina soon came across her and Latrell's tickets, and she followed Monica's lead. The fellas couldn't help but feel proud making the women in their lives so happy. With the quickness, both girls started thinking about what they would wear on the trip. They were almost in a panic.

Before the joyful night came to an end, Monica was blessed with an eighteen-carat white gold watch encrusted with tiny diamonds, and a wine-colored baseball-style mink jacket. Quinton even had the store monogram her initials in the silk lining. No gift that the guys received from Monica or Kanina could compare to the ones that they provided, but all that mattered was that the girls were satisfied. After all the time the couples spent together, the right hand still had no idea what the left was doing. However, that would soon change.

Monica hit every boutique and upscale designer shop in the small suburban town she had driven to. She was amazed by the lack of security in most.

There were no guards in uniforms to intimidate her. There were no signs of outrageously large sensors attached to even a small belt, and the salespeople were nonchalant, acting as if working there were a hobby, not a job. Monica eagerly made it her business to take complete and full advantage of the circumstances and put a major dent in their stock.

Store after store, she left her mark. Even stopping to have a brief discussion about the weather with one store manager, Monica then successfully strolled out the door without so much as a second glance. She jumped inside her car, confidently driving away. When she got home, she surveyed her new inventory of stolen goods. *Damn! I never knew that borrowing would be so easy!* There was no doubt that she and Kanina would be fresh, chillin' in that hot Miami sunshine.

Chapter Thirteen

The day of the trip quickly arrived. Getting an early start, they checked in at the airport an hour ahead of time. The couples were definitely anxious to be on their way. Soon the airline started to board passengers. Of the four, Monica was the only one who had never flown. Deep down she was a nervous wreck, but she did her best to play it off. Her leg was shaking and trembling.

Quinton knew his girl and could tell she was scared. He held her hand most of the flight and reassured her of his love. Before she knew it, they had landed and were getting a rental. The palm trees and humid air were welcome changes from home. Monica was in awe as they pulled up to the high-priced, top-of-the-line resort they had reservations at.

Hotel Mystic was the tallest building on the Miami coastline. They checked in and had their luggage taken to their rooms. Monica and Quinton's room was decorated in turquoise and various shades of blues, while Latrell and Kanina had a tan and rose theme going on. The beach was visible from each room, and the girls couldn't wait to put on their new bathing suits. Kanina and Monica whispered softly to each other about the sleeping arrangements. This would be the first time that Quinton and Monica would share a bed.

"Listen, ladies. We have a meeting to get to in about forty-five minutes," Latrell blurted out. "So why don't we grab some lunch now?"

"Good thinking, honey. You must have been reading my mind. I'm starving." Kanina kissed him on his cheek as they all darted to the elevator.

"Are you all right, Monica?" Quinton wrapped his arms around her and pulled her close.

"I'm tight. I just can't believe my black ass was on an airplane. I swear to God I'm still dizzy."

They all enjoyed a laugh at Monica's expense as they ate lunch. They had crab legs, jumbo grilled shrimp, and fresh lobster that Quinton had hand-picked right out of the tank in the restaurant's lobby. When lunch was just about over, Latrell's cell phone started to ring. He shot a look over at Quinton, who was already pulling out some dough to pay the bill.

"Listen, Monica, we need to go handle some thangs. It shouldn't take any more than a few hours, and then we can go have some fun." Quinton was getting up from the table and talking at the same time. "Take this and go shopping until I get back. Y'all can take the car. We gonna catch a cab." He slipped Monica a knot of cash and headed toward the door.

Latrell, not to be outdone, gave Kanina something to play with too. Before any objections could be made by either of the ladies, the fellas were ghost. The women were far from crazy. They knew their men were both off into some illegal type of shit, but they cared not to make a big deal about it. As long as they were reaping the benefits of the game, they were good with it.

The girls couldn't wait to hit the streets and spend their newly gained revenue. Latrell had given up close to $1,400, and Quinton was out two grand even. Monica stopped along the way and bought a postcard to send to Sandra. She wanted to make sure to let her know where she was and why she wasn't home to accept her weekly call. Sandra worried about Monica as if she were her own daughter.

The pair of girls rode around sightseeing and talking shit until they found a store that caught their attention. They swerved in front of traffic and parked in front. Your World was a store where everyone who was anyone shopped. It was featured in all the fashion magazines around the globe. Pictures of musicians, models, and movie stars all graced its doors. It had marble pillars on each side of the building and a red carpet on the walkway. Plush custom-designed couches and a solid gold champagne fountain in the middle of the store made it the talk of the town. It was off the hook. People who were considered well-to-do owned homes that weren't as out cold as this spot.

Kanina and Monica had stepped into paradise. They made themselves right at home and filled crystal flutes, sipping the good stuff while they browsed. Some of the prices were reasonable, but others were just downright ridiculous, which caused Monica to go into full borrow mode. She and Kanina both had money to spend and loved nice things, but they weren't really accustomed to paying the price.

Latrell and Quinton sat back in red crushed-velvet chairs. There they listened to Malik give several weak-sounding explanations of why he was late with the payment of $22,000 that he owed Quinton for a drug debt. He started with his sick mama, whined about his three-legged dog, and almost dug up his great-granddaddy from the grave. He was sweating bullets and terrified.

"Look, Malik. Do you think we came all the way down here just to hear you bitch about all ya problems?" Latrell was pissed, slamming his fist on the oak desk. "I want my man's motherfucking dough, and I ain't bullshitting with ya ass, either.

You betta check my pedigree, you sissy bitch nigga. I ain't no joke."

Malik was shaking as he looked to Quinton for some sort of sympathy or pity, but there was none. The clock was ticking on his good health.

"Look here, dude. We gonna be in town until Sunday morning." Malik listened intently as Quinton spoke, giving him a chance. "By that time it will be twenty-five thousand. You better try to make something happen by then, or that's your ass. I can only hold Latrell up off you for so long."

Malik was scared shitless and in the middle of still trying to buy himself a little more time when Tami, a girl who worked for him, came in the office and whispered something in his ear. He reached for the remote that was on the desk and turned on the security monitors that scanned his entire store. "This is a disgrace. I'm shocked and offended," Malik shrieked while fanning his face like he was going to faint. "How dare they take from me?"

Latrell and Quinton watched Malik acting like a bitch, and they shook their heads. *Why would a fag like him even try to sell dope?* Quinton thought as he got closer to examine the screen. That's when the real drama started. He was at a complete loss for words. Right there in living color he was watching his woman Monica stealing her ass off, while Kanina watched her back, acting as the lookout.

Latrell noticed his boy's facial expression, and he leaned over to take a look at what was so fuck-

ing interesting that was holding everyone's attention hostage. Once gaining access to the monitor,
Latrell joined the dazed Quinton. They both sat
stunned while Malik still ranted and raved.

"Call the authorities. I want these scandalous
bandits arrested and punished severely," he pouted
as he folded his arms and tapped his foot.

"Calm the fuck down, Miss Malik. Have your
security escort the women up here to your office. I
want to talk to them." Quinton smirked.

"Yeah, bring they hot asses up here," Latrell
agreed. "I want a few words with Thelma and
Louise."

Malik was still performing as if he had been
stabbed and raped, but he followed Quinton's
instructions anyway. Besides, it wasn't a request. It
was a demand.

Monica had just finished casually borrowing a
silk scarf for Mrs. Cooper when a short, muscular,
overly tanned man approached her. He was wearing tight, neatly pressed slacks and a T-shirt that
was at least two sizes too small.

"Hello, Miss Thang." He snapped his fingers and
twisted his lips. "Can you follow me?"

Monica's heart raced. "Follow you for what?"
she asked while searching the store for Kanina's
whereabouts.

"Listen, you lil' bitch, stealing what don't belong to you. Stop all the drama and come with me," he demanded. "Why don't you play nice like your friend and don't make a scene?"

Monica made eye contact with Kanina, who was being led up some stairs. She refused to let her girl be bullied alone. That wasn't her style. Kanina would break down as soon as they asked her one question anyway, so Monica had no choice but to go along without causing any sort of disturbance. "Yeah, all right."

"You've made a wise decision, little girl. Now come on and hurry up." He rolled his eyes like a diva.

Monica headed to the stairs and caught up with Kanina.

Malik waited eagerly at the door for the girls to enter. Even though he wanted to scratch their eyes out, all Malik could do was give them a dirty look. Quinton already told him to remain silent while he handled the situation. Monica stepped inside the office first and froze dead in her tracks as she stared into Quinton's face. Kanina, right behind her, got teary-eyed as soon as she saw Latrell. They were busted and humiliated that the fellas had found out their awful secret. Months had flown by, and they had managed to keep their fronts up. Now it was out in the open. They were caught up in their shit.

"Hi, baby. What a coincidence running into you here," Quinton said sarcastically. "What have you been up to, Monica?"

"Listen, Quinton. Before you start tripping, Kanina ain't have shit to do with anything now or ever."

"Okay, Monica, that's fine and all, but the question was, what has your sassy ass been up to?"

Kanina was holding her face in her hands, crying, as Monica stood strong. Latrell couldn't take seeing his wifey being distraught, and he walked over to hug her. She almost collapsed in his arms, while Monica never blinked an eyelash. Malik was confused about how the group of people in his office were connected, and he sat down behind his desk, puzzled.

"Let me see your purse, Monica. I need a tissue."

She was not scared or impressed by Quinton trying to be slick. "See my purse for what? Is there something you want out of my purse? Do you wear silk scarfs, women's perfume, or knitted tank tops?" Monica was bugging out and heated as she snatched the items out of her purse and threw them on the floor at Quinton's feet, awaiting his response.

"Damn, baby, slow ya roll. I was only playing with you." He smiled. "Your ass went straight gangsta on a brother. This is Malik. He owns this overpriced store."

At that point, Monica couldn't have cared less and didn't even look twice at Malik, who now had his hand out to shake hers.

"Well, excuse me." Malik switched away, sucking his teeth. "What nerve. She done stole my shit, and she's got the audacity to cop an attitude. Bitches kill me."

Latrell decided to ease the tension in the office and started cracking jokes. After a few minutes of coaxing from Quinton, Monica was back to her old self and promised to tell him everything about her past. He pledged the same.

Before they left to return to the hotel to get things out in the open, Quinton put his hand around Malik's throat and reinforced the importance of him paying his debt by Sunday. "This is your last chance! Don't fuck up!"

Malik had to think of something quick. His cash was all tied up his store, and the last thing he wanted was to feel Latrell's wrath. The way he was known to act a fool when pressed to that point was legendary. Besides, what was understood didn't need to get explained.

Chapter Fourteen

Monica and Quinton went back to the hotel and locked themselves in the room. It was time for both to face the music, so to speak. Normally it would be ladies first, but Quinton decided to forgo manners and start.

He explained that he and Latrell were and had been slinging drugs since they were young kids. Spending some time in prison was also on his resume. His parents had both been killed in a car accident, and he was homeless for a year. Malik owed him close to thirty grand, and if he didn't pay up, he would have him dealt with.

With Quinton breaking the ice with confessions of drugs and death, Monica felt at ease when her turn rolled around. Gradually Monica began to come clean. Hours passed as Quinton watched the love of his life fall apart. He always thought his life was rough, but Monica had cornered the market. Her shit was harsh from the get-go. He kissed her face as he consoled her.

Monica was exhausted from the combination of talking and crying, and she wanted nothing more than to take a nap. She reached out for Quinton's hand, leading him over to the bed and pulling him on top of her. "Please hold me. I need you," she begged. "I want you to make love to me."

Quinton wasted no time fulfilling her request. All the years of her imagining what it would be like paled in comparison to reality. Monica felt pleasure and pain together. Quinton took his time and caressed every inch of her virgin body. With each touch of his strong hands, she got weaker. With every thrust, she became more in tune with his body, and they soon moved as one. Just when Monica thought it was over Quinton kept going. He had been patient, and now he wanted his reward: Monica.

The next morning at breakfast, Monica had a strange look on her face, and Kanina noticed. "Oh my God. Y'all did it," she screamed.

Monica blushed as Quinton gave Latrell a stupid expression of getting caught being naughty. "Damn, dawg, get ya girl. She's on the nut."

They all burst out with laughter because Latrell's nosy ass also wanted the answer to the million-dollar question.

Finishing up with their meals and all feeling good, they decided to go for a walk along the beach.

As Quinton and Monica walked, she revealed that one day she hoped to open her very own clothing store and name it after her brother. Quinton promised that sometime in the near future he would help her achieve her dream so she would feel secure and could stop shoplifting.

Over the next few days they spent in Miami, they went clubbing every night and ate like kings and queens. By the time Sunday morning arrived the group was worn out and ready to go back home. Quinton and Latrell let the girls sleep in while they went to finish their business dealings with Malik. Latrell started cracking his knuckles as soon as he got in the car, but Quinton had something else in mind.

The plane ride home was bumpy as they flew through some turbulence. Monica was hysterical, causing everyone else aboard to panic. She was breathing hard, crying, waving her hand in front of her face, and behaving as if there were no air circulating. Monica had easily become a virus. She even had grown-ass men acting cowardly in their seats. Quinton and Kanina tried everything to calm her down, but they were unsuccessful. Latrell told all the jokes he knew and still no cigar. There was only one thing that Quinton hadn't tried. He'd wanted to wait until they got home, but this was an emergency.

"If I give you a present, will you be quiet?" he reasoned with Monica. "It's something you want." Monica, like most females, loved gifts, so she wiped her tears and acted brave. Quinton went in his pocket and gave her a slip of paper with some numbers scribbled on it.

"What are these numbers for? What kind of present is this? I'm lost."

"They're the confirmation numbers of the first shipment of clothes and accessories that are due to arrive at your apartment tomorrow." Quinton beamed. "The rest will be delivered when you pick out your location."

"I love you," she shouted loudly.

"You promised to be quiet!" everyone on the plane yelled in unison. "So shut up!"

Monica asked Quinton a thousand questions. She was baffled about where he had gotten all of the stuff from. That's when he informed her that he had struck a deal with Malik. He explained that Malik traded him $30,000 worth of merchandise at cost and plugged him in with his overseas distributor in exchange for the cash that he owed him. Monica was elated. The only thing she had to do was search for the perfect spot.

When the plane landed, all the passengers thanked Quinton for revealing his surprise early and shutting his woman down from acting a fool. When Monica and Kanina returned to their apartment, Monica started going through the pile of mail and found a letter from Sandra waiting. It said that she was getting released in ninety days and needed a place to stay. Monica was happy to find out that her friend would soon be home. Sandra wrote that she had over $475 saved that Monica had sent, to help with first month's rent and security. Sandra ended the letter with the good news that after all these years she had gotten her GED. Monica was overjoyed. Now all she had to do was find an apartment and a storefront.

Chapter Fifteen

After weeks of searching for what Monica thought would be located on the uppity side of town where Kanina had grown up, she found the building for her new store right on the edge of her old neighborhood. Sure, there was a lot of poverty and hopelessness. Monica knew that part all too well. But contrary to belief, there were hundreds of good, God-fearing, hardworking people who lived and spent their paychecks in the hood.

The building was in desperate need of repair. It had stood abandoned for several years, and the elements had taken over. A pipe had burst, causing major water damage, the roof had a bad leak, and the crackheads and scrapers had stolen most of the fixtures.

Quinton had four different contractors come in and bid on the work that needed to be done to get Monica's store up and running. When they found one who had the same vision as Monica, they hired him, and the transformation began. Carpenters, electricians, and plumbers joined forces to put the project together as soon as possible. Monica explained in great detail what she wanted, how she wanted it, and when she wanted it done. She planned on her store being the shit.

Monica was still in school, and she was trying to oversee the work crew at the same time. She had homework every week, and exams from time to time, causing Quinton to have to step up to the plate to sign for deliveries and see to it that the project stayed on schedule. He was used to helping Monica ease her worries. He loved her and only wanted her to have a happy, stress-free life.

When Monica came to him and explained that her good friend Sandra would soon be released from prison and needed a place to live, once again he saved the day. He offered a solution. Quinton owned some houses that he rented out for legitimate income. One was a brick two-family duplex on the west side of town. It was vacant, and he suggested that it would be just right for Sandra. The block was quiet with very few kids.

Monica jumped at the idea and took it one step further. Sandra would be occupying only one side of the house. Monica went back to her old building, and after days and nights of begging, she finally convinced Miss Lila to move into the other side. She was getting up in years and was a constant easy target, being victimized by the neighborhood junkies.

Day by day Monica and Kanina's apartment was getting overrun by boxes and boxes of clothes and accessories for the store. The extra room was packed to the ceiling, and there was only a tiny walk space in the already-small hallway. The delivery man was a constant visitor and knew both girls on a first-name basis. He was at the door more than Quinton or Latrell. For that matter, he might as well have had a key to the apartment and a toothbrush.

One day, the girls sat in the living room and remembered the night that they had first met the fellas. Kanina said, "Girl, that was the best night of my fucking life."

"Your life? What about mine?" Monica replied.

"You right. That nigga Quinton done put your ass on the map."

"That's my baby for real. He has hooked a chick up. If I had known that Negro laid like that, I would have been gave up the pussy."

"Stop playing, Monica. You know that your ass had a combination lock, a padlock, and a choke hold on that kitty cat, so stop frontin', bitch."

"I was just waiting for the right man to come along, that's all," Monica laughed loudly.

"Yeah, right." Kanina smiled. "He just happens to be clocking them dollars, huh?"

"Well, who wants to be poor but happy? Fuck what ya heard. The poor ain't hardly happy."

***

It was early April, and Monica and Kanina were preparing to fly to Las Vegas to attend a huge fashion trade show. The Magic Show had every major distributor and well over 3,000 up-and-coming designers who would be showcasing their latest lines for the season. Latrell had given Kanina a healthy clothing allowance, and she planned on spending it all. Monica was going so that she could make contacts and possibly do business with some of them. Yet the one thing at the top of her list was trying to find a unique gown for Kayla.

Although she was only a sophomore, Kayla was one of the most popular girls in school. She'd received three different invitations to the senior prom. So Monica was on the double alert of business as well as pleasure. Lucky for Monica, she and Kayla both owned the latest smartphones. Monica could take pictures of the dresses that she thought Kayla would like and send them to her via the phone.

Monica sent over twenty-five different snapshots of gowns. She still didn't get the green light to buy one. Monica gave up on her little sister for that trip. She went on to focus on the store and the little extras she could find that would set it off.

Kayla was front and center at the door, waiting for the girls to come over for Mrs. Cooper's

Thursday night dinner of pot roast and peas. She had poor Mrs. Cooper drive her all around town to every boutique and dress shop they could think of. At every store they visited, Kayla saw one of her fellow classmates trying on dresses. Being spoiled, she would storm out without even taking the time to look. She wanted to be special.

"Hey, Monica. Hey, Kanina." Kayla waved while grinning. "Can one of you do your little sister a gigantic favor?"

"I hate to hear what this is about." Monica nudged Kanina.

"Yeah, you're right. Ain't no telling with this one," Kanina joined in with Monica. Both peered suspiciously at Kayla, waiting for her to drop the bombshell.

"Stop playing, y'all." Kayla hugged them at the same time. "I just need a ride somewhere after school tomorrow."

Kanina snapped her fingers and waved her hand in a circular motion. "Well cool. That lets me off the hook. I have classes all afternoon."

"Dang, G." Monica broke loose from Kayla's grip. "Where your little behind need to go?"

"You'll be sorry," Mrs. Cooper yelled from the kitchen. "That child done made me age ten years driving around looking for a dress." All three of the girls laughed at her comments as they walked into the kitchen. They started opening the oven and lifting tops off the pots that were simmering on the stove. "You girls know it's the same thing every Thursday. Now go wash your hands and, Kanina, get your father. Dinner's ready."

At exactly two thirty on the nose, Monica pulled up in the high school parking lot. The bell was just ringing, and all the students were starting to pour out the doors. They all stood around and took notice of the car Monica was driving. Quinton had just put brand new rims on the Vette and installed a state-of-the-art sound system.

When it seemed no one else was left inside, Kayla casually walked out and headed toward the car. She wanted everyone in school to see the sweet car that she was about to ride in.

"Did you forget I was picking you up or what?" asked Monica.

"No, I didn't forget." Kayla reached in the back and set her books on the seat. "I had to double back to my locker. I left my social studies notes."

"Yeah, I bet." Monica put the car in gear and backed out slowly. "Your li'l ass just wanna floss."

"So damn what, Monica? Stop acting like you don't like to show off too," Kayla pouted.

Monica gave in and blasted the sounds loudly as they burned rubber peeling out of the parking lot and into the street. All the kids stood amazed and jealous, wishing that they were Kayla.

"Now are you happy? You got your big shot on. You big ol' pimp. You mack. You playa."

"Monica, quit doing that. You know you wrong."

"Dang, Queen Kayla, can I be like you when I grow up?" Monica kept kidding her sister.

"Be quiet and drive me to my desired locale, and make it snappy."

The two sisters joked with each other all the way to a small, out-of-the-way dress shop that Kayla had found in the yellow pages. She was dead serious about having a different dress. Monica tried her best to convince Kayla to get one of the gowns there, but she insisted that they were too tacky.

"Listen, Kayla, time is ticking. You gotta get a dress if you plan on going. Now what you gonna do? You gotta do something! You ain't 'bout to run ya big sister all around."

"Can we go to that mall out past the other side of the interstate? I know for a fact no one went that far to get their dress."

Monica was instantly thrown off by Kayla's question. She was talking about the very same mall where Saks was, the very same mall where she had been caught shoplifting, arrested, and dragged off to jail. Just thinking about that awful day gave Monica chills. She racked her brain to come up with any other shops to go check out, but her mind went blank.

"Well, Monica, can we go out there? Pleaseeee?"
Kayla pleaded with her sister and gave her a sad
look while acting like she was crying.

"Are you sure there's nowhere else you can check?
That's a long drive, baby girl!"

"Come on, Monica. I promise I'll find one."

Monica once again gave in to Kayla's spoiled act.
She turned onto the street that would lead them to
the interstate and face-to-face with a place Monica
had chosen to forget.

Chapter Sixteen

The long drive on the interstate brought back the harsh memories of that day. Monica remembered Kanina begging her to go to the other mall. While Kayla was relaxed in her seat listening to the radio, all Monica could hear was the sound of the security guard's voices yelling and screaming at her before she was handcuffed.

When they turned off at the mall exit, she saw the huge sign on the marquee that read Saks. Monica could feel her heart pounding as she waited her turn in line for valet parking. She tried to keep her eyes focused straight ahead and not even glance at the spot where she had lost her freedom. It seemed like just yesterday she had those prom dresses in her hands and was home free.

When they stepped inside the doors, Monica felt a little dizzy and light-headed. She placed her hand on Kayla's shoulder while they walked. The store's interior was just about the same as Monica had remembered. From the pictures that hung on the pastel walls to the crystal chandeliers that lit the aisle, it was pretty much unchanged.

The girls got onto the escalator and made the trip up to the formal-wear department. Once again, Monica had flashbacks and started looking around, observing her surroundings for any signs of security. As hard as she tried to shake the feeling of always being watched, she couldn't.

Kayla was in her own world as they approached the section that could be the answer to all of her problems. She looked over at her sister's face and finally took notice that something was wrong. "Are you all right, Monica?" Kayla quizzed.

"Yeah. Let's find you a dress." She smiled. Monica was trying to play it off the best she possibly could, considering the circumstances.

The closer they got to the gowns, the more Kayla's excitement grew in size with each step. She went from walking to skipping to an almost full-fledged sprint toward the high-priced, elegant department. "Wow, Monica. Look at this one." Kayla was like a kid in a candy store with money to burn. "Ahhh, man! This one is sweet too!"

Monica watched her sister quickly fly through every display on the floor. There were red dresses with tiny white pearls attached. Some were mint green lace with big sashes, and there was an entire section devoted to black gowns in every style one could imagine. "Well take your time, Kayla, and find a few that you really, truly like, and then try them on."

"It's so hard. I have to make sure to have the perfect one," Kayla responded as Monica looked across the aisle at the other side of the store: the half-off side, the discontinued side, the throwback side.

After ten short minutes of shopping, Kayla found the dress of her dreams. It was hanging up high on display with several others as if they were show-cased in a fashion parade. Monica could tell that they weren't the average gowns on the racks.

"Oh my God, Monica." Kayla pointed. "That's the dress I want right there. That's the one." It was a strapless off-white and pink dress with a long train that was detachable. It was directly in the center as if it were the main attraction.

"Are you sure that's the one you want? Don't have me have someone get it down and you change your mind." Monica put her hands on her hips and stared Kayla in the eyes.

"Yes, it's the one I want. I promise."

"All right then, let me go and find a salesperson." Of course, Monica was a little frightened of who she might run into, but she found instant relief when a young female approached them.

"Hello, how are you ladies doing today?" she inquired with a bright smile and pleasant dispo-sition.

"We're great, and thanks for asking," Monica returned her greeting. "My little sister would like to try that dress on please."

Kayla was hopping around from one foot to the other in eager anticipation of having the gown off display and on her body. Her praise for the dress was endless, as she couldn't and wouldn't be quiet.

"No problem. It is a gorgeous gown, isn't it? If you can give me a few moments, I just have to get my senior manager. She has the keys to the fitting lounge."

The young girl walked away and within sixty seconds returned with her manager directly on her heels. Monica slowly turned around and was face-to-face with the same old bitch who'd had her chased and arrested.

"Yes, can I help you two?"

"Yes, my sister would like to try that dress on please." Monica hesitated to speak, but to her surprise, the lady didn't seem to recognize her. "She also will be in need of some accessories."

"I'm sorry. What dress did you mean?" she asked sarcastically, acting as if she were in shock.

"That one hanging up there," Monica once again stated, this time with a little more bass in her tone.

"I'm very sorry, but those dresses up there are very special and very, very expensive." The woman looked over her eyeglasses at Kayla and Monica.

"The salesgirl should have told you that. She's new. You have to forgive her."

The young girl stood idle as the older woman degraded Monica. She hated mistreating people.

"Listen, I'm not trying to be rude, but that's the dress my sister wants." Monica folded her arms, enraged. "Now if you don't mind, can someone get it down for us?"

The older saleslady seemed to get angry at being asked to do her job. "There must be some sort of misunderstanding of what I just said, so let me go slow so you can comprehend. I know Detroit's public schools aren't what they used to be." She took her glasses off her face and clenched her teeth as she spoke. "You and your little friend, sister, or whoever she is, are on the wrong side of the store. The gowns that are over here all are very expensive." She smiled wickedly as if she was enjoying herself. "That means they cost a whole lot of money. Now, if you go on the other side, you two might be able to find something that can fit your budget on clearance. Oh, and by the way, if she didn't inform you," she said, referencing the young, innocent salesgirl standing by, "we don't take layaways!"

Kayla, Monica, and the young girl stood flabbergasted at the woman's bitter and derogatory statements. Monica hastily made her way around the rack and got in the woman's face. Before she could get one word out of her mouth, Kayla came in between the two.

"Naw, Monica, chill. I got this." She used her arm to move her big sister and usual protector out of the way. She stood toe-to-toe with the woman who was old enough to be her great-grandmother, and she eyed the name tag on her blazer.

"Excuse me, Ms. Solomon, but there must be some sort of a serious mistake to cause you to be so rude. My sister made a simple request for you to complete a task that I am very certain falls in line with your job description and responsibilities. It's obvious and painfully clear that you are past your prime and bitter, but so goes life. Now if for some obscure reason you are feeling even the slightest bit disgruntled or dissatisfied with your current choice of employment, then, by all means, I sincerely beseech you to immediately seek other means to support your cranky old self."

Kayla's face was close to touching the woman's glasses. "As a customer of this corporate-owned establishment, I help provide revenue to pay your salary, and I expect to be treated with respect, not verbally assaulted in such an outrageous manner. So if you find it demeaning to assist someone such as myself, a product of the Detroit Public School system, then shame on you." Kayla bucked her eyes and snapped her fingers at the old woman. "Now like my older sister asked your senile ass five minutes ago, do ya job, old woman, and go fetch the dress, bitch!"

Monica had never been prouder of Kayla in her whole life as they awaited the woman's next move. The lady was in a trance after getting deservedly put in her place by a teenager. She had no choice but to reluctantly allow Kayla to try the dress on.

"Go over there and get that dress down for them," she ordered the young salesgirl, who had started giggling.

"Excuse me, Ms. Solomon, but she told you to go fetch, not me." The girl went from giggling to flat-out laughing her ass off.

"Oh, you find something funny? Well, let's see how amused you are about this. You're fired. You can go back to working at the beer and wine store you came from."

"Fired? Bitch, I quit," she yelled, spitting dead in Ms. Solomon's wrinkled face. "You got me all fucked up." She grabbed her purse from under the counter and stormed out, but not before Monica handed her a flyer from the store she was opening, telling her that there was a job for her there if she wanted it.

Ms. Solomon reached over and snatched a costly blouse off the rack and wiped the big glob of saliva that was dripping down the middle of her face. It was then that she recognized Monica as the same girl who had last spat on her. Before she was able to make a scene, the district manager appeared and wasted no time reprimanding her for her actions.

"Ms. Solomon, I need a minute please."

"Just a moment, sir."

"No, right now." He was frustrated, and his anger was apparent as he shouted. "I was observing, on our security monitors and from behind a rack of clothing, the altercation that just took place. I am appalled at your treatment of these customers." He pointed at Kayla and Monica.

"How dare you speak like that to anyone who patronizes this store? Throughout the years we've received numerous complaints about you and your awful, condescending behavior, yet they've been overlooked. Well not today, Ms. Solomon," he huffed. "Clean your locker out and gather your personal belongings. Your services are no longer required here. Oh, and by the way, that three-hun-dred-dollar blouse you used to clean your face will most certainly be taken out of your final paycheck." He gave both girls his sincere apologies as he called the guards to escort Ms. Solomon off the store premises.

Kayla couldn't help herself as she gave her a devilish grin. "In case you don't understand English, he means you're fired."

The district manager then sent his best salespeo-ple over to cater to Monica and Kayla on hand and foot. The dress fit Kayla like a glove and required only a few minor alterations. The manager promised to have Kayla's dress specially delivered to her front door.

The dress was indeed expensive. It was an original from Egypt that retailed for over $4,500. With the shoes and accessories, Monica had to dig deep, but nothing was too good for her baby sister. When asked how she was paying, Monica proudly responded, "Cash."

Chapter Seventeen

The whole town was completely saturated with flyers announcing the store's grand opening. Monica had thought of every avenue of advertisement she possibly could. The local newspaper had a full-page color ad. Radio commercials were blaring, and she had a short spot on a public access program. Monica was doing everything humanly possible to make the day a total success.

Gossip was running rampant throughout the streets. Every barbershop and hair salon client filled their time in the chair or under the dryer speculating about what was going to happen the big night of the grand opening. The rumors spread like wildfire. They began with the food that was going to be served. There were supposed to be free bottles of Moët in the take-home goodie bags that Quinton had provided. The most outlandish rumor of them all was the his-and-hers full-length mink coat giveaway.

If all that talk weren't enough, the speculations regarding the interior were ridiculous and funny to both Monica and Quinton. African artwork flown in from Mali, European wallpaper gracing the store walls, along with a collection of vintage clothes that were once worn by Janet Jackson topped them. One thing was for certain, whatever it looked like inside the new store would be the main point of conversation for some time to come. Even the females Latrell and Quinton used to kick it with wouldn't think of missing out on coming. Jealous or not, they'd be there. There was no way in hell that anyone who called themselves rolling, balling, slinging, pimping, or being pimped was gonna be left out.

It was two days before the big day, and Quinton and Latrell were exhausted. They had been working overtime to make sure that everything would go as planned. Quinton didn't want to leave anything to chance. He hired extra security for the night and also two valet attendants to park the cars.

"Hey, baby. Do you two want to go out to dinner?" Latrell winked at Kanina.

"Yeah, let's get dressed and go back down to Tina's Tavern. We ain't been there since we met."

Latrell put his arms around Kanina's waist and hugged her. "Go put on something sexy for me and let's roll out." He smacked her playfully on her ass and sent her in the other room to get ready. "I'm gonna wear that shit out later," he yelled out to her.

Quinton walked over to Monica, who was working on the computer, and he kissed her on the neck.

"Hey, baby." Monica leaned back and smiled.

"Come on, sweetie. That's enough work for tonight. Let's go out and get some drinks and relax before this store opens and shit's really off the chain."

"All right, daddy, just give me a few minutes to take a shower and get my clothes on, and I'll be good to go." She made sure to rub his dick and grin. Monica ran to her room, and Quinton followed her.

"Damn, this room is getting smaller and smaller. You need some more space or something." He plopped on the bed, watching her get undressed. Less than three minutes after she got in the steam-filled shower and lathered her body with soap, Quinton stepped inside, pinning Monica's wet, slippery body against the wall. Covering her mouth with his, he held her tightly as his dick throbbed. Quinton took his fingers and slowly stuck them inside of Monica as she felt her knees get weak. The hot water pounded on their bodies as he grabbed her legs, lifting her off the ground in one motion. He slipped her down on his manhood and slowly started to grind hard in her pussy. The two stayed in the shower, fucking like animals, until they heard Kanina calling their names.

Tina's Tavern was packed. There was a long line of people waiting for the valet, but that had nothing to do with them. Quinton and Latrell were top-notch VIP in that motherfucker. They didn't stand in lines or worry about finding a seat whenever they came. Tina and Quinton went way back to her slinging forty ounces out of her car trunk after regular business hours. He and Latrell always looked out for her. They said that Tina was good people. She treated them both like her sons and wasn't nothing too good for them or their women.

Quinton had Monica drive up on the curb and park smack dead in front of the entrance. The crowd at the door had no choice but to move over toward the wall. Kanina and Latrell quickly pulled up behind them, and they all walked in the door ahead of the line. It was like that everywhere the foursome would go. The fellas gangsta was deeply respected.

"Hey, Q! What up, Trell?" The bouncer reached over and unhooked the black velvet rope that separated the hallway from the club.

"You got the best hand, my nigga." Latrell gave him a pound as he helped usher the girls in. Them getting searched was totally out of the question. Latrell stayed strapped, and everyone knew it.

"What's good wit' ya, son?" Quinton nodded and threw his hands in the air.

Monica and Kanina left them all to do their "guy thang" and went to get a booth. The waitress soon came over, and the girls ended up placing the food and drink orders for the fellas because they were still across the way, talking shit. When the food did arrive, Quinton and Latrell had just sat down. Monica had Quinton's favorite drink, rum and Coke, on the table, while Kanina made sure that her man was well stocked with a couple of Corona beers and a shot of Crown Royal. They had come to relax, and that's exactly what the group planned on doing.

After dinner, the partying began. The music was bumping, and the dance floor was overflowing with people having a good time. For once there was no arguing about dumb shit. Nobody stepped on anyone's shoes or stared at somebody else's girl or just plain wilded the fuck out. One by one, all the wannabe folks made sure to stop by the table and speak to Quinton and Latrell. It was as if they were a couple of hood dons. They were used to that type of bullshit.

Every girl from around the way who Monica had grown up with on the block all went out of their way to speak to her. Back in the day, they all talked shit about her and her family, yet here they paraded by, kissing her ass. Kanina and Monica tried their best to ignore some of them, but others wanted to be seen talking with Latrell and Quinton so badly that they refused to take a hint and had to be asked to move on by the waitress, whose way they were blocking. Bitches that night were straight-up brazen as fuck.

The evening was drawing to a close, and the crowd was starting to thin out. Quinton was holding Monica's hand, professing his love for her. He was still drinking and getting his buzz on when Kanina and Latrell returned from the dance floor. Latrell had the DJ play a special request just for them. Latrell was usually rough and rugged, but when it came to dancing, he was smooth. He twirled Kanina around as everyone watched.

"You two look so nice out there," Monica chuckled. "I would break my neck with all that spinning."

"I would have caught ya pretty ass." Quinton kept a hold of her hand.

Latrell called the waitress back over to the table and ordered a bottle of Dom Pérignon along with four glasses. She quickly returned and poured the champagne in the glasses. The waitress then signaled the DJ to dim the lights. Then he turned the sounds down very low.

"Can y'all give my mans a minute or two?"

When the few patrons left in the club were quiet, Latrell stood up and made a toast. Monica, Quinton, and Kanina kept their eyes glued on him.

"I want everyone in here to raise their glasses in respect and toast Kanina Tanay Cooper, my woman, my love, and soon to be my wife."

Kanina dropped the glass, and it shattered on the table. Monica's jaw dropped to the ground in disbelief. Quinton looked on proudly as his road dawg went down on one knee and pulled a small box from his jacket pocket. The room was silent as small tears flowed from Kanina's eyes.

"Kanina, baby, I love ya ass like I ain't never loved another. I want you to be my wife and shit. Will you marry me?" He opened the small box and took the ring out. "Please, boo boo." He grabbed her hand and slid the ring on her trembling finger as she nodded yes!

The room went freaking bananas as all the females gathered around gawking at the six-carat diamond ring that graced Kanina's slender finger. The fellas all clowned Latrell for being so soft and sensitive.

"I can't believe it. He really asked me to marry him. Imagine that, me somebody's wife. Wait 'til my mother finds this out." Kanina waved her hand in the light, making the diamond sparkle even more.

"Girl, it is so pretty. I can't believe it either." Monica was hyped. "We got a wedding to plan."

The girls huddled together. They started talking about colors, dates, and even what Latrell and Kanina would name their firstborn. They finally got up to go to the bathroom and were still gabbing as they left the table.

While the girls were in the bathroom running off at the mouth planning shit, Quinton and Latrell had an unexpected visitor at the table. It was a cat who ran one of Quinton's dope houses. He was a loyal soldier and had been down with them for three or four years. No matter what the task was, he was down with his peoples. He kept shit in order.

"What's up, man?" Latrell showed the guy some love, giving him a pound.

"It ain't nothing. I just need to holler at ya for a minute," he replied, looking over his shoulder at the ladies' bathroom.

"Damn, is it that serious? What's happening?" Quinton looked at him hard. "Don't hold me up, nigga. What's the deal?"

"Man, it's that chick you over here chilling with. I knew your girl's name was Monica, but I didn't know it was the same Monica I grew up with from around the way." He rubbed his face.

"Dig this here, Black Billy. If you got something to say, then spit that shit out and give it to a nigga raw." Latrell was tired of riddles.

"Remember that night that shit jumped off with that crackhead broad on Dexter and Davison Avenue?"

"Yeah, and so what? That was over two fucking years ago," Quinton said, and then downed a swallow of beer. "The police been stopped asking questions about that old, played-out bullshit."

Black Billy glanced once more at the bathroom door. "Well, Monica is that bitch's daughter!"

"What the fuck did you say?"

"Listen, Quinton, that's ya girl's mom."

"This shit is wild." Latrell shook his head.

Latrell and Quinton both couldn't believe what Black Billy had just told them. Just like that, the party was over. Black Billy left and went back to the spot to wait for further instructions as he was ordered. Moments later the girls emerged from the bathroom, still talking. They had something to keep them occupied for hours. Between the grand opening in two days, Sandra getting released from prison, and now planning a wedding, they wouldn't even bitch about the fellas claiming to have to handle some business.

Quinton immediately paid the tab and sent both girls home in his car. He jumped into the car with Latrell and headed to the hood. They had to figure this madness out.

Chapter Eighteen

It was the morning of the grand opening, and it was going to be hectic for everyone involved. Monica had to drive up to the prison and pick up Sandra. After years of waiting, her ex-cellmate would once again be free. Monica had yet to fill her in on the new shop Quinton had blessed her with or that she had no intention of ever stealing again. She wanted it all to be one big surprise to Sandra.

Monica had gotten an early start and was pulling up about twenty minutes before Sandra was scheduled to walk through the prison gates. She grabbed her purse off the passenger seat and took her cell phone out. Monica flipped it open, pressed number two on speed dial, and patiently waited for her girl Kanina to answer.

"Hey, chick." Monica reached over and turned the radio volume down a little. "Are you already at the salon or what?"

"Girl, I've been here ever since seven thirty this morning. You know Tasia's ass stays booked up."

Kanina sucked her teeth as she looked around. "Plus all these fake hoes in here trying to get they wigs tight for tonight."

"I heard that. Them bitches betta come correct." Monica and her girl were talking cash shit.

"Whatever they do, it ain't gonna matter. We the headliners for tonight. Believe that." Kanina twisted her face at the females who were in her mouth listening to her conversation and hanging on her every word. She made sure to move the hair out of her face so that they could see the rock she was sporting on her finger. She rolled her eyes. "Let me go, Monica. I'll holler at you later."

They got off the phone just in time for Monica to see the gates open and Sandra to step out with her green duffle bag in tow on her shoulder.

"I can't believe she's here. That child kept her word," Sandra mumbled under her breath. She was almost paralyzed with shock that Monica was outside the walls, parked and waiting for her just like she promised. The day that Monica got released was the last day that Sandra expected to see her cellmate ever again in life, but she was now fooled. Monica had written long letters, sent cards, and put money in her account on the regular, and now she was here in the flesh to pick her up.

"Thank God." Sandra looked toward the sky.

The friends exchanged hugs and headed back to the city. "You are looking good, Monica, and look at what you're driving. You must be putting a killing on them stores." Sandra was truly impressed.

"Naw, Sandra. It's something else, a big surprise."

When they pulled up in the driveway of the two-family flat that Quinton owned, Monica jumped out. "Come on, Sandra. You're home."

"Here? In this nice house?" Sandra was crying her eyes out for being blessed with a friend like Monica.

Miss Lila came outside to greet her new neighbor and introduce herself. After five minutes of listening to them talk, Monica knew that the situation would work.

"Listen, Sandra. I have to run. I've got a lot of things to do. There's plenty of food in the refrigerator, and brand-new bath towels and linens. Plus the phone is already on." Monica handed her the keys to her new home.

"And don't worry, honey." Miss Lila patted Monica on her shoulder. "They delivered the furniture late last night."

Sandra put the key in the lock and couldn't believe her eyes. Monica had the whole house completely furnished and new wall-to-wall carpeting put down. She had toothpaste in the cabinets and toilet paper on the roll. She had thought of everything.

"The closet has a few different outfits for you until we go shopping next week. Pick one out for the big surprise later, and I'll be back to get you. Your hair appointment is at ten. So be ready."

Sandra stood speechless as Monica backed out of the driveway and drove off.

Chapter Nineteen

"This is it, sweetheart. Are you happy?" Quinton and Monica parked in a spot that was specially reserved for the owner. They looked at the huge, flashing neon lights that could be seen across town.

"You don't even have to ask me. You already know I'm happy." She leaned over and kissed him gently on his lips.

The two had gotten there well over three hours early to supervise with the food and drink setup. Monica wanted everything just so. The napkins, the glasses, the plates, the forks, and the spoons had to be placed on the tables just right, with style. The clothes that were in the windows were originals and custom-made. Monica even went so far as to hire a makeup artist to ensure that the mannequins were as lifelike as humanly possible, with their nails and toes painted and extra-long eyelashes to boot.

Ever since Megan originally began helping her and Kanina unpack clothes and arrange displays, Monica was glad that she had given her a flyer at Saks. Even though the district manager had offered Megan a raise to stay after the incident with Ms. Solomon, she turned him down flat and decided to come and work with Monica. Megan knew all the ins and outs of the retail business, including promotions and other things to do to entice customers to spend money. She was up on all the behind-the-scenes stuff that Monica had no idea went on to run a successful store.

At seven o'clock the doors were open for business. Quinton and Monica were like two proud parents who'd just had a baby. Quinton checked his watch and nervously awaited the crowd that was sure to arrive soon. As always, Latrell was posted by his boy's side, and Kanina stuck close to Monica, who paced the floor back and forth. This night was full of tension. This was do or die, make or break for her.

"Girl, don't worry. You know how niggas like to be late and make a big entrance."

"Kanina, I ain't worried. If don't nobody show they punk asses up, we'll wear all this bullshit our goddamn self."

The pair of them were clowning around, messing with the waiters, when the first people walked in the door. Of course, they were some females Quinton and Latrell knew. Kayla and the Coopers came in next and surrounded Monica with love. Five seconds later Miss Lila strolled in with Sandra, who'd had no idea where she was going. After getting her hair done and getting all dressed up, she was let in on the surprise. Monica beamed with pride as all her family wished her well and got acquainted with Sandra.

By the time the clock read eight, the store was getting packed beyond belief. All the clubs in town had to be empty and weren't making a dime, because all the party people were at Monica's. There was no question that her new store was going to be a success. She and Quinton were ecstatic.

Black Billy and his entourage soon entered the store. Everyone in his crew came with their pockets on bump. They were ready to get their hands on some of the new clothes everyone in the town had been speculating about. Quinton watched Monica from the corner of his eye, while Latrell signaled for Black Billy to make his way over to where they were standing.

"What's up, son?" Quinton tilted his head sideways. "Did you handle that or what?"

"Dawg, I'm telling you. We couldn't find that cracked-out bitch nowhere!"

"Listen, guy, I don't wanna hear that dumb shit. I don't need that little slimy dopefiend throwing salt in a nigga's game."

Black Billy hated to disappoint Quinton, but he was at the end of his rope searching for Jenette's drug-addicted ass. There were over a thousand abandoned buildings in the city where she could have been sleeping and getting high. After all, everybody had a sack these days and called themselves getting paid. The gym teacher at the neighborhood junior high, the telephone repairman, and even the little Korean lady at the corner cleaners were all doing a li'l somethin'-somethin'.

"Look, dude, we ain't seen the ho fall through any of the regular spots. Plus, those other tricks her ass rip and run the streets with claim they haven't seen her in a minute."

"I feel you, Black Billy, but keep looking for ya mans." Quinton gave him a pound as Monica walked toward the trio.

"Hey, Black Billy. I'm glad you came." Monica smiled and wrapped her arms around Quinton. "I didn't know you three knew each other." She threw her hip to the side as she bobbed her head.

Latrell grabbed a glass of champagne and stood mute.

"What's up, Monica? Long time no see, baby girl." Black Billy leaned over and gave her a brief but respectful hug. "How ya been? Ya looking good as always."

"I didn't know that you knew my man," she said again, still not getting an answer.

Finally, after a good ten-second delay, Quinton replied, "This dude looks out for my loot around the way. He's good people straight up."

Monica got a terrible feeling in the pit of her stomach when he said that because she knew Black Billy knew the real, true, honest-to-God 411 on her mother and what all grimy bullshit she was capable of. Even though Monica had already told Quinton about her miserable childhood, she chose to leave some of the more humiliating things out of the confession, and hopefully, if she was lucky and blessed, Black Billy would too.

The grand opening was in full swing, and everyone was having a good time. The waiters were on top of their job, keeping all the glasses filled and the buffet looking inviting to the eye. The shrimp was chilled, and the chicken was hot. Megan was on the cash register, ringing up and charging sale after sale. Things couldn't get any better. Monica was living a fairy tale, and nothing could bring her down. Kanina and Latrell were occupied by showing her flawless engagement ring off to all their friends who hadn't had the opportunity to see it yet. They were the picture-perfect couple, madly in love.

Kayla was busy running around the boutique, entertaining some of her classmates who showed up to get a firsthand look at her sister's shop. Kayla had been bragging about the grand opening for weeks and wanted to make sure that the girls from her school would all see how her older sister was living large and doing it big. Come Monday morning she would be the talk of the entire school.

Sandra and Miss Lila were spending their time gawking and whispering to one another about the lack of clothing that most of the young women at the grand opening were wearing. Most gave the appearance of common street hookers. Both older women thought it was a damn shame that they came outside the house in such clothes, and they agreed that most of them would end up with pneumonia before the night's end. Black Billy and his crew were spread out in every corner, picking out new gear that Monica was bringing out of the store room hourly. She was making money hand over fist and had barely four hours to go before it was over.

Mr. and Mrs. Cooper requested that each and every person in attendance, with the exception of the minors, have their glasses filled with champagne. Not only was this the occasion of the grand opening, but a new beginning for their entire family.

"Excuse me, everyone. Excuse me." Mr. Cooper tried his best to get the crowd's attention.

"Yoo-hoo, everyone," Mrs. Cooper assisted him in quieting the noise as she clapped her hands. "Can you turn the music off please?" Without the music playing, the people soon focused on the older couple. The waiters were still passing out glasses as Mrs. Cooper began to speak.

"Hello, everyone. For those of you who don't know my husband or me, we are the proud parents of Kanina and our special adopted daughters, Kayla and Monica. Can all three of them please come and join us up front?" Mrs. Cooper watched proudly as Kayla pranced front and center, followed by Kanina, who was holding hands with Latrell, and finally a shy Monica, who navigated her way through the thick crowd standing by her family. It was a picture-perfect moment. Everything was golden.

Mrs. Cooper raised her tall, slender crystal flute high. "I would like all of you good people here to join me in saluting my three gorgeous daughters on the accomplishments and spectacular milestones in their lives. To our youngest, Kayla, on being selected for the National Honor Society. To our devoted Kanina and our soon-to-be son-in-law, Latrell, we wish you well. And to our little girl of the evening, Monica, on the grand opening of DH Designs, named after her late brother, Dennis Howard. May God bless you all and grant you every wish you ever wished. Cheers." Mrs. Cooper took a sip, and the crowd cheered and drank.

Then, out of nowhere, chaos started.

"Oh, hell to the naw, ladybug! You and all these fake Negros got me twisted." An enraged Jenette abruptly burst through the middle of the crowd, going ballistic. The people standing near her were practically gagging from her repulsive odor.

Without hesitation each quickly moved to the side, making a path. Allowing the visible freak of nature to brush by them as she slurred obscenities loudly, the crowd was stunned.

Jenette was a 100 percent hot fucking-ass mess from head to toe. Jenette was dressed in a pair of old stonewashed blue jeans that were torn on one leg and badly wrinkled. She wore a soiled tan sweatshirt that was three sizes too big. It hung off of her skinny skeleton-like frame. The pumpkin-seed sneakers on her feet had no shoelaces. And, as for her hair, it was all over her head as if it hadn't been combed in months.

"Bitch, you got the game messed up. Them is my daughters you standing up there claiming. Mine! Not yours, damn you. Mine!" Jenette had one of the grand opening flyers crumbled up and clutched in her bony fist as she got closer to Monica and her newly formed family. Mr. and Mrs. Cooper watched in horror as Jenette neared the group. The whole room was silent as she continued with her rampage.

"Monica is my motherfucking baby, not yours! My firstborn! I gave birth to her sorry ass." Her lips were dry and cracked, and the few teeth she had in her mouth were visibly yellow. "Who do y'all think y'all is, trying to claim my child? This store is half mines, too. I raised the backstabbing bitch. She owes me that much at least. Ain't that right, Monica?"

Jenette snatched a glass of champagne off a waiter's tray and guzzled it down in one quick swallow. She then stumbled to the floor and landed at a stunned Kayla's feet. "Hey, mama's baby." She grinned while reaching out her arm, which was infested with needle scars. "Don't just stand there. Help ya mama up." Jenette blew a kiss to her youngest child.

Kayla was completely beyond mortified. The roomful of people, including her classmates, covered their mouths and turned their heads in disgust at the open sores that were on Jenette's wrist. Breaking out in tears, she wanted to die on the spot. Kayla buried her hands in her face and leaned over into Mrs. Cooper's arms.

The security guards on duty rushed over to the scene of the commotion. Hesitantly they picked the troublemaker up off the ground, holding their breath. However, Jenette wasn't finished yet with her outburst. Somehow, she found more strength in her malnourished body. Yanking away and spitting as she screamed out in a violent rage of fury, Jenette continued tripping. "Let me go, motherfuckers! My daughter owns this joint! I'll have all y'all fired." Her breath smelled just like she looked: rotten. "Monica, you betta tell these niggas something! Monica, do you hear me?" Jenette demanded a response from her oldest child.

Monica was stiff as a statue. She hadn't moved one inch. Mortified by what was taking place, she'd failed to mutter a single word since her mother had entered the premises going wild.

Latrell had somehow managed to get back over to where Quinton and Black Billy were standing. All the searching his boys had done for Jenette's low-down ass didn't turn up shit, and here she was.

"What the hell are we gonna do now?" Quinton started sweating and shaking his head. "I swear to God if this dopefiend fucks up my shit with Monica, I'm gonna kill that bitch. That's my word."

"Chill, guy. Her ass is always high as a kite. Maybe she done forgot about that bullshit." Black Billy tried calming a frantic Quinton down.

"Yeah, Quinton," Latrell optimistically weighed in. "He's probably right. Just chill and let's see how this whole thang plays out."

They all decided to play the background and blend in with the rest of the crowd. Quinton rubbed his hands together nervously as he watched Monica start to tremble with anger. He wanted to rush to her side and take all the pain off her shoulders, but his hands were tied. There was no way in hell he wanted Jenette to lay eyes on him or Latrell. That's when the shit would really hit the fan.

"Oh, it's like that? You two little bastard bitches is too good to help y'all's own mama now?" Jenette pointed her finger back and forth at Kayla and

Monica. "I should have killed both of y'all ungrateful asses. Having y'all fucked my life up. That's why I couldn't keep a man. I hated all three of y'all since conception." Jenette ripped another glass of champagne out of a stunned Mr. Cooper's hands and poured it down her throat.

Sandra couldn't take the hurtful words that were coming out of Jenette's foul mouth, and she intervened. "What is wrong with you? What kind of mother speaks to her children like that? You should be ashamed of yourself. Jenette, you need some serious help. You're a total disgrace."

"Excuse me, bitch! Do I know you? And how do you know my fucking name?" Jenette shrieked.

"I was locked up with your daughter and watched her cry herself to sleep at night, worrying about her brother and sister eating because you ain't shit."

"Oh, so you a jailbird bitch like my Monica, huh?" Jenette laughed, showing the full extent of her urgent need of a dentist. "Well if this don't beat all. My own flesh and blood wanna chose all these no-good sons of bitches over me." Jenette was in rare form and on attack mode once again.

"First these uppity assholes, trying to be white, steal my little Kayla from me and make me lose all my benefits and food stamps." The Coopers and Kanina had blank expressions on their faces as Jenette singled them out. "Then this old jail ho right here wants to tell me about mines." Sandra rolled her eyes at Jenette. Her skin was tough, and unlike the Coopers, Jenette's words didn't affect her at all. "And then if that ain't all bad enough," Jenette said, making sure to look Monica directly in her eyes, "you wanna choose that dope-slinging nigga who murdered your little brother over me!"

Monica was shaken out of her horrified trance as the words out of Jenette's mouth hit her like a ton of bricks. Everyone's attention immediately turned on a shameful Quinton, who slowly walked up to Monica in hopes of clearing up Jenette's statement.

"Say what now?" someone blurted out from the crowd.

"Yeah, here he comes, the dirty, punk-ass nigga who killed my son out on the street. Now you got the nerve to be fucking his sister. You ain't shit!" Jenette had the roomful of people mesmerized by her accusations. Monica was starting to get short of breath as she listened like everyone else. "He shot Dennis right in his head, and half of it was laid in the street. Yeah, that's right, Monica. He gunned ya brother down, and you running around here, sucking his little dick! You ain't shit either!" Jenette was stomping her feet and waving her arms, putting on a show as she tried to make her point.

All listening dropped their jaws. Monica had to restrain herself and try to regain her composure after what she had just heard. She knew that Jenette was high and drunk, but how could she make up some bullshit like this? She braced herself.

Quinton took Monica's limp hand and held it tightly. He could feel that she wasn't squeezing his hand back, and she had a look of resentment written across her face. He gently touched her face with his other hand and began shedding light on the events of that senseless evening that could possibly cause the end of their relationship.

"Baby, let me start by telling you that I love you with all my heart and would never ever do anything intentionally to hurt you. It's always gonna be me and you against the world," he pleaded with sincerity. "I would never betray you or lie to you. Now it is true, I was there the night your brother got killed, but it wasn't my fault. I didn't even know that the young dude that night was related to you until the other night when Black Billy told me and Latrell. I've been sick about it ever since. You gotta believe me."

Quinton shook his head and turned his lip up as he glared hatefully at Jenette. "Listen, Monica, I know that this is your old girl and all, and I don't want to drag her name through the fucking mud, but this here bitch is straight-up foul!" Although everyone agreed with his opinion of Jenette, they still were awaiting his explanation. "The night that the shit jumped off, me and Latrell were on our way to meet up with Black Billy to take care of some business. When we pulled up on the block, she was out in front of the old building across the street, begging the fellas for some credit. The guys were shooting dice and weren't paying her any attention. Anyway, me and Latrell got out of the car and got in the game. We were drinking and chillin' about a good twenty minutes before your mother walked in the middle of the game completely naked and acting a fool."

Quinton looked over at Monica's adopted family, who were standing around astonished at what was taking place on a night that was supposed to be a joyous occasion. Mr. and Mrs. Cooper couldn't help but start to fear for their daughter's personal safety being involved with Latrell and Quinton, who they were led to believe by their daughters were computer engineers they'd met at school.

Quinton felt compassion for Monica having to hear all the malicious things that took place that night, but he had no choice but to try to clear his name. "Monica, believe me, ain't nan one of us touch ya mom or lay a hand on her." The crowd sighed with relief at that revelation. "We was all distracted by her antics and was straight clowning her ass, when out of nowhere this young guy jumped out with a big 9 mm and started talking shit," Quinton proclaimed. "She set us up! Your old girl grabbed all the money off the ground, and dude made Black Billy and 'em hand over they chains. Him and her took off running down the dark block, and of course, some of the fellas pulled they shit out and started busting at they asses."

Quinton watched as tears poured out of Monica's eyes. "Your brother shot back and hit Jaron and Duke before he took a few bullets himself and hit the ground. Before we could rush down the block and get our loot back, your fucked-up-ass mother was bending over his body going through his pockets, and then she disappeared in the alley." Everyone in the room was stunned. "That's the last I'd seen of her scandalous ass until tonight. The fellas be having her work the spots sometimes to pay off the debt of all that money she and your brother robbed us of, but I don't deal with her at all. Black Billy had mercy on her because he said he had known her ever since he was a little kid."

Quinton was finished enlightening her with his version of the events. He prayed that Monica understood that he was helpless in the whole situation. Jenette had no shame whatsoever about what was just said and didn't even try to deny it. Monica had yet to utter one single word. Every eye in the store was focused on her. She wanted to be the star of the grand opening, and she indeed was.

"Monica, please, baby, say something," Quinton begged and was now holding both of her hands.

After a long stretch of silence, Monica finally spoke. "Quinton, are you telling me my little brother was out there in the streets, running with her?" She glanced at Jenette. "They were sticking people up together? Is that what you're telling me?"

Before Quinton had a chance to answer, Miss Lila interrupted them. "Monica, you know I done known Jenette and y'all kids y'all's whole life, and I ain't never tried to do nothing but help. So I'd be wrong if I didn't speak up right now and stop all this madness once and for all."

Miss Lila took a long, hard look into Jenette's cold face and shook her fist. "You should be locked up and the key thrown away. Monica, this boy here is telling the truth. I don't know how many times your black-hearted mama and Dennis had folks banging on that apartment door, looking for them about something they stole."

Miss Lila then turned to Monica. "I was looking out my bedroom window that night, and I seen them right underneath the streetlight, scheming as usual. I'm sorry, baby, but I saw Dennis robbing them boys." Miss Lila was infuriated, and she cursed in the loudest tone that she could force out of her old body. "You a low-down, pathetic piece of nothing, Jenette Howard! Your terrible ass gonna burn in hell for getting your son turned out on drugs like you did! Mark my words! You gonna suffer the wrath of the Almighty Creator! It wasn't bad enough that you always been a drug addict. You had to bring that poor boy down to your level, introducing him to that garbage!"

Quinton felt Monica snatch her hands out of his. He watched her head toward Jenette's direction.

"Who you gonna believe, Monica, huh? I'm your mother. I had you," Jenette screamed. "You and me is blood," she slurred as she tried to hug her daughter, who snatched away. "You and me is just alike. I always liked you the best anyhow, not that snotty Kayla or your stupid brother who got himself killed. You know he always did run slow as fuck." Jenette showed no remorse and was brazen with her words. She didn't care who they harmed.

Monica was done feeling sorry for Jenette. Something in her mind finally clicked. The once-young Monica, forced to grow up too early, was suddenly no more in her own eyes. The art of making excuses for all the awful things her mother took them through as kids was corrupted.

"Yes, security, can you please step over here? I need assistance with an apparent problem. I need you to remove this worthless thing from my sight. Something extremely foul stinks in here," Monica demanded as she motioned toward Jenette. "By the looks of things, it's this piece of garbage. I don't want to see jack shit but this trifling bitch's back leaving through that doorway."

Security swiftly obliged. They rushed back over toward Jenette. They strong-armed Monica's mother, who was shocked herself for once that night.

"Monica, is your ass crazy, talking about me like that? Have you lost your damn mind?" Jenette screamed, bucking against the men's forceful grip.

Monica gave her mother the serious side-eye as the amazed crowd looked on in disbelief. Refocusing on her hired security team, she firmly reinforced her wishes. "Will you guys just please hurry up and do as I requested? The smell in here is getting worse."

"Bitch, you done let the nut you been sucking out that killer's dick drive you crazy. I should kick your black ass for the way you talking to me right about now. Have you forgotten I'm your fucking mother?" Jenette evilly hissed once again, trying to snatch her arm away from the men.

Monica was not moved by her mother's empty threats. The days of her being a child and intimidated were gone. With conviction she posted up, ready to do battle. As she stood directly in Jenette's face, she smiled. Monica's smile soon turned into laughter. "My mother? Did you say you're my mother? I'm sorry, there must be some sort of mistake. I don't know what you mean. My mother died a long, long, long time ago. She had me and my brother and sister living in turmoil constantly. She had all three of our minds fucked up so bad I thought we'd never be right in the head. But sadly my brother is dead. He died out in them streets just like my mother. So now it's just me and my little sister and our new family. And guess what, bitch. We good. So please, lady, don't show up around here now shit is Gucci, talking about you somebody's mother. Get the fuck on! Like I said, my mother is dead. Now, security, please do your job like I asked. Get this deranged trick outta my sight."

"Monica, wait. I'm starving out there. Shit is fucked up for me. What do you want me to do? I need y'all to at least give a bitch a few dollars until I get back on my feet," Jenette shouted out as she struggled to break free.

"I guess you could do just like me, Dennis, and Kayla had to do all these years. Get it how ya live," Monica announced coldheartedly, turning her back. As they threw Jenette out the doors and onto the curb, she took a deep breath. Without reservation, she held her head high.

Proudly Monica marched back to Quinton's side. Kissing him on the cheek, she rubbed his arm, reassuring him all was and would be well with them. Pouring herself another glass of champagne, Monica looked into the still-speechless crowd. With a huge smile plastered on her face, she spoke. "I'd like to propose a toast to Mrs. Cooper, Miss

Lila, and Sandra, the best three mothers a girl could have in life. Blood doesn't always make you family. Love does. Cheers!"

Even though Jenette's slimeball performance left them all flabbergasted, her three surrogate mothers still felt proud and truly blessed to be a part of Monica's life. This was a night that they would never forget. How could they?

As everyone in the shocked crowd hesitantly sipped from their glasses, Monica, Kayla, Quinton, and the Coopers all tried putting on happy faces. But they all shared the same thought, and that was the score they had to settle with Jenette's snake ass. The next time each would lay eyes on her and their paths crossed, rest assured it would certainly mean nothing nice. Jenette had it coming one way or another someday. Bitches like her always got theirs in the long run.

The End

You Can't Break Us

by

Treasure Hernandez

Chapter One

We were the last of a dying breed. Me and mines were on some old-school Bonnie and Clyde gangster-type shit. Young, crazy, money hungry, and bloodthirsty if need be. We did things most lames only dreamed about. But to us it was normal. We came from the hood, did dirt in the hood, and sadly, would probably die in the hood. That was our life. We lived it fast. Then just like that, in the blink of an eye, the team was no more. Damn, it seemed like it was only yesterday!

Moni

"Twerk, bitch! Work for these dollars!" Voodo loved the limelight. He tossed big bills into the air at the hole-in-the-wall strip club we were flossing hard in. Strippers flocked toward the three-person party that included me, him, and his right-hand man, Jerell. "Aye yo, ma, give my pretty girl over here a dance." He winked at the light-skinned, dancer with the big booty, whom everyone in the club was checking heavy for. "There's real moneymakers over here in this section."

"Here he goes with this shit," I mumbled under my breath so he couldn't hear. Tucking my phone into the compartment of my new Dooney & Bourke purse, the text conversation I was having with my best friend, Unique, would have to wait. Whatever my man wanted to make him happy, he got. There would never be a day on this green earth when I'd not try to satisfy him.

Looking over at Jerell, I knew he'd heard me complain underneath my breath, but he wouldn't dare throw me under the bus. For one, he was too consumed with the pussy parade going down before his devilish eyes. And for two, he knew Voodo honored me like a queen and would never put his word over mine. Our connection and bond to one another has been unbreakable since the first day we met.

His name is Shawn "Voodo" James, and I am Simone "Moni" Allen. The two of us have been inseparable as boyfriend and girlfriend for about two years. And for those whole two years, we've been nothing but terrorists of the city of Detroit as crime artists. It started the first day we hooked up.

The day I met Voodo was the best and most exciting day of my life. Me and my girl Unique were chilling at a greasy spoon eatery one morning,

stuffing our faces, when he walked in setting it off.
I didn't know how his facial features were set up
because his face was covered with a black mask,
but I was fascinated by his thuggish demeanor
nonetheless. I'd never been attracted to preppy
boys who kept their pants around their waists
secured with a belt. Those dudes never made
me tingle like roughnecks did. Anyhow, Voodo
ordered everyone to the floor and ordered the
cashier to empty the register without hesitation.
As employees and patrons, including Unique, panicked following his directions, I folded my arms
and threw on the best "come fuck me" expression
I could muster up. My confidence was through the
roof, so I knew he was gonna eat me up on sight.

"Hey, ma, you didn't hear me tell everyone to
get the fuck on the floor?" Despite him looking at
me like a child who was disobeying her father, I
returned his hard stare.

I smartly hit him with a comeback. "Yeah, I heard
you, playa. What I didn't hear was you tell everyone to empty their pockets on the way down. Don't
half ass do the job. You might as well hit all of us up."
Knowing that I was walking a fine line with a man I
didn't know, I made sure to bite my lip and let the
flirtatiousness in my voice lead my words. I didn't
want to catch a bullet from his gun just in case he
wasn't feeling my ego or style. Unique tugged on my

ankle, whispering for me to cooperate and shut up, but I was too far in at this point.

He snickered at my wit. "A'ight, li'l gangster boo. If you want it, then you got it. Everyone on the floor and empty your pockets, 'cause she wants a piece of the action too." They hurried to follow his orders as I stood still with my mouth turned up into a smirk. "Whatcha waiting on, li'l mama? Grab that shit up so we can make a move."

I smiled at hearing the words "we can make a move," and then I made mine, collecting everything of value from every person's hand except for Unique. It didn't matter to me that I was in on a robbery. I was trying to see what was up with the man behind the mask. "Now what?"

"You see what type of life I'm living, so that's your call, ma." He grabbed the bag from my hand and pulled down his mask. "If you wanna roll with a nigga, let's go. If not, I'll see you around the city fa'sho."

There was no thought necessary once I laid eyes on his face. Not only was he hardcore, but he was sexy as fuck. After picking up the few pieces of bacon that were left on my plate, I picked Unique up by the hand so she could ride out too. "I'm down. Let's be out." I'd been the Bonnie to his Clyde ever since.

With the DJ spinning one club banger after the next, the subwoofers and the floorboards were

rocking. Ace of Spades was the place to be tonight.
Every pole had a dancer swinging from it, every
baller in Detroit was out in packs showboating,
and no hot-seat, paying lap was empty. Even the
C-list celebrity host was getting tipped out of her
mind for barely twirling. The consumers got their
fixes while the workers got their cash. It all worked
out grand.

Voodo was throwing his weight, and it showed.
Draped in diamonds and gold chains, he was
standing firm like a boss, commanding the attention
from men and women alike. Even I was shining the
way a woman ought to, with diamonds, Christian
Louboutin heels, and a custom-made outfit that
stunted on every wannabe bad bitch in attendance.
Everyone knew our story and that we weren't the
couple to be fucked with. Instead of us having to
demand respect, it was given to us with ease.

Taking a look at the gold Rolex on his arm,
Voodo called the dancer out even louder than
before. "Yo, ma, what's up? You with making this
money or not?" He waved impatiently for the prettiest dancer to move faster and grace us with her
presence. As he sipped from his personal bottle of Moët, careful not to spill any on his blue
Versace shirt, he strategically made sure the dia-
mond-studded bezel on his watch stood out.

"Um, I'm good on that, babe," I finally spoke
up to him. "She ain't gotta dance for me. Matter

of fact, I can dance on you later," I cooed to him seductively. "I'm cooling over here in my corner, actually ready to go." I was playing it cool, because I hated not to please him, but low-key I was fed up seeing the love of my life smack asses and slide dollars between the legs of other women. Now don't get me wrong, I knew where his heart was and that he'd never dare cheat on me, but I hated seeing his hands touch other women the way he touched me. I might've been hardcore when it came to living a life of crime, but I was soft and jealous when it came to my man.

"Come on now, Moni, I already know what you're thinking, but it ain't like that tonight. This is more business than pleasure, so do me a favor by falling in line." He gave me the look I'd seen more than a hundred times. Voodo was up to no good. He was up to what we did best: making motherfucking moves at the expense of others.

"Oh, well that's all you had to say, baby." I smiled slyly, automatically falling into my position. I wasn't caught up in the matrix. I was willingly part of the conspiracy. My role was simple, and that was to hold him down and take charge if necessary. I'd never failed him before, and tonight wasn't about to be the start of that trend.

"That's my girl." He blew a kiss my way. "Ain't nothing better than having my best friend by my side. I couldn't have asked for a better partner in crime."

Damn this nigga melted my heart. Smiling from ear to ear, I wanted to fuck him on the floor of the strip club. I loved when he was gangster and affectionate with me at the same time. "Neither could I, baby boy. Trust and believe we'll be partners forever after."

Voodo gave Jerell a high five then a firm nod to signal things were about to get turned up to another level. Jerell didn't ride with us on all of our missions to get money, but when he did, I knew to expect a full-blown war. Jerell was reckless, unpredictable, and the last person to give a fuck about bodying a nigga. See, me and Voodo had unconditional love for one another. Jerell only loved blood. Popping another bottle of champagne, he surveyed the club, trying to peep whatever mission Voodo was trying to be on while continuing to enjoy his lap dance. I was sure he wasn't worried about making a move when it was absolutely necessary. His gutter ass stayed ready.

Nina, known to the underground strip world of D-Town as Naughty, was on the paper-chase stroll toward our booth, ready to call Voodo out on his bossiness. She knew about Voodo. Everyone in the city of Detroit did. So she was well aware that she was about to get paid or set the hell up. Either way, making money was the name of the game in her world. Just like us, she was knee-deep in trying to win.

All eyes were locked on her as she moved throughout the club in a pair of eight-inch sparkling silver thigh-highs that made her ass pop. The slim-thick dancer reveled in looking like a redbone hood version of a Barbie doll, in her custom studded teal two-piece, which barely covered her nipples and hairless vagina. With a fiercely cut blond bob, perfectly applied matching makeup, and long lashes she could fly away with, Naughty stood out among the crowd, demanding attention. In the past, she'd been able to pay for her car note, rent, and even custom dancer outfits from the amount of cash Voodo paid into her pile. Once she spotted me in the crew, though, she knew the payout might not as grand. I kept a close tab on my nigga and his pockets, like all women from the hood ought to do.

"What's up, boo? You called for me?" she questioned, stepping inside the roped-off booth into Voodo's face.

I growled to myself, hating he was so close to her. But I fell back because I knew his mind was on making money instead of getting twerked on. *Hurry this shit up, nigga, before I catch a 'tude I can't fade.*

"Hell yeah, I called for you," he replied to her too anxiously.

Although I overlooked it and Voodo was trying not to, he was almost drooling as he stared Naughty's tantalizing tattooed body up and down.

Hell, even I had to give the chick her props for being a bad bitch. When he looked over at me and caught my eyes staring him down, he knew what time it was and that he'd been busted for checking out eye candy in my face. "Get to work," I mouthed.

"Bend over and pop that fatty for my girl, ma! Put on a show for my baby right quick." To add flair to his overkill, he dropped stack of a hundred singles over Naughty's head before she had the opportunity to even twerk an ass cheek. He invited Jerell into the limelight as well. "Money is nothing over here! Let her know, nigga."

"Oh, yeah, baby girl, my man does it up fa'sho," Jerell commented, but he was busy putting two and two together of what was about to go down. By this time, he'd pushed his own private dancer off his lap and was tipping Naughty out heavy as well.

Naughty was in a stripper's heaven. The more money that fell over her head, the harder she danced. Then she popped back onto my lap, working for her cash even more. For a second I enjoyed the dance, then I blocked out everything within the strip club by keeping my eyes focused on Voodo. He was up to something and about to make a move on someone. I just wasn't sure about the particulars of what and to whom.

Playing my part well, I leaned back so the dancer could do her job. I even swayed to the beat and stuffed a few bills of my own into her G-string.

Whenever there was a setup in place, I always made sure the mark never saw it coming. And since everyone in the club knew that Voodo and I rolled like Bonnie and Clyde, I fa'sho had to leave her unsuspecting.

"Yeah, that's what the fuck I'm talking 'bout! Let me get some more of you pretty ladies this way." Voodo broke another rubber band then threw the whole stack into the air. He was ready to turn the heat up to hell in the Ace of Spades bar. I knew him well. This was all a diversion from what his plan actually was. "Cheers, my baby. We have arrived, and it's lights out to any chump who's looking to knock us down." He looked across the room with a pair of killer eyes. Being his wifey, my eyes followed his, and that's when they marked the target.

Jerell might've been giving his boy props for doing it big, but he too picked up on Voodo's eye movements and stance. No words had been exchanged, but all three of us were marking the same target with venom in our eyes. *If it ain't ol' Felix out in the open, wearing his heart on his sleeve. Niggas always go wrong leading with their emotions.* The longer Jerell simultaneously watched Felix and Voodo discreetly checking for one another, it was easy to tell with my experience with them that blood was getting ready to be shed.

Jerell's stance went from laidback to tense within seconds. My gut rumbled with anticipation. I was ready to get it popping too.

Naughty never picked up on any of this. While she smacked her firm backside and kept occupied, Felix Stewart, better known as Felix the Snitch, stood across the Ace of Spades in his own VIP section, watching the love of his life get preyed upon.

He knew what was up. He knew the hood didn't take well to snitches, and once one person found out he'd had a roundtable with the Detroit Police Department earlier this week about crimes me and Voodo were responsible for, there'd be consequences. The news had spread like fire. Running into him tonight wasn't a coincidence. It was planned out by Voodo especially for payback, and ultimately it was a way to keep our freedom intact.

With a single gold chain lying on top of his white tee, Felix stood tightlipped beside his bootleg street soldiers with regret etched across his face. I'd already pieced together what my babe's plot was: to use Felix's woman as his weak spot. I wasn't sure if he felt bad for Naughty or felt bad he was about to get dealt with. What I did know was that if he reached for his cell, I'd be pushing his girl off my lap and reaching for my pistol to pop him. His mark buster ass could only call one person for protection, and that was his connect at the precinct. By no means necessary was I gonna let him get the club raided and shut down before my man's plan was fully played out. Then a sudden move was made.

"Hey, Voodo, chin check to your left." Jerell was the first one to mention that Felix was cutting through the crowd.

"I'm on it, bro, trust and believe. I knew that sissy, soft nigga wouldn't be able to hold his nuts for much longer with the pussy parade his girl is the star of. I've been waiting on his froggish ass to leap." Pocketing the rest of his stacks, Voodo eyeballed me to make sure I was paying attention, and then he felt for the revolver I knew he kept nestled underneath his shirt. He was more than prepared to reveal his true intentions for the night.

"Me too. That snitching-ass nigga deserves whatever you've got planned for him for trying to take you and Moni down. And by walking into your trap, he deserves even more. These young fools get so caught up in their mark emotions and can't think straight."

"Consider his ass on countdown," Voodo grimly spoke, then whipped the pistol from his waistband with ease. "It's time to get it popping with these lame, duck-ass clowns. I don't play when a nigga comes for me and my girl. Never have and never will."

"One hundred grand, my man. You know I'ma hold both of you down." Reaching under his shirt for the concealed weapon he never left home without either, Jerell maneuvered it out discreetly then held it straight down at his side. For all intents and purposes, he was ready to go to war with his right hand.

"Hey, ma, get your ass off ol' girl and back to working the stage. This private party bullshit you got popping over here with this joker is over." Felix, accompanied by his two-man crew, called themselves intruding our party without problems. Felix already knew what trouble he was in and that Voodo was well aware of him snitching, so I wasn't sure why he thought shit was about to roll over easy.

"Naw, nigga, it don't look like she sweating to leave. She good, my manz." Voodo was more than cocky, responding before Naughty had a chance to. It was all a game to Voodo, to deflate Felix's ego even more by proving loyalty would fuck you over if you couldn't remain loyal to the hood code.

"I ain't yo' muthafuckin manz, and this here ain't the streets." Looking Voodo up and down in his name-brand tags, Red Bottom kicks, and money-loaded pockets, it was obvious the snitching street runner was feeling some type of way. "What the fuck, ma? You heard ya man. Get up off that bitch and let's be out!" Pushing past Voodo, Felix bumped him intentionally before yanking Naughty by the arm up off of me.

"Yo, my nigga, apologize to my lady." Voodo became the divider between him and Naughty. "I don't fucking play when it comes to me and mine. You ain't get the memo after all these years? Don't be coming over here on no shit with your li'l play bodyguards, my dude." Ready for war, Voodo knew when he walked through the door he was gonna end up shutting the club down.

"Nigga, what? I ain't apologizing to that yellow-bone ho," Felix cockily disrespected me before his head snapped back.

Voodo shattered the glass Moët bottle over Felix's head, and he fell to the ground, flopping like a fish. "Get them bitch niggas, Jerell! I got this clown." He stomped and kicked ol' boy into the ground. His head bounced up and down off the floor as blood splattered from his mouth. "No to an apology? It's bad enough you're a snitching-ass nigga, but I'ma make it so you don't ever speak an ill word about my fam again."

Red Bottom shoes ruined, Voodo was proving a point to Felix while Naughty watched with disbelieving eyes. Even with my pistol loaded with one up top, I was feeling more in love than ever before. My man always rode for me. For his actions tonight, I was gonna make sure my jaws locked up from sucking his dick once we got home. Shifting my attention to Jerell, I saw he was manhandling two men at the same time, eventually cold cocking them both in the head and making them fall to the ground motionless.

Naughty hurriedly scooped the money up off the floor, then rushed alongside the other dancers scattering like roaches to the locker room and exits nearest them. She wasn't the least bit concerned about her man getting beaten to a pulp. Felix might've been her man, but she wasn't ready to meet her Maker, nor did she have unconditional love for him like I did for mine. I would've run after her, but Voodo never gave me the word to do so. This was his plan, which meant I was to follow his lead.

Random shots rang throughout the club, making the scene hotter than ever. I gripped my piece and aimed around the room, ready to light up whoever was busting shots.

"Hold back, baby girl." Voodo looked up at me from stomping Felix. "We good. Trust and believe that we'll always be good."

"A'ight, big boss man, what now? I'm sure the cops are on their way," Jerell shouted, swiftly stomping one of Felix's men in the back with the hard sole of his Timb boot.

"Slang them lightweight punks over your shoulder and put them in your car. I'll handle this disrespectful snitch." Voodo threw out the command, preparing to abduct three unsuspecting men. Jerell, large in statue and well over 220 pounds, moved like a beast, grabbing both of Felix's guys up and getting them out of the club. Knocking over tables that stood in his path, he was out the door in no time.

"Yo, Moni babe, let's be out! Pull the truck around to the door!"

After giving him a quick peck on the lips, I rushed to get our whip as he wanted. I was never planning to give my hood nigga up. I loved his gangster ass to the depth of me.

Chapter Two

Voodo

Two Years Ago

"Is Alexis dressed so we can roll out for the weekend?"

"Well, good morning to you too, Voodo." Yolanda rolled her eyes. "She can be ready in a hot second if you've got my child support payment." She gave me the "bitch, better have my money" look. I knew this morning was about to turn sour.

Reaching in my pocket, I dug out one of the last fifty dollar bills I'd earned from my job this week and slid it through the mail slot. She watched the bill fall to the floor, then she turned her nose up in disgust.

"These little nickel and dimes you keep dropping off ain't doing shit for your daughter, nigga. You're gonna have to come better than this," Yolanda barked through the locked gate of her door. "You think the hood ain't talking? I know you've got enough cash to smoke, drink, and club with Jerell's lame ass. So I know you've got enough dough to buy Alexis some shoes, clothes, and new toys. Not to mention give me a few dollars for raising her ass. You only come through on weekends, and that leaves me babysitting with no life five out of seven days." Yolanda took being a mother as a jail sentence or torture. Some women shouldn't be blessed with the gift to have kids.

I'd been going through hell for the last three years with my baby's mom. Nothing I ever did for our daughter was good enough for her to feel satisfied. The measly job I had couldn't even be considered a real job because it only paid out a few hundred bucks a week. That wasn't enough for me to live life like a man, let alone give her the stipend she felt was fair.

"There's some shit in the game if you can't make fifty a week pop for a three-year-old, Yolanda. You know a nigga ain't making shit at that punk-ass car wash. Plus I've gotta pay for a roof to remain over my head. Give a nigga a break," I spat, irritated that my morning was starting off so roughly.

"Naw, you've got life fucked up, Voodo. There's some shit in the game if you can't find a job better than washing cars. Just 'cause you choose to be a piece of shit doesn't mean our daughter's life deserves to be on the same level. I suggest you step your game up."

As I looked Yolanda up and down, my hand was itching to reach out and slap the spit from her mouth. As disrespectful as she was, I couldn't believe I was still sticking my dick in her from time to time. Watching her mouth move as she continued to spit disrespectful shit, my mind was starting to crank up with ideas on how I could make more cash. My daughter Alexis was the only good thing I had going on in my pitiful life. I could admit as a real dude that me not seeing her was gonna drive me insane.

"So what's your game plan with your lame ass? Are you gonna go slang on the corner or what? You've gotta at least double this whack-ass fifty spot per week in order for me to let her leave with you," she threatened. "And that's only temporarily. Each month I think I'll raise it a few bucks to keep you on your toes." She smirked devilishly, knowing my heart's weak spot for our child.

"Don't worry about what a nigga gonna do to eat, Yolanda. Have my daughter ready in a few hours when I return. If you don't, I'ma kick ya fucking door in," I threatened her back, meaning every word I growled.

"You'll be paying for that too, if you dare with ya punk ass." She was resilient at disrespecting me. That only sent my rage into overdrive more.

I'd never been the hustling-and-bustling type for fast cash like many of the dudes in the hood were. That's probably why Yolanda dissed and dismissed me in the first place. Sure, I thought about slanging after my inexperienced ass got fired from one job after another, but my pride wasn't about to let me slang dope on a corner.

Don't get me wrong, I didn't feel like getting the community high was a profession that was beneath me, I just couldn't stoop to the level of begging another nigga with a humongous ego to let me slang Baggies for them. I wanted to start off on top. Fuck working my way up from the bottom. I was twenty-five, not sixteen or seventeen like most of the runners of the hood were. If I couldn't be a boss, I'd rather not be shit but a beer-guzzling, weed-smoking, car-washing nigga forever. I wasn't about to deal with being mocked or belittled. Judge my choice however you want. Everybody's got reasons for how they operate.

Jumping in the hoop ride I could barely call a car, I revved the oil-needing engine before whipping off from in front of Yolanda's house. If the only way she was gonna let me see Alexis was to double that fifty, I was gonna have to make it happen.

"What up, Voodo? I ain't know you worked today." Jerell gave me dap as soon as I clocked in. "I thought it was daddy/daughter day."

Jerell and I were aces. I'd met him the first day I started working at this hell hole, which was his first day out of jail from bodying a nigga. Each day we worked the same shift, we shot the shit and got high to pass the time. Just like me, he didn't slang dope. But that's because his big ass would stand out to the cops, probably landing him back behind bars.

"I didn't, but my ho-ass baby mama on that bull-shit again about cash. I'ma try to make it in tips real fast then shoot a move back through there." I dropped my head. "I swear it be times I wanna put my fist through her face for using Alexis as a pawn."

"That's why I only stick it to these bitches with rubbers on and bounce. I can't trust no chick with the rest of my life. A kid is too permanent," he said, keeping it real.

The afternoon was bumping as usual. It was a hot summer day in Detroit. No matter if their car was a piece of junk or glamour on wheels, every-one was pulling up to get their whips shined up. Me and Jerell were on the tail end, drying cars off for the lame dollar tips we sometimes got. At the rate things were going, it was gonna take me dry-ing fifty cars to make the double-up Yolanda was demanding.

"What up, nigga? I've got five dollars if you can put a little pep in ya step. I've got some hot pussy waiting on me." A dope boy from the hood tossed five singles my way like I was a trick dancer.

Usually, I kept my ego under wraps, but today wasn't one of those days, especially since I couldn't grab a bag of weed to help zone me out. Ol' boy had just treaded into grimy territory with me. Looking at him from head to toe, I spit on the ground then walked up into his face.

"You better watch who the fuck you speaking to like that, blood. I ain't ya lackey." I was caught up in my emotions.

"You ain't a boss, either," he disrespectfully cut into me.

Before I knew it, I'd two pieced his ass in the jaw. I'd reached my limit today of being belittled as a man. He stumbled back, then reached for his pistol, a move I already knew was in the making. Before he could get it whipped out all the way, I grabbed it myself and cold cocked his ass on the left side of his head. Adrenaline was rushing through my body.

"Yo, Voodo, stomp that clown-ass nigga out," Jerell cheered me on. "Teach that fuck boy a lesson." He too hated cats to stunt on us. The amount of jokes that came our way for us being car washers was always a bit much to digest.

By now, everyone was watching me spazz out on the nigga with the flashy clothes, flashy whip, and big mouth. I didn't care, though. I was lost in whipping his ass so he'd never speak down to me again. As powerful as he was in the streets, he couldn't match me scrapping man-to-man. Blood was spewing from his mouth and nose with each blow I served his ass.

"You're fired. Stop and get the hell off my property, Voodo," the owner of the car wash yelled, finally appearing from the back. All he did was collect the cash folks paid when they initially drove up. I was shocked to see him up front, but word must've spread.

"Fuck this ho-ass job, fool. I'm out," I yelled back at him. Even though I didn't want to, I regretted the words as soon as they left my mouth. I didn't have anything to fall back on. And I only had twenty dollars in my pocket from the tips I'd earned drying cars. Glancing down at ol' boy on the ground, my mind clicked, and from that point on I made moves that were unlike me but felt comfortable.

Digging in his pocket, I pulled out the small wad of cash he had folded up, and I stuffed it into my own. For him to be such a big shit talker, he sure didn't have what I assumed he'd have. Then I got even bossier. Jumping in his whip, I threw the running car into drive and damn near hit every oncoming driver in traffic as I pulled out. I'd just pulled off my first robbery. The rush made me realize it was a life I could get used to.

Moni

Present Day

I pulled Voodo's black Yukon truck to the curb of Felix's historic-looking home. I waited for Jerell's headlights to shut off behind me. I then turned off the ignition, waiting patiently for Voodo to tell me what was next. Crime gave me a rush. I was most definitely feeling my heart flutter. Looking to the back seat where Voodo sat with his hollow point centered to the side of Felix's jaw, I surveyed the damage he'd done by whipping ol' boy out in the club. Besides the look of fear on his face, it was lumped up and bruised badly. Part of that was because he'd disrespected me, and my dude stayed taking up for me.

Grinning at how dedicated he was to holding me down, I couldn't help but stroke his ego. "You know I love you, right?"

"Yeah, baby girl. You always have and always will," he said, taking the time to show me some affection. Up until now, he'd been busy making sure Felix stayed coherent and under control. "Now let's do what we do and get to work. Here's his keys. When we get to the front door, open it up for me and Jerell." Voodo dangled them in front of my face, knowing I'd eagerly snatch them.

"Did you make sure the coast would be clear in the house, babe? Or do you want me to run in and make sure there aren't any surprises?" I was more than ready for game time.

"Naw, we good. I've been trailing this nigga for the last couple of days, and he keeps the same moves. The only riders his ass has are those two pitiful punks Jerell got resting in his trunk. This is about to be a gravy payout for us." After kissing me on the forehead, he opened the truck door and dragged Felix out onto the pavement.

I jumped out and made it five paces ahead of them. If my man said we were gravy, I didn't have a reason to second-guess or question him again. I had the door unlocked and was holding it open just as both Voodo and Jerell dragged the men onto the porch. It was well after one in the morning, plus we were on a damn near destitute block. I was sure no one but the rats were watching us. Once they got both men inside, I slammed and locked the door behind us then waited for Voodo's next command.

"A'ight, baby girl, me and my ace are gonna take care of these clowns. Your job is to clean this house out from top to bottom. He's got cash, product, and all kinds of shit I can add to my wardrobe. Take it all!"

"No doubt, babe. I'm on it." I eagerly jumped at hearing there was cash and product for us to steal. We'd be able to shop in the morning plus make more of a profit with whatever dope he was sitting on. Voodo was absolutely right. Tonight was nothing but a win-win for us.

"Hold up, Moni," Voodo stopped me before I darted off. "I think this ho-ass nigga gotta say something to you before you go." Loading one up top of his pistol, Voodo put his piece to Felix's head then spoke each syllable slowly. "Now like I said back at the club, apologize to my lady. I don't take too kindly to disrespect, so I'm more than ready to blow ya head off if you get to showing her some."

"My bad. I'm so sorry," Felix stuttered while trembling. "It'll never happen again."

"You're damn right it won't." Voodo pistol whipped him, gashing his head wide open. Blood immediately poured out as a bloodcurdling scream left Felix's mouth. "Do you accept his apology, baby?" At this point, he was mocking Felix, but I didn't care. It was turning me on.

"Yes, baby. Thank you for always making sure folks don't get out of line." I walked over to Voodo, giving him another soft kiss on the lips.

"You ain't never gotta look behind you with me having your back." He smacked me on the ass. "Now you can go handle business."

"Can y'all cut all that mushy shit out? I'm ready to start shedding blood or something," Jerell impatiently cut into us both.

"Yeah, dude, let's be on it," Voodo laughed. "Once you find you a hood girl like Moni, you'll be distracted and on some ride-or-die shit too. Now back to Felix the Snitch. I know all about the roundtable you had with the cops the other day. And like you've already heard, I've been trailing you, so I know about the cash you copped from ol' boy you sold some heavy weight to. The only thing I don't know is where the cash is stashed. Spare my girl some time and tell me where it's at."

"A'ight, bro." Felix spit out blood onto his own shiny hardwood floors. "Let's make a deal. Spare me and I'll not only give you the cash you're asking for, but more monthly. I'll even recant my story to the cops. Just let me have my life, man."

It was too late for excuses and begging. It was what it was.

"Shut the fuck up with that begging shit, Felix. I can't take it." Jerell put two bullets each into the chests of Felix's ride-or-die friends. They went from barely moving to lifeless within seconds.

"We all know you can't take back shit that's been said to the cops. We also know if I let you out of here alive, you'll run right back to the pigs and request to be moved out of the state into a witness protection program. You and I both know I ain't taking no chances on you. Ain't shit loyal about you, Felix. You're more punk made than Detroit made. The answer is a bold no about making deals with yo' chickenshit ass," Voodo firmly said.

"Then it looks like you're on your own. I'm not telling you, yo' homeboy, or that bitch shit. May the next man you cross be damn the last." Felix wished that bad drama toward Voodo through his gritted bloody teeth then closed his eyes. He knew the grim reaper was coming. Seconds later, Voodo signed off on the two bullets that ripped through his skull. It would have to be a closed-casket funeral for Felix.

Chapter Three

Moni

The sun hadn't crept up yet after our long night, but it wouldn't have mattered if it had. Until my man was satisfied, we weren't getting out of bed. Smooth sounds of R&B were playing softly through the iDeck speakers, elevating both of our moods. I was kissing, sucking, slobbering, and bobbing for every nut Voodo could give me. For every time he jerked, he made my body jerk too. He was dining on my kitty cat hungrily. Getting freaky in the sixty-nine position, our bodies stayed in unison. When his dick swelled and the veins got bigger, I could tell he was ready to cum. That made me grind down harder on his face so I could cum too. We were both sexual freaks.

After setting Felix's house on fire with him and his crew inside, we came home and blew through about five blunts with Jerell, while divvying up the cash and product. The payout was one of the best we'd seen come out of Detroit. Despite the cops having a heads-up about me and Voodo being responsible for many robberies in the city, Felix snitching was a very profitable situation for us. If he'd never brought attention to himself, Voodo would've never tailed him to see he was actually connecting a lot of cats to dope from an even bigger supplier. The lick we'd stolen was the payback and re-up he hadn't made yet. So not only did we take his life, but we were temporarily drying out the streets from dope, too. No connect meant no supply. It wasn't us who gave a fuck, though.

"Damn, baby girl, you were trying to put it on me." Voodo wiped my cum off his face, then propped himself up with a pillow. Reaching for the half-smoked blunt we'd blown before getting in a sex session, he lit it then passed it my way.

"Don't front. I always put it on yo' ass. You can't handle me for real for real," I joked, hitting the blunt hard.

"A'ight now, your mouth is gonna get that pussy in trouble," he replied. "You already know this monster will wear you out."

I laughed, knowing he was right. Voodo never slacked when it came to giving me grade A dick. Unlike some men who jacked off to pornos or let hustling slow down how often they fed women sex, Voodo always made sure I was sexually pleased. In return, I never turned him down when he was horny, and I kept our bedroom life spiced up. Not only was our relationship wild in the streets, with our chosen lives of crime, but in the bedroom, too. There wasn't a position, sex toy, or role I wasn't willing to play with to keep him satisfied.

"You ain't ready, so g'on in that kitchen and whip me up something right quick." He took my silence as a hint that my coochie was probably tender and sore.

"I'ma fix you something to eat. But please believe I'll be back for another dose." I bit my lip then took another hard hit of the blunt while taking Voodo's sexiness in. For him to be straight raw and gangster, he was fine and flawless. You couldn't find an imperfection on his body if you were paid to. At least I couldn't. With dark chocolate skin, perfectly aligned teeth, and a thick fade gracing his head, he would've easily picked up a conceited college girl if that was his type. But that wasn't the case. I considered myself lucky to be the woman of his choice. Therefore, I kept my tongue licking on his ripped six-pack of muscles, tattoos representing the street life he loved, and his thick black dick whenever possible.

Out of my zone and ready to please, it was time to freshen up a bit before putting my man together a hood-style breakfast. The lady in me wouldn't allow me to prance around the kitchen with dick on my breath and cum dripping from my vagina. Taking a quick ho bath and brushing my teeth, I brushed my weave out and swooped it on top of my head, making a bun. It was the best I could do since my curls were sweated out. Afterward, I slid on a fresh black bra and panty set from Victoria's Secret, along with a pair of sexy black pumps. If he crept out of bed and into the kitchen, I wanted to make sure he was pleased with me on sight.

I wasn't the type of chick who didn't keep it cute for her man. Voodo was too fine for me to have bad days and slipups, no matter how loyal he vowed he was to me. There was always a chick lurking to take my place, so it was best to always have my A game presented. That meant I cooked and cleaned half nude in pumps and even dolled myself up on sick days that should've been reserved for looking like a peasant. It wasn't hard, though. I was already a bad chick. The milk to Voodo's black coffee skin, I was a redbone. But I wasn't accompanied by green eyes and long hair. I had dark brown doe eyes, cute features that I kept well maintained, curves in all the right places, and I always rocked the best weave. I was perfect for Voodo, and he was certainly perfect for me.

Whipping up damn near a whole pack of sausage, a few cheesy eggs seasoned with salt and pepper the way he liked them, a huge pot of buttery grits with parmesan, and some freshly cut hash browns with onions, I was done within thirty minutes and waltzing back into the bedroom with his breakfast on a platter. He was half asleep with the video game remote in his hand playing basketball.

"Wake ya ass up, boo. I didn't cook all this food for you for it to get cold." I shook him, setting the platter down.

"Oh, shit, girl, you weren't playing in there. You ain't gotta worry. I'm about to smash on all of this goodness." He dug in immediately. "And don't think I didn't notice your spicy lingerie or forgot about giving you another round. After I get this energy up in me, I'ma put it on yo' ass so we both can pass out."

"We'll see about that, daddy." I climbed into the bed beside him, diving into my own plate.

Stirred from my sleep by someone pounding on the door, I rolled over to wake Voodo, but he was already reaching into the nightstand drawer for his piece. "I see someone is amped and disrespectful this morning." I yawned, rolling back over.

"Too bad I'm not in the mood," he grunted, sliding on his boxers then walking toward the front door.

I rolled over, ready to doze back off, but I was disturbed by my vibrating phone. "Damn, I guess no one cares about me getting some beauty rest," I complained to myself, reaching over to see who was calling. I almost sent my girl Unique to voicemail but thought against it because it was so early. She too didn't usually rise and grind before eleven, so for her to be up at nine must've meant there was something going down that I needed to be aware of. "What's up, girl?"

"I can't call it, but I'm sure you can," she responded, sounding wide awake. "Turn the TV on to the news."

I found the remote, flicked the TV off the PlayStation to channel four, and tuned in attentively to the news reporter broadcasting live from in front of Felix's burned-down house. It wasn't that I wasn't expecting the news and police of Detroit to be swarming all over this story. Hell, it was a burned-down house with three bodies inside, one of which belonged to an informant. But I didn't think I'd wake up to it being breaking news on every local channel.

"There's been a string of violent crimes in the metro-Detroit area last night. A house on the south-west side was set ablaze, and there were three bodies found inside. It's believed but not confirmed that those three bodies and the killers are connected to the shootout we earlier reported at the Ace of Spades strip club. Reporters are live, and we will continue to keep you updated."

"Wow, I see there was some harsh stuff going down in the D last night," I spoke calmly into the phone. "That's messed up. The city can't catch a break when it comes to crime," I said, making sure

I didn't incriminate myself. It was against code and protocol to speak about anything with value via telephones. In the line of business I was in, I didn't talk, text, or post pictures on Instagram or statuses on Facebook. Those were all methods that were considered snitching on yourself. If the cops wanted to catch me up, they'd have to send a person with a live wire taped to their chests to implicate me face-to-face.

"I know, right? I've been seriously thinking about moving to another state once I get my paper up." Unique played along with it. She knew about my lifestyle and lived by hood-coded rules too. "But enough of that depressing shit. I know you and Voodo are cuddled up together so just hit me up later."

"A'ight, I'll holla at you in a few hours. Thanks for keeping me current on the news," I continued to play it off, then hung up.

Unique and I had only been best friends for a couple of years, but I trusted her more than I trusted myself on some days. She wasn't into the life of crime like I was, but she didn't frown upon how I got down. Nor did she run her mouth like females were known to do. Whenever Voodo and I did dirt, she kept her ear to the street for news on who might've been jealous or feeling froggish enough to leap or snitch. And when Voodo and I were ready to move in together, she offered to put everything in her name so nothing could be traced to us. I wasn't sure why she trusted me so much, but I took her loyalty to heart and returned the friendship twofold.

Getting up about to put my robe on to see what was taking Voodo so long, I stopped in my tracks when he walked back in. "I was just getting ready to come looking for you. Who was it?"

"Yolanda's crazy ass dropping off Alexis." He rolled his eyes. "I already went off on her about coming over here without calling and banging like the police, so don't trip."

"Ugh, your baby mama makes me sick," I huffed. "She's always trying to ruin someone's day with her trifling behind." Not only was I irritated by Yolanda popping up at our house, but I was irked because she'd permanently have strings to Voodo. Because they shared a child, she'd always be the other woman in his life. I hated the sound of her name. I hated whenever I was reminded of her role.

"Yeah, I know, but don't you be the one to start on my day now, Moni. We had a great night that ended even better, so let's not bump heads over something I can't change."

"Don't worry, I won't. Besides, I've gotta get up and prepare myself to play mama to Alexis. Where's she at anyway?" Although I was ready to move on, the hint of animosity could be heard in my voice. Not about Alexis, but because of her ratchet-ass mom.

"In her bedroom, watching cartoons." He waved me off, sitting on the side of the bed and preparing to roll a blunt. He was always stressed after dealing with Yolanda, especially when her appearances could strike up a bitter beef between us.

"Call me when you're done rolling so I can hit it a few times. You're not the only one who needs their morning attitude reversed for the better. Oh, and by the way, before it slips my mind, what we pulled off last night is on every reporting news channel in Detroit." With that, I left him in the room to digest the information I'd just relayed. We were both used to our crimes making the news, so this was nothing but another notch on our belts. The only difference this time was that there was a dead informant and a lot of witnesses who saw Voodo and Jerell flexing on Felix and his crew at the strip club.

"Hi, Alexis. Are you hungry, sweetheart?" Putting on my sweet voice, I was always kind and loving to Voodo's only daughter. Although I hated his ghetto-ass, trifling baby mama, I wouldn't dare take it out on his five-year-old. Having smooth chocolate skin, puffy cheeks when she smiled, and a shimmer in her eye, she favored Voodo and not Miss Ratchet Yolanda, and I was glad.

"Yes, Miss Moni." She smiled, showing a little mouthful of yellow teeth, a sign that Yolanda hadn't touched her teeth with even a hint of Colgate. "Can I have a cheese sandwich?"

It was hard to keep myself from frowning. I never spoke negatively of her mother around her, because that wasn't my place. However, Yolanda didn't deserve to be a mom, in my opinion. I didn't even know what Voodo was attracted to for him to lie up and bust nuts in her. Yet and still they made a beautiful little girl, so I always made it my business to doll her up and treat her like the princess she deserved to be treated as. Yolanda rarely combed her hair. She fed her Ramen noodles each time her stomach grumbled, and the money Voodo would give her to dress Alexis like a baby diva, she spent on herself. I truly felt bad for Alexis.

Voodo was a man, so he wasn't prepared to be a full-time dad. But as his soulmate, I allowed my mother's intuition to kick in, and I picked up whatever responsibility I could. You couldn't love a man without loving his child. So I loved both him and Alexis unconditionally. "Let's get you some bacon, toast with grape jelly, and a bowl of grits to sit on your stomach. If you're still hungry after that, I'll get you a cheese sandwich, too." I smiled, seeing her smile.

"Okay, Miss Moni. Can I come in the kitchen with you?"

"Sure you can, baby." I put my hand out so she felt more than welcome. Smelling the weed burning from Voodo's session, I didn't even bother taking a break for a few pulls. His daughter needed nurturing, plus I could tell she loved being around me. And truth be told, I liked being loving to her. Alexis was too sweet and innocent for all the grown, roughneck shit going on around her.

I cooked her breakfast, gave her a bath, combed her hair up in pretty ponytails, and dressed her in all pink so she'd resemble a baby doll. When I was done, I sat her in front of the TV to watch cartoons so I could get dolled up too. Whether Voodo eagerly agreed or not, all three of us were going on a shopping spree and to lunch, and then Alexis and I would get our nails done. I might've not had kids of my own or wanted any, but spending time with his daughter was a good compromise.

Voodo

"What up, doe? Is everything good on your end?"

"Ain't nothing but slow motion this way. I already know what tip you're on, but niggas ain't gonna be checking heavy for that shit, dude. His ass was a goner when he signed his name up for the police payroll," Jerell chuckled into the phone.

"Say word." I agreed with Jerell's rationale about Felix's final unfortunate circumstances. When he chose to be a mark buster, he should've gone into hiding. You couldn't fuck with a nigga's livelihood then walk around like it was nothing. "Keep ya ears open and make sure you silence any bird trying to chirp," I spoke in code. Jerell was a villain, so he knew that meant dead any nigga on sight if they wanted to bring any heat our way. Just like me, he was married to crime.

"That goes without saying. I'm about to get my big ass up, grab some breakfast, and get at one of them strippers from last night to see what's up. I'll get at you later."

"Shit, I wish I could still be moving at my own pace. Yolanda's ass came through here trying to break the door down with Alexis. Me and Moni are already up and making moves," I sighed. "But get at me, ace. One." Ending the call with Jerell, I set my phone back on the nightstand, then I made sure my pistol was loaded and ready just in case any heat came our way. I was doubtful, but it would've been an amateur move for me not to be prepared.

The money we'd swiped from Felix last night was more than worth the risk. Hell, if I could, I'd have taken all the credit for killing him and his crew, because I hated a snitch to the depth of me. I'd never touched that nigga, so he should've never come for me.

After hearing the news reporter give her version of what she assumed happened, I flicked the TV off without worry. Even the police could go down behind my gun smoke if they wanted to come for me and Moni behind his murder. Fuck people who went against the grain. Fuck the law. And fuck peace if it came down to it. Like Tupac rapped, "All I need in this life of sin, is me and my girlfriend." In my case, that was my rider, Moni.

Two Years Ago

"Damn that was a rush." She was hyper like a schoolgirl as I drove the stolen vehicle away from the restaurant I'd just robbed.

"You're a trip, girl." I shook my head, still in disbelief of myself. "Do you talk yourself into being an accomplice all the time, or was this a first for you?"

She giggled before replying. "I've never robbed actual people before. I usually stick to shoplifting so I can stay fly. But naw, I don't work with a partner."

"Then what the hell made you so cocky back there? You do know your pretty face can be identified." I hit her with some knowledge she might've not considered. See, I'd already become a menace to Detroit. Since leaving ol' boy in his own puddle of blood at the car wash, I'd been on a robbing spree. I went for small businesses, legal moneymakers who were on the wrong side of town unprepared, and young dope runners who got too cocky by staying out way past curfew. The cash I'd been bringing in over the last few months was more than enough to keep Yolanda off my back and for me to live like a man. It sure beat out slanging dope on the corner.

"Sometimes you've gotta say fuck it and go for the thrill. And hell, I'd rather be hitting a lick than getting my lick stolen." She kept it real. "You can do one of two things: turn me down, or be attracted to the feistiness I have."

"That's real talk, ma. I like the way you think."

"And I like the way you operate." She looked up at me flirtatiously.

"How old are you? Do you know what you're getting yourself into by running with a nigga with a resume like mine?"

"I just turned twenty-one, but my mental is way older. And nope, I don't know for certain, but I'm game to find out. If you're down to take me for the ride, I'm down to ride out."

She didn't have to say another word. From that moment on, she'd been the one riding shotgun with me.

Present Day

"Bring your fine ass over here, girl, and give me a kiss," I greeted Moni once she finally came back into our bedroom. I smelled her cooking for my daughter. I saw her playing with her while she gave her a bath, and I even heard my baby girl say she looked like a princess once Moni got done combing her hair. It was essential for me to let my wifey know how lucky I was to have her on my team. If it weren't for Moni, Alexis wouldn't know how a mother's love was supposed to feel.

Yolanda was the typical nightmare every man experienced with a hood-rat baby mama. Of course, she was a brick house, stacked with breasts, a big booty, and a tight waist. But what accompanied that body couldn't be faded. She was rude, trifling, and always looking to use our daughter as a pay-out. When I didn't drop bills on demand into her outstretched hand, she was threatening to call the cops on me. If it weren't for me loving Alexis to death, I would've wished our relationship never occurred. The only thing beneficial she did besides give birth to my baby girl was give me the juice to go into work two years ago, which ended in me robbing a nigga, hence my life today.

Waltzing over and laying a big, juicy one on my lips, Moni slipped her tongue inside of my mouth then pounced on my lap. "Is that all you want? Alexis is all into cartoons, so if you want a quickie, we can get freaky right quick," she purred, always eager to please.

"Slip that robe off and push those panties to the side," I spoke like a true bad boy. I couldn't deny her juices even if I wanted to. Moni was addictive. She was the all-around package, the perfect prototype for any hood nigga looking for a down-ass chick who'd cook, clean, and live a life of crime. Since finding her, I hadn't thought about stepping out even once. Sure, I eye fucked pretty girls and tricked out cash at the strip club, but Moni would never have to worry about anything other than being my number one.

"Oooh, daddy, give it to me good," she moaned as I gripped her plump cheeks while puffing on a fat Kush blunt at the same time. The more she ground up and down on me, the harder I pounded her so we'd both bust fat nuts.

"Take a few hits off this, girl." I passed her our only drug of choice.

Watching her hit the blunt was a turn-on. I wasn't the type of dude who hated for his girl to smoke. Matter of fact, I loved the thuggish qualities she had. We could blow weed plus blow niggas' heads off together. Moni and I were a perfect link. It was us versus everybody. Once she'd finished taking her hits, I took total control so I could pound her juiciness with my stroke. It was time to give her the business for real. Flipping her over, I spread her booty cheeks then ground into her until she screamed my name. With one hand on her waist and the other holding the blunt, I got even more turned on by how her pussy creamed on my rod. She didn't even have to say it. I knew I was the best man she'd ever had.

Alexis was still consumed with television, so me and Moni took a shower together then got dressed for our day. We still needed to converse about last night and how we'd handle things if trouble came our way behind smoking Felix and his boys, but for now, neither of us mentioned it. We were too busy being in love and showing Alexis how a family was supposed to be. Plus, I'd already gotten with Jerell for him to keep his eyes and ears open.

"Listen up, Voodo, I don't want to hear you complaining while I'm tearing the mall up. We have more than enough money from last night for me to feel comfortable shopping in every store all through Great Lakes," Moni said, sounding like the typical spoiled woman.

"Just hurry up and get dressed. You won't hear me utter one complaint. It's gonna feel good buying the mall out for my girls with someone else's dough." I might've been a criminal, but I was putty in both Alexis's and Moni's hands. If they wanted to shop, I'd shop. There ain't nothing like feeling like a top dog for taking care of the jewels in my life. Sliding on a fresh outfit and a pair of Red Bottom sneakers, I left Moni to finish getting ready so we could hit the streets.

Chapter Four

Voodo

"Daddy! Moni did my hair. Do I look pretty?" Alexis ran and jumped in my arms with the widest smile ever. I swore her innocence warmed my heart. It was hard to believe a dude of my caliber created something so exquisite.

"You're absolutely gorgeous, baby. Are you ready to go get some new clothes, shoes, and your nails done with Moni? We're all about to go out for a few hours before your mom comes back to pick you up."

"I don't wanna go back home with Mommy. I want to stay with you," she whined. At only five, my precious baby knew her mom was nothing worth being around.

"You don't think Mommy will be sad if you don't live with her?" Questioning her to see how she felt and how much she truly knew, I could tell Alexis took after me when it came to picking up on a person's demeanor. Yolanda couldn't fool me, and she for sure wasn't fooling our daughter.

"Mommy has a boyfriend. All I do is watch TV in my room and play with my toys alone. She never takes me to Chuck E. Cheese's or to get my nails done like Moni does, either. I have fun with you, Daddy." Her truth broke me down.

"Daddy will see about letting you spend the night. I have fun with you too, baby love." I gave her a big hug. I couldn't tell her there was no way Yolanda would let me have her full-time, and that no judge in America would give a dude with a rap sheet like mine custody of a kid. All I could do was try my best at making her happy while she was with me and attempt to keep Yolanda financially straight so she could provide. I was glad I had Moni riding for me now. That way I'd never have to deal with a hood rat like my baby's mom again.

It might've still been early, but folks in the hood stayed up on their grind. Whether it was chasing a rock or the almighty dollar, every day was a struggle to survive and maintain. That meant every second was accounted for, being that their mentality was to get it how they lived. Stepping on the porch with my girls close behind, I took in my surroundings to make sure there wasn't anything out of place. Since my life consisted of crime, I stayed watching my back and being prepared for the worse. Rarely did cats test me, because they were well aware of my thug pedigree, but I never wanted to be caught slipping off my game.

"What up, Voodo? I see you're looking casket sharp and shit," a dude from around the way said, giving me props.

"I've always gotta keep it crisp." I gave him dap, then continued to keep it moving. Usually, I'd kick it with folks from the hood, but Moni was giving me the eye not to keep her waiting. She was eager to burn miles through the mall. Of course, my lady always came first, so it was time-out for hood shenanigans for now.

"Y'all heard about Felix the Snitch? That nigga and his crew are no longer factors," he said, dropping the bomb I'd been seeing all over the news.

"It was only a matter of time someone took him out of the game with the bad reputation he made for himself." I shook my head. "Maybe he'll do right by either the demons he's living with in hell or the angels watching over us all in heaven."

"Word up," he replied. "The real nigga suffering is ol' dude who gave him some cash to cop a heavy package. That's his fault, though, for letting Felix sit on the cash instead of getting his product immediately."

"We all have faults, my dude. I ain't the one to judge." It was crucial for me to keep my responses short. I didn't know what team this dude was playing for, since he was so willingly giving up tidbits of information.

"I feel you, Voodo. Anyway, get at me when you and your family get back. Maybe we can get a card game going or something."

"Fa'sho, we'll link up." I bid him a farewell and then climbed into the truck beside Moni.

"Damn, these niggas stay thirsty for a story," Moni spoke, reading my mind.

"No doubt. You know some of these lazy mutha-fuckas would work for the news station themselves if they could pass a piss test. I'ma fa'sho get at ol' boy later, though. By the time we get back, he ought to have more than a mouthful. But right now, it's officially family time." Leaning back in the passenger seat while Moni whipped through traffic, I wiped my mind clear and cancelled everything that was weighing heavy on my shoulders, so I could give her and Alexis the world.

We hit up a mall located about thirty-five minutes outside of Detroit. It hosted many outlet stores, a sea-life aquarium, restaurants, and even a movie theater. I was able to show my little family a wonderful day. They were all smiles as we tore the mall up for hours, spending part of the stolen cash swiped from Felix. It felt kind of foreign to not be shoplifting the finer things in life we desired, since that's usually how Moni and I got down. But I was feeling it nonetheless. There wasn't a single store that didn't get a taste of our attention. I even got Alexis a small pair of diamond earrings, which I hoped Yolanda wouldn't pawn, and I treated both of my ladies to lunch. We might've been crooks, Moni and I, but we were like Mr. and Mrs. Claus this day. It was truly Christmas in the summertime.

Once we left, I found the closest toy store so Alexis could go crazy on her daddy's pockets even more. Whatever doll, Power Wheels, playhouse, or toy caught her eye I purchased without question. I didn't rob niggas only to keep me and Moni fresh from head to toe but for Alexis to have the world. With bright and sparkling eyes, she'd never grow up thinking her daddy didn't care about her happiness.

"Pay the ticket so I can grab this call." I handed Moni a stack of bills then made a move to the truck for privacy. "What up, my nigga? What's the word?"

He cut straight to the point. "Are you at the crib or still shooting moves with the fam? I need to holler at you."

"We're still out making moves, so keep it brief. I'm listening." I didn't want to cut family time with Moni and Alexis short, but that was totally dependent on what Jerell was about to say.

"Ol' boy who Felix was working with ain't taking lightly coming up dry without a package. He's put the word out about putting a ticket on whoever's responsible." That meant that the guy Felix took the money from in exchange for dope wanted whoever killed Felix delivered to his doorstep. He didn't care about Felix personally. He was just feeling salty about not having his cash or any product. I didn't blame him, but I wasn't about to make amends. I was a robber, not a saint.

"He'll get caught slipping, and hopefully it's sooner rather than later, ya feel me?" Jerell knew that I meant we'd have to body his ass too. When it came to casualties or my life, I always chose to be put on a pedestal.

"No doubt. Get at me once you're back around the way."

"Fa'sho, my dude." I ended the call just as my girls climbed into the truck. I knew Moni could tell there was drama lingering from the look she cut me, but she chose to hold off on questioning me. To ease her mind and give her a little comfort, I returned the stare, speaking volumes with my eyes. She knew we'd kick it when the time was right.

Moni

Whatever information Voodo was holding out on, I knew he wasn't gonna hold out long before sharing it with me. He was probably trying to process it to see how it should be played out. Instead of grilling him, I played my position and continued with our family day. There was still one stop left to make, and I wasn't about to miss out on a manicure and pedicure.

The nail shop was swamped with women waiting to get lashes, their eyebrows waxed, or their claws and paws worked on. Voodo had chosen to stay in the car, blowing weed, while me and Alexis got our girl time on. I was cool with that. He wasn't the type of man who liked to get pampered, and I wasn't the type of chick who wanted him to.

While we waited to get serviced, I couldn't help my wandering eyes from taking note of all the ritzy well-to-do women among us. Before I met Voodo, I used to pick pockets and shoplift with ease. Since meeting him, I'd put my trade on the backburner and stepped it up a few notches. Let's just say I was ready to get reunited. The first thing I did was get friendlier with the women I was interested in stealing from and those who took to the prettiness of Alexis. Once they took the bait, they became easy targets.

It was like taking candy from a baby. I swiped wallets and spare cash from their purses, jewelry they took off so file dust wouldn't ruin the sparkles of their gold and diamonds, and even a few cell phones they carelessly left lying around to go on bathroom trips or to wash their hands. By the time I was done, my nail polish was ruined because I never gave them a chance to dry. But my oversized purse was filled with new trinkets that the stolen cash from Felix could buy if my thirst for stealing weren't in need of being quenched.

"Buckle up, baby. We've gotta make it out of suburbia quick." I slammed the car door after putting Alexis in the back seat.

"Your ass must've been up to no good," he chuckled.

"You already know I couldn't help myself." I didn't bother lying. "There was too much of an opportunity to get over to just sit back chilling. I cleaned up, too."

"That's my girl. I love it when you live dangerously. Now just get us back to the hood safely. We fa'sho can't get caught up out here. They'll hang us without question."

"You ain't never lied, baby. The last thing we need is to get caught slipping. Alexis baby, hold on and don't get scared." Whipping out of the parking lot headed to the expressway, I couldn't wait to cross into Detroit City.

Chapter Five

Nina aka Naughty

"New developments have come in about the fire in which three males were brutally killed and burned. Detroit police have been working tirelessly to get those responsible off the streets."

My phone had been blowing up nonstop since the news stations began broadcasting the murder of Felix and his two friends. The other dancers at Ace of Spades were fools if they thought I was getting ready to answer and give my opinion about the multiple headlining news reports about their death. Naw, not me. No matter how much I loved Felix, I loved my life more. I wasn't ready to reconnect in the afterlife. Being a product of the streets and familiar with how Voodo and Moni got down, I knew the consequences behind trying to vindicate Felix's gruesome death would be me in a body bag. Hell to the naw, that wasn't about to be my ending!

Making sure I had enough food, smokes, liquor, and painkillers to pop so I could sleep, I was prepared for the long haul of me hiding out. One of these days I'd have to come out of hiding and get back to grinding. I didn't need any enemies trying to set me up. Honestly speaking, I was lucky they hadn't killed me that night.

I'd personally watched Voodo and Jerell drag Felix and his boys all through the club in the worst way. But what was I supposed to do? Jump in with the losing team, getting my ass beat too? Or call the cops, becoming a snitch and the next victim on their list? Nope, my mama didn't raise a fool. I had to do the best thing for Nina: stay living! I wasn't getting ready to get caught up in the middle of no gangster bullshit when Felix brought negative karma on himself.

Just like Felix tried to get me off the pole, I tried to keep him out of the police department. He wasn't trying to hear me, though. At least once a week he was adamant about bringing down cats who were either an actual or a feared threat to him and his hustle. Either way, I couldn't understand why he was so scared to handle his beefs on the streets. That's how real bosses in the game got down. When you're married to the streets, you handle your grievances in the streets as well.

Unfortunately, Felix thought he could outsmart the game and take hustlers from the hood down without a hint being dropped that he was an informant. But people in the hood dropped more information than CNN. Granted, no one had brought any heat his way over the last few months of him working with the cops, but death for him was inevitable. Emotional I was. Surprised I wasn't.

Hearing my notifications on my phone go off, I was hesitant to check my voicemails, but I couldn't help but want to know what the streets were screaming. I knew the chicks I worked with weren't gonna rat out Voodo or his team, since they wanted to continue hustling. In our profession, we saw a lot of shit go down, but it wasn't our place to report it. If we did, we'd be taking money from our own pockets.

"Hey, ma, this is Tone. Get at me about ya dude. I'm trying to see if you're good or you need a few dollars to hold you down."

That was the guy Felix was supplying dope to. Deleting his voicemail quickly, I knew better than to return the call. He wasn't concerned about how I was doing. He was more concerned about the money I'd seen him give Felix in exchange for some dope he was supposed to collect today. I wasn't dumb. I knew his intention was to hem me up to see what I knew. Not only was I not about to rat out Voodo, but I wasn't about to join forces with Tone. The only person I could trust right about now was me.

Blocking his number so I wouldn't get any more calls, I made sure the locks on my door were secured, then slid a chair underneath the doorknob for added protection. The eerie feeling I couldn't get out of my gut was that someone was gonna try running in on me. It was time for me to blow through a fat blunt so I could try easing my rattled nerves.

Moni

We were finally close to home. The three of us had been shopping, to the aquarium, out to eat, and on a little stealing spree while getting my and Alexis's nails done. My body was drained and exhausted, but the wheels in my brain were turning. I hated to ruin the good vibes of the day, but I needed to find out how we were gonna do damage control so nothing came our way from killing Felix and his dudes. In the back of mind, I couldn't help but wonder if that's what Voodo's private call earlier was all about. Since Alexis was in the back seat fast asleep, I figured this was the best time to bring it up.

"So, what's your thoughts on handling the witnesses from last night? Not only did everyone know we were balling out at the club last night, but Felix's ol' lady is probably feeling some sort of way about us using her to set her sponsor up for death."

"I've been thinking on that, babe. Truth is I should've snatched that punk up when he was leaving the titty bar last night instead of causing a scene. But I couldn't help myself." He sounded a little on the regretful side. "I seriously doubt a cat will snitch us out, though, seeing that we took Felix and 'em out of the game."

"What if they want some type of incentive?" Being his teammate, my job was to make sure we covered all of our bases. If he went down, I went down. I'd do anything under the sun to make sure that never happened.

"Well I fa'damn sure ain't paying nobody to keep their mouths closed, nor will I be admitting to killing them niggas. That would be putting all of us in a trick bag," he spoke sternly. "The only thing that people can for certain testify to is that we stomped those fools out."

"Word up. So there's nothing left for us to do but send a strong message to everyone at the same damn time."

"Okay, keep talking. What do you think we should do?"

"Blow that bitch up the same way we blew up Felix's house. Fuck it." I sounded relentless.

"Listen to my gangster boo," Voodo laughed at my response. "You're not about any games or moving lightly, huh?"

"Nope, not at all. Whatever cops are investigating the murder will more than likely be up there tonight to question all of the dancers who worked last night, including ol' girl, Naughty. So the best time to make a move will be when the owner first opens the doors for business this evening. Everyone will know in one swift motion to keep their lips tight."

"There's nothing to it but to do it. I'm with you, boo."

"Then it's settled. Let's hurry home and get Alexis straight so we can ride out," I spoke excitedly. Relief flooded my body seeing he was game for the plan I'd low-key had been plotting all day. If we made a grand move like setting the strip club on fire, folks would know not to test us or they'd end up in flames too.

Dropping him and Alexis off at home so he could get her to bed, I drove to a dollar store a few miles away for the extra supply of lighter fluid we'd need to pull the job off. Thought I was pissed that I had to put a hat on my cute, curled-up hair, I knew that was an easy sacrifice for not being easily recognizable on camera. After sliding on a pair of bogus reading glasses that made me look nerdish, I walked in and blended in with other customers.

Being careful not to look like an arsonist, I purchased a grill along with lighter fluid and charcoal, plus a blow-up pool with cheap toys for a little girl.

That way, it would seem like I was prepping for a grilling/pool day with my family as opposed to setting something on fire. To seal the deal just in case any cops came lurking, I paid with a prepaid debit card I'd put in someone else's name. I was skilled at being a delinquent, so making amateur moves wasn't something listed on my resume.

The minute I made it home, I was thrown for a loop seeing that Alexis was wide awake, playing with her new toys. She was so hyper it seemed like she was high off sugar. "I thought you were putting her down for the night, babe. What happened?"

"She popped up as soon as I carried her through the door." He shrugged his shoulders, chuckling. "With all the new toys spread throughout the living room, I couldn't make her cry by telling her it was bedtime."

"I swear she's got you wrapped around her pinky finger." I shook my head.

"She's not the only one," he shot back at me.

"Whatever, Voodo. You already know I'm not about to go word for word with you about how you treat your daughter. All I want to know is what we're gonna do now about taking care of business."

"Shit, we'll just have to take her with us, in addition to a few of these new dolls and the portable DVD player. She'll be so occupied with them and a cartoon that we can make our moves and be right back to the truck before she realizes we left her alone." He sounded certain.

"If you say so." I wasn't sure if it was the best idea for Alexis to accompany us, but so be it if he was cool with taking his daughter on a mission. I guessed she'd be introduced to a life of crime very early on. "Well, the lighter fluid is in the Yukon. How about I handle all of the dirty work while you stay in the truck with Alexis? I can sprint around the perimeter of the club, dousing it where security never watches."

"Are you sure you want to make it a one-person job?" he questioned me with uncertainty. "We can do far more damage if both of us go to work."

"You know I'll be good, baby. As much as I love us doing damage as a team, I wouldn't feel comfortable with Alexis in the truck alone. That's too much of a risk," I said, giving him my honest opinion.

"Maybe I can call Jerell up so he and I can cause the damage while you keep an eye on Alexis."

He was coming up with every possible way for me not to be alone getting my hands dirty, but I wasn't worried about doing the job solo-dolo. I should've been happy that he cared that much to not want to put me in harm's way alone, but I wasn't. "We don't have to call him. Don't offend me, Voodo. You and I have been riding as a two-person team since we hooked up in the diner. Don't start sleeping on my skills or underestimating me now."

"Never that, baby. Trust and believe that I know you're about that life when it comes to holding me down, us down, and handling business. I'll let you have it your way, but you know I'll be watching your back." He pulled me close, caressing my backside.

"You better be." I put my face into his chest, loving the smell of his cologne. If I didn't have to set the Ace of Spades on fire, I would've stayed in his arms all night. There had to be an emotion stronger than love, 'cause I was in deep with Voodo. We innocently made out for a few seconds, then parted ways to prepare for the run.

Voodo

On our way to the club, with Jeezy playing through the speakers, neither of us spoke a word as we were mentally preparing for what was about to go down. Usually, there would've been a blunt in rotation, but with Alexis in the truck, we couldn't act out our normal ritual. I knew I'd come up with the plan of her riding out with us, but I wasn't about to get her high off of secondhand smoke, too. Yolanda might've been a trifling-ass mom, but I wasn't the recipient of the father-of-the-year award right about now either. Yet and still, there was a mission to be completed. If the ball was dropped when it came to silencing witnesses, she wouldn't even have a part-time dad.

Dressed in all black from head to toe, I was ready to make a move, although Moni really didn't want me to. She was sometimes so bullheaded that it irritated me. Don't get me wrong, I loved her for being a down-ass chick who wasn't scared of anything but us breaking up. However, I wasn't the type of nigga who liked to leave his woman on her own. If something happened that she couldn't control, it would be like I threw her to the wolves. I didn't try to change her mind at the crib just to keep an argument from popping off between us, since the mission had to be completed. But that didn't mean I wouldn't switch up the game plan. She was confident one person could do the job efficiently and just as well. Nevertheless, I wanted to make sure we'd never have to touch base with the problem of Felix again.

"You ready to make this move, baby?" I questioned her, pulling up few feet away from the club. It was dark, and other than the many cars lining the street of patrons who were in the Ace of Spades, the block was empty. Detroit's Public Lighting Authority not making sure the street lights worked was always a bonus for us.

"Yup. The next time you see me, it'll be with dust behind my feet and flames behind my back." She leaned over, giving me a kiss while rubbing my manhood through my pants. "Make sure you have him ready to please me tonight as my reward. I'm about to make you proud to claim me as your woman."

"You were already gonna get this dick, girl. I saw the lingerie you tried to sneak and buy earlier." I kissed her back. "And for the record, I've been proud of yo' thuggish ass since day one."

She hopped out of the truck, sliding her mask on like she was ready for war. I was lucky to have Moni, hardheaded or not. I was sure there wasn't a girl in Detroit or anywhere else similar to her.

Moni

Walking quickly toward the club, I didn't want to draw attention to myself by running before the job was done. I'd save that energy 'til after the fire was started. With tight black leggings on, a fitted black long-sleeved shirt, and black track shoes laced tightly, I carried a bag in each gloved hand consisting of two bottles of lighter fluid each. The matches were tucked under the wrists of my sleeve for easy access. It was about to be easy as one, two, three to complete this mission.

Once I peeped the alleyway was absolutely clear, I darted to the back of the club, getting right to work. The longer I lingered, the more of a chance there'd be that I'd get caught. Opening all of the bottles of fluid, I put one in each hand and began tossing the flammable liquid all over the building. Once those two bottles were empty, I put them back in the bag then spread the fluid from the other two just the same. For the finale, I pulled out the matches, struck them, and tossed them right toward the building, seeing instant flames from the contact. The blazes began spreading quickly by shooting up, down, left, and right of the building. "Bingo," I whispered quietly. "I told Voodo's ass that I had this."

Satisfied with my work, I turned and sprinted back toward the truck. I was running like my life depended on it, because it really did. If I was caught setting a fire, my freedom would be snatched for arson plus probably the murder of Felix and his two-man crew. Before I could get back to where Voodo was parked, he swerved up on me with the door already open, making it easy for me to jump straight in. "I told you not to underestimate me, baby." I smiled, sliding my gloves off and mask down.

"I never did. Good job, baby," he responded. Burning rubber by pulling off, he swerved up to the side of the strip club where the fire had spread to, pulled out a gas can, and tossed it out of the window.

The loud noise from part of the building exploding made even Alexis jump. He'd shocked the both of us. Initially, I thought about lighting the club on fire with gasoline, but we were just trying to prove a point, not leave the whole club of dancers and patrons dead. I guessed Voodo didn't care about casualties. "What the fuck, Voodo?"

"Don't question me, girl. Just take these gloves and put them with yours to dispose of." He slid off the pair he was wearing as he drove like a racecar driver to get away from the scene of the crime. "And we'll be at the used dealership tomorrow getting a new whip. This Yukon has become too hot."

I didn't dare question my man. If he thought spreading the fire with gasoline was the best move to be made, I trusted him on that. The only things left to do now were get home, get Alexis to bed, and get my brains fucked out.

Naughty

"Breaking news! The Ace of Spades nightclub is currently on fire. We'll have a live report as soon as our reporter makes it to the scene. Stay tuned."

My eyes bucked wide open. I went from being high from a Kush blunt to wired with even more fear and stress. You couldn't tell me the fire at the titty bar wasn't the aftermath of Voodo and Moni. Those two were relentless at killing, robbing, and covering their tracks. I swore they were like a modern-day Bonnie and Clyde made from Detroit blood. Struck with regret that I'd danced in their section that night, I knew without a doubt I was on their radar. My greed helped them set Felix up, and I'd seen the beginning of what was the end of all three of the victims' lives. If they'd set the bar on fire as a statement, I couldn't imagine what they'd do to me. Damn!

Chapter Six

Voodo

The morning had started off good with Moni cooking breakfast for all three of us. We sat around smashing while watching cartoons. Everything seemed so simple, in place and ordinary. One day I'd have to retire from living a life of crime so each day could be this calm. That peace was short-lived, though. Once my baby's mom showed up, all hell broke loose.

"Look, Yolanda, I'm not about to battle you over Alexis. When she's with me, she's with me. I don't come at you sideways about how you and her spend mother/daughter time." I tried keeping my voice down. She'd seen the news and figured it was the handiwork of me, Jerell, and Moni, and she was trying to chastise me in addition to bank a few dollars to buy her silence.

"That's because your ass knows better, Voodo. Besides, I keep her at home where a child is supposed to be. Not running the streets at night, blowing shit up." Yolanda jumped up in my face. "You and that bitch Moni ain't no good, and I don't want her around my child."

"First and foremost, Yolanda, you better jump back from my face before I knock you back. But most importantly, you're not about to be telling me who I can have my daughter around when you keep a different nigga in her face whenever your hot-ass pussy purrs for attention. Get the hell on with all of that." By now I didn't care how amped my voice got. Our conversation was no longer mild or easily tamable. We'd both struck hard and were drawing bad blood, again. Yolanda and I rarely saw eye to eye, and she'd never accepted that I'd moved on with Moni.

"Don't bring up my pussy, Voodo. You're the one who left me high and dry for that wannabe gangster ho," she yelled with animosity in her voice.

She'd caught me off guard spitting that bullshit. She knew good and well our relationship had ended long before Moni came into the picture. Matter of fact, she was the whole reason why I turned to a life of crime. Had I not been trying to appease her money-hungry ass, I would've never met Moni at the diner two years ago. Before I could respond, Moni broke out from the back in rare form.

"I'm not gonna be another ho, bitch, or wannabe, Yolanda," Moni said, barging into the living room.

"I'm tired of trying to be the bigger woman and letting you and Voodo handle parenthood when the only person you're really concerned about is me."

Yolanda looked back and forth between me and Moni like I was supposed to intervene, but I wasn't. Throwing my hands up like "fuck it," I wasn't about to put Moni back on a leash. Although I didn't like them bumping heads, since it always caused turmoil for me and potentially Alexis, maybe Moni needed to put Yolanda in her place once and for all.

"So you're gonna let her come for me, Voodo? I'm the mother of your only child last time I checked. I'm owed a certain level of respect." Yolanda turned her back to Moni.

Tapping Yolanda on her shoulder, Moni wasn't about to be ignored any further. At this point she wanted all the attention focused on her. "Ummm, I think you're the one who keeps coming for me. So now that I'm here, don't turn your back on me. Say what you've gotta say to my face so from this point forward you can keep my name out of your mouth. 'Cause trust, you don't want none of this."

"Miss Thang, please. I'm not worried about you. And for the record, I can say whatever I want, when I want, to my baby daddy. You ain't nothing but the girlfriend, boo. You'll be gone once the next rider introduces herself. That's how it goes. You betta buy a clue!"

"If you were as worried about Alexis as you are about my relationship with Voodo, you'd be a better mother," Moni said, going for the jugular.

"Oh, no, the hell you didn't." Yolanda was shrieking. "I ought to lay hands on you." It was easy to tell Moni had gotten underneath her skin.

"That'll be the last time you raise either of those weak-ass hands." Moni folded hers, not seeming the least bit concerned over Yolanda's threat. It might've been time for me to intervene.

"Okay! Okay! That's enough. It's clear you two don't like one another, but I ain't trying to have y'all scrap it out. Yolanda, you need to respect Moni as my girl. And, Moni, you need to respect Yolanda as Alexis's mom. All this hormonal bullshit ain't necessary."

"Yeah, whatever, Voodo. I ain't trying to hear you on that tip." Yolanda waved me off. "Alexis, come on so we can get home. Daddy time is over." Calling after our daughter, she was about to use her against me. Her next words proved me right. "Until you get this chick under control, Voodo, Alexis won't be over here. If you want to spend time with her, you'll have to do it on my terms at my house."

"You can't keep using my daughter as a pawn against me." I was disgusted with Yolanda.

"Watch me," she vindictively spat, then stormed out of the house with Alexis's tiny arm and body dragging behind. "And if you think that's all I'm capable of doing, you're underestimating the bitch in me. I know things that'll get you got," she threatened before pulling off.

Not only did my heart sink because I didn't know when I'd see my little girl again, but because I truly didn't underestimate Yolanda's spiteful ways.

Moni

Yolanda made my skin crawl. Her mangy weave, basic attire, and rat-like attitude always made me side-eye Voodo for giving her the time of day. Sure, I might've been a thief, but I was ten times a better quality of woman than she'd ever be. Just like Voodo, I hated sending Alexis home with her.

"Damn, Voodo. I don't know what else to say but I dropped the ball, and I'm sorry about not being able to stay in the back or hold my tongue while you and Yolanda conversed. But that trick wasn't gonna keep disrespecting and coming for me."

"Yeah, it's all good, baby." He threw up his hand. "I could've deaded the argument before any words were exchanged, but I was tired of her threats and constant disrespect too."

"Do you really think she won't let you see Alexis but on her terms?" I was hoping that really wouldn't be the circumstance. Granted, I didn't think he'd go back to her or get caught up sticking his dick in her while on a visitation, but I didn't want him on her territory at all. Any chick who used her child as a pawn and was as trifling as Yolanda couldn't be trusted any day of the week. She was bitter, cruel, and spiteful, the wickedest type of bitch to cross. Hell, I knew firsthand since I was bred from those emotions.

"Knowing Yolanda, she's dead serious. I'm not even sure if a few dollars will be able to calm her down, either," he spoke, sounding defeated. "I hate playing by her rules!"

"I know, boo. It's fucked up you've gotta jump through hoops just to be around your daughter and be a good father to her. Women like her make me sick. Regardless, though, I'll step back so I won't be the reason you can't be there for Alexis. It's clear that she's got a beef with me that's causing more confusion between you and her." I was willing to bid out like a woman for the sake of my love for Voodo.

"I respect that, babe. Instead of jumping the gun, we'll just play it by ear and see what trick Yolanda pulls out of her sleeve. Just do me a solid by grabbing me a beer and rolling me a fat Cigarillo so I can calm my nerves and think. I'm about to jump into a game of *Black Ops* so I can relieve a little stress." Men loved their video games like kids loved toys. As long as he wasn't trying to run up out of here to another woman, I wasn't about to clown about his pastime.

"I got you, babe. No matter what you need, I got you." I was speaking from the heart to Voodo. "But um, just for a heads-up, is there anything she has over your head that I need to know about? It doesn't sound like her threats were just in regard to you visiting with Alexis." I trusted Voodo to handle her like a man would, but I was a woman. That meant I was well aware of how emotions played into our revenge. I admitted it was hard, but Yolanda's words sounded vicious.

"I won't lie and say I didn't feel the weight of her words, babe. You already know she stays giving me the option of doing things her way or going to jail. But don't worry your pretty little head about it. I'm gonna handle my baby mama drama before it blows up either of our faces." If only I could believe his words.

Sitting down to break the buds of weed down so I could roll him a fat one, my mind began cranking on how I would stop Yolanda from getting beside herself by stirring up unnecessary drama. If things were bad for Voodo, they were bad for me. "Whatever happens, you won't have to deal with the consequences alone. I'm with you when times are good, and I'll be there when they're rocky as well."

From the tight hug he gave me before heading back toward the bedroom, I knew he truly believed in my words. Our hood love was one of a kind. I was gonna do whatever I could to preserve it, and keep his baby mama from ruining it.

Once I got Voodo squared away, I took a long, hot shower and got dressed in a comfortable peach maxi dress with a matching pair of BeDazzled sandals. Pulling my weave into a tight ponytail and accessorizing with gold bangles and big hoop earrings to set off my natural makeup, I couldn't help but smile at my pretty reflection in the mirror. There was no need to get flashy or fly since I was only going to kick it with Unique. Nevertheless, I had to keep it cute. She didn't do the club scene, so I knew we weren't going any farther than her front porch. Overdoing it would've been a waste. Making sure I had enough blunts to last me a few hours, I was set to roll out.

"Damn, I can't believe you're not up under Voodo. The world must be about to end," Unique joked, pouring me a glass of wine. We were having girl time, which we hadn't had in a few months, and I'd missed it. She was right. I stayed up under my man day in and day out.

"It just might," I laughed. "That nigga slangs good dick and keeps me thrilled. There's no reason for me to run the streets if he's not."

"I feel that, and I don't blame you. Y'all two are made for one another. I couldn't believe you turned into his shooter at the diner that day, but obviously it was meant to be."

"Hell yeah, it was." My grin stretched from ear to ear. It was easy to tell I was in love.

"So um, let a sister know what happened that night at the Ace of Spades and after that. At first, we were texting about jokes on Instagram, then you dropped off. Put me up on what the news doesn't know to report." She sipped her wine like it was tea, eager for the gossip.

"You're always trying to live vicariously through the rush of my and Voodo's life. Why don't you find you a gangster to ride out with too? Then we can go on double dates."

"Girl, bye, you know that I'm not cut out for running from the police and shooting shit up. Not to mention dealing with ratchet-ass baby mommas. Besides, I've gotta keep it clean so you can have someone to fall back on. Who else is gonna let you use their name or keep money on your books if you go to jail?" She giggled at my expense.

"Bitch, bye! Don't burn bread on me. Besides, it'll be a cold day in hell before I get locked down. Me and Voodo keep our tracks covered at all times."

"Aww, don't go getting soft on me now, Moni. You already know you're my bestie, so I'd never burn bread on you. I'm just keeping it real." She was getting tipsy.

"Yeah, yeah, whatever. I love you too, just slow down on that glass of wine so you can drive me past his baby mom's house. I wanna see if there's any action over there and with whom, so I can report back to Voodo. She came over with a mouthful of threats, and if she's planning to get a nigga on my dude, I want us to either be prepared or moving first."

"You know I'm down, but um, why can't he play the private eye? That chick was his problem before he met you." Trying to rationalize my motives, Unique wouldn't understand since she didn't have a man.

"The answer is simple. Voodo has a connection with her through Alexis, so even though he knows she's trifling, he still wants to give her the benefit of the doubt. I, however, couldn't care less about Yolanda. Besides, Unique, you can't draw a line when you're in a relationship about what problems you'll take ownership of. When I tell him it's us against the world, I mean it. You'll understand once you finally meet a man who'll knock the dust off your ol', cooped-up pussy," I said jokingly, but I was dead serious.

"If I've gotta do all that to prove my loyalty, I'll be on team single forever." She rolled her eyes then guzzled down her glass of wine. "Come on so we can take that ride. I swear we can never have a girl's day without Voodo interrupting."

"Aww, look who's getting in their emotions now," I mocked her then gave her a friendly hug. "Get your keys so we can ride past Yolanda's. Then we'll grab another bottle of wine to guzzle while you catch me up on your lame life."

"Forget you, Moni," she said playfully.

"Yeah, yeah, I love you too."

Chapter Seven

Voodo

As soon as Moni walked out the door to go have girl time with Unique, I hopped on the phone to invite Jerell over. We needed to kick it face-to-face about everything he'd heard surrounding us murking Felix and his crew. Plus, I wanted to know if there were any developments pertaining to Tone, the guy Felix was supplying.

"Ain't nothing different from earlier, my dude. That punk is only running through the hood, whining about getting caught up and got for stacks. We got him sick to his stomach," Jerell said, relaying what he'd heard. "You wanna sell him some of the weight we swiped that he already paid for to shut him up?" Jerell never chose the calm route. I was slightly caught off guard.

"Naw, we shouldn't go that route, because he might put two and two together that it's from the same supplier. Then we'll be putting ourselves out there as the ones who killed Felix."

"True that. Then how should we handle it? You still wanna make a move to body his ass before a problem potentially presents itself?"

"I think that'll be the best plan. I know we ain't never stacked this many bodies in a week, but I ain't trying to have random cats on my head," I honestly stated, taking a swig of my beer.

"It's better us than them any day of the week. You know I'm game to take a nigga down." Jerell sounded like his normal self. "Now throw me the other controller so I can start blasting these fags on this game."

Moni

I knew I'd promised Unique we'd continue our girl time once we finished riding past Yolanda's crib, but I couldn't chill when I'd seen so much going down. Doing damn near eighty miles per hour, I was feverishly trying to get home so I could put Voodo up on game. His baby's mom had about five niggas posted on her porch, and they didn't look like they were there to trick. My street sense and women's intuition told me they were part of her earlier threat.

"Voodo baby," I yelled, running through our front door, out of breath.

"What's wrong, Moni?" he panicked, reaching for his pistol. Jerell was there too and was also going for his weapon.

"Oh, damn, I didn't know you had company. Hey, dawg," I greeted him, still gasping for air.

"Enough of the small talk, sis. Is everything good or is there a problem outside?"

"No, it's more like a problem with Yolanda," I said, looking Voodo directly in the eyes. "Me and Unique did a drive-by about fifteen minutes ago, and she was posted with about five dudes on the porch, running her mouth recklessly. If you couple that with what she said running out of here, I sense trouble."

My eyes stayed locked with Voodo's while Jerell sat back, putting his pistol back underneath his shirt. I could tell Voodo's mind was racing to see how he should digest the news I'd just blurted out. And I knew he could tell I was ready to make a move because I didn't trust her.

"Can you run down how they look or what they were driving? Maybe I know them cats and it's not what you're thinking." He made me sick giving her more credit than she deserved.

I was glad I'd thought on my toes and could present him with more than just my word. "Here's a few pictures I snapped. I even took a video, even though the sound didn't pick up that well with so much commotion going on over there." Handing him my phone, I knew that was all the evidence he'd need to feel just as I felt.

"Oh, shit, sis, yo' ass must love this nigga's stale-ass balls for real," Jerell clowned me. "You better hold on to her for real, Voodo. She ain't letting Yolanda breathe or make a move without her being on top of it. Y'all two take that thuggin' and lovin' shit serious."

"Hell, motherfuckin' yeah." I playfully punched Jerell.

"A'ight, enough playing, y'all two." Voodo gritted his teeth while still staring at the phone. "As bad as I don't want to admit it, I think ol' girl has gotten even grittier than I'd expected."

As he handed the phone over to Jerell, I was happy that he was no longer giving Yolanda the benefit of the doubt, but I was pissed that she was such a thorn in both our sides. What I wasn't expecting was for Jerell to get so amped up.

"Yo, nigga, why in the fuck is your baby's mom posted up with Tone?"

Damn near throwing my phone onto the ground, Jerell's eyes turned bloodshot. Who the hell was Tone? Why were both of them getting so pissed at the video and pictures? I understood why Voodo might've been ticked, but I was clueless as to why Jerell was taking it so personally.

"That's exactly why I told y'all two to quit playing. This bitch has gone too far." Voodo was so mad he was spitting.

"Okay, um, I know I'm the one who brought the pictures to you, but who is this Tone cat and what's the word?"

"That's what I never got to discuss with you, Moni. Tone is the cat who was getting drugs through Felix. We stole a part of his money that night. According to the buzz Jerell heard in the hood, he's been trying to find out who killed Felix so he can even the score. He's dry on dope and out of money," Voodo said, breaking it down to me.

"And let me guess the rest," I sighed, shaking my head. "Your baby mama is probably dropping dimes on us as we speak." I didn't want to tell Voodo "I told you so," but the words were burning to fly off my tongue. I held them in to keep the peace between us, although I knew my body movements spoke volumes.

"Hey, man, I know that shit has gotten hella personal for you all of a sudden, but how do you want to proceed? If you really think Yolanda would pull a snake move like that, we can't hibernate over here, waiting on them to pull up." Jerell was preparing for war.

"You already know I want to handle Tone. But I can't give the heat to Yolanda. She's Alexis's mom," Voodo stated, sounding conflicted. "How could I look my daughter in the face for serving her up with bullets?"

I'd held my tongue enough. "You're the only one giving a fuck, Voodo. You don't see her over there screaming you're Alexis's dad and she can't screw you over. From what it looks like, she's conspiring with the enemy. Like I said earlier, you can't take her threats lightly."

"Stand the hell down, Moni, damn!" Voodo never yelled at me, so I felt weird that he was doing so now. Pissed actually, seeing that it was over Yolanda. "Yo, money, give me and Moni a second to get geared up and we'll meet you outside. If them niggas are still posted over Yolanda's crib, we'll follow them until they're off her block, then handle our business. If they're gone, we'll make our rounds until we find them. I'ma keep it real, bro, I don't know if she dropped a dime about us, because I never tell her my business. But it ain't sitting well with me that she's conversing with him so shortly after storming out of here with a mouthful of threats."

"No problem, bro. I'll be outside ready to make moves. I ain't trying to make shit worse or nothing, but it might be time to start looking to make a move out of the D. Thangs been getting real messy around here," Jerell said, speaking his piece. "Chill out, sis, it'll be cool." He nodded toward me before walking out to give me and Voodo our private moment.

"Look, Moni, I know you're caught up in this by default, and that's my bad. If you wanna fall back while we ride out, I understand." Voodo looked at me understandingly.

"I wish I would fall back while she's coming hard." I rolled my eyes at him. "You're the one who told me to stand down. I've been ready to go hard since she was standing in our living room being extra disrespectful. Don't get me wrong, I can't jump first because she's your baby mama. But I can jump with you."

"Don't misplace what I'm about to say, baby, 'cause I appreciate and love the way you're so loyal to me. Nonetheless, I'm still gonna be the one who handles Yolanda. Our history is too deep and gritty for me to allow you to get confused in it. But I will need your rider skills for ol' boy as our driver. Me and Jerell will need all our focus to be scoping for Tone. If she did drop him some hints, he'll be looking for us, so we've gotta strike first."

"Say no more. Let me slip on some shorts and a wife beater and I'll be ready to rock and roll."

Voodo

I'd called Yolanda a dozen times, but she hadn't answered one call. Not once did I tell her my eyes were set on killing Felix, but she knew how gritty I got down in the streets. In addition to that, she'd already asked for some hush money after hearing the news about the fire at Ace of Spades and little Alexis telling her about the super loud noise she'd heard with Daddy. Yolanda might've been ratchet, but putting two and two together was never hard for her to do. The more I thought about it and the more she sent me to voicemail, the harder it was for me to stomach that she'd cross me without giving a fuck. No matter how many days I lived a life of crime, I'd never understand a woman's wrath.

Me, Moni, and Jerell were riding through the hood in Jerell's whip with the windows up and the air conditioner bumping. A blunt was in rotation, but none of us were really blowing it. All six of our eyes were zoning in and out, trying to peep Tone and four of his dudes. Since Moni had brought us photos and a video of them from today, it made our search a little easier. They'd stand out quicker.

Pulling up on Yolanda's street, we didn't need to look any farther. Tone and his crew were still posted on her porch right out in the open. Moni parked about a block down so we could watch and wait for them to leave. In the meantime, we made sure every pistol within the car had one in the chamber, was fully loaded with ammunition, and the locks were off. We didn't need any hesitation when it was time to strike.

After about fifteen minutes of being posted up, Tone finally made a move. He gave my baby mama a hug and what looked like a few dollars of cash, then walked off the porch and to his car. Chills ran down my spine because I knew Moni was absolutely right. It was definitely fuck me. So once Alexis was finally back with me, it was gonna be fuck her. Neither Jerell nor Moni said anything, but I knew they'd peeped it all. I was embarrassed, pissed, and sad for Alexis. One day I'd have to tell her all about her mom.

We kept a close tail on Tone as he rode away from her house. I was ready to bust bullets, but the time we struck had to be perfect. They needed to be as off guard as possible. When they swerved up into a driveway and hopped out posting on another porch, we all knew it was time to make a move. Moni dropped her speed and rolled up slowly as Jerell and I rolled down our windows, aiming both our pistols at all five men. They didn't have time to blink before we began lighting the porch up. One by one they all fell down.

"Stop the car, Moni," I commanded, then hopped out running toward the porch. I didn't even know Jerell was behind me until I felt bullets zooming past my shoulder. I guessed I wasn't the only one who needed to make sure they were dead. Each guy had caught hot ones, but only three appeared lifeless. Tone and two others were still squirming and fighting for their lives.

Jerell shot the two who were dead twice more to make sure they'd have funerals, and I popped one bullet each into the other two, leaving Tone to go last. Part of me wanted to leave him alive so he could be a living vegetable who would spook Yolanda, but I knew the game didn't go that way. Once he was dead, the ticket on me would expire. That's all that really mattered at this point. Bending down, I whispered in his ear a personal message to take with him. "Felix will confirm that I'm not the nigga to come for."

One bullet to his head. Another one connected to Felix had been sent to either heaven or hell.

Chapter Eight

Officer Hubbard, Detroit Police

Three Days Later

No matter what the season was, a dark gray cloud seemed to sit over Detroit, Michigan. No matter how much money the rich white folks poured into downtown, the inner city was still struggling with high crime rates, poverty, and drugs selling themselves. Chaos and murderous plots were always being played out within the urban communities of the D, but this case that my partner and I were working was irking me more than others. We'd been assigned to find out who killed Felix Carter, our informant about crimes that were taking place, and two of his friends, Jeffery "Rich" Richardson and David Cook.

My gut feeling told me the guilty party was the couple he'd given information about a week earlier, but we didn't have anything to stick them with for even arrests. It was hard getting leads since none of the strippers wanted to snitch, the owner of the club claimed he wasn't there the night of the incident, and the known girlfriend of Felix was staying locked in her apartment like she wasn't there. I knew the fire at the strip club was a message sent. I just had to find a way to connect all the dots.

1300 Beaubien might've already been over-crowded with thieves, con artists, and straight-up hardcore criminals, but that wasn't about to stop me from getting suited and booted to bring the heat to the perps responsible for the three-body murder and double charges of arson. I took to heart my oath to protect and serve the city of Detroit, despite how many cops were dirty and in bed with hoodlums.

"Richard, Hubbard, I need an update on that burning snitch case," my boss, Captain Williams, shouted out of his office at me and my partner.

"Yo, this chump be crazy as hell for calling ol' dude that. I know he was a certified police's bitch and all by solving unknown cases in the hood, but that's just wrong," my partner chuckled, sliding his chair back, ready to report.

"The only reason he gives a fuck is 'cause Felix the Snitch put money in his pocket by splitting the reward to ensure his safety and the security of his identity. And with him gone, Williams's pockets are feeling lighter. That nigga is taking it personal."

Grabbing the manila folder full of Felix's phone records and surveillance photos done on Naughty to prove she was in fact in her apartment, I led the way into Captain Williams's office with my partner close behind.

"Close the door behind you," Williams commanded. "Please tell me you have some new developments on this case."

"I know we've been hitting a dead end with the leads not wanting to talk, but I think we've made a breakthrough." I slid the manila envelope across the desk. I'd been working for a couple days straight without sleep, trying to break the case. "Those are arrest warrants for a few of the dancers on charges that they have pending, ranging from traffic violations to prostitution. Plus there's one in there for the owner because his liquor license was expired. I'm sure one of those warrants will lead to someone talking. No one wants to do jail time behind someone else's bullshit," I reported with confidence.

"Good work, Hubbard and Richard. I'm glad you two didn't come in here empty-handed or feeding me some bullshit." He looked over the warrants with a nod. "Now what about the girlfriend? She hasn't broken her silence? It's not sitting well with me that she doesn't want her man to rest in peace by turning in the killer. If she's in hiding and not banging our door down trying to find out why we haven't found his killer or killers, I'm sure she knows something."

"Those photographs behind the warrants are a few shots we were able to get of her peeking from her blinds time to time over the last few days. She's locked in her apartment, refusing to answer the phone. Unfortunately, she's clean when it comes to any pending charges within the system, so I couldn't pull a warrant for her."

He looked at the pictures while rubbing his salt-and-pepper goatee. "Lie and tell her she's a suspect in the case. Like I said, she should be trying to avenge her boyfriend's death. The fact that she's not makes it seem like she's guilty or at least knows who murdered them. I want her walking through these doors today." He got loud, handing over the manila folder and its contents. "Do whatever you have to do!"

"We're on it. Let's go, Richard. I'll drive." I was more than ready to solve this case.

Voodo

Posted on the porch, I was puffing on a Kush blunt and barbequing the meat Moni seasoned like a chef. I couldn't wait until the food was done so I could stuff my face. The hood was live, especially our block. Everyone was out grilling, chilling, and enjoying the warm sun of June. Summertime had officially arrived.

If Alexis wasn't gone back home with her mom, I would've been watching her run through the sprinklers or riding her bike up and down the block. It was a bitter feeling not having my li'l one around, but I knew all that would change sooner or later. Once Yolanda touched base with me again, I'd be manipulating her into a trick bag. My mind was officially made up to body her, because I couldn't trust her slick ass. For now I felt cool, because I knew Tone's death was a message she'd heard loud and clear.

"What up, doe boss? Let's get a game of dominoes or cards going." Ol' boy from around the way walked up. We weren't friends, just associates of the hood. I didn't keep dudes around because niggas were known to get envious. The only cat I considered my ace was Jerell.

"Pull out some paper and let's make it happen." Since Alexis was gone and Moni was in the house yapping on the phone with her girl, I figured this was the perfect time to hear what'd been buzzing around the way. "Sit down and get the game set up while I flip the meat, my dude."

Most houses in the hood had small tables on the porch because many of the families didn't work but sat outside day in and out, drinking and gambling with what little change they had to their names.

Although Moni and I kept cash, we also had a table because it was easier for me to roll up on and for her to set out the hair products she needed to braid hair with.

Starting a domino game up, I was enjoying the free time. I hadn't robbed a nigga or caused turmoil within the city for the last three days. Not only was I lying low until everything surrounding all the murders I'd committed blew over, but me and Moni were financially set with the cash we'd stolen from Felix. We'd been looking at spots to have an extended vacation in, too. Both of us had heard Jerell's suggestion and knew he was right about Detroit being hot.

"Man, I know you heard about that titty bar getting set on fire. That shit was mad crazy. I ain't never seen a bunch of naked bitches before on the news, but they aired all that shit that night," he laughed, then waited for my response.

"Yeah, dude, I was bugging out about that too." We took a few turns back and forth without passing conversation between us, then he was right back on it.

"Word on the street is that they're having a memorial for Felix in a couple of days. His family had to get some cash together to bury him. You would think his stripping-ass girlfriend would've come up with the dough to help his family, but the rumor is that bitch left town."

"Oh, straight up? I hadn't heard." Cutting him a look then taking a sip of my beer, I was starting to feel uneasy about this guy even being around me. In another few seconds, he was about to get dismissed from my presence despite the game not being over. I didn't like feeling apprehensive, especially at my own crib.

"But whatever, I know you're happy that nigga is iced out. He can't be a threat to you or your ol' lady with all that snitching shit now." He peeked up at me, waiting for a reaction.

"What the fuck, nigga? Are you the Feds or some shit?" Getting loud and sliding my dominos to the side, I was giving him a clear indication that the game was over.

"Huh? Hell naw. I was just talking, bro. Chill out." He seemed shocked by my sudden outburst.

"Well, you know what they say about mother-fuckas who run their mouths too much. I think it's time for you to rise up out of here. I don't feel like company or being friendly, ya feel me?" Looking him square in the eye, I wanted him to know I was dead-ass serious about him pushing on. And if he didn't kick rocks fast, I was gonna throw his ass off my porch by his throat. I didn't care about me not getting any info about whether folks had identified me and Jerell as being responsible for Tone. This mark buster was no longer welcome.

"Hold up, Voodo man, I feel you. I don't want any problems. I swear to G it wasn't like that." He stumbled over his words, rushing to get up. Fear was easily recognized in his voice and eyes. That same fear should've warned him not to question or test my gangster.

"You better make sure it wasn't like that," I warned, leaving the hint of a threat lingering. "Don't come back around here with all those damn questions and accusations again. I don't like it when niggas run their mouths like diarrhea."

"I got you, boss. And I swear I didn't mean no disrespect. I ain't trying to step on your toes or cross no lines. I'm out, and I'll see you around." He got off my porch with the quickness.

I watched him rush up the street with anger bleeding through my eyes. If it weren't broad daylight, I might've shot him in the ass to scare him even more. I was beyond irked by the feeling he'd given me. No longer did I have peace of mind. If cats from the hood couldn't let Felix's murder die down, I knew the cops probably couldn't either. Leaving the meat unattended, I went in the house to cut Moni's conversation short. Me and my girl had to talk.

Moni

"Whoa, whoa, hold on, Unique. I'ma call you back in a minute." I cut my girl off, seeing Voodo walk in looking frantic. "What's wrong with you, baby?"

"This cat I was just playing dominoes with rubbed me the wrong way by bringing up Felix. Niggas around here are too nosey and can't let shit die down." Moving from the living room to the kitchen, he grabbed a beer then plopped down on the couch. "I was itching to pop that nigga. He made me feel edgy and uncomfortable with the way he was talking."

"Are you sure you just aren't tripping because the news has still been reporting what went down? Or that you and dude had to body them niggas behind Yolanda? Usually you don't care about niggas from the hood," I rightfully questioned.

"Don't get me wrong, I don't like that a Crime Stoppers ad is getting run multiple times daily, but ol' boy was acting real suspect, like he was working with the cops."

"I don't think he'd be gutsy enough to sit in your face and work with the cops at the same time, babe. Everyone knows yo' ass got a short temper without good sense. Not to mention, if he thinks you had something to do with Felix, he knows it wouldn't be in his best interest to even tempt you to feel like he's a snitch too," I tried rationalizing with him.

"You're probably right." He still didn't seem all the way persuaded to calm down. Quiet for a few seconds in deep thought, when he spoke again his words made me ready to react. "He did drop the dime on Felix's chick, though. Ol' girl Naughty who was dancing on you that night to help lure Felix over, people talking about she left the city or disappeared. I think we should cruise by her crib and check out the scene to see what's up for ourselves."

"Oh, so now you know where the bitch lives at?" I got jealous immediately. The first thought that crossed my mind was that he'd tricked with her before, after a night at the bar with Jerell. The second thing I wondered was why we hadn't ridden out to her spot to see what was popping.

"Calm down, girl. You know I followed every move Felix made days leading up to murdering him. It's cute that you're jealous, but this ain't the time." Voodo seemed slightly annoyed by me trying to snap on him.

"That's my bad." I took a cop, feeling foolish that I'd even popped off. He was absolutely right. This wasn't the time to trip on him even if I thought he was up to no good. "Anyway, you already know we can go check out the scene. Pull the meat off the grill and give me fifteen minutes to get dressed."

Sitting in front of Naughty's apartment, we were waiting and watching for any movement. Voodo said that ol' boy told him folks were saying she left the city, but we were trying to confirm that. I wasn't really worried about the guy or this chick, because the cops would've beaten down our door if she'd snitched us out. Just like everyone else who was staying tightlipped and not getting mixed up in some shit that could get them killed, I was almost sure she didn't want any part of my and Voodo's wrath. Regardless of my feelings, though, we needed proof in order to feel settled.

Naughty

At first I thought I could mentally handle Felix's death, but it'd been eating me up inside. I wasn't sure if it was because his family kept leaving voice-mails asking for cash to help bury him, or if not dropping the dime on Voodo, Moni, and ol' boy was eating me up because Felix's killers were still living free. That night kept playing over and over in my head, and being honest, I felt partially responsible for the love of my life being taken up out of the game.

He'd been begging me to quit stripping for months since we'd hooked up, but I loved my grind and money too much. With rent alone topping $1,000, my credit card bills almost maxed out, and a shopping habit like crackheads fiend at the last of the month, twirling on the pole and twerking for my lifestyle was a must. My love for the hustle and his love for me were the reasons he'd been caught slipping. Strapped with anxiety, sorrow, and worry from thinking retaliation would be brought to my doorstep, the only solution I could think of was to break free from Detroit for a long-term vacation.

"What up, cousin? Do those cats down there tip heavy? I might be looking to make a move." Finally getting an answer from my stripper cousin, I was trying to check on how the dancing business was treating her down South. With the heat turned up in Detroit, I wasn't sure I'd be able to grind on the pole here anymore. Hell, as of now I was too scared to walk out of my front door.

"I ain't struggling to eat out here, ya feel me? What's going on up there? Them cats acting stingy with their coins, or has the city dried up of hustlers?"

"Yeah, something like that." I didn't want to get into details over the phone. "I'm kind of down on my luck here. A bitch gotta get up out of here fast before I dry up even further. Is your club hiring dancers?"

"I can get the manager to give you an audition. The rest is on you. I can't completely nurse no bitch's hustle with mine fully on the table," she honestly responded, willing to help me but with limited conditions.

"That's what's up. I might need a place to crash, too, just 'til I get my bread up," I said, pushing my luck.

"Uh naw, you know I can't let no bad bitch lie up," she laughed. "But there's a Motel 7 up the street from the club. The best I can do on that tip is let you bum a ride. Don't be salty, 'cause you know this is how I gotta play it."

"It's cool. I guess a bitch can't be choosy, but damn, they ain't got no Holiday Inn down there at least? I can't be slumming it!" Shaking my head, I said a silent prayer to Felix for him to cover my back. I was trying not to be secretly pissed at him for leaving me on this cold earth alone, but since he'd gotten murked for snitching and trying to be tough fronting Voodo off, how else was I supposed to feel?

"Yeah um, as a matter of fact, you can stay at the Ritz-Carlton, popping champagne for all I care. You just won't be prancing all up and through my condo for my nigga to get any bright ideas. Hit me up when you touch down, though, 'cause I got you on the job tip."

I wasn't mad at my cousin. She was keeping it real with me. We both used our bodies to get cash and make things happen. She could and should consider me a threat. "Cool. I'm about to be on the next plane out of here. The D is mad hot!" Geeked as hell, I was finally starting to feel like I had a chance to get back out here right.

Suddenly there were several loud knocks on the door followed by shouting voices. "Detroit Police. We're looking for a Miss Nina Sanders! We know you're in there. Open up! If you don't, we'll be forced to kick the door in."

Jumping up from the couch, I quickly looked around the room for somewhere to hide. What in the fuck did they want with me? I knew these niggas weren't about to blame me for Felix's death! Not wanting to open the door, I was backed up against the wall. Sounds of an *Empire* rerun played over the TV's factory speakers, as my cousin kept yelling, "Hello?" into the phone. I knew them slick cocksuckers were standing by the door, listening to my conversation. What in the hell was I going to do now?

Moni

Naughty's apartment might've been still with movement from her, but it wasn't still from visitors. At least two strippers came by within the time we'd posted up, yet they left without anyone answering the door or cracking open the blinds. That didn't move us, though. Whether she'd left the city or was just hiding out still hadn't been confirmed.

"Do you want me to break in and see if she's in there, Voodo? If so, you know I'll snap her neck within a matter of minutes. And if she isn't, I'll sneak back out." I was growing slightly impatient. At first I wasn't concerned about Felix's death biting us in the ass after setting the club on fire, but for some reason, my gut was starting to make me feel slightly nervous.

"Put a hold on your thuggish ways, baby love," he chuckled. "You know real bad boys move in silence, and we can't make any more rash decisions. If she's in there on alert waiting for one of us to run up and happens to put a cap in you first, we're fucked. We're doing what's best right about now."

My only response was a nod in agreement. I knew Voodo was right, but I wanted everything surrounding that robbery and murder to be over. So much so that I wasn't thinking clearly. We'd never had one of our crimes taunt us like this one was doing.

"Shoot a move right quick to the store so I can grab another pack of blunts. We can blaze through at least ano-ther one before heading back to the crib." Voodo leaned back in the passenger seat.

"Are you sure you want to make a move? We might miss something."

"Yeah. I know her crib has been dry for the last couple of hours, but I want to stake it out for a few more. I can't do that without having something to blaze up. And you obviously need something to calm your nerves as well."

I pulled off toward the store so he could grab the Cigarillos plus a few snacks for us to nibble on to get by. Neither of us had eaten, since the meat he was grilling wasn't done by the time we'd left home. My stomach was grumbling like a homeless man's. I couldn't wait to get within the comfort of our home and smash out.

We were only gone from watching Naughty's apartment complex for about ten minutes, but that's all the time it took for the whole scene to change. There was a police car parked directly outside, a few feet from where we once were.

"Look what we have here." I pulled into a parking spot a few complexes away from the one Naughty rented in. It was a good thing we'd gotten a new vehicle so no one would be checking for it. The Yukon had been involved in many of our actions of corruption, so Voodo felt it was necessary to have it totaled. We were now whipping a silver truck.

"Yup, it looks like us and those strippers aren't the only people checking for Naughty. Let's see how this all plays out."

We sat, waited, and watched. It didn't long for both of us to shake our heads, totally disturbed about what we were witnessing. Naughty was being escorted willingly out of her complex by two cops. Dressed in a baseball cap, oversized shades, and wrinkled clothes, she kept looking around frantically like she was worried about someone seeing her. She should've been. From what it seemed like, Naughty wasn't under arrest but working with the boys in blue, just like her boyfriend Felix had been.

"Let's get out of here and to the crib. We need to pack and lie low for a couple of days at a hotel or something, until whatever her snitching ass tells the cops unfolds in the streets," Voodo instructed. "I'm about to call Jerell and put him up on everything so he can watch his back as well."

"All right, babe." I swiftly followed his directions.

Chapter Nine

Voodo

Packing a few outfits, shoes, a couple of pistols, and most importantly all the product and cash I'd swiped from Felix, my luggage was by the front door. Once Moni got done getting everything she needed together, we'd head out to go check in at the hotel. My plan was for us to stay low-key until I saw exactly what was going to happen with Naughty. Me not taking her out of the game initially was a slipup that I'd made, but I never thought her money-hungry ass would snitch. Apparently, I was hella wrong. Her walking with the cops was all the confirmation I needed to know she always deserved the same treatment as Felix. Because of me breaking a cardinal rule of the game, all of us could possibly be screwed. It was up to me to at least make sure Moni's and Jerell's freedom was spared if at all possible. Unbeknownst to Moni, I'd already put a plan in motion.

I paced my living room back and forth, from looking out the window to checking the time on my Rolex watch. I hated the feeling of nervousness. The information Naughty knew about that night was enough for the police to issue arrests for all three of us. I swore on Alexis that if they pulled up with the intention of dragging me and Moni out of here, I'd go down spraying bullets. "Hurry up, Moni babe. I'm sure we can buy whatever you don't have packed."

"I'm ready, Voodo." She finally came out of the bedroom we shared with enough baggage to last her a year. Women could never travel lightly.

Locking up and leaving out the back, we didn't want any of the neighbors to see us exiting with luggage. For one, if the wrong person was watching us, they would break in knowing our house wouldn't be secure for days. And for two, if the police did come snooping, we didn't want them to know we were one step ahead of them. From this point on, I was trying to stay on my toes as opposed to giving motherfuckas chances to screw me first.

Moni's best friend Unique checked us into the Atheneum Suite Hotel near Greektown Casino in downtown Detroit. We paid her a full grand and promised a grand more if she remained loyal and silent. Although I was wary about trusting anyone, I felt a little at ease that she turned down the extra grand, saying we were family and she'd always have Moni's back. In addition to that, she already knew how her best friend got down and never breathed a word before.

"This suite is nice as hell. I wish we could fully relax and take advantage of having a break from the hood." Moni fell back onto the pillow-soft king-sized bed.

"We might can't relax all the way, but I'm sure there will be times none of this mess will be on our minds." I hinted toward when we'd have sex. "Don't get me wrong, this is fucked up, and I know playing the waiting game to see what will pop off ain't no vacation. Nevertheless, you deserve a break from the home front and so do I. We'll be getting freaky in the Jacuzzi, maybe hitting the casino for a few table games late at night, and drinking the best champagne this hotel has to offer, while fucking in this top-of-the-line bed." I lay down beside her.

"As nice as all of that sounds, Voodo, what if that bitch snitches us out? I mean, she wasn't handcuffed while getting escorted to the cop car. That means she wasn't under arrest or forced to go. I don't want to get too far gone enjoying this getaway when we really need to be pulling off a real getaway." Moni sounded worried.

"Jerell is watching her crib as we speak. As soon as she returns, he'll be touching base with me. If Naughty does talk, we'll be making sure her testimony never makes it to court. They can't make charges stick to us if the witness disappears."

"You always think of everything, don't you?"

"That's what a nigga from the hood involved in crime does, baby love."

She rolled over and mounted me. My dick grew hard instantly. It was time to fuck Moni's brains out so we could both release some endorphins and feel a little more at ease.

Officer Hubbard

Stepping into the interrogation room with a Faygo orange pop, a bag of chips, and a candy bar as requested by Nina, I was burning with anticipation to question her as our witness. I knew she was holding on to pertinent information when she hesitated to open the door, making us threaten to kick it down at her apartment.

"Tell me everything you know surrounding your boyfriend's death, Nina," I said as I sat down across from the stripper I knew was hiding something.

"Like I told you at the apartment, I don't know anything." She moved her hands off the table into her lap.

"Come on now, Nina. I know you're a headliner at the Ace of Spades, and I also know that Felix,

Jeffery, and David were all there the night of their murder. We know pandemonium broke out and gunshots were fired. So maybe we should start there. Tell me about that night." Letting her know I knew bits and pieces of what went down that night, I was hoping that was enough for her to bite the bait and get to talking. After speaking with a couple of the strippers who worked that night who had warrants, they stuck to their stories but said Naughty for sure knew who murdered Felix and his crew.

She took a deep breath then looked away. After about ten seconds of silence, she began talking. "Yeah, I worked that night. I work damn near every night the doors are open. I'm a hustler." She paused then continued. "Felix couldn't handle that. He hated men to eye fuck me, touch me, and say crude things to me. So much so that he wanted me to quit stripping. But you know a hustler never gives up their only means of survival. Anyway, he came to the club each night to monitor how far my hustle would go.

"That particular night, he watched me dance the stage and for a few guys wanting private dances in their booths. One minute I could see him across the room staring at me in disgust, and the next minute I couldn't find him. But that didn't stop me from hustling, Officer. The only thing that stopped me from hustling was the gunshots that rung out.

So yeah, there was pandemonium of course. The whole club was trying to find the closest exit. I was among the runners. I didn't have time to scope out where Felix was at."

"So you don't know what caused the pandemonium?"

"Nope," she replied without blinking an eye.

"You didn't see anything out of the ordinary?"

"Not at all, Officer."

Rubbing my temples, frustrated with the game she was playing, I knew her story was fabricated. This interrogation was gonna take longer than I thought. "Would you consider Felix having a confrontation or argument with someone something out of the ordinary?"

"Come on now, Officer. You and I both know Felix made his money in the streets and had a lot of enemies. That's why he was working with you guys as an informant. Him having a confrontation or argument wasn't something odd. It was part of his daily routine. But now that we're speaking on that, wasn't an exchange of protection from y'all part of his agreement to be a snitch? If y'all would've had undercover cops watching his every move like the captain promised, I wouldn't be in here getting grilled. And my boyfriend would fa'damn sure still be alive," she smartly commented, looking me square in the eyes.

Initially, Nina didn't have courage and was afraid to speak with us. Now she was attacking me and blaming the entire squad for his death. I couldn't lie. Her words caught me off guard and had me thinking. They must've had my partner thinking too, because he excused himself from the interrogation room. We were supposed to protect Felix by tailing his every move since he was an informant. Nina was absolutely correct. He might've been alive if the captain had made sure everyone was doing their jobs. But the truth was, all we wanted was Felix's information. We really didn't care about his life as a man hustling in the urban neighborhoods of Detroit.

Despite her throwing me for a loop, I had to keep my game face on. "I'm going to ask you one final time, Nina, because two people have made statements that you know who killed Felix Carter and those other two men."

"Well, since you put it like that, this will be final time that I'll tell you I don't know. The first time I knew trouble had found Felix and his friends was when the news reported it. If that'll be all and you're not formally pressing charges, I'd like to be sent home by taxi."

Moni

"Fuck me harder. Pull my hair. Give it to me, daddy," I screamed into the pillow. Voodo wasn't having an ounce of mercy on me, and I knew exactly why. He wanted me to forget about everything going on outside of our hotel room so I wouldn't be stressed or worried. It was partially working.

"Throw that ass in a circle, girl. Push it back on this stiff dick." He grabbed at my weave, yanking my head back.

My back arched immediately, making him slide deeper inside of me. I screamed out again but this time couldn't muffle my voice within the pillow. Doing just what he wanted, I began sexing him back just as hard as he was sexing me. The louder he moaned, told me my pussy was amazing, and smacked me hard to the point where I knew a handprint was left behind, I pushed myself on him even more. I'd never been the type of female who liked it soft. And Voodo had never been the type of dude to give it to me soft. Even our love-making sessions consisted of vulgar talking. And right about now, we were both trying to outdo one another.

The competition didn't last too much longer. I couldn't hold back cumming any longer. Letting all of my senses go, I quivered until my body was exhausted. "I love you 'til the death of me, Voodo. Oh my God, I love you," I whispered lovingly. Falling onto the bed, I was out of breath, sweaty, and completely satisfied. All I remembered after that was drifting off to sleep.

When I woke back up, I wasn't sure how much time had passed. Sitting up and pulling the sheets over my naked body, my heart almost pounded out of my chest. The room was dark, and I was alone. Where in the hell was Voodo?

Voodo

Downtown Detroit was the only part of the city that had restaurants, nightlife, an influx of hotels, and gangs of white people walking around freely. Within the last few years, I'd seen the area change from nothing but bums and young black people flossing in shiny cars up and down Jefferson and through the Greektown area, to black folks as a whole actually seeming like the minority. The ages of the Caucasian persuasion being afraid to cross over Eight Mile was a thing of the past. This was both a good and bad thing. Good because it gave me access to rob citizens or visitors who had money, without leaving the comfort of my city. But bad because my color now stuck out like a sore thumb. Tonight was like many of the nights I was invested in being the leader of corruption. I didn't care.

Dressed in a fitted cap with the brim pulled down and clothes that weren't flashy so I wouldn't draw attention to myself, I walked inside of Greektown casino with a concealed mission. I wasn't here to gamble, meet chicks, or drink. I was here to find Moni an engagement ring. Somewhere between the fucking we were doing and her proclaiming her love for me, I knew it was time to permanently make her mine. The way we held one another down meant a lot to me. And no matter how many hood chicks were made in Detroit, I knew she couldn't be replaced. Moni was an original. In addition to all of that, if ol' girl from the club turned out to be a snitch and we'd have to go on the run, I wanted to run as husband and wife.

With a malicious plot brewing in my head, I inconspicuously scoped the scene out. I played a few slot machines so I could fit in with the crowd. But instead of being interested in whether I won a jackpot, I was trying to find a woman who looked to have cash. One of these high rollers within this casino tonight was about to be a victim of a robbery.

There were a few reasons why I didn't just go and purchase her a ring that would be accompanied with a receipt. First, I didn't want to take the chance of getting flicked by the cops if they were looking for me. Second, I didn't want to spend too much money on a ring when I didn't know if we'd have to use it to break out of Detroit. And lastly, I was a robber, so this was the type of life I lived for. Stealing gave me a rush. It was a thrill for me.

After about twenty minutes of scoping the gambling floor out, I was getting restless because it was dry. Plus, Moni was starting to blow my phone up.

As soon as I answered the phone, her questions began rolling out. "Is everything okay? Are you good?" I could tell by her voice that she was worried I'd gotten caught up.

"Yeah, baby, I'm straight. Either go back to sleep or enjoy the comfort of the room. I'll be right back," I replied, hoping that was enough to end her concern.

"Naw, not until you get your ass back here. You better not be working, Voodo. Especially if I'm not by your side." She went from sounding concerned to sounding pissed.

I couldn't help but laugh. This was the whole reason I wanted to marry her in the first place. She wouldn't dream of breaking our duo up. "I'm not working, baby, so like I said, chill out and be easy. All I'm doing is grabbing something, so I'll be back to you in a few."

"If you're not back in thirty minutes, I'll be calling you back, nigga." She disconnected the call. She wasn't exaggerating, either. Moni stayed on my head tighter than a fitted cap.

With a time limit on my head, I had to put a rush on things. Making my way to the bar, I ordered a drink, and I scanned the area for a woman who looked like she wanted some male attention and

had a ring on her finger. It didn't take but a second
to find one. The blonde who was already guzzling
drinks was tall, blue-eyed, and dressed scantily. In
a sequined, cropped top, high-top spandex pants,
shiny stilettos, and big hoop earrings, it was easy to
tell she was looking for some attention. She looked
to be a middle-age white woman, but I wasn't sure.
Not trying to be funny, but black women aged
much more gracefully than some white women.
So she could've been young and I wouldn't have
known. Either way, she looked tipsy enough for me
to feel comfortable trying my luck. "Can I buy you
a drink?" I approached her flirtatiously.

"I can buy my own, but if you're treating, of
course." Her words made me thirstier for a thrill.
The more money she had, the more I could rob her
for. "I'll have a martini on this man, bartender."

After three more martinis, two shots of tequila, a
meaningless conversation that was full of lies from
me, and a lot of leg rubs, she'd agreed to accompany
me back to my hotel room for drunken sex. From
the emotions she'd spilled out to me, her husband
was a cheater who never paid her any attention,
and that was why she'd chosen to step out tonight
for a breath of fresh air. Even I couldn't believe my
luck at finding such a vulnerable woman.

What I thought was going to be a semi-hard task
to pull off was ending up being way too simple.
Part of me wanted to cancel my plan because it

could've been a setup. But I couldn't. The bling on her finger, the studded-out Rolex on her wrist, and the Celine purse sitting in the chair beside her made the lick too inviting. If everything went without a problem robbing her, and I walked away from killing Felix, I'd have to start picking women up at the casino more often.

"I've never had a black dick in me before." She sounded eager yet dumb.

"I guess tonight is your lucky night then. I'm gonna make it worth your wait," I whispered in her ear, forcing myself to kiss it gently. I damn near gagged at my lips touching her, but laying it on thick was a requirement of the job.

We walked out of the casino hand in hand, with my phone vibrating off the hook. I knew it was Moni, but I couldn't chance answering because her voice would be too loud yelling, which would throw off my game plan. Hopefully, it wasn't Jerell, but he knew better than to make a move without my word or let Naughty out of his sight. So regardless of who it was, they'd have to wait.

"My room is a few blocks from here. Are you good to walk, or do you want me to carry you on my back?"

"Oh, you're so nasty," she flirted. "You must want to feel the warmth between my legs. Bend down so I can climb on."

I did just that, happy that she was a dumb blonde. A few blocks away from the casino, I felt comfortable to put my mission into full play. I began acting like she was slightly heavy and I was too tipsy to keep carrying her without taking a break. Conveniently, I'd stopped right beside an alleyway. It was dark, and by a quick glance, I didn't see many people or bums around. Plus, there was loud music blaring from the clubs, which were packed. That would drown out her voice if she got a chance to call for help.

"Don't tell me you're weak and can't handle me already," she playfully said, sliding down my back.

I turned around in full attack mode. "Naw, bitch, I can handle you just fine."

"What?" She was caught off guard with surprise.

I didn't respond verbally. I covered her mouth and snatched her into the alleyway. She tried putting up a fight but was no match for my strength. The only thing she did was manage to scratch my arms with her acrylic nails. I was mad at myself for not wearing long sleeves. Ready to get the robbery over with, I made sure we were backed against a wall beside a Dumpster before hitting her on the side of the head as hard as I could. After two blows to the same spot, she fell out cold.

Moving swiftly, I slipped the rock off her finger, snatched the necklace from around her neck, unclipped the Rolex on her wrist, and snatched her

Celine bag, which I knew Moni would love. After tucking the jewelry deep in my pocket, I took off walking briskly toward the hotel. I was well aware I'd look suspicious walking with a woman's purse, so I kept it tucked close hoping no one would take notice. Luck was still on my side as I reached the Atheneum Hotel without a problem.

Before I could pull the keycard from out the door, Moni swung it open with her attitude on ten. "Where in the hell have you been, Voodo? And why haven't you been answering the phone? You better not have been with a bitch. Drop your pants, nigga, so I can smell ya dick." She hadn't taken a breath and was already reaching for my pants to unbutton them.

"Chill out, babe." I pushed her back lightly, slammed the door, and put the chain on. "I lied when I said I wasn't out working, but I got you something. Here." I handed her the bag.

She looked up at me, confused. "Why'd your ass lie?"

"Because I didn't feel like hearing your mouth throwing me off my square. Don't you like the bag?" Trying to throw her a diversion, I wasn't ready to propose to her just yet. This wasn't the most romantic moment in my opinion.

"Hell yeah, I like the bag. It costs about three grand in the stores." She eyed it then opened it up, inspecting the contents. "But why did you go out chancing getting caught for a purse? We've got cash, plus there's real shit on the table with ol' girl." She was truly on top of her game today.

"You fell asleep and I needed some air to think, so it started out as just a walk around downtown. The rest is history. You know how I get down."

She backed up from the door with her eyes fixated on me the whole time, dumped the contents of the purse on the bed, then called herself getting tough with me. "Don't leave this room without me again, Voodo. If you do, we're gonna have a serious fucking problem. And that's my word."

Chapter Ten

Moni

I was still slightly upset at Voodo for leaving me in the hotel room and not answering my calls, but I couldn't smother him nor continue beefing. It wasn't worth it. Besides, he hadn't cheated on me while out because he didn't fuck with white women, and the wallet within the purse proved he'd stolen it from one. Voodo was lying across the bed watching television while I was busy running us some water in the Jacuzzi. Since he told me we could take full advantage of being down here, I'd ordered fruit and champagne from room service and was ready for some romantic time with my man.

"The water is ready, babe," I sweetly called him. Sliding off my clothes, I slipped inside the warm water, feeling relief take over.

"Damn you look so sexy." He came in, biting his lip.

He took his shirt off, exposing his muscles and thuggish tattoos. I was turned on. The minute he was fully naked, he climbed in behind me and began massaging my shoulders. His touch felt amazing. It felt so good sitting between Voodo's legs. His kisses sent tingles down my spine. And the hardness of his dick on my back made my kitty cat purr with anticipation of what he'd serve me with soon enough. Leaning back on his chest, I was ready to completely melt into him.

"I love you so much, Voodo. I'm sorry for hounding you earlier, but I got scared. Imagining my life without you drives me crazy. I might be tough out here in the streets, but I'm putty when it comes to you." I honestly shared my feelings with him.

"It's cool, baby. I know how you feel, and I know that you're genuine. I love you right back." He leaned his head down on mine. We were definitely having a moment. I was eating it up, savoring it in my heart. "Turn around and straddle me. I wanna suck on your tits and lick your nipples 'til you cum." He was ready to get nasty.

Standing up so he could admire my body, I stood in front of him, dancing a little bit to turn him on even more. There was nothing but lust in his eyes as his hands grabbed on my thick thighs, finally pulling me down onto his lap by my waist. Caught up with the sensation of him kissing and licking all over my breasts and nibbling on my neck, I could barely open my eyes. "You are the best thing that's ever happened to me," I moaned slowly.

"And you're the best thing that's ever happened to me, Moni. I don't ever want you to forget how good you feel right now. Open your eyes, baby love."

It was hard, but I managed to open them, and I gasped louder than when I came earlier. Holding out a diamond ring that could blind a bitch, he spoke the four words I'd been wanting to hear him say only days after we hooked up for the first time.

"Will you marry me?" Slipping the ring off his pinky finger, he held it up with a look of seriousness on his face. Voodo wanted to know if I'd spend the rest of my life with him.

"Yes, yes, yes! Over and over and over again." I excitedly put my hand out so he could slide the ring onto my finger. Then I did something he'd never seen me do. I cried.

Naughty

If I didn't hate cops before, I despised their asses now. They had me down at the station, questioning me damn near all day, but I hadn't told them shit relevant. If they thought I was about to snitch like Felix and end up dead, they were straight fools. I'd rather serve time, which couldn't happen since I hadn't bodied anyone. Peeking through the blinds, I watched the two busters pull off in their unmarked car. I'd requested they send me home in a taxi, but the cheap bastards refused. Low-key they probably thought I'd have a change of heart. But nope, Moni and Voodo scared me more than them.

It was time to make a move to get the hell out of Detroit before more bad luck showed up on my doorstep again. Escaping to live a new life in my cousin's town, even if it was temporary, was the only option I had. Slightly paranoid that someone could've been listening at the door, I tiptoed through my apartment, gathering small items that I could take in my carry-on. I needed to travel lightly so I could get the fuck out of dodge quickly. The longer I took, the worse it would be for me. Hiding out in the D was no longer an option.

Once I stuffed as many clothes, personal documents, and most needed necessities into my matching Louis Vuitton purse and small rolling suitcase, I plopped down on the bed and called my neighbor for a huge favor. When I got the green light that they'd run me to the airport, I rushed to the door, ready to say good-bye for good. I'd worry about getting a ticket once I got there, and I didn't care how much it would cost. Swinging the door open, feeling free, I damn near jumped out of my skin. "Ahhh," I shouted before the guy who was with Voodo that night grabbed my throat and forced me back inside.

"Shut the fuck up," he commanded, with the craziest look I'd ever seen a man have on his face.

Voodo

The sex we had in the Jacuzzi was mind-blowing for the both of us. I swore Moni had always been a freak, but it was like she turned into a seasoned porn star once that ring was nestled on her finger. Not only did she suck and swallow me under the water, only coming up a few times for breath, but she rode me until I dropped my load off into her deeply. The water that was once within the tub had splashed over onto the bathroom floor. That's how wild the sex had gotten.

"So that bag wasn't the only thing you ripped off from ol' girl, huh?" Moni wasn't a fool by a long shot. She'd put two and two together with ease, but I didn't have any secrets to hide, so I hurriedly admitted the truth.

"Nope. I got you a necklace and watch, too." I smiled devilishly, getting up to retrieve them from my pants pocket. "The only bad thing is that we probably can't hit the casino as planned, just in case the white girl woke up and went back to report me. I picked her up as my prey from the bar." Now that Moni had the ring on her finger, I didn't care about exposing the whole truth. I wasn't worried about her judging me or being upset since we were one in the same.

"Well, aren't you a sly dog?" she laughed, throwing her hand up to admire the ring. "I love you as a thug, baby. This ring is bomb as hell. It must've cost ol' girl or the dude who brought it for her a grip. I'm not sure how many karats it is, but the Cartier band alone is rocked out. That bitch's finger gotta be feeling hella light without it. But from the stuff I found inside of her purse, she'll be able to replace everything you stole. You know white girls insure pretty much everything they buy."

"And if she can't, who cares? The only woman I'm concerned about pleasing and being happy is you. She should've never trusted a random nigga anyway." I laughed at her expense. "I'm just happy you ain't tripping over it being ripped off and not brand new from the jewelry store." Despite me not wanting to ruin her cheerfulness or the moment, I didn't want Moni to feel cheated out of something she deserved. She held me down too much. Her having a secret chip on her shoulder wouldn't be good for either of us in the long run.

"Hell to the naw, Voodo! First and foremost, this ring is bad as hell, and I know it cost just as much as a down payment on a house. But most importantly, I know the cash we got from Felix won't last forever, and we might have to make moves to get out of Detroit with it. I'm no fool. I know how the game goes. We were already planning to break out of Detroit for a while anyway. I'm just overwhelmed with pleasure that you thought about making us one hundred percent official even though so much shit is going on."

I was relieved. Everything was playing out the way I wanted it to. "It's always gonna be like that, baby. No matter what is popping off in the streets, you're always gonna be my first priority. You and Alexis." Interrupted by my phone vibrating, I rushed to pull it out of my pocket. "What's the word, nigga?" It was Jerell, so I knew he was calling about business.

"It's time to make a move," he spoke in a low tone.

"Say no more," I responded, then disconnected the call. "Hurry up and get dressed, Moni. Jerell has eyes on Naughty. It's time to find out what has been said and what to expect."

"That bitch better be able to prove she didn't snitch like Felix, or I'm icing her without anyone's approval. There's not a soul on this earth who is gonna keep me from marrying you."

Trying to talk sense into Moni or getting her to calm down was pointless. The vicious look in her eye was easily recognizable, because I usually looked the same way when I was ready to attack. When either of us got into the mindset that someone needed to get it, no one could stop us. That was the bottom and final line.

The drive to Naughty's apartment wasn't tense nor were we sitting in silence. The radio DJ was spinning a mix of Detroit artists that had us both in the zone. Plus each of us was puffing on our own blunt. I guessed both of us were feeling good about finding out what popped off with Naughty at the police station.

"There's Jerell's hoop ride. I'm about to call him, 'cause he must be up in the apartment with ol' girl."

Naughty

My wrists were sore from the cords ol' boy used to restrain me. I could barely breathe since my mouth was taped shut daring me to whimper. And I was sure I was getting ready to go into cardiac arrest from my heart pounding a million beats per second. I was extremely terrified. I didn't want to die. I wasn't ready to see Felix or my lost loved ones or meet my Maker. Closing my eyes, I prayed hard for God to have mercy on me by allowing a way out.

The crazy dude answered his phone. "Yeah, it's clear to come up." He was short with whoever he was talking to, who was probably Voodo.

Sixty seconds later, there were a few light taps on my door, and then the crazy dude opened it up. Although I wasn't a snitch, I was hoping it was the cops so I'd be saved. My luck wasn't that great. In walked Voodo and Moni. Even restrained, with fear pumping through my veins, I took notice of the humungous rock on her finger. They must've hit a helluva lick since the other night. Before I could close my eyes again to pray, Moni stormed over to where I was, damn near slapping me unconscious.

"We saw you walking with the cops. I'm gonna give you only a few seconds to tell me all about it and what you said before I leave your ass dead. If you scream, those seconds will be voided, and I'll leave a bullet in your dome." Snatching the tape from my mouth, she put the gun to my head, daring me not to believe her words.

"I didn't tell them anything, I swear," I wheezed, happy to at least be able to breathe easier. "They'd been pounding on my door since Felix got killed, finally forcing me to answer. I only went because they were acting like I was under arrest. Yet when I got down there, they didn't have shit but some hearsay from some other dancers."

"Yeah, the fuck right." Moni put one in the chamber of her gun. "Just like I'm made for my nigga, you were made for yours. Two motherfuckin' snitches."

I saw my life flash before my eyes. All the dancing, hustling, and tricks I pulled were about to be over. I could feel it. "Please no, don't kill me. I promise I didn't say anything." I begged for my life. "I know Felix was snitching, but that type of shit don't run in my blood. I was just using him for his cash. That was it."

"Whoa, baby, slow down." Voodo walked up behind her, putting his hand on her waist.

My life was worth fighting for so I begged even more. "I know the shit don't look good, but I swear on everything I didn't talk. The last thing I want is to end up in a body bag. Think about it for a second. They're gone, and I'm not in witness protection. I won't lie and say y'all two don't terrify me, 'cause I've heard of how y'all get down. I wouldn't have snitched and come back here. Please believe me!"

"I caught the bitch just as she was getting ready to run out the door with her luggage," the crazy dude spoke up, making me seem slightly guilty.

Voodo had gotten Moni to calm down at first, but because of the words the crazy dude had spoken, she was back amped. "Oh, really? You were about to shoot a move out of the city?" Laughing like a crazy woman, she rubbed the gun against my lips with a cold look in her eye. "I should put this bullet down your throat, silencing you forever."

Afraid to speak and set her off, I couldn't sit in silence knowing I was innocent. I hadn't done anything to deserve to be murdered. I'd been loyal to them, although I should've been loyal to my man. My pleas continued. "Only because I was trying to get the hell out of Detroit before the cops tried badgering me again. If they know anything about the murder and y'all being responsible for it, they didn't get that information from me. Hell, I don't even know for sure if y'all took Felix and his boys out."

Tears were streaming down my face as I tried rationalizing with them. I couldn't tell if they were believing me, though. Moni's expression was menacing, Voodo looked deep in thought but not about sparing me my soul, and the crazy dude looked like he was ready to strangle the life from my body with his bare hands. If this was the end for me, it was a sad way to go. I could only imagine how Felix and his crew suffered.

Officer Hubbard

"What in the hell do you mean you let her go?" Captain Williams was screaming at the top of his lungs. Slamming his fists on his desk, enraged, both my partner and I slid our chairs back to avoid the stuff that was falling. "Please tell me why you let her walk out of this station without charges. You know that woman was lying through her teeth and withholding information."

"We kept her for hours, sir, but she wouldn't break. In addition to that, she brought up the point that we'd failed at our job of protecting Felix since he was our informant. And honestly speaking, boss, we did. We couldn't hold her without any evidence," I spoke up, knowing he wasn't going to accept my answer easily.

"Tell me one thing, if you don't mind. Why in the fuck do you have a badge if you can't throw around your power? All I see before me are two punk-ass cops scared to go hard and get the evidence we need to find out who killed those men. I don't care that we dropped the ball on protecting Felix. As far as our trail of paperwork says, we did. So the only thing left for y'all to do is to bring the killers in. Why in the fuck is that so hard?"

"Because no one wants to talk. We're lucky Felix wanted to sell the folks out in his hood. There's not many cats on his level willing to take a risk like that for obvious reasons," my partner, Richard, spoke up. "People from the hoods of Detroit like to handle matters without the police being involved. They don't trust us, because they fear we'll arrest them for anything they've got pending on their head. They don't believe in our skills to protect their lives. And with so much police brutality going on across the globe, it's us versus them in their minds."

"Thanks for your speech, you piece of shit, but you're not enlightening me. I'm well aware how those bums feel, but I just don't give a fuck. Now instead of being in here feeding me crap about not being able to do your jobs, get out there to find who killed our informant. Make the first stop his girlfriend's house. Your job is to escort her into this station with her wrists in handcuffs. Maybe a little time in a cell with hardcore murderers will make her talk."

"What will we bring her in for, boss?" Questioning him although I knew he was irate, I wasn't trying to lose my badge by arresting Nina under false pretenses.

"I swear y'all are getting transferred after this case, because y'all are dumb and not worth the hassle. If that woman won't tell us what happened to Felix, she was in on it. Bring her in as the lead suspect of the case. Now get the hell out of my office before I fire y'all asses right here and now!"

Despite me wanting to punch the captain in his throat for talking to me like I was less than a man, I got up to follow his orders. I needed my job. With a family to feed at home, there was nothing else I could do. My partner, however, had other plans.

"Yo, Williams, fuck you and this job. You ain't gotta transfer or fire me, because I quit. If you want that trick brought in or this case solved, you better get out from behind your desk and do it yourself. I'm out. It's been real, Hubbard." My partner of two years threw his badge on Captain's desk, gave me dap, and slammed the door on his way out.

Chapter Eleven

Moni

Voodo had proposed. In spite of the how he'd gotten the engagement ring, it was sitting on my finger as a symbol of his love and loyalty to me. Not only did he truly have strings to my heart, but I had them to his as well. In a few months, I wanted to give up my last name and become his Mrs. James. The thought of having a white princess wedding dress, Alexis as the flower girl, and him waiting for me in front of a preacher to recite our vows made me melt. It didn't matter if our relationship wasn't written as a fairy tale, it was our story and I wanted to create sequel after sequel until death found my soul. With dreams so big, I couldn't let Naughty spoil them. She had to go.

"Please, you've gotta believe me." Her voice annoyed me. I regretted even taking the tape off her mouth.

I didn't believe her. And even if I did, I couldn't give her the chance to go snitch now that we'd run up in her apartment, threatening her life. If she didn't know for a fact that we were responsible for Felix's and his crew's deaths, she knew now. Plus, we'd made things more personal with Naughty by holding her hostage within her own apartment. I'd never be comfortable with knowing a bitch on the streets held guilt over my head. There was only one thing to do. "If you haven't made peace with your sins, I'll see you in hell." My words were concrete. My mind was made up, and there was no turning back. I swiftly handled my business.

"Oh, shit, Moni!" I could tell in Voodo's voice that he was shocked by my decision to shoot Naughty.

Standing in front of Naughty's now-slumped body, I waited to see if I'd feel an ounce of regret for sending two bullets into her neck, but I didn't. If either Voodo or I had gone to jail over her giving the cops any information, I would've spent my days looking to gun her down or counting down the days of my sentence so I could gun her down. If anyone else wanted to test us or try taking away the life I wanted with Voodo, they'd end up with the same fate.

"Give me the gun, baby." Voodo slid the weapon from my hands. "I can't believe you iced her out like that."

"Fuck taking a chance, baby. Like I told you at the room, I'm not letting her or anyone ruin what we're trying to build. It's us versus everybody."

"That rock has made you crazier than you were before." He laughed lightly. "Come on, though, we've gotta get out of here before the cops come. I know someone had to have called them after hearing those gunshots."

Jerell untied Naughty's body from the chair she was tied down to, threw her over his shoulders, and ordered Voodo to grab the used cords because his fingerprints were on them. Questions didn't need to be asked about what Jerell was doing. We both knew he was cleaning up as much evidence as he could. The job we'd pulled on Naughty was messy. Me murdering her made it worse.

The small hallway of the floor her apartment was on was quiet, but that didn't mean no one was peeping out their peepholes or hadn't heard the shots fired. I'd killed a witness, but we were making a few more in the process of trying to get rid of her. At this point, my decision was starting to seem a bit too rash. Hopefully, my impulsiveness hadn't fucked us in the game, because it was too late to go back in time.

Officer Hubbard

It felt weird having the captain ride shotgun with me out on duty. We weren't supposed to be working the streets side by side. My job was to take

orders from him and report about my progress or
lack thereof. But Richard had shocked us both by
saying screw the police force. With no partner but
an open investigation, I was stuck with the man
who'd help the victim become a target in the first
place. As we rode in silence toward Nina's apartment, her words and Richard's speech were the
only things on my mind. My honor to the badge
and my oath were starting to seem irrelevant and
nothing but a heap of bullshit. At this point, all I
was protecting and serving was my dickhead boss.

"Gunshots reported at 2407 Glendale Drive, unit
2M. We need a squad car to follow up."

The captain didn't pick up on the address as
quickly as I did, probably because I'd been working
this case and sitting on Nina's property waiting for
movement for days. While he looked on, oblivious
and uncaring, I responded to the operator sourly.
I knew it was time to prepare for the worst. "One-
two. This is Officer Hubbard. Captain Williams
and I will respond."

"What the fuck, Hubbard? We've got a mission.
Let some other cops get on their jobs," he snapped.
"I ain't got time to be out here playing in the field
with a whole squad to manage."

Ignoring him while I flipped my siren on, I
pulled my gun from its holster so I'd be prepared
the instant we arrived. "That address belongs to
Nina Carter, boss. You might want to start famil-

iarizing yourself with the case you want solved so badly."

Voodo

There was nothing else I could do but blame myself for how things were unraveling. I wasn't the one who'd put the two bullets into Naughty, but I hadn't been smooth or quick enough to talk Moni up out of it, either. Not calming her down before leaving the hotel was my first mistake. Then not taking total control over the situation once I noticed she was leading with emotions was the second. Matter of fact, I should've let Jerell take care of cleaning up the dirty work altogether.

Me wanting to judge for myself if Naughty snitched was the reason things had gotten so sloppy. I wasn't emotional or regretful over her death. I was pissed that all three of us now had more monkeys on our back. If anyone in that apartment saw our faces, that could only add up to more bullshit for us to deal with. In trying to fix a problem, we'd been creating more.

Jerell dropped Naughty's dead body into his trunk like she was lightweight luggage, then slid into the driver's side of his car without a word. I didn't know where he was taking the body, nor did I need to ask. He was efficient when it came to washing his hands clean. So wherever her corpse ended up, I knew the Detroit police would never recover it. "Get at me, ace." I threw my hand up at him.

"No doubt," he responded. Jerell was most definitely loyal, true to the game, and grounded when it came to reacting without emotion.

"Come on, baby. By the sound of those sirens, the cops ain't far at all," Moni's paranoid voice rang out. "We've gotta bust a move and fast."

Rushing to the truck, we both jumped in prepared to get out of dodge. With each second that passed, the sirens were getting closer. I couldn't tell by ear if there was more than one squad car, but I didn't want to be around to find out. Having murders under our belt along with a long list of other wrongdoings we'd pulled off, I was sure Moni and I were highly wanted. Arresting us for one charge would lead to many crimes being solved, which meant several years of jail time for us apiece. Fuck that option! With the car started and Moni yelling at me to pull off, I couldn't hit the gas yet, and my nerves were rattled because Jerell still hadn't driven away.

"I can't leave my ace with a dead body in the car, Moni. Fall back and be cool for a second. Everything is gonna be okay." I tried sounding confident when in fact I wasn't. The louder and clearer the sirens rang in my ears, the less I wholeheartedly believed we'd make a clean break.

"Hurry up and get that piece of junk started and let's go." Moni slammed her hand on the dashboard, screaming at Jerell as if he could hear her. Hell, as loud as she was, he just might've. Shaking with paranoia, she was in the passenger seat going crazy. I'd never seen her trip out so hard, but I understood why. My girl was falling apart before my eyes.

After a few more failed attempts at getting the car going and screams from Moni out the window at Jerell, the doom buggy turned over. It seemed like all three of us had a chance. The engine of his hoop ride sputtered a couple of times then finally became strong enough for him to pull off. By the time he whipped from his parking spot, Moni and I were revving up to burn rubber away from the scene. That's when the cop car we'd heard bent the corner on two wheels, swerving up to Naughty's apartment complex.

"Fuck, fuck, fuck." I shook my head, but I was trying to be cool. There was no way either of us could get away without passing the cops. I stalled to see what they were gonna do, because bringing attention to us was the last thing I wanted. But Jerell kept driving without wavering. Probably because he didn't want his car to cut back off with a body in the trunk.

Before both officers could climb out of their squad cars, a woman's voice rang out. "There's the shooters right there. They killed that poor girl and took her body."

The cops followed which way Naughty's neighbor was pointing and screaming, with their stares landing on Moni and me. One of the cops lifted his weapon without hesitation and let off four quick shots toward the truck. The windshield shattered immediately.

"Ahhh!" A bloodcurdling scream came from Moni's mouth.

Glancing over at her, I saw Moni wiggling in pain. She'd been shot. My heart sank to the pit of my stomach. I might as well have caught one of those bullets. I didn't have time to see how bad the wound was or hold my baby love. The feeling was horrible. "Hold on, baby. Don't let that bullet or some bitch-ass cop stop you from marrying me. Be strong," I howled at her. "We're forever after, and this ain't the end!"

"Put your hands up," the cops yelled out.

Looking up at both cops running my way on foot, I pulled my chrome piece from under my shirt then pushed my foot down on the gas pedal. They weren't about to take us down, and I wasn't about to let my fiancée die. I didn't know if she was still breathing, but I wasn't about to admit she was dead. I went into sheer murder zone. Gunshots didn't stop ringing until all of my clips were unloaded. Although I'd caught three bullets that felt like they were burning through my flesh, I didn't take my foot off the pedal. In the rearview mirror, I could see both cops laid out in the middle of the street.

"Moni, baby, answer me, girl. Moni!" For the first time in my life, I was shaken up and kind of scared. I didn't want to look over and see the love of my life dead. I needed her to respond. "Moni!" I kept screaming her name as I drove faster away from the scene of the crime.

For us to have the hottest love in Detroit, we couldn't have the coldest ending. In the blink of an eye, the team was no more.

The End

So Far Gone

by

Katt

Chapter One

It was Friday. I woke up to go to school. I brushed my teeth, washed my face, took a shower, and got dressed. This all took place after I woke up at 5:30 a.m. That sounds early right? I was always done by 6:00 a.m. because school started at 6:30 a.m., but it was only a couple blocks from my house. I walked there every day and after school walked back home.

I started looking in the mirror to see my reflection. I saw dark brown hair, light skin, and dark brown eyes. I was normal height for a fifteen-year-old girl in the tenth grade. I would always look in the mirror for a while before I was done. Not for any conceited reasons at all but just because that was my time when I would wonder, why? Why me? Why do I have to be dealt this hand in life? I don't deserve this. No one does. I was done getting ready early today, so I ate breakfast at home.

"Renee, honey, your pancakes are done!" I heard my mom yelling from the kitchen.

"Okay, I'm coming, Mom."

"Good morning, honey." My mom smiled as she hugged me before kissing me on the forehead.

My mom was a little thick as they say. Standing around five feet five inches, she had dark brown eyes just like me. Her name was Theresa, but she had golden blond hair unlike me. Her hair wasn't dark brown like mine because she dyed her hair all the time. Yet surprisingly she had stayed with blond for a while now. She used to have the biggest, brightest smile, but sadly nowadays she hardly ever smiles anymore. Giving birth to me when she was a teen, her life was stressful. But Tyrone made it a lot worse when he came around.

I loved my mother more than anything, but I couldn't lie. The life she had us living was terrible. I guessed she was trying her best, but sometimes it didn't really seem like it. My mom was almost hitting thirty-one. That was a little too old for her not to have her shit together. In a few more years I'd be an adult, and my worst nightmare was ending up like her. I didn't want to end up as a stripper with a kid I couldn't take care of and a deadbeat husband who hit me and took all of my money. Naw, I wasn't interested in that way of life at all.

"Good morning," I said, sitting down at the small yellow table in the kitchen. We had a small kitchen, too, but actually just a tiny house, period. Sometimes I would catch my mom with a lot of money, but not for long because she would pay the rent, then my stepdad, Tyrone, would take the rest from her. Sometimes we would even be late on the rent because Tyrone would take my mother's money before she could pay the rent.

I never knew my mom was a stripper until one night. I was like thirteen years old. This was a little after Tyrone first started drinking and acting crazy. I woke up out of my sleep and looked at the time. It was 12:30 a.m.

"Listen here, bitch." I heard Tyrone yelling out, so I got out of bed. Slowly I cracked my door open. I could see my mom with her makeup and hair all done and this long coat on.

"Tyrone, leave me alone. I just got off work," she told him calmly as she took off her coat. All I could see was my mom wearing a black studded bra and matching bottoms. I didn't understand why she was wearing that.

"You were out whoring around all night, stripping for money, and you mean to tell me this is all you made? All you made was fifty dollars?"

"Stripping?" I mumbled in a very low voice.

Tyrone backhanded my mom twice. And just like that, she fell on the floor sobbing.

Without hesitation, I bolted out of my room. Like a crazed lunatic, I jumped on Tyrone's back. Using every bit of strength I had, I balled up my fist tight. Wildly, I started punching the back of his head, demanding he stop his actions. "Leave my damn mother alone! Don't touch her! Don't put your hands back on her!"

Tyrone reached over his shoulder. In what seemed like one swift movement, he grabbed at my wrist. With brutal force, he snatched me off of his back by my arms. Before I knew what was taking place next, he threw me on the floor. I tried to get up to attack him again. Yet this time he was having no part of it. Raising his leg, he kicked dead me in the face. I couldn't believe it. I was dizzy. I was out of breath, and I felt so defeated. In agony, I crawled to the far side of the room to recover from the disrespectful blow. Balled up under the table, I cried for myself and my mother as Tyrone's rage continued. By daybreak, it was finally over. It was back to quiet in the house.

I went to school the whole next week with a bunch of makeup on. I attempted to cover up the black eye that evil bastard gave me by kicking me in the face. After that fateful night, my mom told me if I ever saw Tyrone hit her again, then just close my door. She advised me to stay in my room. Why she didn't just leave him, I'd never understand. However, I listened to her after that. I did as I was told. Well, at least for a long time.

He was slightly taller than my mom and overweight. Tyrone was in his mid-forties now, which was about fifteen years older than my mom. I honestly thought my mom only went with him because she thought he was going to take care of us, which he didn't. He and my mom had been married for about four years now. You could see his age was kicking in because he was starting to go bald. His skin was starting to look dry with light wrinkles. But maybe it was the alcohol that was kicking in, not his age.

Mom and Tyrone met at his old job. I was about eleven years old at the time. Tyrone was a fire-fighter. My mom used to tell me that one day she was walking past the fire station where he would mostly work if they did not move his location around so much. This day Tyrone happened to be on break. He was outside of the fire station, smok-ing a cigarette. My mom told me she gave him her number and they went on a really nice date. Then it was history from there. It would have been nice if their relationship stayed like when they first met, but it surely didn't.

I ate my pancakes and drank my orange juice. I looked around. Straight from the table where I sat were the silver oven and the stovetop right next to each other, connected together. A little ways down was the sink, lined up against the wall. There was also a window above the sink. The kitchen was a tan color with pink marble tiles on the floor. Across from the sink was our white refrigerator. Our kitchen was connected to the living room.

I drank the rest of my orange juice then said goodbye to my mom. I then left for school. As I started walking, I could feel the cold Cleveland morning air from this fall season hit my face. Across the street was a group of kids who lived on my block. They always walked to school together. My block wasn't that bad compared to most neighborhoods in Cleveland, Ohio. The only bad thing, in my opinion, was the small one-floor houses everyone around here lived in.

I never walked with the group of kids. I never really made a lot of friends because of the way my stepdad acted. I never wanted to take them to my house to experience what I did almost every day. If I did take that chance and he clowned, this would bring more attention to my horrible life outside of school.

Hours passed, and it was 3:30 p.m. Time to get out of school. The weather warmed up a little compared to that cold breeze this morning. I started walking back home. I saw the same group of kids who were walking earlier to school now walking home. I saw these kids walking almost every day since school has started.

"Renee," I heard someone call out from behind me. It was one of the girls walking with the group of kids. Her name was Maria. I had my fourth and fifth hours with her.

"Yeah? What?" I spun around and stopped as Maria and the group of kids walked closer to me.

There were three people walking with Maria: one boy and two girls. I knew the boy because he was Maria's twin brother, but I didn't know the girls they were with. Maria and her twin brother were both tall, with light brown hair, and African American.

Finally, they caught up to me. "Renee, can you come to my sleepover tomorrow for my birthday?"

"I want to but I can't. I have to go see my grandma in the hospital tomorrow," I told her, knowing I was lying about this.

"Okay, well, maybe I could come over to your house on Sunday and we can hang out?" Maria wouldn't take no for an answer.

"Maybe, but I don't think so, because I have to go to church in the morning. The rest of the day I have to spend time with my grandma," I lied once more.

"Okay then." Maria sadly gave up, then I walked away.

I even stopped talking to Cedric, my old boy-friend. At this time, I was staying away from every-one, and I knew if I did not talk to him, I really did not want to talk to Maria.

I wasn't that far ahead of them, and I could hear them whisper. "Maria, why would you want to invite her anyway? I heard she is weird and she never really talks to anyone anymore," the Mexican girl said.

"She just lied to you. You know that right?" the other girl told Maria. She was a mixed girl. She looked Indian and black. I kept walking but continued to listen to them talk.

"She is not weird, and I know. I could kind of tell she was lying. But she's really cool. We were super close in the summer, and I would always go over to her house. But once her mom married that guy she stopped talking to me," Maria explained to them.

This was the truth. Maybe I shouldn't have stopped talking to Maria, but I knew she would want to start coming over to my house more often. I could not let her. If I told her no, then she would start asking why, and then what would I tell her? Maybe I was a little paranoid, but ever since my mom had been getting hit by Tyrone, it has just been driving me crazy. I just was not talking to anyone now that Tyrone was starting to hit my mom more and more.

I sped up as I walked home because I didn't really care about listening to their conversation anymore. If I stayed to listen to more, I probably would have punched one of the girls Maria was walking with. How could they have all bad things to say about me when they didn't even know?

I finally made it home. I walked in the house and closed the door behind me. I was still standing at the door in the living room. Tyrone was yelling at my mom. I could tell he was drunk, and this was actually early for him. Tyrone at least waited until 6:00 p.m. or later to drink.

Overweight, black, and bald was always the best way for me to explain how Tyrone looked. Every damn time I looked at Tyrone, those three words went in my head. Tyrone was a big guy with big muscles. But even though he had muscles, he was out of shape with a big belly. I didn't know what my mom saw in him. He wasn't even cute.

Their conversation didn't seem that bad, so I walked down the small hallway from the living room into my room. I set my book bag on my floor and lay in my bed. I put my headphones on because I did not want to hear my mom and Tyrone arguing about him drinking too much or them arguing about my mom not giving him all her money. That was all they ever really argued about. I was pretty sure they did not even notice I entered the house.

I continued listening to my music. I loved being in my room. It was my escape place from all the arguing and fighting that happened every night at my house. My room was small, but I didn't care. I loved it. We lived here for a little while now. My room was painted pink. My mom and I did it when we first moved in this house, and even Tyrone helped.

He was not always a drunk. He and my mom had been together for five years now. The first year he was a nice guy and never drank. But shortly after that year passed, they got married, and he started to drink. It went downhill from there, because after the drinking then followed the arguing. After that started, he started to hit her. I never really knew what to do because I was not strong enough to help her. I would beg her to leave him, but time and time again she would never listen to me. She stayed.

Sometimes I would catch my mom watching talk shows about abusive relationships in the living room when Tyrone would leave the house. At that point, the bum did not have a job. However, most days around noon he would leave, then come back around 2:00 p.m. Then he'd strangely leave again at around 6:00 p.m. and come back around 7:00 p.m. I never knew where he went, but I knew once he left at 6:00 p.m. he would always come back drunk. The weekends were different, though, because those days Tyrone didn't have a set schedule at all.

Chapter Two

Some people would have said I had the killer instinct of a wolf when it came to my mother, but I always knew, in reality, I was as fragile as a sheet of paper. I had hatred in my heart and in my soul, and Tyrone made me like this. All this time I had to deal with Tyrone hitting my mom. Sometimes I would even get mad at my mom for not leaving him, but at the end of the day, I could not stay mad at my mom because I loved her so much. Sometimes I would hear people calling me crazy or weird, but they could not say I didn't love hard. All my life I had felt this way. Maybe that was what made me the "psycho" the judge, jury, and everyone else in America labeled me as today.

Living with Tyrone had gotten even worse. Not all the time, but a couple times when my mom was not home, he would even try to do things to me. But he never actually did it because I would wake up while he was trying, which scared me even more. For some reason, I was attractive in my sick stepfather's eyes. All I could feel was a hand mov-

ing down my arm really slow and softly. I thought
I was dreaming, but I woke up to the strong scent
of beer. There Tyrone was with bloodshot eyes,
sitting on the side of my bed and touching my arm.

"Get away—"

"Shhh," he sinisterly responded as I tried to
finish my sentence.

My heart was racing. I didn't know what was
about to happen. But all Tyrone did was tell me
to be quiet. Then he just got up and walked out of
my room. I never told my mom because I knew the
look in his conniving eyes. It was an evil look. He
didn't want me to tell her. And truth be told, with a
look like that there was no way in hell I was going
to tell her. As long as he didn't touch me, I felt okay
with the thought of not telling her. It wouldn't help
anyway if I did tell her.

My childhood was a nail and a hammer. Although I was the nail, life itself hammered me down.
Those days coming home from school were worse
than stepping foot in school. Even though I stopped
talking to my friends and was becoming an outcast,
I still did not enjoy going back home. Every day I
would come home from school and Tyrone would
be sitting there in the brown wooden chair in the
living room almost straight across from the front
door, waiting to bother me. Tyrone would almost
all the time have a whisky bottle next to him that
he chucked down before my mom and I had gotten home.

He would say to me when I walked in, "Take your ass in the room. I'm not babysitting no kids!"

I would always listen to his commands. One reason was because I was very scared of him, but I hated being around him anyway, so I didn't mind listening to him. I thought since he hit my mom that I might be next, especially since he hit me once before. I stayed in my room until my mother got home every day to avoid being in the same room as him. I always asked my mother, "I don't understand, Mom. You are a very attractive woman. Why did you settle for a scum like him?"

She always came back with the same response. "Never say that around him. He would kill us and not think anything of it."

I believed her, and when my mom told me this, it was my first time when I knew Tyrone was more dangerous than I ever thought before. I could always hear him slapping her late at night when they argued about something. Sometimes it also sounded like he was choking her, and I would just put my headphones on. Sometimes he would do it right in front of me. He knew I was too young to do anything about it, and Tyrone knew I was scared that he might hit me again. I would cry all the time with her when he left the house, and I knew she was hurting. I was too. She would sometimes have big black scars around her cheekbones, and she tried hiding them with pounds of makeup.

I sat in my room every day, staring at the four pink walls, just thinking about running away and never coming back here. But I knew I couldn't do that. I would never leave my mom behind with this man. But sometimes I would even daydream about being a princess, waiting for my knight in shining armor to come and rescue me from this dungeon. Sounds cheesy, huh? But it was better than thinking about this terrible life.

Everything I thought of in my room, from the time I came home to the time my mother got home, was escaping this house. I had no games. I had no television to keep my attention. All my mother's earnings from her job were wasted on Tyrone for more beers and cigarettes. My room was the only place in the house that did not reek of beer and cigarettes. So I stayed in my room until my mom came back from work. I would be asleep or just listen to my music while lying in my bed. I'd peek out of the room. From there I could see the whole living room, and I could see Tyrone in the chair.

One night, I saw him dozing off in the chair, which gave me a chance to grab a bite to eat out of the kitchen. I realized two seconds after I walked to the kitchen that Tyrone staring right at me.

In a loud tone, he said, "What the hell do you think you're doing, huh?"

I was startled and answered, "I'm just going to get something to eat. I have not eaten since lunch."

"You ask me first, or you wait until your mom gets home. Whatever is in this house is mine. You have to ask," Tyrone barked. He took a chocolate bar out of his pocket and said, "Here, you can have this. I won't eat it anyway."

I stayed in the same spot. I did not know whether to run or approach him and take the candy bar. But I was pretty hungry, and I could not wait until my mother got home.

"Hurry up before I change my mind!" Tyrone said loudly.

I start to walk toward him, but then he dropped the candy bar between his legs. At that moment I walked back to my room.

"So you're not hungry anymore, huh, dumb little bitch?" Tyrone angrily hissed.

A few hours later I could hear from my room my mother coming in from work. I could hear almost every night my mom worked from Tyrone's loud, deep voice. He would always ask my mother for money before she could even settle in.

"I only have a hundred and twenty dollars. It was a slow night tonight," my mother mumbled.

"It was a slow night, huh? Do you think I'm stupid, Theresa?" Tyrone's voice grew louder.

At that moment I knew he would hit her. I put in my headphones on and started listening to music because I hated to hear my mother scream. Music was always my escape. I waited a good two minutes before unplugging my headphones, and I heard nothing. There was a strong silence in the house. I had gotten curious why it was so quiet. I went out of my room, and I saw Tyrone just sitting in the chair, falling asleep. I walked into the kitchen and saw my mother wiping her eyes on her gray sweater.

"Are you okay, Mom? What did he do to you?"

"Yes, I am okay, Renee. Just go into your room until I'm done with dinner."

I followed orders and returned to my room. It was then I heard my mother scream and Tyrone yelling. "I told you, you bring your fucking earnings to me. All of the earnings, not just some," he demanded.

I ran out of the room just in time to see Tyrone hitting my mother in the head with a pan repeatedly. This was the worst he'd ever been. So many thoughts were going through my mind. I never had been so scared in my life, but I also never felt so much hatred in my heart.

I snatched a knife off of the coffee table to try to stop him from harming her any further. My mom lay unconscious on the floor with blood spewing from her skull. I was livid. I was terrified. I had so much hurt in my heart that I could not deal. My emotions became overwhelming. I'd never felt this kind of inner rage before, but it was empowering.

"Oh my God, oh my God! You killed her! You killed my mother!"

"So fucking what if I did?" he taunted me. "Renee, what are you doing with that knife? Little girls are not supposed to have sharp things in their hands." He slyly smirked, walking slowly toward me.

My eyes filled up with tears as I clenched the knife handle. I could feel the hard rubber handle of the knife bruising my palm. "Don't come near me. You better not come anywhere near me," I shouted, pointing the sharp end of the knife toward him.

"All right now, you little bitch. I'm done playing games with your crazy ass. Now like I said, put that damn shit down before you be laid out on the floor next to your hardheaded, no-making-money mother."

Suddenly, in the blink of an eye, he attacked me. I was overpowered. My back hit the corner of the coffee table as he body-slammed me to the floor. The impact made the knife fly out of my hand toward my bedroom door. He dragged me away from the knife as I tried fighting him off.

"You want to be an adult? Well, I'll show you what adults do." Tyrone snickered.

When the monster turned me over on my stomach, this gave me an advantage to grab the knife. I reached for the shiny blade and hid it under my stomach. When I heard him unbuckle his pants, I turned over. With no remorse, I leaned up and repeatedly stabbed my mother's tormentor in his chest. His eyes grew wider. He didn't speak. He was silent until he took a huge gasp then fell to his knees. His oversized frame then collapsed on top of me.

After a bit of a struggle, I got up from underneath him. The rush was intense but exciting. Blood gushed out of his chest to the floor. Just to make sure my mother and I were really rid of him, I gripped the handle of the knife once more. I continued plunging it into Tyrone's chest and rib cage until his soul was no more. Tonight I was going to make sure he was dead. There was no way he was going to kill my mom and get away with it. I hated Tyrone so much.

I finally stopped and began to breathe heavy. I went to my mother, but at that time I thought she was already gone. I called the police, but dumbly at the age of fifteen, I did not know I'd committed a crime. I had no idea I could and would be punished, when all I felt like what I was doing was protecting myself from an evil asshole.

Later, I found out that my mom was not dead on the floor as I'd presumed. However, later that night, at the hospital, she did actually take her last breath. But I did not care one bit about killing Tyrone, let alone being punished for the heinous act. I was what the old folks in the South called blood-thirsty.

See, the feeling of killing my mother's killer did not leave me. Even now as I thought about it, the ill thought of doing it again excited me. But then the thought of my mother dying killed me inside. I would never get the painful heartache of my mom dying out of my system.

Chapter Three

Calming Meadows. That sounded nice, right? You would think it was a peaceful place, but it wasn't. It was the name of the mental hospital I was sent to after committing murder. Well, the second one I was sent to because the first one I hardly remembered anything about. They had me so drugged up. For some reason, they thought I was going to kill anyone I came in contact with. But I wouldn't. Murdering random people wasn't in me. To be honest, I did not even remember the name of that place. All I remembered was that I spent half a year of my life in there. When I was almost sixteen, I was moving to another mental house because the last one closed. Maybe it was a good thing that the last place closed, because I would not be so dependent on drugs. Or just my luck, maybe it was a bad thing just like everything else in my life.

White walls with flowers on them were what I saw as I followed the woman down the hall to my room. Behind these pretty walls were pain, murder, confusion, and cries for help. I entered my room and saw a girl lying on one of the beds in the room.

"Hello," I softly spoke to the girl on the bed.

"Don't waste your time or breath on that one. She doesn't speak to anyone," the woman coldly announced as if the girl were not there in the room. "Her name is Shondra, and Miss Thang has not spoken to anyone since she arrived here about six months ago."

I looked over to her, watching her every move, but she didn't make a move. She just kept staring at a picture on the wall of people sitting on the grass at a picnic. Shondra was a thick Italian girl with long black hair, pale skin, brown eyes, and a longer nose.

"Have fun you two." The woman sarcastically snickered as she walked out of the room.

I started looking at the walls in the hallway again through the door in my room. I was lost in the screams of tragedy. Each and every flower I could see on the wall had so much meaning behind them. Out of nowhere, I heard a girl screaming a loud and very intense scream. My roommate who supposedly never ever talked once in the last six months of her being here jumped up.

"It's happening again," Shondra screamed as she continued to look at the picture. I did not think she knew she said it out loud.

"What, Shondra? What's happening?" I asked. I didn't get answer. Shondra just lay back down in her bed as if she'd said nothing.

Hours passed, and it was time for dinner. I left my room, and to the dining room I went. As I sat down to eat, I overheard two workers talking. It was about the scream. I heard the workers say, "A girl found her roommate dead after she committed suicide." I immediately thought, *why is this happening to me? I hate this place already*. After I was done eating I went to my room.

Exactly an hour later a man came by saying, "Lights out, ladies."

Shondra had already gone to sleep. I turned off the lights and lay in my bed. I could not go to sleep at all, and all I could think about was Tyrone's face, his voice, and the way he looked at me. I started to feel the same surge of anger I felt that night. The truth was if I had the chance I would do it all over again. My soul wept, and my heart was dying. My mom was gone. I couldn't stop thinking about her. I never knew how much hatred you could have for one person. I tried to protect myself, and all I got as a reward was to be stuck in a crazy house for the rest of my life. These thoughts made me so angry, but I finally fell asleep.

The next day I woke up. Today I was told I had to go speak to someone once a week. I actually felt like this was a great idea because I did not have anyone else to talk to. My roommate never spoke, and everyone else was a little too insane to talk to. Demented, deranged, mad, or whatever you wanted to call it.

I walked along with some random lady I hadn't met before. I entered Mrs. Sims's office. Mrs. Sims was a dark-skinned African American woman. She was very overweight, and she was short and had very short hair.

"Hi, Renee, please take a seat." She smiled.

"I didn't know we were already on a first-name basis. Call me Miss Turner, please," I rudely stated as I sat down. Only a friend could call me Renee, and I trusted no one in this place.

"How is your day so far?" she asked with this fake happiness in her voice.

I studied her for a while before I answered. I could tell she wasn't sincere. She had done this a million times before. "As good as it could possibly be living in this place."

After our session, Mrs. Sims gave me a notebook so I could start writing about my emotions. "I will surely put this to great use," I said sarcastically as I walked out of her office. In my head, I could already tell she knew I wasn't going to write in this bullshit. I thought it would be nice to talk to someone around here, but why would I want to talk to someone who wasn't genuine with me? *No, thanks. I'd rather not speak to anyone at all.*

***

A week later, Tuesday morning, it was time to visit Mrs. Sims again. I sat in her office with the notebook in my hand.

Mrs. Sims asked, "Have you written anything yet?"

"Why should I?" I replied. Then I added quietly, "I can see right through you."

"What was that, Renee?" Mrs. Sims asked.

"I asked you not to call me Renee!" I repeated. At this point I was angry. My mom was the only person who mainly called me Renee. I remembered a couple times Tyrone called me Nae. I calmed down a little because at least she didn't call me Nae. "I'm sorry. Please just don't call me Renee," I said.

She reassuringly smiled. "Okay, Miss Turner. Is that better?"

I thought she was happy to see I had a little self-control. I had so much anger inside of me. Why did I have to be in here? I asked myself that even though I knew the answer to that question.

Mrs. Sims started talking about religion. "Do you believe in God?" she asked.

"I did believe in God once before. Why?"

"Well, why do you not believe in God anymore?" she quizzed as she wrote some notes down about me.

I really did not like talking to a stranger about personal things, especially when she was only talking to me because she was getting paid. But there was something about her that made me want to keep talking. "Because I was a good child. I respected my mother and believed in God but . . ." I could not finish my sentence.

"But what, Miss Turner? Go ahead. You can tell me."

"But my mom got killed by my stepfather, and now I'm stuck in this place." I paused for a second. "So why should I believe in Him? He ain't did shit to help me when I needed Him."

"You need to open up your heart and let all these evil emotions out."

When our time was up, Mrs. Sims said she wanted to see me Friday, too. Of course, she reminded me to write in my notebook. I went to my room and noticed Shondra staring at the picture on the wall. She wasn't making a sound, as usual. I continued to look at her for a minute, and it actually looked like she was counting the people in the picture on the wall.

I started seeing Mrs. Sims twice a week after that. A lot of time went by. I didn't know how much. It seemed like weeks, or maybe months. But maybe it was just a few days. I was so confused. I

started to think about how I wasn't open to letting
God in my life yet. But I was starting to trust Mrs.
Sims. I gained so much respect for her in such a
little amount of time. I felt an ounce of happiness.
This feeling was weird and unusual because I had
been pissed for what seemed so long now.

The time between sessions sometimes went by
so slowly. Wednesday, Thursday, and now it was
finally Friday. I was ready to talk to Mrs. Sims, but
it was still twenty minutes before the time for me
to go. I couldn't wait anymore. I was walking down
these halls finding myself looking at the flowers on
the walls once again.

I finally reached her office after walking these
long halls thinking about the stories behind
these flowers. I stopped because I could see that
her door to her office was mostly closed but open
just a little. I could hear voices inside. I started to
walk away, but I heard my name. "Renee," I heard
Mrs. Sims say. She knew I didn't like being called
Renee. I told her that time after time. So I did not
walk away. I stayed and listen to their conversation.

"She's making progress," Mrs. Sims said. I smiled
with joy even though I was mad she had called
me Renee. "But she's a brat with an attitude problem." The other lady laughed as Mrs. Sims went
on. "I don't think I can help this one. She is a fire-
cracker. We talked about God. She doesn't believe
in Him." Mrs. Sims went on and on telling this
lady my business.

I was angry, annoyed, and irritated. I trusted this bitch. How could she do this to me?

I heard the lady say, "It's almost time. I'm going to be back to talk about the rest later!"

She started walking toward the door. I noticed her face. She was an Asian lady with long hair, and she was very short, just about Mrs. Sims's height. I knew this lady's face. I'd seen her before. It just came to me that she was the same random lady who took me to Mrs. Sims's office the first time I went.

I ran to my room so annoyed. I hated her now, and I never wanted to speak to her again. I punched the wall and left a hole in it. My fist started to bleed. Shondra stared at me with no lifelike emotions, then she started looking at the picture on the wall again. This time I could even hear her in a light and very low voice counting the people in the picture.

Chapter Four

I always thought of times I shared with my father, Juan, and my mother, Theresa. My dad was Mexican and Mom was African American, so I always had different backgrounds as a kid, at least before my father left us. The best time I had with my mom and my dad was when I was nine, but it was also the last time I saw my father.

Oh, yeah, I remembered those days my father and mother and I would go to the amusement park. We would always get on the Ferris wheel two times before playing in the arcade. Oh, how I missed sitting between my mother and father on the Ferris wheel. It felt like the safest place in the world. But like all good days, there are always bad days to come. The day my father left was a tragic moment in my life for me. It made me feel empty, like there would always be something missing. And I knew it would feel like that for my mother too.

It was early Saturday morning. I had just woken up from the sound of my mother crying. I walked into the living room and saw my mother with over fifty tissues around her on the floor.

"What's wrong, Mama?" I looked wide-eyed sitting beside her.

"Nothing, honey. Just a little tired, that's all." My mom wiped the tears from her eyes.

"Then why are you crying, Mom? Do you cry when you're tired?" I asked, knowing she was lying.

"I'm just tired, hon, that's all. Nothing is wrong with me," she repeated in an annoyed tone of voice.

My dad walked through the door with a lady with long, blond hair. She was very short and very skinny. She had on a blue sleeveless shirt and a short skirt.

"So this is her? This is the woman you put over your wife and daughter?" My mother was heated, crying even harder.

"Theresa, please do not start this with me. We have talked about this a thousand times before. We have grown apart from each other, and its time we move on," my father replied.

I was still baffled. I had no idea what was happening and why they were arguing. My father looked at me but said nothing at all. He looked ashamed.

"What's going on? Why are you two arguing?" I looked toward my mother and father for answers.

"You're too young to understand, Renee. You will understand someday," my father told me, wanting to shut me up.

"No, she is not too young. Your father is leaving us, Renee. He is not going to live here anymore."

"Well, Mom, where is he going to live then?"

"With that home-wrecking whore over there." My mother pointed to the short lady with fever in her voice.

"Why are you leaving, Daddy? I don't want you to go."

"Look, sweetheart, Daddy will always love you, and I will always be right here for you. But Mommy and Daddy need to be apart for a while to clear our heads. There's more to it than that, but I can't tell you just yet. But in the future, you will understand, when you're older. You will still see me but just on the weekends. Or I will come visit you a lot. It will be as if I were still living here," my dad claimed, kneeling down and hugging me.

As my dad continued, I did not listen anymore. I felt like he did not even care about me anymore. My dad never even gave me a good reason for him leaving, if you asked me. "No, I want you to stay. Don't go! Don't go, Daddy. Don't go!" I said and started crying. I truly did not want my dad to leave us, and I just could not understand why he was leaving.

"See? Look what you have done. How could you sit there and let your daughter cry? You are really just going to leave us like this?" my mother yelled at my father.

"I have to go. You act like you don't get it, but I explained all of this to you, Theresa. What don't you understand? Sorry, Renee, but I just have to go," my father said, getting off the ground.

I hated this, and it felt like someone was stealing my most precious gift in the world right out of my hands. It was hard even thinking of my parents not being together.

My dad walked out the door without even looking back, and this was why I felt like my father did not have even an inch of care for me. After that day I never saw him. He never called or came over like he said he would. Everything that my dad said about coming to see me on the weekends and coming to visit was all a lie. And this did not help with me thinking that my dad did not care about me. He missed my birthday and Christmas, Thanksgivings, Halloween. He basically missed my whole life. Even though I hated him for this, I still missed him deep down in my heart. I loved him. But I could not help but think that if he were still with my mother, the things I had dealt with in my life would probably have not happened. Still, to this day, I thought of the day my dad left and how that changed me, and how that was another part in my life that made me who I was today.

Chapter Five

I never went to the meeting with Mrs. Sims. I could not take seeing her backstabbing face anymore. A guard came to my room to ask me why I was not at the meeting. I lied and told him that I could not go because I wasn't feeling well.

The nurse still always came in my room every day to bring me my daily medication. I never knew the nurse's name, which was sad because I saw her every day since I'd been here. I always acted like I took the medicine that the nurse would bring to me every day. However, when she would leave my room, I would take the pills out of my mouth, wrap them up in a piece of paper, and put them under my bed in my room.

The pills really started to add up. First, there were about ten pills under my bed, but after a while, it seemed like a couple hundred. I only took the medicine once, and it was the first night I stayed in here. But I never took the pills again. When I took them my first day I felt sleepy and like I had no control over myself. It kind of felt like I was in a dream world and could not wake up. I had more control of my anger issues when I took those pills, but I didn't have control over anything else in my life.

I stayed in my room for a week straight. The only time I left my room was when I needed to shower, use the restroom, or eat. I did not do any extra activities that week. Shondra always stayed in our room as well. So we saw a lot of each other that week, more than usual. Shondra was looking at that picture on the wall again, counting the people over and over again in a low voice.

"Shondra," I shouted to see her response. But she just ignored me and continued to count. "Shut the fuck up," I screamed. Of course, she didn't listen and continued to count. "Why the only time I ever hear you talk is when you are counting those fucking people in that picture?"

I'd spent about a week and a half listening to this mumbo-jumbo bullshit, and I was fed the fuck up. This was enough time to drive someone crazy if they weren't already. She did not reply. She just continued to count, and when she was done counting the people in the picture, she would just start right back over and count the people again.

I marched over to Shondra's bed. Wanting her to stop driving me nuts, I grabbed her shoulders and started to shake her hard. While I repeatedly called out her name, she still ignored me and kept at it

"Three, four, five, and six," Shondra mumbled in a trance.

I stopped shaking her, got up, and knocked the picture off the wall. I held each end of the picture, and I broke it against my knee. Shondra stopped counting because there was no longer a picture there to look at. I walked over and put the broken picture underneath my bed. If one of the workers here saw it, they would probably start asking us questions.

Then Shondra started to look at me since the picture was not on the wall anymore. "What do you wannna do, Shondra? What you want?" I bossed up as I sat on my bed. "You did not want to talk two minutes ago."

"Want? Huh," Shondra said. "There's nothing you could give me that I would possibly want."

I was stunned to hear her speak. You could see that I was shocked by looking at my face. My mouth dropped, my eyes became wide, and my eyebrows were lifted. After a moment of being silent, I spoke. "Shondra, I'm sorry for breaking that picture, but you don't understand how much I hate this place! You really don't."

"If we can agree on one thing it's our hatred for this place," Shondra agreed.

"Why do you barely speak, Shondra?" I asked, glancing over at the door as if we were doing something against the rules.

"I never want to make friends here or become comfortable with this place or these people." Shondra paused for a second then continued. "I wanted to talk to you, Renee, but I needed to know I could trust you."

Surprisingly I was not bothered by her calling me Renee. I actually enjoyed it a lot. Shondra reminded me of what was once home, being with my mother. Shondra's voice sounded a lot like my mother's voice.

"I stay quiet, and I listened to a lot. I know a lot more than most of these employees here, and when I'm not listening I'm counting," Shondra said. "I know what happened to you with Mrs. Sims."

"How do you know what happened?"

"Oh see, Renee, I was in the hall when you were at Mrs. Sims's door listening to their conversation. I'm everywhere but nowhere. Most people think I stay in this room all day, but I don't. If I did, I would have killed myself by now." Shondra took a breath then continued. "I see images in my head of places I've never been before, but I know exactly how the place is set up. I know this place from top to bottom, and I've never even been through this whole building. I know you are wondering why I count the people in the picture. I count the people in the picture to keep my mind off of thinking about how lonely I am and what I have seen here since I've been here."

This was the most I'd ever heard Shondra speak, and she spoke a lot, I tell you, a lot.

"How do you know if you never looked through this place to see?" I asked, and I had a million more questions in my head I wanted to ask her.

"Follow me, girl. I'll show you." She motioned as we left the room.

We were standing at the bottom of some stairs in the hallway. Shondra kept quiet until the hallway was fully cleared. I could tell she didn't want anyone to hear us talking as the hall was finally cleared.

Shondra spoke very quietly. "Upstairs is a big room with blue walls, and three windows on each one of the four walls up there. Glitter on the wooden floor. How odd is that? Wait! I can see something else. Come on!"

We went through the door, which was unlocked. Everything looked as she'd explained. We made a right and kept walking straight until we got in front of the first window on the nearest wall. "This is what I saw, Renee. There's a map underneath that piece of wood in the floor. Underneath," Shondra repeated.

I picked up the piece of wood. "All I see is an empty bag." I picked up the bag, and in there was a very small map of this entire place.

Later that night we were in our room. I had the map underneath my pillow.

"Why are you here? What did you do?" I finally asked Shondra.

"I see things, like I said earlier. One time I was watching the news in my classroom at school. The teacher and a cop were explaining how you need to be safe. The news showed a picture of a man they were looking for. He was last seen at a park taking two kids and putting them in the back of his car. Out of nowhere, I could see his face in my head. 'There he is,' I yelled out loud. 'There he is.' I couldn't control myself. Everyone started to stare at me. I knew they all thought I was crazy. He killed the little boy, and I could see the room he and the little girl were in. They were in a basement, an empty basement. And three months later I'm here. They made me come here, but I wanted to help. I'm only fifteen, and I'm stuck in this place. After they found the kids in a basement, just like I told them, I got locked up in this mental house, so I stopped talking. What was the point of helping them if they weren't helping me? All they were doing was hurting me by making me come here."

"Girl, that's messed up. Where is all your family?"

"I don't know. At first, they were coming to see me here. But I wasn't talking to anyone, so I guess they stopped coming to see me. In reality, I just wish they had fought harder to keep me out of this place. My family did not even try at all." Shondra answered my question with a disappointed voice.

***

A few days passed. It was time for me to go to Mrs. Sims again. Of course, I didn't want to go, but they forced me.

"You were doing so well for a while. Why did you stop coming?" Mrs. Sims asked.

"Bullshit!" I rolled my eyes.

"What?" Mrs. Sims responded in a surprised voice.

"I know exactly what you did. I trusted you not to tell my business," I said with anger in my voice.

"I didn't. I didn't, Miss Turner," Mrs. Sims argued.

"I heard you with my own ears. I hate you! You're going to lie to my face, too?" Mrs. Sims was quiet for a while. "Is there anyone I can trust?" I frowned, but she did not respond. "Ha, that is exactly what I thought." I smirked as I walked out of her office.

I went back to my room and lay in my bed. "I want to leave, Shondra. Get all my stuff and leave," I said, even though I knew I didn't have much. I'd been there a long time, and I thought I would never like it there, let alone get comfortable. "You wanna come with me?"

"No, I can't. But I will help you use the map to escape," Shondra said.

I never knew why she said she couldn't come, but I never thought to ask and find out. It took us a week to plan my escape. I was thin, but the basement window was a little too small, so for that whole week at lunch, Shondra would eat my food at lunch time. This was the only way we could try to make me lose a little weight in order to fit through that basement window.

I would put my food in a napkin then hand it to her under the table. One time we almost got caught. "What are you doing, ladies?" a lady in a black suit asked us.

"Nothing," I responded as I slowly dropped the napkin on the floor, the cornbread muffin wrapped inside of it.

"Well, do not keep your hands under the table. Leave them on top of the table," the lady told me.

I put my hand on top of the table. She looked at them then walked off.

The next day it was time for me to go through with this escape. This day felt like it took forever to come. Shondra had the gate outside already cracked open for me from the day before. All I had to do was make it outside without getting caught.

I picked the lock on our room door with my bobby pin I had in my hair. It was ten o'clock and dark outside. The big male security guard in the hallway was asleep in his chair. I stole the keys to the basement, which were on the floor right next to him.

I stared off at the walls again but for a while this time. Flowers were everywhere. I could feel the emotions behind these flowers again. They were so intense, even more intense than usual. Why did it take me so long to find out what these flowers and emotions represented? Well, I knew now. All these flowers represented the people in here, including me.

"Are you coming?" Shondra said very quietly from down the hall, standing in front of the basement door.

"Yeah, yeah, I'm coming." I snapped out of my thoughts about these flowers. I walked down the stairs. "Bye, girl. I promise this will not be the last time I see you."

"You promise, Renee?" Shondra asked me.

"I swear on my life."

I walked down the basement stairs. It was pretty dark. I took my time walking down the stairs so I would not make a lot of noise and so I would not fall. I could hardly see. The only light was from the open door at the top of the stairs where Shondra was standing.

I walked over to the window and opened it. I looked back for the last time, then I left. It was the spring, so the weather was pretty nice, but still, the night air hit me with a chill. Lights were flashing on the entire building. The lights flashed my way. I hit the ground so fast. I lay in the grass for a quick second while my heart was beating as fast as lightning. Once the light moved, I got up and stayed as low and close to the ground as possible. I quickly walked through the gate, closing it behind me and not looking back.

Overall, I had spent a few months of my life at Calming Meadows. I kept running. Starting to feel dizzy from not eating this entire week, I still continued to run. The air was hitting my body as I ran and ran. The air made me feel so free and happy even though my body was ready to give out.

Chapter Six

I would say hiding out for so long was the hardest thing I had ever done in my life. I had been away from the hospital for some months now, I thought. I hadn't really been able to keep up with time. It was weird not having anyone to talk to but myself. I never thought I needed the medication from the hospital until now. I was starting to actually feel a little crazy.

I had been living in an abandoned building behind the subway. I ate from garbage cans, I had not taken a bath, and I accompanied the rats. I did not even know what part of Cleveland I was in. I couldn't even remember the last time I had a good meal. Even when I was at the hospital, they served food that tasted like garbage. But I had to say the hospitals meals sure sounded good to me right now. I craved that dry roast beef and mashed potatoes with a side of garlic bread.

The place was dark and deserted. It had nothing but me and the rats and roaches living in the walls. I was scared of rats and roaches when I was a little kid, but at this point in my life, I did not believe I was scared of anything anymore. I was going crazy just sitting in the dark with no one to talk to. I started to have conversations with myself, and it sounded crazy, but finally, someone was listening to me.

It was in the evening, I guessed around 8:00 p.m., and I knew this because it started to get dark outside. Every day at this time a little mouse would come from a little hole in the wall. He would nibble around for food as I watched out of boredom. He never did notice I was right behind him every time. If he had, he would have run away. He ran out of the hole in the wall fast, looking for food to eat, blinded by the huge human figure behind it. The mouse stopped at a small piece of meat I had from the trashcan earlier. I never knew if the mouse was a boy or a girl, so I just called the mouse a boy all the time.

The mouse stayed there on top of the meat, nibbling around it. I got up as quiet as I could to sneak up and grab it. I got close, and just before he could run, I grabbed his tail and held it upside down. I let the mouse go, and the mouse ran back into the hole in the wall.

"I guess I scared it," I said to myself.

I was alone and was losing my mind just sitting in the dark with no food to eat and no one to talk to. I left the empty house and went to the nearby store.

I didn't know what day it was and what exact time it was. I hadn't been around a clock or calendar in a very long time. I entered the store and saw the clock on the wall. It was 9:05 p.m. I felt like everyone in the store was looking at me.

"What the fuck are you guys looking at? I'm not an alien," I said loudly.

"Brazen-ass crackheads these days," I heard this lady say under her breath.

I just ignored her and went up to the man who worked at the store. "What year is it?" I asked.

"It's 2018, miss," the store clerk responded.

"2018? There's no way two years passed that fast," I said louder than I thought.

"Excuse me?" the store clerk asked as everyone in the store looked at me.

"Nothing. Thanks a lot, sir."

I started walking to the door of the store. "I'm pretty hungry. I wonder what has been thrown out in the trash," I said to myself.

I couldn't believe that it was 2018. I'd spent two whole years hiding out, two whole birthdays that I wasn't aware of. I must have been going crazy, but I didn't care too much because I was so hungry. I checked to see if anyone was around before going outside to dig in the trash. Even though I wanted food, it was kind of embarrassing to dig in trash. I found a half-eaten sandwich, and I ate it as if I had not eaten for days. My feet stuck out from the black trashcan because I had failed attempting to grab the rest of the sandwich.

All of a sudden I heard two deep male voices behind me. "Excuse me, young lady. Please get out of the trash and come here," one of the men said.

I got out of the trashcan, and I saw two male officers. One was very tall, kind of heavyset, and had a long brown beard. The other had a very nice defined face with green eyes. He was pretty muscular with dark short hair. The heavyset white officer pointed the flashlight at me to see my face.

"Step forward, miss, and take your hands out of your pockets," the heavyset officer said.

To be truthful, I was kind of scared. I thought they would take me to jail because they might have known who I was. Hell, eventually they would return me to the mental hospital. I had seen both of their name tags when I walked up. The heavyset officer was Tanner Braylock, and the cute officer was Keithon James.

"How old are you, miss?" Officer James asked me.

"I'm eighteen," I said. If two years had gone by, I'd be close enough.

"Why are you out in this kind of neighborhood digging through garbage? You don't have a home?"

Officer Braylock quizzed, looking at my filthy appearance.

"No, I don't. I'm homeless, sir," I told the officer.

"Where are your mother and your father? We can't just leave you here. You are too young to be out here in these streets," said James.

"Oh, come on, James. She looks fine to me, and she's eighteen anyway," Braylock said jokingly.

"I'm okay here. You guys can just leave. I'm good. I was just a little hungry, that's all."

"I can't have that on my conscience, that I left a woman on the street digging through trashcans. I can take you to a shelter right up the block from here," Officer James kindly urged.

We walked to the police car. He opened the door for me and closed it before we took off.

"So you never answered our question. Where is your parents?" He seemed honestly concerned.

"My parents are both dead. I don't have any." I was telling half the truth at least. Of course, I lied about my father being dead, because he was alive. But after he left I didn't have a father. So yup, he was as good as dead because he was not in my life or there for me.

"Oh, I'm so sorry. So tell me what happened for a girl like you to become homeless?" Tanner Braylock finally got involved in the conversation.

"All bad luck I guess," I said jokingly.

"I hear that. Shit happens," Tanner Braylock replied, laughing.

"What is your name?" Officer James continued with the twenty questions.

"Renee. My name is Renee."

"Cool. My name is Keithon James. This is my partner, Tanner Braylock," he told me as he looked back at me from the front of the police car.

We pulled up in front of an old, dingy, flat building. There were a lot of homeless people walking around the place. If I could describe how it looked, I would say it looked like a project.

"Well, we're here. It's not that bad, Renee, and it's better than being homeless."

I exited the car, but Officer James ran behind me to give me something. "Hey, here is my contact card. If you have any questions or need help with anything at all, just call me and I'll be here." I could tell he meant every word he said.

"Why are you helping me? You don't even know me," I said.

"Well, a young, beautiful girl such as you should not be on the streets. It is not safe. Now promise me you are going to call me if you have any trouble. I'm just up the block, remember that, okay?" He grinned while holding the shelter door open for me. "And if I don't hear from you, I'm gonna come looking."

Obviously, he was a nice guy and nice looking, too. His words kind of made me feel a way I had not felt in a long time.

True to his word, Officer James started to visit the shelter to check up on me every other day. The more he came to visit me, the more we connected. Then, feelings started to show. We were on more than a first-name basis, but I still couldn't reveal my true identity.

Chapter Seven

Waking up this morning actually felt good for once in a very long time. I was happy, but the last time I trusted someone it didn't work out. The walls in this place were dirty, and the paint was chipped, but for some reason it was beautiful. Or maybe just the thought of seeing Keithon's face almost every day was beautiful. This was so much better than seeing those flowers on the walls at the mental house. Most people stayed on the first floor, but since Keithon knew the owners, I was able to sleep upstairs last night by myself. I walked downstairs only to see him in the kitchen. I could hear him from upstairs. I wondered why he was here.

"What are you doing?" I laughed, standing at the bottom of the stairs. The kitchen was right across from the stairs.

Keithon turned around and replied, "Want something to eat?" with a smile on his face.

"Yeah, of course I want something to eat," I said. My stomach was hurting from hunger.

We sat at the small, dusty table that was in the room connected to the kitchen. This shelter didn't look terrible. It looked like it used to be nice a very long time ago. Keithon put the food on the table. It was nothing but some canned peaches, chili, and bread. It was not much, but it was the best thing I'd eaten in a long time.

"So, Renee, did you rest well?"

"Yes, I did. How about you?"

"Yeah, but I was wondering if you were going to try to run away since you've been living on the streets."

This was awkward, so I changed the subject since he didn't actually know I ran away from the mental hospital. "So how did you become a police officer?"

"Well, when I was a child my grandfather was a police officer. I looked up to him." He continued as I drifted off. He was so cute, the way he smiled. I could not help to think about how much I was attracted to him.

"You are so cute," I giggled out loud, not knowing that I did.

"Thank you," Keithon told me as he blushed.

I finally noticed that I said it out loud. "Oh, Jesus," I said, knowing inside my head that calling on Jesus was wrong because He never helped me before in my life.

Keithon James stood up and grabbed my hand. "Come on."

I got up and followed him. We walked upstairs, and Keithon just stood in the middle of the hall. I looked up, and I saw him reaching for the door. Keithon opened up the door, and a ladder fell down. He grabbed my hand and helped me climb up them as he followed me. I had a lot of questions in my head, but I stopped myself from asking. When we got to the top, there was a room that kind of looked like a hideout to me. Keithon started telling me how he believed a drug dealer lived here because usually, that was what these hidden rooms in neighborhoods like this were used for. This was hard to believe since it was a shelter.

Keithon grabbed my hand and said, "I want to show you something else that I found out about this shelter."

We walked to the end of the room, and Keithon grabbed a chair. He stood on top of it and pushed on the wall. A big square of the wall came off. I looked up at the missing piece of the wall, and all I could see was the sky. We went on the roof. It was early in the morning, so the sun was just starting to rise. We sat on the roof, watching the sunrise.

"This is beautiful," I told Keithon.

"You are beautiful, Renee Turner. I just don't understand you. I'm trying to figure you out. You seem like you have a beautiful soul."

At this time my smile was no longer on my face. I stared off at the sky as the sun continued to rise. I knew he could feel me becoming distance. I could feel myself falling for this guy, but I couldn't handle someone else hurting me. This was the most confusing thing ever, wanting someone but not knowing if it was worth the risk of being hurt again.

Keithon moved in closer to me, so close to where his leg was touching mine. His body was slightly turned, and he put his hand on my cheek, turning my head to him. Then he looked me in my eyes. No one ever looked at me like this before.

"It's going to be okay," he softly whispered in my ear. He did not let me go. But this was the first time I ever felt 100 percent safe in my whole life.

Hours passed, and later I was in my room, lying in bed and trying to go to sleep, but for some reason, I could not go to sleep. I walked downstairs where I saw his fine ass sitting on the couch in the back room that was separated from the main room of the shelter. I went to lie next to him, and I put my head on his chest as he wrapped his arm around me. I fell asleep in his arms, and that was when I knew I was catching feelings for my knight in shining armor.

Chapter Eight

Keithon and I bonded a lot over the next month. Every morning I would wake up to a warm cooked breakfast of eggs, bacon, buttered toast, and orange juice. Keithon really did take care of me, as if I were his wife or child. He even bought me clothes because the last things I had looked like dirty rags on me.

I started to have deep feelings for him. I thought Keithon started to have deep feelings for me too. Well, at least that was how it felt. I felt weird thinking this way. I guessed it was because I had not felt compassion in a very long time. I loved everything about Officer Keithon James: his smile, his personality, the way he took care of me, and I love that I found someone I could connect with. And, for this moment, I felt that God had not forgotten about me, and God put Keithon in my life to show me He really hadn't forgotten. This gave me a warm feeling in my heart. Maybe I was starting to believe in God again. Religion was something I left behind for a long time once my mom died, and

I didn't notice this until Mrs. Sims talked to me about it. I guessed that was one thing Mrs. Sims was good for.

Today Keithon made plans for me to meet his mother and his father at their house. He told me so much about his parents. In fact, he talked about them every day. He said his mother and father were very wealthy, and that they owned their own bank called Credit One in New York. They lived in New York, too. That was where he and all his family were born. That was a great thing, but I came from no wealthy family, and I lived in Cleveland. What if they looked down on me? What if they asked about my occupation and I couldn't answer? All these questions were going in and out of my head. I was pretty nervous going to meet his parents.

I tried to wear the best sundress Keithon bought me. I tried on both dresses. First I tried on the orange dress with the orange and white lined bolero and the all-black flat sandals. But I did not like that one so much, so I tried on another dress, which was the black-and-white sundress with my white flat shoes, which showed most of my feet but were not open-toed. I loved it.

"I think this will be okay. What do you think, bae?" I asked.

Keithon was looking at me through the mirror, standing right behind me. "I think it looks perfect on you, but you do not have to dress up to meet my parents. All you have to do is smile, and they will love you."

"Oh, I know. I'm just very nervous meeting your parents," I said as I turned around to hug Keithon.

"Why are you so nervous? My parents are nice. You can trust me. I would not lie to you. But I am an only child, and if my parents show you too much attention, I may get kind of jealous," Keithon replied jokingly.

We hugged and kissed then got ready to leave. I was still pretty nervous but not as much as before now. He was wearing khaki pants and a navy blue sweater, with navy blue dress shoes.

At Keithon's red Charger, he opened my door and waited until I got in. It was eight hours driving from Ohio to where Keithon parents still lived in New York. I never knew why Keithon moved from New York to Cleveland when his family still stays in New York. I thought about asking, but I was not sure if he wanted to talk about it. About three and a half hours passed. I could tell Keithon was getting a little tired of driving, but I was still wondering about why he moved to Cleveland and did not stay in New York anymore. Ten more minutes passed, and I finally got the courage to ask.

"Keithon?"

"Yes? What is wrong?"

"Nothing. I was just wondering, why did you leave New York and move to Cleveland?" I asked.

"Well, one of the reasons was I was grown, and I wanted to be a cop, and I thought Cleveland would be a new start and a good place to protect people. All the crime here is just really exciting."

I thought how there were other cities full of crime he could have gone to, and especially in New York, there was a lot of crime. But I just ignored my thoughts. "Why did you need a new start?"

"It is just a long story, and I do not feel like talking about it," Keithon told me.

I knew a drive to New York from Cleveland was about an eight-hour drive, so we had more than enough time for him to tell me about whatever had happened. But I just left it alone, because I knew he just did not want to talk about it right now. I thought we were close enough to talk about anything and everything, but maybe he just needed time. I did not know, but of course, I was overthinking it, wondering what Keithon wasn't telling me. It was a long, boring car ride, and I had nothing else to think about.

"How old are you, Keithon?" I finally asked, because I'd never thought before to ask him this question, even though he knew my age already.

"I'm twenty-seven years old. What is with all the questions, Renee?"

"I don't know. There's just a lot of stuff I don't know about you, so I wanted to find out."

"All right, well, anything you want to know you can ask me, and I'll let you know," Keithon told me while he reached to hold my left hand with his right.

Thirty minutes passed, and he never let go of my hand until we saw a motel. He had to park the car in the motel parking lot.

"Wait here. I will be back." He left the car and walked to the little office building for this motel.

The Paradise Motel was the name. It was written on the side of the dirty building. The building had once been painted cream but was now turning brownish. This was not paradise at all. Matter of fact, that was a silly name to give any motel. Motels were usually dirty and nothing like paradise. When I thought of paradise, I thought of some beautiful place off the beach, not a dirty motel. I could go on and on about how dirty this place was, but to be honest, it was way better than that abandoned house I was staying in.

Keithon walked back to the car. "Come on, let's go," he told me as he grabbed my bag and his bag. I followed him to a motel room we had to walk up some stairs to get to. It was room 208. Keithon unlocked the door, and we went inside. It was a small room, with one bed on the left side of the room. There was a tiny TV across from the bed on the right side of the room. The TV was on top of the one dresser in the room. I took out my stuff on the side of the bed and sat on the bed. There was no reason to put my things in the dresser because we were not going to stay long. We were just going to sleep here then leave tomorrow.

There was a small space between the bed and the TV, and Keithon walked straight through it to the small bathroom. The bathroom had just enough room for the small shower, the toilet, and the sink.

When Keithon went to the bathroom, I just was sitting on the bed, looking around. This was not that bad. Well yes, it was a small room, but it was really clean, unlike the outside of the building. I guessed that's why they say to never judge a book by its cover. While Keithon was still in the bathroom, I couldn't help but think, *what if he tries something?* This was going to be our first time sleeping in a bed together, but nothing happened, thank God. I wasn't ready for that. Keithon and I fell asleep in each other's arms.

The next day came up fast. I got in the shower then got dressed. Keithon went in after me, and after we were both dressed, we headed out. It was 6:00 a.m. when we left the motel. We drove the last four and a half hours to New York only stopping to get gas and to use the bathroom. When we were finally in New York, we stopped and got a motel room there so we could stay low-key and put our clothes there so they would not be noticeable in Keithon's back seat.

After we relaxed for about an hour, we left the motel and headed to his parents' house. We pulled out from the driveway. It was about two in the afternoon, and during this time I had gotten even more nervous.

"Hey, I'm getting very nervous. Do you think we should just go another time?" I cried.

"No, you'll be just fine. I'll be right here for you, okay? If they say anything mean to you, I'll fix them, promise."

"Okay, I guess. I'm just overreacting. I'll try not to be so scared," I replied. "Where do your mother and father live?"

"They live right in the city, about a twenty-minute drive from here. Here, you can rest until then, and don't think about being nervous."

I laid my head cocked sideways against the seat, and I stared out the window. I was not tired since I'd rested at the motel, so I watched as cars drove past. Buildings looked as if they were running backward. This took my mind off of being nervous, and it was pretty relaxing. Then, when Keithon turned on the radio to the jazz station, I felt even more relaxed. I took deep breaths in and out. I closed my eyes for five minutes and thought of my mother and me playing in the sprinklers.

The city was crowded as usual with cars and millions of people. The buildings were high up, touching the blue sky. The streets were so crowded that people had to walk in the streets.

"We are here, Renee."

The condos looked huge. They were big and built upward. The windows were wide, and probably looking down from them you could see a lot of New York outside. We walked to the elevators because his parents lived at the very top of one building. He told me that the more you go up, the bigger the rooms are. So I was guessing they lived in the biggest condo here, and my God, I guessed they were very rich. We exited the see-through elevator and knocked on the black-and-white door.

"You will be fine, I promise," he said, putting his arm over my shoulder.

When the door opened, a petite white woman opened the door, serving hugs to me and Keithon. "Now, Keithon, you have to introduce me to this beautiful girl standing here," Mrs. James said.

"Well, Mom, this is Renee."

"Renee, it's so nice to meet you, dear. Both of you come inside and have a seat in the living room."

We walked into the living room, and a big window showed the whole world when you looked from it.

"What would you guys like to drink?" Keithon's mother asked, walking into the kitchen.

"Do you like lemon tea, Renee?" Keithon asked me.

"Yes, that's my favorite."

"We will both have tea, Mom," Keithon screamed to her.

"I love this condo. It looks amazing, and it's very big," I said.

"Oh, yeah, it's pretty big. I love it too. Imagine growing up in it."

Mrs. James came out of the kitchen and handed us our lemon teas. She sat next to me and watched us as we took the first sip. "How does it taste? It's not too sweet, is it?" Mrs. James asked.

"No, it's fine," Keithon and I both responded at the same time.

"So, Renee, tell me about yourself. How old are you? Where do you work? Do you have any kids?" Keithon's mother asked.

"Mom, come on now," Keithon said, cutting her off and smiling at me.

"I'm just curious. Renee, I've heard so much about you, but Keithon never told me how beautiful you are," Mrs. James said while holding my hand.

"Oh, thank you, Mrs. James," I said, smiling.

"Um, Mom, where is Dad?" Keithon asked while sipping the lemon tea.

"He went goofing around with a couple of friends from work. He will be back in a few hours. If he's not back in time to meet you, I'll tell him you came over," Mrs. James replied.

We sat and talked for hours. I even saw old pictures of Keithon when he was a baby. Keithon was always cute, even when he was a baby.

Keithon's mother treated me nice the whole time. She asked questions that were a little weird, but overall she was very sweet. But then the question came up that scared me.

Mrs. James asked me, "So where did you two meet?"

I was ready to tell the truth when Keithon said, "Um, we met in the grocery store. She dropped her wallet, and when I picked it up, we looked into each other's eyes. And from then on we have talked ever since."

He saved my life with a big lie, but it looked as if Mrs. James did not believe him. "Wow that's something," Mrs. James replied sarcastically.

Then we all spent a couple more hours on small talk.

"I'll see you later, Mother. Don't forget to tell Dad I was here," Keithon told his mother.

"Okay, and it was so nice to meet you, Renee," Mrs. James said, hugging us both then letting us out the door.

Back on the way to the motel, I asked him why he told that lie to his mother for me. He told me he would do anything for me, and he thought he found the one woman he could spend the rest of his life with.

This meant a lot to me. I felt the same way about Keithon.

As we drove, I looked out the window at the houses, big ones and little ones. One stood out to me. It looked a lot like my grandmother's house I went to when I was really young. It was a normal-sized house with bricks. It had a pink door, and the windows were outlined with pink. I never knew why I never saw my grandmother again, but I'd never forget that house for some reason. Maybe she'd died, or maybe she moved far away where she could not visit.

As we passed the house, I turned my head to see it once more. "That is her house!" I said to myself. I knew it was my grandmother's house at this point because I noticed the paint drawing on the side of the house of my name and the name of one of my childhood friends. "Renee and Todd" was written on her house. Maybe this was why I hardly saw my grandmother. I never knew when we went to her house it was all the way in New York. But then again if we went a lot when I was little, that was not a good reason to just stop going.

I remembered that day because Todd and I got in a lot of trouble for painting on her house. It was around the time she first moved in this house, and it was one of the first times my mom ever got mad at me. My mom was always a nice lady and hardly ever got herself upset, other than the time my dad left us. Even when Tyrone hit her, she was hardly ever upset. Maybe she just knew that once my dad

left, our life was going to go downhill from there.
Maybe that's why she was so upset with my dad.
He was the first love of her life.

This made me just continue to think about how
much I was loving my life right now and how I felt
the same about Keithon. But I hoped he'd never
just leave me like my dad did to my mom. I did not
know how I could deal with something like that.
That was why I would always know how strong of a
person my mom was.

But where my grandmother was, I guess I
would never know. My mom never told me why
we stopped going to see her. Maybe I was just too
young to understand.

Chapter Nine

Keithon and I went to see his mother and father again. We arrived, and Keithon's father answered the door.

"Oh, hey, son," Mr. James said.

"Hello, Dad, how are you?"

"Hey, Mr. James, I'm Renee," I said.

He replied, "Hello, young lady. Nice to meet you finally."

His mom was cooking. You could smell the food from the front door.

"This smell is amazing," I said as Mrs. James walked out of the kitchen to the front door.

"Well, thank you very much, Renee," Mrs. James responded.

We sat down at the table. Ten minutes in we were all eating at the table. Mrs. James seemed a little quiet. This was kind of weird, but I ignored it and continued to eat. Two more minutes passed, and I had to use the bathroom.

"Please excuse me," I said, and I asked where their bathroom was located.

"Go straight up the stairs, then make a right, and you will see the bathroom," Mrs. James told me.

I walked upstairs and entered the bathroom. As I was using the bathroom, I could not help but hear voices through the heat vent in the bathroom. I got up and washed my hands fast. I cracked the door open, and I could hear the voices more clearly.

"She is no good, son!" Mrs. James told Keithon. "I invited you here to let you know the cops have been coming around here more and more lately asking questions about her."

"She was in a mental hospital and escaped! We told the police she's with you. But did you know this?" Mr. James asked.

After I heard Mr. James say that, I walked down the stairs, nervous because I knew Keithon did not know about me escaping the mental house. Of course, the first thing I thought as I walked down the stairs was whether Keithon would judge me and no longer care about me since I lied to him.

Keithon came over to me and grabbed my hand tight. He walked me to the elevator. As the elevator door was closing, Mrs. James yelled, "Where are you going, Keithon? Come back!"

Once we got out of their condo building, Keithon opened the car door for me and walked to the other side and got into the car. I could see Mr. James standing at the door in his blue jeans and black-and-white button-up shirt. He was right next to

Mrs. James in her yellow and white floral dress, looking at us as we drove off.

I hadn't paid attention to how Mr. James looked until now, seeing him at the door with a disappointing look. He was a fairly tall man with black hair with light amount of gray. He had a really thick head of hair for someone as old as him. His eyes were really dark brown, almost black. I could tell right in that moment, looking at Mr. James's face, how much Keithon looked like him. I never ever wanted him to look at me the way his father was looking at us right now.

Why was this happening? Bad things were always happening to me. Keithon was silent the whole time we were driving.

"Hey, where are we going? Are you going to turn me in?" I asked him.

"I love you so much," Keithon remarked.

I could hear power in his voice, but there was also sadness. I replayed those words back-to-back in my head. He loved me, and I loved him too.

Keithon never answered my question. So I did not know where we were going, but I assumed it wasn't to go turn me in.

An hour and a half passed. I still did not know where we were going. I could see that the gas was pretty low. It was right above E. At some point, Keithon had to stop and get some gas. What made me notice the gas was low was that every two minutes Keithon would take his eyes off the road and look at the gas. It was starting to get dark outside. With the headlights on and shining bright, I could see a gas station not too far ahead of us. Keithon started to slow the car down as we got closer and closer to the gas station. Keithon turned into the gas station and parked by a gas pump.

"Stay in the car," Keithon said, and he got out of the car and walked in the gas station.

Keithon took a couple of minutes staying in the gas station. So I started looking around. There was only one car other than ours in the station. It was blue and small, and an old Asian lady was sitting in it. I could see into the lady's car, but I was only looking because I had nothing else to do while waiting for Keithon.

He finally came out of the gas station. He started pumping the gas. As the gas was pumping, he got in the car and sat down. Keithon had two bags full of things in his hand. He left the bags in the car when he got out to finish pumping the gas.

"This may be a while, so I bought some food for us to eat," he said to me, looking deep into my eyes for a second.

We stopped at the motel. Keithon went in and got all our clothes as I sat in the car waiting for him. He finally came back out two minutes later, and we started to drive again.

Chapter Ten

There I was again, hiding out, but this time I wasn't alone. I was tired of hiding and tired of running away. I still believed in God even though this was happening. And I thanked God for not turning me in and staying by my side through these last couple of days.

Keithon and I had only known each other for a little while, but to us, it felt like we knew each other for a lifetime. At this point, I knew in my heart and in my soul that Keithon loved me, and I would never second-guess this again. He and I were hiding out at his second house. Only his mother and father knew where it was. He'd never come to this house before, so he assumed that the police would not find us here or even think of this house as an option of us being here.

We kept the house very dark and stayed in the basement to make it seem like no one was here. This almost felt like I was back in the abandoned building like before where there were no lights. But at least I had food and a fellow person to keep me safe. This thought made me a little happy inside. We both stayed in the house at all times, and Keithon was still on his vacation, so he didn't have to go to work.

After years of Keithon being a police officer, he had never gone on vacation until now. He let me know that he did not think it was safe for him to go into work anyway because the police were already coming to his parents' house asking questions. He still answered his calls so everything could seem normal so the cops wouldn't think anything about him possibly having me with him somewhere. But he did avoid actually seeing the cops so he would not have to answer any questions.

"Why do you think the officers asked your parents about you and me?" I pondered.

"I really don't know, but maybe because once Officer Tanner found out who you were he told the cops he and I were the last two to see you, and how I wanted to take you to the shelter."

"Oh, okay, that is probably it. I did not even think about how Officer Tanner was there when we met," I responded.

"Yeah, Renee. I've been avoiding asking you this, but why would you lie to me? I love you, and that's why I took you here instead of turning you in, but what you did was messed up," Keithon said to me. Then silence hit the room like a wrecking ball.

I finally responded to Keithon. "Because I didn't want you to judge me and leave me. What guy wants to be with someone from a psychiatric hospital?"

"Damn, Renee. How can you make a decision like that for me?" he fumed then turned his back to me.

A few moments later he turned back around and said, "Oh, and by the way, I would have chosen you."

He and I didn't talk to each other for the rest of that night, but we connected a lot during that time of us hiding out. We told each other stories that happened in our life. It was there I told Keithon exactly why I was in the mental hospital. I literally told him almost everything from Tyrone killing my mom to how I killed Tyrone when I was trying to defend my mom. But I even told him about everything that happened while I was in the mental house. He knew everything about Shondra and how she was the only friend I made in all the time I spent in the mental house. Keithon also told me of the time he found his ex-wife with another man and that day she died in a car accident. It was a long story he told.

"That is why I wanted to move to Cleveland to get a new start," Keithon explained. "I did not feel like telling you before because it was a dark time in my life and I hate thinking about it. But my wife cheated on me a bunch of times. I found out she even cheated once with my cousin John. John and I were best friends as children, but I never talked to him again after I found out he slept with my wife. I hated her so much for hurting me like that. When she died, I felt so bad for hating her even though she had hurt me so much. But she did not deserve to die," Keithon told me then paused for a second.

Keithon took a deep breath then continued. "I'm still hurt today, but I'm a lot better. I slept with strippers and even one of my lady coworkers. I knew all of this was wrong, but I just did not know how to deal with my wife cheating and her dying soon after. I wanted to be loved, but I knew all that was not real love," Keithon told me as he started to cry, remembering all the pain he went through with his wife.

"I'm sorry," I sobbed as I hugged him tight. "I will never cheat on you."

After a couple minutes of Keithon crying, he wiped his eyes and told me how he was still legally married to his wife because she died right after he found out she was cheating, so he did not file for divorce.

In his basement, there were three rooms. We stayed in the back room with a lock on the door. In the room were packs of food, a refrigerator, our clothes, one bed, a toilet, and a lit candle. We also had a window that the sunlight would shine through every morning to wake us up. We had a small sink to wash up in and to hand wash our clothes. It was nighttime now, and Keithon and I were lying down and talking as usual.

"We are going to be just fine. I promise you I will protect you if it kills me," Keithon said while kissing my forehead.

"I feel safe in your arms, and I know you will. But how long do you think we will have to hide? I'm not saying this is not nice being with you, but I'm just tired of hiding," I said, sitting up and looking Keithon in the eyes.

"I don't know, Renee. I really do not know how long we will need to hide. But until then we will be safe down here. We have food, a toilet, things to wash up with, and each other. You do not have to worry. This will all be over soon, and we can live a normal life together," Keithon said, holding me in his arms.

After all of what he just said to me, all I really heard him say was "together," and I loved the sound of that. Us together always was nice to me. I wasn't alone. I knew he was there for me. Millions search their lives for someone who cares for them as much as Keithon cared for me. And I, a woman from a mental hospital, had found a man who would do anything for me. I loved this man with all of my heart, and I knew he loved me with all of his.

"Maybe you should turn me in. All I'm doing is getting you into more trouble, and I do not want to do that to you," I told him in a serious voice.

"No. Why would you say something like that? You have been hurt your whole life, Renee, and hearing and seeing you hurt, it also hurts me," Keithon replied with an angry reaction.

"I'm just saying this has gone too far. I don't want you to lose your job or go to jail for me. I know you care about me, and I really do care about you, but you have a mother and father who love you, and I don't. Don't waste your life on me. I'm nothing special. I can't imagine hurting you, and if you don't let me go now, you will probably get hurt."

"I love you too much for me to do that, Renee. I do not have control over how I get hurt, but I do have control over who I let hurt me."

Keithon began kissing me on my lips. I enjoyed it then did the same. It was then we began undressing and holding each other close, unable to unlock our lips. Keithon unlatched my bra. I returned the favor and unbuckled his pants. We locked tongues and were in the motion of intimacy.

"Stop, Keithon," I said eagerly.

"What's wrong, Renee?"

"This is the second time so go slow."

Keithon laid me down slowly and kissed me from my neck to my navel. The feeling was amazing. I felt like I was in a dream. We lay in bed naked and ready to pursue intimacy. I saw a bright light flash into the window of the basement.

"Keithon, stop. I saw something in the window."

"It's probably just an animal," Keithon said while kissing my neck.

Outside the door began breaking down and this startled us.

"Shit, Renee, come on," Keithon screamed and ran out of the room.

"It's the police. Come out with your hands up!" They had finally found where we were hiding.

Keithon and I tried running out the back door to go under the porch. We both were naked, and this was very uncomfortable as we tried running through the bushes. Three officers tackled Keithon and me to the ground and put handcuffs on us. In this moment I knew it was all over. We had been caught. The officers gave us clothes then put us into the cop car.

"Renee, do not tell them anything. When they ask you questions, say you don't know."

I started crying because I knew after this Keithon and I would not see each other for a while.

"I love you, Renee. Do not worry. This will work itself out," Keithon said in a worried tone as the officers drove away.

I blocked out the sounds of the police sirens as I sat there and cried tears into my lap. I put my head in my lap and tried closing my eyes to forget what was happening. I had gotten very curious about how the police found out about this house. Who told them we were here? The only people who knew about this house were Keithon's parents, Keithon, and I. Of course, it had to be his parents who told, because when we left it was clear they wanted their son to have nothing to do with me.

The officers drove away with me in the back seat of the car. I watched as the house we just made love in was far gone into the dark distance. I had never been in the back of a police car before, so I was a little scared. It started to rain and become gloomy outside. There was a thick fog against the window, making it hard to see out. The memories, the passion, and the love we shared for this short amount of time would always be with me.

Chapter Eleven

Interrogation. I never thought about it before. Maybe when I was little and my mom and I would sit and watch interrogation shows. But I never thought of interrogation until now. The cops took Keithon and me to separate rooms. As Keithon and I were walking the opposite way from each other, the cop was holding my arm as he walked me to a room. I turned around and looked at Keithon.

Keithon silently said, "I love you." I could read his lips so clearly. This hurt me because this could be the last time he ever said those words to me.

I entered the room, then the cop pulled the chair out for me. I didn't know the cop's name, but he was a big white guy with dark hair. He looked like he was about to bust out of his uniform. As I sat down, the cop left the room. I never saw that man again.

The room was empty except for a table and three chairs. The walls were a light shade of gray. As I waited for someone to come into the room, I continued to look around. Of course, I compared everything to how it looked on the shows my mom and I used to watch. And everything seemed to be the same.

Two guys with suits and ties on walked in. They both sat down and said, "Hello." I could tell one of the guys was trying to read me by the way he kept looking at me.

"My name is Thomas, and this is Officer Robinson," Officer Thomas told me.

About an hour passed. It felt like I was asked a million unnecessary questions, like how I felt, what my height was, and what I was interested in. I could tell they were just trying to get to know me better overall as an person. This was nothing like what I watched in the shows. In the shows there was always a good cop and a bad cop, but not here. They were really serious but not mean or bad people.

Officer Thomas stopped talking, and Officer Robinson began. This is when the serious questions started. "Are you attracted to Officer James?" Officer Robinson asked.

I didn't respond to the question. Officer Robinson gave me a look like he already knew the answer.

"Why won't you answer the question? Do you have something to hide? What's wrong?" the officer asked.

I continued to be quiet.

"Okay, how about we take a break? Want some water?" Officer Robinson asked.

"Yes! I would love some," I responded.

I drank some of my water and told myself that I loved Keithon so much. At least I thought I had said it to myself, until I saw the officers' eyes widen. My face changed with a look of wonder.

Officer Robinson said, "Yes, Ms. Turner, you did say that out loud."

I never said anything else to the officers that day. I felt like crying. I knew I did something wrong.

Officer Thomas told Officer Robinson, "I guess this interrogation is over."

Chapter Twelve

Keithon

I couldn't believe we were caught. I'd spent my whole life putting criminals in these interrogation rooms, and now I was in one. I hoped Renee was okay, and I hoped she would not tell those officers anything at all. Maybe we still had a chance to get out free with a clean slate. But deep inside I knew it was not that easy, especially since we were caught in my parents' house together.

The door opened. My own partner, Officer Tanner Braylock, and some other officer named Marcus were going to ask me questions about the situation. They both were wearing blue police uniforms, which made me think of how I was just a cop and now I was a criminal. I sat in silence at the big, round brown desk, tapping my feet and avoiding looking Braylock in the eyes. I could feel them both staring at me, disappointed, but who gave a damn?

"Hello, Keithon. Funny seeing you here," Officer Braylock said.

"Whatever, you piece of shit. Get this over with," I said, annoyed.

"Hey, wise ass, we're giving orders here, okay?" Officer Marcus said angrily.

"Why didn't you report in when you had her? If I had known she was a runaway that night, I would have," Officer Braylock said.

"I plead the Fifth," I said jokingly.

"Listen here, you little shit—" Officer Marcus said.

"Marcus, I got this. Just go stand outside. Give us a couple of minutes," Braylock said.

I was glad Braylock said something. I was starting to get angry. How the hell was this officer I didn't even know giving me orders?

Marcus left the room and slammed the door behind him. I could tell Officer Marcus really did not want to leave the room, but I guessed he left out of respect for Braylock.

"Now listen, Keithon, you could go to prison for a long time. I could see to it that your time in prison is short if you just cooperate with me," Braylock said calmly.

"Oh, so you're returning favors after all I've done for you. Oh, like the time I saved your life or maybe the time I got you this job," I said, annoyed by his response.

"Stop, Keithon, don't play the blackmail game. You did this to yourself. I'm just following orders," Officer Braylock said, angry.

I sat there, angry. I hated that I missed Renee, and I hated that I did not know how she was. And this made me hurt, and I took this out on Officer Braylock, but at this time I did not care at all.

"You love her, don't you? You did not bring her back once you found out who she was because you fell in love. Am I right or wrong?" Officer Braylock asked me.

"That's none of your business, okay?" I said, annoyed.

"You did. The moment you saw her that night you fell in love with her!" Officer Braylock said with confidence in his voice like he knew actually how I felt that night.

"Finish your questions so I can go to my cell," I responded to Officer Braylock.

"I'm done. Follow me," Officer Braylock said as he stood up.

I got up and followed him out the door as he grabbed on to my handcuffs. As we walked into the hall, I saw Officer Marcus standing by the door, looking at me with a smile. Officer Marcus was an asshole. I knew this with all my heart and soul. It was like Officer Marcus was getting a high off of seeing me hurt, but I just looked away and kept walking. He followed Officer Braylock and me.

But then I could not help myself. We walked to a cell block, and out of anger, I spat into Officer Marcus's face then shook apart from Officer Braylock's grip. I hit Officer Marcus in the nose with my shoulder as hard as I could. I tried pounding him with my fist as he leaned to the side trying to contain me. Trying to pound him with my fist did not work out that well, so I just kicked him in his privates.

Another officer saw this and tackled me to the ground. I hit my head on the cell door. I was knocked unconscious, because when I woke up, I was in a dark room called the hole. This was where all criminals went if they committed crimes in jail.

"Keithon, because you tried to pull a fast one you will be in here for three weeks," Officer Braylock said outside the door.

Braylock closed the slit where the light from the outside beamed through. The place was dark and scary. I screamed, "Help, help. Someone help me!" But no one came. "You fucking no-good cops. I was the best y'all ever had!" I shouted this over and over until I could not do it anymore. I began to feel lonely. I started talking to myself. I was losing my grip on reality. I felt hopeless and afraid. I had no one but this cold-ass chill I kept feeling in the air. And even that kept coming and going, and this was making me lose my mind.

I thought about Renee all the time. I started to imagine her everywhere. I even started asking the image of Renee that I saw questions like, "Is that really you, Renee? Do you still love me? Are you here with me?" The crazy part was that Renee would respond. She would answer, "I'm here, honey. I do love you. I am right here with you." Those were the answers I wanted to hear anyway.

I did not eat for at least two days, did not sleep for one, and had not washed up in three. Even when they did try to give me food, I would not eat it at first. I sat in my own filth. I reeked of shit and urine. After a week I could not see Renee's image in the cell anymore. It hurt me not to see Renee's image anymore, even though I knew the image was not real. It was still nice to see her.

After I started to get my sleep and started to eat, I did not focus on thoughts of her that much. The three grueling weeks were up, and after I was arraigned, I got a cell with a bed and a roommate. We did not talk those first four days, but he was very respectful by staying on his side of the cell.

I also had a few personal items, which were a notebook that I wrote in, my toothbrush, and a picture of Renee that hung on the side of my bed. Those things I had were the only things I had there besides thoughts of my beloved. I grabbed the pen from my back pocket and started to write in my notebook.

Entry 1

February 25, 2018

Renee, wherever you are, I hope you are okay, and I hope you are staying to yourself. I miss you so much and this pain I feel in my heart is overwhelming. Sometimes I feel like what's the point of living because of how much stress I'm under. But the thought of leaving you is what drives my mind before I take my life. I cannot leave you behind, and I will not do that. I know you need me even more than I need you. I love you so much, and I hope one day that we will be together in a place where it is just us.

I closed the book and put it under my pillow then fell straight to sleep.

Chapter Thirteen

Renee

It was 9:00 a.m. I was in the back of a cop car on my way back to Calming Meadows. A mental house because I was mental, right? Wait! Don't answer that. I wouldn't lie. I kind of thought I was mental after my mom died but only because I had so much hate in my soul, and I know that's not normal. But after meeting Keithon, I knew I wasn't mental. Well, at least I thought I wasn't. To be honest, I did not even know what mental meant exactly. But I knew I wasn't the same as the other people in that place.

We pulled in the parking lot of the place. I smiled because the one and only good thing about this place was that I would hopefully get to see Shondra. I had not seen her in a couple months.

It was different now. I'd never been on this side of the building before. The walls were the same with the flowers on them, but . . . Wait, never mind.

We went through two doors, and I was back on the side I lived on before I ran away. I went back to my same room. Shondra was nowhere to be found. A lady dressed all in white came in and gave me something to put on. It was a plain blue top that said "Sunshine" on it, and the lady gave me a pair of pants, too. She walked me to the bathroom.

Before I entered, I said, "I've been here before. I know where the bathroom is."

The lady replied, "Look, whatever. I'm told I have to watch you. You ran away once, and we do not want that to happen again."

I went into the bathroom and changed into my uniform. Once I was finished, I came out of the bathroom.

"I'm sorry for being rude. My name is Ms. Taylor. If you need anything while you're here, come to me."

"Okay, I will." I shrugged my shoulders. I guessed I'd be seeing a lot of her while I was here, since she went out of her way to tell me her name.

Back in the room, we found Shondra lying on the bed. I was so surprised to see her.

"Okay, my office is down the hall, make a right, and it's the first door on the left. So if you need anything, come to me," Ms. Taylor told me.

"Okay, cool. I will."

"Also, early tomorrow we have to ask you some questions. I will come by your room early, around ten. One last thing, after tonight this will no longer be your room," Ms. Taylor told me.

"Wait! Where will I go?" I begged to know intensely with a great amount of curiosity.

"We will talk about it tomorrow." Ms. Taylor smiled.

Ms. Taylor finally walked away. I went to our room door and peeked around to make sure she had left. We couldn't close the door because there was a rule now that you could not close the door during the daytime.

So I walked to Shondra's bed, hugged her, and said, "I missed you so much!" very quietly but with power in my voice because I really meant it.

"I missed you too, Renee! Why are you back? What happened?" Shondra asked. I knew she was eager to know. I could hear it in her voice.

"It's a long story."

"Renee, you have to tell me."

"Okay, I will," I said as I lowered my voice. "After I ran away I met this guy. He's a cop. He found me but didn't know I ran away, but even when he did find out, he didn't turn me in. I fell in love with him. I never cared about anyone as much as I cared about him!"

"Wow! Well, how did they catch you? Did the cop end up turning you in?" Shondra asked.

"No! Keithon would never do that."

"Well, who did?"

"The police found us in a house where we were staying, but I knew it was just a matter of time," I replied.

Shondra followed up by asking, "What do you mean, a matter of time?"

"His parents found out who I was because the cops were coming to their house asking questions. So I figured they were going to find me," I replied. "Okay, enough about me. What's going on with you? Have you talked to anyone?" I asked.

"No. I am the same. I still never talk to anyone here. But I will admit I got lonely without you here. You are my only friend. I've been seeing people lately who are not really there. I think it's from me being so lonely."

"Yeah, I missed you too. You are the one thing I regret leaving behind," I replied, kind of looking past the last thing she said.

"Is that bad?" Shondra inquired.

"Is what bad?"

"Wishing you were here even though I knew you hated this place?"

"No, that is not bad at all. Hey, girl, I haven't seen Mrs. Sims. Where is she?" I asked with old feelings coming back to my mind.

"She doesn't work here anymore. She quit."

"What?" I said in shock of the news I was hearing. "Why'd she quit? I mean, I'm happy the bitch is gone, but why?"

"She never did tell anyone why. With you gone I did a lot of listening, and I actually overheard three workers while I was at lunch one day talking about how she never told anyone, even the people she was close to. It is kind of weird."

"Yeah, it is, but I'm happy that she is gone and I won't have to see her while I am here."

She and I talked for hours, and it was finally time for us to go to sleep. Shondra got up and turned off the lights. Ten minutes passed, and I was still up and couldn't go to sleep. I was just thinking about a lot of things. It felt nice to know Shondra cared about me enough to want me back here. This was the last thing on my mind before I fell asleep.

Chapter Fourteen

Keithon

Even though I was a cop, I started to adapt to prison life. But I had to say, I wasn't used to taking orders from cops who had worked right beside me in the precinct. People I worked with, cops who put in good words for me to the chief, were now telling me what to do. I'd never imagined this day would happen, when I could not even talk to my buddy Braylock without him treating me like a criminal.

It took three months before I even felt comfortable to walk outside the cell. I stayed posted in the small box, writing poems and avoiding other prisoners. I tried to make sure to avoid prisoners because I put some of them in this prison. And if they recognized me they would have probably beaten me to death. So my cell was the only safe place to stay.

Some of the officers around the cell blocks were nice to me. They would let me stay in the cell and also bring me lunch so I would not eat with the prisoners. Yes, even though it was prison, and I was now a criminal, I also had advantages. I kept to myself and only talked to my cellmate. I would share things with him about me and Renee and what I went through to save her.

He would say, "Why so much for a crazy bitch?"

I told him, "I never thought Renee was mental. She was a lost little girl who searched for the love she never had."

He would laugh and tell me she had me hooked like a fish and if I were rich, she would probably steal my money. But what the hell did he know? He was a damn criminal and was used to people around him stealing.

Today I wanted to do something in prison that I had not done, and that was walk to the basketball court. Usually at 12:30 p.m. no one was there, and today the officers would make sure no one would be there so I could play a little basketball by myself without worrying about getting stabbed or hit. I knew personally that prison was a little rough, and it would be especially if someone found out I put them in jail. So I headed down to the basketball court while the prisoners were at lunch.

I shot around for a long time. It was pretty relaxing and took my mind off of everything. I was just by myself, just shooting the ball around without the sounds of fights and angry police officers. Yeah, I could do this every day. Plus, I could come outside to breathe in the fresh air. So I shot around, but then the door opened and out came ten prisoners. I was pretty scared because they looked straight at me with the eyes of wolves who'd just seen a deer.

Most of them were black and Mexican, but two were white. There was one short man who stood out because I'd put this man in jail not too long ago. Fear came to me. *Oh, shit. He has found me. What will he do to me right now?* His name was Malik Mason, a drug lord I put in jail nearly three years ago. Malik was about five feet three inches, with no hair at all on his head. He was sporting multiple types of tattoos on his body and even a couple on his face, but there was one that stood out the most to me. It was the name "Unique" on his forearm, the lower part of his arm. Right above the name was a little girl's face. I didn't know why this stood out to me, but I was surprised to see any sign of Malik having a heart or caring for someone other than himself.

"So you tried hiding from me? Is that how to treat an old friend?" Malik smirked sarcastically.

"I'm just playing a simple game of basketball, dude. I don't want any problems."

"Dude, I'm not trying anything. Plus, you have your cops on your side," Malik said laughing to his friends.

Malik came toward my ear then whispered in it, saying, "I heard about your little bitch Renee and how she was a fucking nut. So you like your women crazy?"

That moment I turned to him and struck him with every bit of strength I had. It happened so fast that I was on the ground being stomped by his group until the officers stopped them.

As Malik's friends pulled back a little, he said, "You're damn lucky you have them cops to protect you, or you would have been killed already!"

I was shocked at what all just happened. This made me hope that once I went to court, I would not be proven guilty, because if I was, I would have to stay in this place for years. I didn't think I would live to see another day. Either I would take my life or the prisoners would.

I stayed and shot around until it was time for me to come back in. And that was when all the prisoners went back to their cells. I walked past the cells and blocked out the loud noises. It was clear to me that a lot of people now knew I was once a cop. I started to think of Renee's smile as I walked past. The thought of Renee took my mind off a lot, but it also made me sad thinking about her. But I knew somehow or someway we would see each other again.

Chapter Fifteen

Renee

I woke up missing Keithon, but I just put that in the back of my head.

An hour after I woke up, Ms. Taylor came down and took me back to her office. We talked for hours about how different it would be from how it used to be when I first started living here and my living situation.

Ms. Taylor ended the conversation with, "This is only because you ran away. We do not want that to happen again."

Ms. Taylor walked me to my new room. We went through the two doors I went through when I first came back. It was just like the other side of the building, but something was unfamiliar. We stopped at room 114. The other rooms on the other side of the building, where I'd stayed before, were not numbered.

As Ms. Taylor unlocked the door, I noticed on this side the rooms were far apart from each other, unlike the old side I was on. Also, the same flowers were on the walls like on the other side of the building, but this time I felt no emotions looking at them, nothing but emptiness.

Ms. Taylor finally got the door open. We entered the room. The walls were bright white, and the carpet was sky blue. I touched the walls in my new room. This room was made to look homey, but it wasn't. This room had extremely hard, cold walls like the ones made in jails, painted over with white paint to make it unnoticeable. My old room had wooden walls and felt like an actual room. As I took my mind off of the walls, I could hear the light sound of Ms. Taylor saying, "This is your new room."

I didn't pay attention because my eyes went to looking at the rest of the room. I noticed there was a sink and a toilet in my room. At this very moment, I started to feel like a prisoner.

Ms. Taylor handed me a piece of paper and began to speak. "This is your new schedule." She pointed at the white cabinet in the room then continued to talk. "Everything you need is in here. Pads, tampons, first aid, water and so on. Here is a cell phone. You can only reach my office, 911, and our medical service on this. If you ever need anything call me. I basically live here." Ms. Taylor laughed for a second.

She gave me five notebooks and a bunch of pencils and pens. "This is just in case you ever get bored. But are you okay?" Ms. Taylor asked.

"Yes," I tried to reply, but I ran to the toilet and threw up.

After I finished, I felt dirty. Ms. Taylor took me to the nurse, who gave me some medication and let me brush my teeth. I lay down in the bed in the nurse's office for about twenty minutes. Then Ms. Taylor walked me down to the dining room.

"Have a good lunch. I'll talk to you about the other things after lunch," Ms. Taylor said.

"Okay, bye." I was just happy. I felt better now.

I went to the lunch line, got my food, then sat next to Shondra at a lunch table. The food was not bad today. We had pizza, salad, and pineapples. As I was drinking my orange juice, she stared at me with the same face she made before she asked me a question. So I knew what was coming.

"What, Shondra?" I asked.

She giggled. "So how is the new room?"

"I feel like I'm in prison."

"What room are you in?"

"Room 114, and yes, we have room numbers. They also lock my door at night."

"Maybe sometimes at night when you're bored I can sneak out of my room and talk to you from the other side of the door. Or we can pass notes under the door," Shondra whispered very quietly.

Before I knew it, it was time for lunch to be over. I saw Ms. Taylor walking up to me at the lunch table.

Shondra nodded good-bye as she got up and walked away.

Ms. Taylor walked me to my new room. She unlocked my door, and as we entered, she showed me this small green light on the inside and outside of the door.

"Whenever you have a meeting, a meal, or it's time to shower, this light will turn green, and this means the door is unlocked."

"Okay. I understand."

"When the light is red, it means I locked the door, so you are not able to leave when you are not supposed to." Ms. Taylor took a small break then said, "That is all for now, but remember we have a meeting in about an hour. It's also written on your schedule." Ms. Taylor walked out of the room and locked the door.

I watched the small green light turn red, then I lay back in my bed, thinking about passing notes under my door. In these few seconds of me thinking about this I remembered that I was the only person Shondra talked to here. I didn't know why I forgot this. I knew she must feel so lonely sometimes. Like how I felt without Keithon in my life.

Chapter Sixteen

Keithon

Today was the first day I met with the lawyer who would work with me on my case. I really
did not want to meet her. Like I told Renee, she
could ask me all the questions she wanted, but
I was not going to say anything. And I hoped
they did not bribe Renee into telling them information. If that did happen, we were toast, dead
meat, roadkill, damn it we were done for. I also
had to keep in mind that Renee would not do
such a thing. She was smarter than most girls.
She had gotten this far. So all I could do for right
now was just relax, have a talk with the lawyer,
and leave, simple and easy.

In came two officers through the door of my
cell to take me to the conference room where the
lawyer and I would speak. I stood next to the bed
and locked my arms so one of the officers could put
me in the handcuffs.

"Damn, what the fuck?" I barked because one of the handcuffs pinched my skin.

We started to walk down the cell block. I looked downward as always, and I imagined Renee in my head to block out all of the noises around me. We approached the room, and I saw an older white woman with gray hair. The woman was very short. She seemed like someone's grandmother.

"Hello, you must be Keithon James. I'm Mrs. Brenda Archer. I will be your lawyer for this case. Please sit down." She greeted me with a handshake, and then we took our seats to begin our meeting.

"Now, Keithon, we will meet one more time before court, which is July fourteenth. Then, I will prepare you."

"When will I be able to see Renee again?" I eagerly spoke up. "It has been four long months since I have seen her. I need to know how she is doing. And just talking over the phone will not satisfy me, even though we can't contact each other through the phone anyway."

"Well, that is not my job to assign visitation. That is the court's job. But are you two married?" Brenda Archer looked up at me.

"Well no, but it was a thought in my head before this situation happened."

"Really, I don't know if there will be any visits assigned, Keithon. If you two are not legal partners, then the court will look at it as nothing."

I was pretty upset at the response I got, but I kept my composure and just listened. I guessed I knew ahead of time that I was not going to be able to see her, because we had done a crime together.

"Keithon, could you tell me your side of the story about what happened with you and Renee?" Brenda Archer asked.

"I'm sorry, Mrs. Archer, but I just do not feel comfortable telling you things when you do not know me," I said with a little anger in my voice.

"Excuse me?" Brenda Archer raised an eyebrow, shocked by my response.

"I just don't feel like talking about it, okay?"

"I know, Keithon, that you are angry right now, but I am here to help you. If you do not tell me the truth, then I can't help you out of this mess."

"I just don't feel like talking about nothing right now. Can you come back tomorrow or in an hour?" I said, holding my tears back from pouring out of my eyes.

Now, stop. I just want to say right now I wasn't just telling her these things just because I didn't want to talk. I was beginning to feel tears pushing to come out of my eyes because right now my thought of Renee was popping in my head, and the thought of never seeing her again was killing me.

"Can someone bring him a tissue? Poor baby. It will be okay."

I walked out of the room and back to my cell, wiping my face so I would not be embarrassed crying in front of any of these criminals, which would be the last thing I needed. So once I got to my cell, I went to sleep.

Two hours later I woke up and the same two officers were standing over me. One said, "Come on, the lawyer is waiting for you." I got up and felt a little better from sleeping, and I headed back to the conference room.

"How are you feeling, Keithon? I hope you're in a more agreeable mood."

"Just fine, I'm good," I lied, sitting back in my seat.

"That is good. Now look, Keithon, you are going to have to tell me something to help you in court. I know that you love Renee, but don't you think if you tell me something, you are possibly helping her? Maybe you will even be able to see her again if you do so."

Well, maybe this would help me to be able to see Renee again. Oh, how I would love to hold her in my arms again and shower her with gifts. I would do anything in this world to see her again and to get out of this place.

"Okay, I will, but it is just between us. I don't want the officers in here to hear while I'm talking if that is okay."

Brenda waved the officers off, and they exited, and I began talking. "It all started when me and my old partner, Officer Braylock, were doing block patrol. We had seen someone digging in the trashcans behind the abandoned building. So we pulled up behind the trashcans and asked the person to exit. When we flashed the light, we saw it was a woman, a very young woman, who was Renee. We both started asking her questions like why was she digging in trash and where her parents were. Renee said she had no parents because they both died when she was young. I took her to a shelter to stay the night so she would not sleep on the streets. Every day I came to see if she was okay and to get to know her better. Couple months later she came and stayed with me, and there we connected and fell in love. I took her to meet my parents in New York, where I was born and where my parents still live. Afterward, everything went downhill. The police were looking for her, and that's when I found out she ran away from the hospital. I loved her so much that I kept quiet and hid her out at my parents' second house where no one goes to. Then we were caught because the police found the house because my parents told them. There's my story."

Wow. I told the whole story, and now I felt horrible. Now it felt like I would never see Renee again. What if she went back and told the judge what I did and I was stuck in prison forever?

"Wow, Keithon, that is some story. It seems like you really love her, but you do know hiding a runaway is a federal offense?"

"I know. I was a cop, Mrs. Archer, but love had me blinded, and it still does," I confessed.

"Keithon, I had a husband who committed a horrible crime. I don't want to say what. But it did not stop me from putting him away."

"But did you love him?" I asked her.

"Yes. I loved him with all my heart."

I thought that she never felt real love if she was quick to lock her husband away. I knew how much I loved Renee, so I had nothing to worry about. "Are we done here, Mrs. Archer?" I asked, getting up and slowly walking away.

"Yes. We will meet before you go to court, Keithon. Have a good rest of the day," Brenda Archer replied.

I left the room and went back to my cell. I grabbed my journal from under my pillow to write an entry for today. I was pretty aggravated today, so my entry would show anger through my writing.

Entry 20

June 29, 2018

Fuck, I can't get a break. It's like as soon as I start to feel happiness, something knocks me off and I get this shitty mood again. I met my lawyer today, and she asked me why I didn't call law enforcement when I

*found Renee. Well, have you ever heard of
this thing called love? I could have just gone
off rocket talking to her today, but I kept my
composure, and I think I did a very good
job at that. At least this meeting is over, and
now I can get some rest.*

*But I don't understand. She is my lawyer,
not my fucking mom or dad. She's supposed
to fight for me, not against me. Maybe I'll
ask to be assigned to a new lawyer. No, I
should just calm down and relax. Maybe it is
not that bad. I am probably just overreacting to this situation. But at the same time, I
told her things I should have kept to myself.
Here I was telling Renee not to tell anything,
but I told on the both of us. Shit, I'm screwed.
What the hell can I do to change what I have
done? Maybe I'll just rest on it. Maybe I will
ask my cellmate what I should do. I'm so
confused and so angry. I don't know what
to do.*

I closed my notebook and slid it up under my
bed as I always did after I was done writing. Only
this time I decided not to go straight to sleep. I got
up and tried praying. I had not prayed in a long
time. I wasn't even sure if I even believed in God.
All my accomplishments in life I had done on my
own. I had never had help from anyone. And if

there was really a God, why would He have me going through what I was going through? But even though I doubted my faith, I still tried praying to see if a good outcome would come from this.

"Dear God, I know we have not talked in a very long time. And you probably won't even answer this prayer, but I'm asking you for a favor, a simple, small favor. I know you can work miracles in people's lives, and I am hoping that you could do one for me. Ever since I got to this prison, and ever since I left Renee, I have had this pain in my heart that leaves me feeling empty inside. God, if you are real, I am begging on a bending knee to help me and Renee back together again. I love her, I need her, and I want to marry her. Amen."

Chapter Seventeen

Renee

Keithon kicked open the door of my room, and he grabbed me. We started to run. Security started to chase us. We ran faster and faster, but they continued to get closer and closer. One security guard yelled out "Stop!" As the security got unbelievably close, Keithon whispered, "I love you!"

I woke up in sweat. It had been a while now since I'd been here. I kept having dreams about Keithon. These dreams felt so real they were starting to scare me.

About ten minutes passed of me sitting in my bed, thinking about these dreams. I finally noticed the red light turn green. Still feeling the sweat on my body, I went to the bathroom to take a shower. This was my first time using these showers on this side of the building because they were open and not private. I'd been washing up in my room for the past few weeks out of the sink.

I walked into the bathroom. The walls were white, but the first thing I noticed when I walked in were two stacks of face cloths and towels. There were also little bottles of body wash that had "A cleaner way could be a brighter day" printed on the bottle. I grabbed one of each and walked through the small hallway that led to one big room with twelve showerheads and a mirror on the side. There were four girls already in here showering. I showered really fast before anyone else could come in. I felt awkward and uncomfortable. And then the worst thing that could possibly happen happened.

"Why are you looking at me?" I heard in a really angry voice.

"I can look where I want to look, but trust me, you ain't much to look at!" someone responded.

I was scared to turn around because the last thing I wanted to see was two naked girls fighting. I finally turned around after a couple minutes of hearing a bunch of noises. I saw one girl hit the other girl's head against the mirror. The girl's nose started to bleed. She had cuts on her face from the glass. I saw blood dripping from her face and flowing down to the drain. I felt sick to my stomach. I had a flashback to the night my mom died when I stabbed Tyrone. I always hated seeing blood. Snapping back to reality as the two big female security guards rushed into the bathroom, I started to feel dizzy.

The one other girl who was in the bathroom yelled out, "Look at her." She shouted it super loud as I was throwing up on the floor.

Once security stopped the fight and took the girls out of the bathroom, I got my strength and wrapped my towel tighter around myself and left the bathroom. I went back to my room. I brushed my teeth then lay down in my bed. The nurse came in to check on me thirty minutes later and brought me some water and crackers.

"You have been sick a lot lately. I've talked to Ms. Taylor, and you can stay in here and rest today. She will meet with you tomorrow. And I'll bring your meals to your room today," the nurse said before she left my room.

The nurse was a small white lady with red hair. I ate some crackers and drank some water. I finally fell asleep after a while.

The next day I felt a lot better, and I didn't have a dream about Keithon last night. Ms. Taylor and I had a meeting today, so I went to her office.

"Hello, Ms. Turner."

"Hello," I responded to Ms. Taylor.

"Please take a seat." I walked over to the chair and sat down as she continued. "We have to talk about a lot today. Are you feeling better?"

"Yes, I'm feeling a lot better."

"I do want to talk to you about the fight you saw yesterday and how you feel about it, but I'm going to talk to you about something that is more important to you first."

I could tell it was something important because she kept talking around it instead of just telling me. "Ms. Taylor, please just tell me!"

"Okay. A month from now you will have to go to court to get questioned for Keithon James's case."

All my bitter emotions changed to happiness but also fear. I stayed quiet thinking of these emotions and what might happen. I started thinking about seeing his beautiful face again.

We talked for a while, then, later on, Ms. Taylor reminded me again about court. "The date is July fourteenth, so mark your calendar. We will finish talking about this tomorrow. Get to lunch." Ms. Taylor handed me a calendar as I walked out the door to lunch.

As I entered the dining room, I saw my only true friend. I sat down and told her all the news about what just happened and about the fight.

"I can't believe it. I don't know how to feel."

"Don't overthink it. Just be happy you get to see him again," Shondra responded.

When lunch was over, I hugged Shondra. "You are a great friend!" I told her then walked back to my room.

When I got to my room, I put a heart on July 14, then marked today.

Chapter Eighteen

Keithon

Over the past month, I had been eyed by every prisoner in this place. I couldn't go anywhere by myself and couldn't leave my cell without officers to protect me. My cellmate helped me by keeping the guys he knew from harming me. I even had a name the prisoners called me. Every prisoner, even my cellmate, called me prison cop. There was one prisoner who wanted me dead and hated that the police had my back, and that was Malik Mason. Little bastard was probably making plans to kill me right now with other inmates.

But today I would not worry a thing about the prisoners. I guessed I'd go shoot the ball around on the basketball court today. I hoped to not have any problems like before, and if I did, I knew the cops would stop anything from getting out of hand.

"Do you want to come to the court with me?" I asked my new cellmate.

"Sure, what the hell? I have nothing else to do."
He was a brave, "fuck these other inmates" type of
dude who didn't mind I was a former cop.

"Well, my name is Anthony Hampton, but you
can call me Tone."

"So, Tone, how long have you been in prison?"

"About five years now in total," Tone replied.

"Damn, that is a long time. Do you have family?"

"Yeah, sure I do. Two sons and two daughters.
They are the love of my life, too. I have a wife who
keeps the kids in line since I'm not there."

"Wow," I said, sitting next to him on the ground.

"So about this Renee you keep mumbling about,
have you talked to her?"

"No, I haven't. I am not allowed to, but I would
rather see her in person anyway. I need to see her."
I was getting depressed.

"I see, man. That's how I feel about my wife and
kids. I hate just talking to them over the phone. I
love when they visit here so I can hug them and tell
them I love them in person," Tone replied.

"What did you get in for, buddy, if you don't
mind my asking?"

"I was drinking, was kind of depressed because I
lost my job. I was driving from the bar and hit two
people with my car and killed them right on impact.
I was sentenced with involuntary manslaughter.
Put in here for twenty years, man. Twenty years
of not seeing my sons and daughters graduate or

go to prom. Recently I heard my son Shawn is in a gang and has been in and out of jail for selling drugs. And my wife cries every night. There is a lot my wife goes through, working two jobs and taking care of four kids on her own. I told her to leave me, get a guy who can love her, be there for her, and who can work. But she loves me too much to leave. She does not know how better off she would be without me," Tone said.

"Wow, I'm sorry," I told Tone. I was in shock but at a loss for words.

"I have not talked with anyone in here about my life outside the bars. You're the first person. You are a cool guy, prison cop, a cool guy indeed."

"Sometimes I need someone to talk to. I'm just returning the favor."

"When is your court date, man?"

"It's in two weeks, on July fourteenth."

"Are you nervous at all?"

"Kind of, but I'm more just happy. I will see Renee again, and I hope that I can talk to her during that time. I will be at peace then," I told him.

We started to head back to our cell because lunch was over. We waited until the prisoners got into their cells before we started going back in.

"Good talk, dude. Whatever you want to talk about is safe with me, I promise. And if I do not have anything else, I have my word, and my word is everything," Anthony told me.

Chapter Nineteen

Renee

Cleveland was not the best place to live with all the crime that happened. But it did not matter where we lived, because the biggest crime to me was happening in my house, under our roof. I remembered one time, out of all the times of my mom being with Tyrone after he started drinking, the only time my mother ever stood up to him. One time when I was just a kid, my mom was at work, and it was only me and Tyrone in the house. I was in the shower for about an hour. I always took long showers because they were relaxing and peaceful. I guessed sometime between this time of me being in the shower and the time I got out, my mom had come home early from work.

I was getting out of the shower, and Tyrone pushed the bathroom door open and came in. I was naked. I grabbed my towel super fast and wrapped it around me. Of course, Tyrone was drunk.

"I have to pee," Tyrone said while looking at me.

I left the bathroom really fast. I was not scared or anything because Tyrone had never sexually harassed me before. I was just feeling really awkward because my stepdad saw me naked. I walked in my room and took my clothes out of my dresser to get changed. Little did I know I did have to worry about him. I put on my lotion as usual before I put my clothes on. I heard a light sound, and I could see the door was slightly open and Tyrone was peeking in through the door. *OMG.* I hurried and tried to put my pajamas on, but Tyrone opened the door all the way once he knew I had noticed him peeking in my room. Tyrone saw me naked in the bathroom, and now he saw me naked again, but this time it was on purpose. What was wrong with this creep?

"Don't make a sound," Tyrone instructed me.

I still slowly reached for my pajama pants. But the bastard gave me an angry look. I knew he did not want me to move. He slowly walked to me, looking me up and down, and he sat next to me on the bed. I could smell all the alcohol that he'd drunk.

He never did touch me that day, but he kept looking at me. I was so scared. I did not know what was about to happen, but I knew I did not want him to touch me, and I did not want to get raped. But to my surprise, he did not do any of those things. He kept looking at me with a blank stare. I heard a sound and looked up. My mom was at my bedroom door.

"Get away from my fucking daughter, you monster," my mother screamed.

I grabbed my clothes and ran out of the room to put them on.

All I could hear was my mom yelling at Tyrone. "You sick fuck. How could you?" My mother was yelling, and I could hear the sound of her punching him.

That day was the first day Tyrone did not hit my mom. I never knew if it was because he knew he was wrong or because he was just too drunk to think to hit back. I did not really ever feel the same after that day. I never really wanted anyone to see my body. For about a month I stayed with my older cousin, who later in life died from cancer. When I came back, I would only shower when my mom was home or when Tyrone was not in the house. It was weird after that situation with Tyrone happened, and we never spoke about it again in our house.

Chapter Twenty

Today was the first time I'd been able to get outside since I'd been here. I was sitting on the grass with my notebook in my lap, and my back was leaning on the tree. Ms. Taylor was sitting on the bench next to the tree.

"I know you never get outside and you're always in that room, so I was thinking some of our meetings should start being outside. Would you like that?" Ms. Taylor asked while smiling at me.

"Sure." I started to look around, and I noticed there was a male security guard not too far away from us, sitting on the bench and looking our way. We were the only people outside at this moment. "Is he here to make sure I don't run away?" I asked Ms. Taylor.

"Yes, he is. You know, if you don't feel like talking, you can write in your notebook," Ms. Taylor told me.

"Okay thanks," I told her before I started writing in my notebook. I spent most of our meeting writing in my notebook, I never talked to Ms. Taylor unless I was spoken to. It was not because I didn't like her or trust her. It was only because I was tired of talking about my problems to strangers. It wasn't going to change anything. But I liked Ms. Taylor. She was a nice lady.

"Okay, it has been an hour. It's time to go back in."

"All right."

"Okay, but you have a visitor so follow me," Ms. Taylor responded as I almost walked off.

I stopped, then followed Ms. Taylor to the visitor room. I'd never had someone visit me here so this was my first time ever being in this room. We entered the room. There was a desk to the far left, where three ladies were signing people in on the computer. I noticed there were security guards standing at different spots by the walls. I also saw about fifteen circular tables with chairs.

"Come on, Ms. Turner, follow me."

Ms. Taylor took me to a table where some man was sitting. He lifted his head. I didn't remember much about my dad, but I knew this was him. I had his same big brown eyes. She walked off, then turned around and said, "Tell me if you need anything." Then she walked away.

I was still standing, and my dad got up real fast. I'd never been hugged so tight in my life, but I did not hug him back.

"I missed you so much. I'm so sorry!" my dad said as tears fell from his eyes. He sat down. I decided to sit down across from him at the table. My mom only told me a little about why he left, so I did not really know much other than he left because of that lady.

"Why? Why now? Why did you leave us? Why!" I bellowed with power in my voice.

My dad had black hair, big brown eyes, and a light brown skin tone but kind of on the pale side. "I'll tell you everything, I promise." My dad went on to tell me about how he left because he was not ready to be a parent, so he left with a lady, but he was ready now. He told me how he could not take care of us and did not have a job at the time. After he left, he joined the military, and he just got back from his latest tour. I was starting to remember the part about him leaving us for that lady.

"I'm better now, and I am so sorry all this happened to you. I cried so much when I found out. I never cried before, but you are my little girl. I'll do anything so you will let me back in your life. And if that devil weren't already in hell, I would kill him myself!" my dad told me.

I just looked at him. I didn't know how to feel, but I was happy he felt the same about Tyrone as I did. Of course, I wondered how he found out about me being here.

"You don't have to decide now, but please just allow me to come here and visit again."

"Okay, you can visit me, but I'm only giving you one more chance. If you mess up again, I'm never giving you another."

Ms. Taylor walked over and said, "Time is up. It's time for you to go now." So I did not have time to ask him about how he found everything out, but I'd ask him the next time I saw him.

"Okay, I love you, Renee. I'll be back tomorrow!"

"All right, bye."

"How do you feel?" Ms. Taylor asked.

"It went okay," I told her, then walked back to my room. I wasn't really in the mood for talking to Ms. Taylor anymore today.

Once lunch came, I told Shondra everything as usual, and then I went back to my room. I wrote in my notebook for some time about everything today. It had been a long day. I put my notebook under my pillow, marked a day off the calendar, then fell asleep.

Chapter Twenty-one

Keithon

Today my parents came to see me. I hadn't seen them since Renee and I ran off after they talked to the police. I didn't really want to see them, but they were my parents. I guessed I could try to forgive them.

I walked down to the phone booth to talk to them. I picked up the phone. My mom picked up theirs so fast.

"Hello, Mom. Hello, Dad."

"How are you, son?" my mom and dad asked at the same time.

"I'm okay, I guess."

"Why haven't you called us?" my dad asked.

Was this a serious fucking question? "I had nothing to say."

My mom said, "That's all you have to say?"

"Honey, not today, okay? Not today!" my dad told my mom.

"Look, why did you come here if you were just going to argue with me?"

"That's not why we came here. We've just been worried about you, son," Dad said.

"I am sorry. I love you so much. I just hate seeing you in here," my mom told me.

"That's funny, because you helped put me in here," I replied with anger in my heart.

"Keithon," my father said.

"No, Dad. You guys helped put me in here."

"Now you listen. Don't go blaming anyone. You knew she was running from the law after we told you, but you chose to stay with her. You should have never fallen in love with her. You are an officer."

I knew there was some truth to that, so I was silent for a second. "Dad, you can't help who you fall in love with. I will never apologize for loving her when no one else did!" I told them while a tear fell from my eye.

"I love you, honey. Everything will work itself out," my mom told me.

"I love you too!" I replied. I was over this whole conversation.

"We heard your court date is July fourteenth. We will be there to support you," my father claimed.

"Okay, thank you!"

"Time is up," I heard in a loud voice.

Chapter Twenty-two

Renee

I woke up super early so I could get in the shower alone. Since that fight in the showers, I asked Ms. Taylor to unlock my door at 5:00 a.m. every day so I could wash up in peace without having to deal with the risk of something like that happening again.

Some hours passed and today my dad came in early to see me. I walked down to the visiting room. Before I entered, Ms. Taylor was standing by the door.

"When you are done talking to your father, come to my office. I need to talk to you about some things," Ms. Taylor said.

"What is it?"

"Just come to my office afterward," Ms. Taylor said, and then she walked off.

I entered the room and sat down across from my dad.

"Hey, Renee. How is your day so far?" my dad asked.

"It's good," I said while smiling. I was more open to letting him in today, maybe because I was happy that soon I'd get to see Keithon.

"Why are you so happy? What is going on, if you don't mind me asking you?" my dad asked.

I was scared to tell him, but I didn't care. "I get to see Keithon soon, and I know you might not agree because he is older than me, but I don't care. I love him," I said very quickly, leaning toward my dad.

"Honey, I might not agree, but the last thing I want to do is judge you. I've never seen you so happy before. I know he has to be a good guy," my dad said to me.

"Keithon is a good guy. He really is!" I said then got up and hugged him. "I love you, Dad," I whispered in his ear while hugging him.

"I love you too, baby girl," my father said while wrapping his arms around me tighter.

As I sat back down, I could see a tear falling from his eye. I was so surprised. My dad whipped the tear off his face real fast, cleared his voice, then asked "So when is this court date? Can I go?"

"It's July fourteenth. I'll have Ms. Taylor send you the information," I told my dad. "Dad?" I spoke.

"Yes, honey?"

"How did you find out about everything?"

"Since I am still your guardian, someone had called me to inform me of everything that was going on and what happened with your mom. Of course, I couldn't just up and leave the military. I had to wait until my time was up. But as soon as I heard about everything, I knew the first thing I was going to do was come find you. I just had to, and I was so sad you had to go through all of this alone. I really wish I could have been there for you. And since I wasn't, I will live with that for the rest of my life. I am so sorry, honey."

"It is okay. If I am willing to work on forgiving you, then it is only fair that you work on forgiving yourself. Promise me you will let that go and stop being mad at yourself. Just worry about how you can work on being a better father now," I told my father with my pinky out. "Pinky promise you will get over it and just worry about today and tomorrow, not yesterday and before then?"

"I promise." My father smiled and put his pinky out and promised me.

I started to think about Ms. Taylor, and I remembered she wanted to talk to me.

"Nice talking to you, but Ms. Taylor wants to talk to me. I just remembered. But I'll let her know to send you the information."

"All right. Love you, Renee. Bye," my dad said.

I started to walk off.

"Renee, no matter what, I'm proud of you!" my dad yelled across the room.

I smiled at him then walked to Ms. Taylor's room. *"Renee, no matter what, I'm proud of you!"* This was in my head the whole time while I walked to Ms. Taylor's office. I never really had anyone tell me they were proud of me before. This was a nice feeling.

I knocked on the door. "Come in!" Ms. Taylor yelled. I entered her office, and I saw dresses everywhere.

"You have to look nice for court, right?" Ms. Taylor said, smiling at me.

"This is for me?" I asked, but I wasn't really looking for an answer.

"Yes, this is for you, Ms. Turner."

"You can call me Renee, Ms. Taylor." I started to look around, then I asked, "Can my friend Shondra help us! And can she come to court with me?"

"Shondra? Shondra, who doesn't talk to anyone in this place?" Ms. Taylor remarked.

"Yeah, but she talks to me. Shondra is my only friend here, the only person I can truly trust."

"Sure, why not?" Ms. Taylor said then went over to her desk. "Shondra, come to Ms. Taylor's office," she announced on the intercom.

Five minutes later we heard someone knocking on the door. Ms. Taylor opened the door, and Shondra walked in. She had a strong look on her face. I knew she was wondering what was going on.

"Shondra, it's okay. I told her to call you down. I want you to go to court with me, and Ms. Taylor got us a bunch of outfits to try on."

"Okay," Shondra said while smiling. I was surprised she responded so fast, but I knew she trusted me. I also could tell Ms. Taylor was just shocked to hear her voice.

We tried on all the clothes, laughing and joking. This was a lot of fun. Finally, we found the ones we wanted to wear.

"Thanks," Shondra and I told Ms. Taylor. I hugged Ms. Taylor then walked to my room. Of course, I wrote everything in my notebook: about how nice Ms. Taylor was, how my dad and I had reconnected, and how I would never find another friend like Shondra.

"Renee, no matter what, I'm proud of you," was on my mind again before I dozed off to sleep.

Chapter Twenty-three

Keithon

It was the afternoon before my court date. I could not stop thinking about Renee, her big brown eyes, and her smile. I couldn't wait any longer. I needed to hear her voice. I had to.

A lot of people left the dining room, but there were still a decent amount of people still in there. Then I finally left the dining room, and I saw an officer I knew. He was a childhood friend, and we went to the academy together.

"Hey, Max. How are you?"

"Hey, buddy, I'm good," he said with a smile on his face.

"Can you do me a favor?"

"Sure, you know I'll almost do anything for a friend like you," Max told me. Max did not ask why I was in here, so I assumed he knew everything. There was no point in saying anything. It was clear. He could see me wearing this baggy orange jumpsuit.

"Can you take me to a phone I can use?" I asked in a low voice.

"Sure, follow me, but only because I know you are a good person. But you can't tell anyone I did this, of course."

I followed him to his office and sat in his seat at his desk. I looked in the phone book to find Calming Meadows, and I saw Ms. Taylor listed under it. I called, and the phone rang about three times. Then someone answered.

"Hello, Ms. Taylor's office. How may I help you?"

"Can I speak to Renee Turner?" I asked.

"May I ask who's calling? And you do know you have to make an appointment? She can't take calls," Ms. Taylor responded.

"No, I did not know this," I said, thinking of a name to say.

"Is this Keithon James?" Ms. Taylor asked.

"That's Keithon! I know it is! Let me speak to him! Please!" I heard loud in the background. I knew it was Renee. I knew that beautiful voice.

"Is that Renee? Please let me talk to her!" I asked, and my heart started beating fast.

"Do you know how many rules I would be breaking if I let y'all two speak to each other? I could lose my job!" Ms. Taylor said in defiance.

"No one will find out. Please, I just love her so much! Please just let us have a couple of minutes?"

"How are you even calling me? Aren't you locked up? Never mind. Okay, you can talk to Renee but just a quick hello. Then I will hang up the phone myself," Ms. Taylor said.

"Keithon? Keithon? Are you there?" Renee gleefully screamed out.

"I'm here, and I love you so much," I responded. Just hearing her voice meant so much to me.

"I love you so much too. I can't wait to see you tomorrow. It is going to take everything in me not to jump in your arms," Renee told me.

"I know, right. But are you okay?"

"Yeah, I've been doing my best. I reconnected with my dad, but I've been feeling really sick lately, throwing up and—" Click. While Renee was talking, the phone hung up.

"Renee?" I yelled.

"Shhh," Max said quietly. "Are you done?"

"Yes, and thanks, man," I told him.

Of course, I was mad that I could not talk to her longer, but I wasn't thinking about that at this moment. I was thinking about how I'd just heard Renee say she was reconnecting with her father. I'd thought her parents were dead. When Renee told me about her mom and everything while we were hiding out in my parents' second house, she never said anything about her dad. So I automatically assumed that he was dead like what she told me the night I first met her. But I guessed that was just a lie, so we would find out just what the truth was.

Chapter Twenty-four

Renee

This was Keithon's second time being in court. The first time he pled not guilty. Today was the day of his trial. The first time I couldn't come to court to see him. But for the trial I could because I was part of this case. Keithon was a former officer, so this case was talked about on TV and on different blogs. When they didn't tell me what was going on with Keithon, I kept up with him through media. This was my way of keeping in touch since I couldn't talk to him on the phone.

I also was reading a lot about the law. One thing I found out was that Keithon could've represented himself, but I could see he didn't choose that.

The judge started talking then called me to the stand. I looked around. I saw the jury. There was a mixed group of blacks and whites, but also two Asians. They seemed to be emotionless.

A guy name Terrell Johnson came in front of me. "What's your name?" he asked me.

"Renee Turner," I responded.

"Are you in love with Officer James? Yes or no?" he asked with anger in his voice.

"Yes."

"That will be all for now," Mr. Johnson said as he walked to sit down. I could see him whisper something to the lady sitting next to him.

Then the lady who represented Keithon walked up before me. Her name was Brenda Archer. "Hello, how's it going?"

"Okay."

"Tell me, how did you meet Mr. James?"

I explained to her how I was in the trash and Office James and the other officer found me and took me to a shelter.

"So you can say that Officer James and Officer Braylock did not know you were a runaway?"

"They did not know," I responded.

"That will be all for now."

The judge told me to go back to my seat.

When it was Ms. Archer's turn to question Officer Braylock, she asked him, "You know Mr. James pretty well, right?"

"Yes."

"Can you say he's a pretty well-rounded, kind-hearted, good person?"

"Yes, definitely. He's one of our best officers," Officer Braylock told the court.

"You both didn't know the state was looking for Ms. Turner?" Keithon's lawyer asked.

"No, we did not!" Officer Braylock responded.

She turned, facing the jury, and said, "Mr. James wasn't aware that she was a runaway when he met her."

There was a small recess. Then everyone came back to the courtroom. It was hard for me to keep my eyes off of Keithon. I missed him so much.

"Keithon James to the stand," I heard the judge say. As Keithon walked to the stand, I could not help but think about me not stressing him anymore. I was starting to feel sick to my stomach again. Seemed like I'd been getting a lot bigger, too, but I'd been stress eating a lot lately.

Once I stopped thinking I got back to reality and noticed Mr. Johnson was getting angry with Keithon. "So at the point you knew she was a runaway, why didn't you turn her in?" he asked loudly.

"I was fully in love with her, but I didn't plan for this to happen," Keithon told him.

"Nothing was planned, but you carried it on," Mr. Johnson said. He was asking all these questions, trying to make Keithon look like a bad guy. This made me so angry.

The day ended when the judge said, "This case will be continued a week from today."

Chapter Twenty-five

For a couple days during this passing time, I started to think about everything in the world. First I started thinking about the time when my mom and dad were together. When I was really little, we went to the park once for July 4th. I started to zone out thinking about this. It was one of the last times I actually saw my family on both sides together. My father's and my mother's families came together at this park on this one night to see fireworks, and we were all happy. Actually, this was one of the only times I remembered ever having a family.

My dad was pushing me on a swing back and forth. I was going higher and higher. The sun was just starting to set, and it was starting to get chilly out. My dad went over to my mom and started to talk to her as I continued to swing. I watched from a close distance as my dad took off his jacket and put it around my mom's arms. I continued to watch as he kissed her on the cheek, and she smiled the biggest smile I ever saw her smile in my life.

I snapped back into reality as I thought about this being the last time I truly saw my mother really happy and her smiling so bright. I really missed her so much. You will never ever feel as much pain as losing someone you love. I started thinking about the time when I was in middle school. My mind started to drift away from reality again. I could see the white walls with poster boards of equations on them. One wall had stars on it, with the name of each student who had an A or B in the class on each star. Cedric Johnson. I would just stare at this gold star with the name Cedric Johnson on it written in green marker.

"Miss Turner, pay attention," Ms. Coleman said.

Ms. Coleman was my sixth-grade math teacher. Ms. Coleman was a black lady in her late forties and wore glasses. Ms. Coleman would always yell at me about not focusing in her class. I was not doing that badly in her class. Even though I was not on the star board, I still was passing. I had a C+ in Ms. Coleman's class.

I could not help but not focus when I had some-one like Cedric on my mind and in the same class with me. Cedric was the first boy I ever liked. Cedric was gorgeous and a smart boy, which was hard to come by. I'd had a crush on him for a whole year. I heard the bell ring. I got up and started walking out of the classroom.

"Hold up, Renee!" I heard coming from behind me, and of course, I knew the voice.

"Yes?" I said as I turned around and looked at Cedric. I was looking right at his cute face. With black curly hair, light brown skin, and beautiful hazel eyes, Cedric was mixed black and Mexican.

"Do you need some extra help in class? If you do, you can stop by my place after school, and I can tutor you," Cedric told me.

I stayed quiet for a minute.

"Well, we don't have to," Cedric told me, and I could hear his confident level dropping as he said that.

"No, no. I would love your help," I told him while standing in the hall. I knew I was going to be late for my last class, but I did not care. I was not about to waste this opportunity. Cedric, the boy I had the biggest crush on, wanted to hang out with me. Every girl in school liked him, which was just an extra bonus.

Cedric started writing his address on a ripped piece of paper, pressing the paper against the wall as he wrote in black pen. I could remember everything about Cedric.

"Here you go. Come right after school if you can. Talk to you later," Cedric said with a smile then walked off.

That day I tried to rush to my last class, but I was late. I made it to the door right as the bell rang, but my teacher closed the door in my face. I knew this meant I had to go to the office.

I did my work in the office, and after school, I went straight to Cedric's house. I did not think to go tell my mom. I knew she would not care anyway with the arguing with my stepdad and stuff.

I arrived at Cedric's house and rang the doorbell.

"What's up? Come in," Cedric said as he let me in. "My parents are not home, but we can still stay in the living room," Cedric continued.

I followed him to the living room. His house looked like an old lady decorated it, but it was still really nice. We both sat on the couch, and we started to do our math homework. Cedric helped me on all the problems I did not know how to do. Finally, we were done with our homework and him showing me example problems.

"I really like you, Renee," Cedric told me, and he leaned in and kissed me.

"You like me?" I asked as I smiled really big. This was my first kiss, and it was with someone I really liked who'd just told me he liked me back. It was amazing.

Cedric and I started dating two days later. We continued to date for years, until not long before Tyrone killed my mom. The reason we stopped talking was because too much was going on in my life with my mom and Tyrone.

I came back to reality. I hated ever thinking about Cedric because it was another thing my stepdad messed up for me. Of course, Cedric did not nearly compare to Keithon, but I couldn't lie. I did miss him a little after all this time. I at least wished I would have told him the reason why I stopped talking to him.

I started to fall asleep once I thought about the final court date for Keithon coming up so soon. I was not exactly ready to hear that I might not be able to see him for a while. After I thought about this my eyes closed and I was asleep.

Chapter Twenty-six

A week passed, and we were back at court. Today I wore the prettiest dress Ms. Taylor gave to me. I was hoping to look good for Keithon, wearing a dress a little above knee length. The dress had sparkles all over it. When I was a kid, I loved sparkles, so of course, I really liked this dress. I saw Keithon sitting down, and his beautiful eyes had fear behind them. You could tell he was scared just by looking at him. This change my mood really fast from thinking he had little time to me thinking I might never get to see him again.

"Mr. Johnson, please give us your closing argument," Judge Monroe said.

"Why should we let this man get away with crime? He might not have known at first, but once he found out, he continued. He is a bad man and obviously a bad officer." As Mr. Johnson spoke, I could really feel anger in my heart.

"You're a liar. He's not a bad guy at all. He is the only who cared when no one else did!" I yelled across the room.

"Order in my court!" the judge said. I sat back in my seat and didn't say another word. I saw Keithon's parents looking at me from across the room.

"It's okay, Renee!" Shondra told me.

Mr. Johnson ended his argument by saying, "He was harboring a fugitive. He committed the crime, and he should do the time."

When it was time for Ms. Archer's argument, she stood in front of the jury with confidence. "Okay, there was a warrant out for Ms. Turner, but Mr. James didn't know that most of the time he was with her. He has no history of committing any crimes, and if you've ever been in love before, you know that you would do anything to be with that person. So when you make your decision, keep this in mind and imagine yourself in his shoes. He's not a bad person. He didn't kill anyone or hurt anyone. All he did was fall in love, and he did not know that she was a runaway until after the fact," Brenda Archer told the jury.

After about thirty minutes of deliberation, the jury came back out and sat down. A black man in his mid-forties stood up with a paper in his hand. The room was completely silent to the point where you could not hear a person take a breath. I looked around and saw my dad, Keithon's parents, and Ms. Taylor, and I could see a bunch of strangers' faces, so I stopped searching the crowd. I was so nervous I could hear my own heartbeat.

"In the case of Ohio v. Keithon James, we find the defendant, Keithon James, guilty of an unlawful act," the guy from the jury said.

My heart dropped. I looked at Keithon and could see tears rolling down his face. His eyes were red and watery.

The judge started to speak. "Keithon James, I considered your clean record and that you are obviously not a terrible person, but I have to punish you for what you did, which was harboring a fugitive. You broke the law, and you are an officer, which kind of makes it even worse. I sentence you to ten years in prison, and you cannot see Ms. Turner even when you get out. Case closed."

I ran over to Keithon so fast. I kissed him and hugged him as tight as I could. "I love you, and I will always love you," I whispered in his ear.

My heart was broken. I felt the same amount of pain as the day my mom died. A cop came over and tried to grab me off of Keithon, but we were holding on so tightly to each other it took another cop to help pull us apart.

"Always," Keithon said, yelling across the room to me as I got damn near dragged away.

"Forever. Forever and a day," I promised him as I sobbed like never before.

Watching the officers handcuff Keithon hurt me so bad. I couldn't take seeing this, let alone knowing that this was the last time I was able to see my beloved. I fell to my knees when I had the last glimpse of his back leaving the courtroom. Ms. Taylor and my father leaned down and hugged me. I could see his parents walking over to me as my dad and Ms. Taylor were hugging me. I let go of my dad and Ms. Taylor so I could figure out what the hell Keithon's parents wanted. Hadn't they done enough to cause our heartbreak?

"I am so sorry, Renee," Keithon's mother claimed.

"Me too," his father said, following his wife's probable lie.

With these words being said, I forgot about anything they had done because I knew at this moment they actually cared. They were Keithon's parents. And I knew he loved them so much, so how could I honestly stay mad at them for what they did, no matter how dirty it was, when I loved Keithon so much?

"I forgive you guys!" As I told them this, I meant every word. I could see tears falling down his mother's face. I was far from blind. I knew she had felt the pain of how she basically threw her own son in jail with the aid of her husband.

Chapter Twenty-seven

An entire day passed since Keithon was sentenced. Today I felt even worse than yesterday. I had not gotten any sleep. It was 4:00 a.m. and Ms. Taylor wouldn't unlock my door until 5:00 a.m. for my early shower. I started going through all the stuff I wrote in my notebook. I thought about all these times: my mother dying, my dad leaving me, Ms. Sims talking about me behind my back, meeting Keithon, talking to Shondra, seeing Keithon getting taken away from me, and so much more. They were mostly bad memories, but when I had a good memory, it was an amazing part of my life. But why did every time something good happen for me, something even worse came behind it? I asked myself this question, but I did not have the answer. No one had it. I usually heard people say, "God gives His biggest battles to His strongest soldiers," but all my strength was gone right now. I was weak. I could tell the truth. I was weak. I'd never said these words before, and I was pretty sure everyone in my life knew this already, but at this point, it was at a different level.

I knew I would not be in this place right now if I actually felt bad about killing Tyrone, but I didn't. Looking back, I wished I just acted like I felt bad. But then again, I would have never met Keithon. But no matter what, I didn't feel bad about killing Tyrone. To this day I still felt this rush going through my heart. If I had to go through it all again, I would still kill. If someone killed your mom and tried to rape you, tell me what you would do.

Almost an hour passed. I started to think about Keithon again, and I knew I didn't want to live without him. I just couldn't! With my mom and my beloved out of my life, there was no point in living. Sure, I was reconnecting with my dad, and he was supposed to see me today, but I did not care. I forgave him and loved him, but he would never mean anything to me like my mom or Keithon. I could never forget him walking out on us.

I spent this hour writing. I wrote a note to Shondra, telling her how much I loved her. I wrote a note to my father, telling him how much I forgive him. I even wrote a note to Ms. Taylor, telling her how much I thanked her for being here for me these last few months.

Finally, I got to the note I wrote to Keithon.

At first, I thought I was evil, but now I know I have the biggest heart. And that is my biggest problem. I'm too young to know any better and running from my pain is probably not right. My mom was killed, and I felt like nothing was worth living for. That's why I killed him. But, Keithon James, you came around and gave me life. I love you so much, and I just can't live without you. No one will ever understand, but just know that after tonight the one thing that won't die is our love!

It was finally 5:00 a.m. and the light on the door turned green. I left all the notes on my bed. I went to the showers. I thought about hanging myself, but I noticed a piece of broken glass from the mirror was on the shower floor. I turned on the shower so everything could seem normal. I sat on the ground and picked up the sharp piece of glass that was on the ground. I started to cut my wrist. It hurt so badly, and I secretly wanted someone to stop me, but I knew I did not want to live without Keithon. I started to cut deeper, and my vision started to blur. In the distance, I heard footsteps coming in the bathroom. Within moments, I saw a girl with red hair staring at me, screaming. Everything went dark.

Next thing I knew I saw a doctor. I thought I was in the hospital, but I wasn't really sure. My vision was still blurry, and it was getting harder for me to breathe. Was this a dream?

"Wait a damn minute! This girl is pregnant, and full term at that!" I heard the doctor yell out to the trauma team. This was the last thing I heard before I died that morning in the hospital.

Later Ms. Taylor found the notes in my room when the cops came. Ms. Taylor told Shondra, and they cried. But once Ms. Taylor got herself together she called my dad and told him to meet her at the prison where Keithon was located. She introduced them first. She knew this would be the way I wanted it, and this was the first time Keithon met my father, since I never really told him that he was actually alive. She gave the notes to both of them at the same time.

"Wait. Before you open them I have to tell you something!" she said.

Both of their faces changed like they knew something serious was up.

"Renee died today, a couple hours ago, but the baby is alive and healthy, thank God," she told them. They both started to cry.

"Baby?" Keithon was confused as tears rolled down his face. "I have a baby?" His sad voice turned angry. Keithon repeated louder and louder, "Where is my baby? Where is my baby?" My dad was in tears, barely even able to read his note, but he still tried. Keithon was a different story. He held the note in his hand but did not read it, at least not that day. Keithon was more concerned about his child and just kept asking Ms. Taylor, "Where is my baby?"

I never meant to cause so much pain. I was just so far gone. He and I both were. And if I were still alive and I knew that I was pregnant, I would have never thought about killing myself in a million years. And when I thought back to that note I wrote Keithon, now I knew there was more than one thing that did not die that day in the emergency room, and it was bigger than our love.